Outside the House of Baal

Seren Classics

Outside the House of Baal

Emyr Humphreys

Seren is the book imprint of
Poetry Wales Press Ltd
57 Nolton Street, Bridgend, Wales, CF31 3AE
www.serenbooks.com
Facebook: facebook.com/SerenBooks
Twitter: @SerenBooks

First published, 1965
This edition, 1996
Reprinted 2019
© Emyr Humphreys, 1965

The right of Emyr Humphreys to be identified as
the author of this work has been asserted in accordance
with the Copyright, Designs and Patents Act, 1988.

ISBN
978-1-85411-102-9

A CIP record for this title is available from the British Library.

The publisher acknowledges the financial assistance of the Welsh Books Council.

Cover painting: 'Fferm Pen y Groes' by Stephen John Owen
courtesy of Oriel Ger-y-Fenai Llanfairpwllgwyngyll.

Printed in Bembo by Bell & Bain Ltd, Scotland.

Outside the House of Baal

Anrheg O Rywfath

I Mam[1]

Preface

There cannot be as many definitions of the novel as there are novels, but every confident example of this portmanteau form tends to set out on its journey with its own map marked with its own rules of the game. The one denominator common to all is the need to tell a story — 'Oh dear yes', sighs E.M. Forster as if this were a plebeian restraint on what would otherwise be a palace of aesthetic delights: a lowly element better hidden in the foundations of the work so that the novelist's imagination be free to soar into the realms of fantasy and the infinite freedoms of outer space. If pressed Forster like most novelists would agree that the story is frequently not so much the novelist's invention as a gift left on his desk or on his doorstep. This is the philosopher's stone that will contain the excited writer's desire to comment on the human condition and transmute his scattered perceptions into a coherent narrative; a written world which any sympathetic reader can inhabit and thereby make his own.

At this distance in time I can assert that in the summer of 1963 I was presented with just such a gift. Only the previous year I had published under that very title a mildly picaresque novel about actors and their metropolitan agonies — unaware perhaps at the time that it was a fond farewell to a brief but beguiling career as a television drama director. In that summer circumstances combined to focus my attention on a far more potent source of creativity flourishing on my own hearth. The gift, so to speak, had been there all the time at my feet. My mother and father-in-law were living with us in our farmhouse oddly marooned in the middle of Penarth. The house itself was a relic of a previous age. Our parents were both in their seventies, which seemed to us in those days a considerable age. They had that wealth of recollection and the more piercing awareness of reality that comes with old age. They had emerged from monoglot Welsh societies and in spite of wars, revolution, famine, mass unemployment and mass communications, their existences and concerns had continued to revolve around chapels, those impregnable citadels of a Welsh nonconformity that had managed to convince itself of being in existence since the world began, rather than a little more than a century and a half. Like the British Empire, of which Welsh nonconformity was a not inconsiderable corner, the illusion of permanence and stability, carefully cemented with good intentions, was fundamental to its structure. Until two catastrophic world wars had destroyed the bourgeois culture of Europe, it had seemed that these myths had a greater influence on the shape of the future than the raw facts of history itself. They certainly had contributed more to the resilience of this older generation than the bewildering rate of change in social and material conditions they had been obliged to witness.

They held on to their faiths and even to their superstitions. Neither of them had ever owned or driven a motor car. Satellites were already in orbit when my mother assured me as we drove at night from Penarth to Prestatyn that it was a bad omen to see the moon through glass, even of a windscreen. My father-in-law at the age of twelve had been apprenticed to a blacksmith at Llanbedrgoch in his native Anglesey. He had seen a 'corpse candle' flicker above a cottage as he hurried along the four miles from the smithy to his home, a small farm in the next parish. So much of what they had to say was a vivid evocation of a lost world and of a period of unparalleled historical change. They were a constant reminder that the wellspring of most literature of consequence is local. It is through the poetry of the particular that we have the easiest access to patterns of the universal. It so often seemed, even then, that if by their fruits we are to know them, in certain vital respects their mythic reality was superior to our anxious uncertainties. But our generation was more acutely aware of the process of decline. We imagined we could see in alarming slow motion the collapse of a wall of mythic certainties; from the subsiding of the flames of hell-fire to the fizzling out of a belief in progress towards a sanitized version of a twentieth century earthly paradise.

There were themes here which called out for some form of epic celebration. The novel was the obvious form through which to explore the splendours and miseries of the Welsh experience. A local variation of Decline and Fall would not be enough. That quality of the stream of living which separates the novel from the monumental marble of well-written history had to be a central element of the work in progress. Furthermore, although the story and the novel were as essential to each other as body and mind, or as our parents would have put, as closely related as body and soul, they were never the same thing. The story had its origins in a monoglot Welsh context. It would seem to follow that the novel waiting to be composed should therefore be written in Welsh. And yet I set to work immediately in English. At first I was not unduly troubled by this inconsistency. The novel is generally accepted as the most international literary form. Whereas poetry notoriously fades away in translation, the novel more often than not survives this gruelling process. The characters of Tolstoy and Dostoievsky, for example, colonise the imaginations of readers who have not a single word of the noble language in which their novels were written. An English critic, John Middleton Murry, managed to write an excellent book on Dostoievsky without knowing a word of Russian.

Alas, my problem was moral as well as aesthetic. I wanted my novel to be a contribution to the life of an ongoing society and not a memorial stone on its grave. I had attempted in *Y Tri Llais* a short novel using first person points of view which in several ways is the simplest form of narrative. What I had in mind now was an altogether larger enterprise. It seemed to me that summer that I was confronted with two inadequacies: my own, and the absence of a developed modern tradition of the long novel in the Welsh language. The Welsh novel had begun late, but in a gloriously substantial form, in the work of Daniel Owen. When he died, the society he celebrated lost the capacity and the self-confidence necessary to nurture a worthy successor. The novel more than any other literary form needs a solid constituency of readers alive to the novelist's preoccupations and open to his way of expressing them. In poetry and in drama and in the short story, and perhaps in the short novel, in spite of the decline of the language, Welsh literature in the twentieth century miraculously managed to keep pace with European modernity: but as far as the novel was concerned, as Welsh nonconformist dominated society declined in power and influence, the novel declined with it.

This was in stark contrast to what happened to the novel in the English language. After the great age of the nineteenth century novel, that we think of as coming to an end in 1914, it was the novel in English, perhaps more than any other literary form, that took the full blast of a hurricane of modernity. This in itself was a curious phenomenon, the originators of the storm, so to speak, great theoreticians like Nietzsche, Karl Marx, and Sigmund Freud, wrote in German; the vital centres of experiment in the arts were Paris and Vienna. It could be argued that there is no accounting for genius and that English was just lucky to have the polarising geniuses of Joyce and Lawrence born and brought up in Dublin and Eastwood. The two greatest practitioners of the modern novel in English were so attached to their respective birthplaces that they could not bear to live in them. In order to dedicate themselves to the celebration of this love-hate relationship, they condemned themselves to live in permanent exile among people who did not speak English. In their distinct and different ways, these geniuses could also be held responsible for bringing about a fatal dichotomy in the novel form. Initially their experiments in form and content alienated them from a large scale readership; so that when the mass media usurped the throne of the popular story-teller, the literary novel was too weakened to put up an effective resistance. After the Second World War, the novel in England could be seen retreating into neo-provincialism and most of the novelists gazing with gloomy envy across the Atlantic towards richer and more exciting pastures.

Wales was not without its universal geniuses. It continued to produce fewer preachers but more than its share of poets and manipulative politicians. Poetry, the lifeblood of Welshness down the ages, produced a galaxy of twentieth century talent in two languages and almost exhausted itself in the process. Between the wars there was a remarkable resurgence of scholarship and criticism led by a posse of knighted scholars and more dissident figures such as Saunders Lewis, Ambrose Bebb, and the maverick W.J. Gruffydd. The short story as a vital and contemporary form broke through the Welsh sound barrier in the unique work of Kate Roberts. But the long novel in Welsh languished undeveloped and largely fossilised. There was a positive renaissance of Welsh prose in the period between the wars but its unifying characteristic was critical and polemic. The abilities of a generation of gifted writers were stretched to the limit in defence of a cultural realm and a way of life under constant threat. These are not the ideal conditions for the development of writing extended fiction, experimental or otherwise.

Most of those who tried their hands at the form in English relied too much on the impulse of rebellion against the shackles of their society to make the efforts required to try and understand it. There needs to be a relationship between the novel as a viable contemporary form and the stability of the society it is intended to serve. In the first half of the twentieth century, because of a basic economic weakness, political indecisiveness and a lack of sustaining institutions, Wales was chronically unstable. It is difficult if not impossible to paint a portrait of society in perspective if the ground is shaking under your easel. Wales was still covered with a network of chapels from end to end, but the manses were either empty or occupied with nervous ministers, wrestling with their consciences, attempting to cope with a ferment of new ideas and the importunities of a dwindling flock and a demanding family. Long before the nineteen-sixties it was apparent to the acute observer that the Welsh condition represented the spiritual crisis of the West in microcosm.

A retired minister and his sister-in-law, widower and widow, share the same somewhat spartan semi-detached house. This would be the source of the form this novel had to take. The retired minister might well have attended my father-in-law's theological college and it was equally possible that his sister-in-law would have been in school with my mother. Parallel lives like parallel lines travel together but never meet. For old people Time is a constant companion and it never ceases to whisper in their ear the legend of their lives. For them the Present is continuously confronted with the Past. The growing awareness of the mystery of the connection between small events and the drama of history can develop into an abiding consolation for the disabilities of old age.

The form of the novel has to be as simple and inevitable as old age itself. The events of one morning, or even part of a morning, should be the ground, in the musical sense, of a polyphonic sequence of events spanning seventy years. Simple solutions to complex problems have a way of dressing themselves up as magic formulas. I have a distinct recollection of shuffling around in the summer of 1963 like a man about to patent a secret method of crystallising the fruit of intense research and introspection into stark scenes that would mean something more set in telling juxtaposition to one another. I remember our youngest son aged nine telling me that time was a device to prevent everything happening at once. I don't know where he read it, but it reinforced my conviction that time could also be adapted to give this novel the exact structure appropriate to it. The events of one morning could confront the events of two lifetimes, which in turn could confront each other for the first time and create a penumbra of meaning that would not otherwise be apparent.

For this to happen it was clear that every character and every occasion should enjoy the maximum possible autonomy. The author should at all times restrain himself from trespassing on the consciousness of any character; otherwise his voice would colour everything and in one way or another invalidate the integrity of the event. He would not presume to know their thoughts or their feelings other than to the extent that they volunteered them by what they said and by what they did. In the convention of this novel the author should abdicate his author-ity as one of the rules of the game. The vacant space should be occupied by the reader as a bench where he could consider at his leisure the evidence of the scene laid in front of him.

This semi-monastic rule would lead to an integrity of expression which at its best would be capable of giving that flavour of authenticity that can only be found when the writer ventures to plunge his hand into the stream of living, and by some alchemy, succeeds in transforming the fluid into the solid; the transient into a lasting artifice. This was a practice more commonly encountered in the short story form than the novel. The short story relies on that flash of revelation that both illuminates a situation and dictates the form of the story itself. This novel could be construed as a sequence of short stories involving the same characters in a variety of situations over a prolonged period of time and the author's absence would make the whole greater than the sum of the parts. In each case the scene had to be brought to life with the minimum of words if only because, as Wittgenstein might have written, 'the fewer words uttered, the more notes are struck on the keyboard of the imagination'.

That year, as I wrestled with these self-imposed restrictions, I threw up a succession of theoretical scaffoldings to support and sustain my efforts. Some of these theories have stood the passage of time, most have collapsed or withered away on the wayside. I cherished the illusion, for example, that the proliferation of the new media would produce a public better trained in the arts of observation. Through the microscopic services of camera and microphone they would have acquired access to wealth of meaning from the mere appearance of the world around them. A whole new vocabulary of gestures, attitudes, tones and undertones would have provided a battery of new skills easily transferred to the business of reading. All sorts of literary conventions would be outdated, including the practice of authorial omniscience, olympian comment, stylistic pyrotechnics, deliberate obscurities. A means would be evolved to close the gap between the popular and the experimental and restore the old information highway between the serious novelist and a wider public.

I could not have been more wrong. Thirty years later it seems that our sensibilities have been coarsened rather than sharpened by the new instruments of communication. Any form of communistic aspiration has been crushed by the triumph of one form or other of capitalism. It would seem that the same potent combination of unbridled commercial greed and technical expertise has also infected the development of the novel. Authorial extravagance predominates among the coterie novel while popular storytelling has deteriorated into the mechanical equivalent of painting by numbers.

A major part of the impulse of writing springs from a belief in the unique properties of the raw material you are privileged to exploit. I consoled myself then that by writing in English I was attempting to give a wider public a better appreciation of the Welsh experience of the transformations of the twentieth century. I still believe that this experience in so many respects prefigures the crises of identity that are beginning to disturb many larger European nations. There is ample evidence by now to show that even the hereditary self-assurance of the English is being shaken. If anything there is less interest than ever now in the Welsh experience of the spiritual crisis of the West. The age of anxiety has given way to the age of indifference. It is possible too that some of our poets and politicians have played so much on stage Welshy-ness to imprison us all in the comic pen reserved for windbags and no good boyos.

Of course these could be the crabbed observations of old age. It may well be the culture of telecommunications is still in its infancy. After all universal literacy in most languages is a recent phenomenon. Every writer has to pin his faith in posterity. He has to assume that somehow or other educative processes will be re-established. A readership may again emerge which will call the author to account for every word he uses. In my own case when *Outside the House of Baal* was finished and a few years later I embarked on a sequence of novels about the progress of a woman from rags to riches and a poet from success to despair, I relaxed my own rules sufficiently to accommodate a treatment of the themes that would exploit more space and a simpler chronology. Rules have to be made like moulds in order to be broken.

I have now reached the age of J.T. Miles and Kate Bannister and I am in a position to vouch for the authenticity of their experiences that morning. From the same vantage point I can also presume in this preface to advise the reader how to read this book to the best advantage, before I look up the details of the next mystery tour of Anglesey, *Frin dirion dir — yr hen ynys uniaith...*

E.H

1

THE VENERABLE HEAD rolled sideways on the pile of pillows. The pillow-case was lightly stained by the halo of white hair. The deep-set eyes opened briefly and closed again. The trimmed eyebrows rose and fell, the high forehead creased, the back arched; there was a stiffening of the whole body, a critical pause, until he broke wind audibly. Then his body relaxed and his brow cleared. He breathed deeply as if more sleep could be induced in this way. His eyelids lifted enough to see his bedroom in a golden haze created by sunlight passing through brown curtains that had washed thin. The light picked out J.T.M., the initials gilded on the collar-box that stood on the chest of drawers. The initials were stamped at a distance from each other across the front of the box. The lid was open showing the dark-blue velvet lining.

Somewhere in the room a clock was ticking, showing what time it was. He stretched his mouth, passing his tongue over his lips. His lips moved in silent speech, shaping words. He coughed. His eyebrows twitched, but his head did not move and his eyelids stayed closed.

The eiderdown had fallen from the single bed. His thin arm poked forward out of the striped pyjama sleeve and felt about for a corner of the eiderdown to pull up and spread again over his body lying peacefully in the centre of the single bed. Under the bed was a chamber-pot which he had used twice during the night. He raised himself sufficiently for the eiderdown to avoid the pot as he drew it back slowly to cover the bed. His mouth opened with the effort and his fingers sank into the warm silk of the eiderdown cover. When it was done his head sank back and his mouth closed.

ON HER KNEES in front of the corner fire-place, Kate put down the worn poker with which she had been raking the coal fire of the previous day. She fumbled in the pocket of her working pinafore for the small handkerchief she kept there rolled into a tight ball. She sat back on her heels and lifted her head, moving it from side to side as if she were looking for something on the mantelpiece. But it was not possible to survey the objects on the mantelpiece in detail without standing up. It was of a height level with her eyes when she stood on tiptoe.

The fire-place was framed in black cast iron on each side of which were embossed for ornament the outlines of two tapered Grecian urns. Inside the frame floral tiles gleamed around the iron arch which contained the grate itself, now obscured by a cloud of settling dust.

Still sitting on her heels, from the pocket of her pinafore she extracted the small handkerchief which she lifted carefully to the socket of her missing eye. Her fingers were stained with grey ash, and as she contrived to wipe yet another deposit of mucus from the socket she rubbed ash into her cheek. She looked up again, stretching her neck, but until she pulled herself up, she would not be able to see what she wanted to see on the mantelpiece.

Slowly she screwed the soiled handkerchief into a ball and pushed it back into the shallow pocket of her pinafore. The pocket needed mending. At one side it had torn loose. Also the tapes that tied the pinafore together at her waist were grey and frayed and ready to be replaced. The pinafore was printed with a fading pattern of flowers. Her hair, still plentiful and dyed black, was held down by a hair net that also covered her ears, which were prominent. In contrast to her thin neck her cheeks were plump and intricately veined. Her small mouth as she went about her work was always pursed as if she would never speak unless there was something worth saying.

She took up the poker and crouched forward with her weight on her thin left arm to resume her fierce raking of the cinders. At her side there was a small shovel and a bucket with which she would remove the ash.

J.T.M.YAWNED. His jaw shuddered as it stretched, and he released a noise that could have been a groan of pain if anybody chanced to hear it. He tilted his head so that his left ear, which heard well, could pick up any sound from downstairs. A door could open or shut. Tap water could suddenly strike the bottom of a heavy kettle. A lavatory seat could fall, or apostle spoons tinkle in bone china saucers. He screwed up his eyes tightly and heard a poker rattle in a grate.

He brought his long bony hands together as he lay in bed.

— Most merciful Father, he said aloud.

He opened his mouth widely like a cat yawning and then shut it firmly into an attitude of intense thought.

SHE RESTED THE tips of her fingers on the edge of the mantel-piece. Within four inches of her face, the clock sliced away at the seconds. The inscription at its base had been polished so much the last number in the year of presentation had been rubbed away. She turned her head first right and then left. She waited. The clock ticked loudly. She stepped back and bent to pick up the ash bucket. Her hands were dirty. She saw her sack apron on the kitchen floor and stood looking at it, the bucket in her right hand. She paused above it, as if deciding whether to wear it or not. Then she opened the back door cautiously and peeped out. As far as could be seen no one was watching through any overlooking window. No one was peering over the wall at the bottom of the back garden or gazing through any of the windows of the new public house that stood boldly staring at all their back gardens from the centre of the asphalt car park that surrounded it. She held her head down to conceal her right eye socket and made for the bin with a stiff westerly breeze blowing against her. The wind caught her breath. It was a dull day in late August and the traffic on the coast road was so far very thin. If the sun had been shining, by now the cars would have been rushing past in their hundreds and everybody in Gorse Avenue would be hurrying about as if the clock had been moved forward two hours. She clamped the bin lid down before the dust could rise. She sniffed quickly and allowed the wind to drive her back to the kitchen door. Still spinning slightly she put down the empty bucket, lifted the latch, stepped inside and picked up the sack apron on the kitchen floor.

LYING IN BED J.T.M. opened his eyes cautiously without looking at the clock. He saw the haze of light that took the colour of warmth and sunshine from the worn curtains, although it was in fact a dull day outside. The travelling clock stood in its leather case in a busi-ness-like stance, ready to be consulted in relation to some course of action. The ticking finally captured J.T.'s attention. His eyes turned in his head and he saw it was seven thirty.

He shut his mouth firmly and swung his legs out of bed. Then he paused to try and pick up some sound that would indicate clearly what stage in her work had been reached by the woman downstairs. It seemed unlikely she would be on her way upstairs. He pushed aside his slippers and patiently bent down to pick up the chamberpot. He carried it carefully to the door, where he paused and placed the pot on top of the books in the bookcase to the left of the door, in order to release both hands to the task of opening the door silently. No. 8, Gorse Avenue, was a thin-walled house.

Crossing the landing with care, the warm soles of his feet sucked against the cold surface of the linoleum. It was only a few steps to get inside the bathroom and once inside he lifted the lavatory seat and tipped the contents of the pot into the pan. He stopped for a moment to listen, no doubt in case Kate should call. Then he flushed the pan, swilling the white interior of the flowered china chamber-pot under the cascade of water and then for good measure rinsing it under the cold-water tap of the bath. Quickly he tiptoed back to his bedroom, closing his door as quietly as he could and replacing the clean pot under his bed. His heart beating faster with the speed and cultivated lightness of his movements he lay back again in the mould from which he had raised himself up. His lips opened and he spoke aloud with breathless speed.

— O Lord, he said, as he still listened for downstairs sounds. Look very favourably upon the efforts of Thy servant, Kate. Melt her heart towards herself and make plain to her. . .

He stopped suddenly as if disturbed by an unfamiliar sound or thought.

— Make plain, he said in a whisper. Make plain. . .

KATE WAS HOLDING the butter-dish in one hand and the short-bladed knife in the other as she had always done to soften the butter before spreading it on the loaf. It was an old habit. The blade of the knife worked in the butter as she held the slippery dish in the other hand. The sudden flushing of the lavatory-pan upstairs made her jump. Her stiff fingers let the butter-dish fall. It bounced first on the marble top taken from the wash-stand that used to be in Pa's bedroom in Argoed. In the kitchen of 8 Gorse Avenue, she used it as a working surface that could be wiped easily with a damp cloth. Her knees bent as if she was attempting a catch, but the butter-dish hit the tiled floor of the little kitchen. The dish was a present from Aunty Addy of Denbigh, given to her thirty-four years ago the first Christmas after her wedding and a token of understanding and forgiveness. It smashed into so many pieces that any part of the half-pound of New Zealand butter could be impregnated with splinters of glass from the dish. She stood with her feet apart contemplating the damage.

Then she looked up at the ceiling.

— Damn you, Joe Miles, she said. You soft old fool!

2

THE GOVERNESS CART had been backed as near as possible to the garden gate. Ma's sister, Aunty Addy of Denbigh, sat in it with a rug already wrapped around her knees. The farm, Argoed,[2] was on a hill-top, and the wind that blew around it, even on this sunny day, made her eyes water.

Wearing a freshly ironed smock, Kate held back the garden gate. When she moved her head from right to left she could watch her mother's slow progress from the wheelchair by the front door down the path. Ma's frail arms lay across the shoulders of her two strongest sons, Dan Llew and Ned. With his hands raised anxiously, Pa hovered behind them. As he muttered warnings and instructions Kate saw his mouth open, making a hole in his beard. Ma was laughing and her teeth looked long in her thin face. She stretched her fingers to try and touch Kate's hair as they carried her forward. Ned and Dan Llew were looking downwards, watching where they placed their feet on the rocky ground outside the garden gate. Aunty Addy spread her arms as if to steady the springs of the governess cart, which rocked as Dan Llew and Ned set their mother down in the seat which had been prepared for her.

Pa decided more rugs were needed. Before he had finished speaking Kate had darted towards the house. He gave her further, louder instructions as she ran. Ma lifted her hand and whispered she really didn't need any more. She turned her head and looked down to see Hugh, her youngest son, clinging with little arms outstretched to the long spokes of the wheel. Pa followed her gaze and before she could speak ordered Griff to take his little brother indoors. Ma shook her head and pointed to her empty wheelchair on the lawn near the front door. Griff nodded eagerly and smiled, dragging Hugh away from the wheel to a new form of entertainment. He spoke mockingly to his brother Rowland who was sitting on the wall buttoning and unbuttoning his breeches below the knee and yet watching everything as it happened. Pa turned and pulled Griff's ear and told him to hold his tongue. Griff passed on his father's irritation by giving Hugh's arm another tug.

Lydia aged seven sat on the mounting stone. She stretched her leg to touch the curving shaft of the governess cart. It was just out of teach. She leaned back and kicked the shaft with the toe-cap of her boot. The startled pony lifted his head and the little bell on his bridle tinkled. Tomi Moch,[3] the farm-hand whom Ma was teaching to read, scolded the pony. Lydia put her hand over her mouth. When Tomi saw this, he pointed at the little girl accusingly. Lydia looked up and saw a twig in an overhanging branch of the pear tree bend downwards under the weight of a bird.

Pa couldn't wait for Kate to reappear with more rugs. Ordering Rowland to get down from the wall, he strode back to the house. It seemed so empty when he called out Kate's name. His voice reverberated through the house when he called again, telling her to hurry even as she clattered anxiously down the carpetless stairs. He took the rugs from her and told her to close the door at the bottom of the stairs even when she had already done it. If this were not done, the stairs would be visible from the yard since the front door was wide open. He seemed to cheer up when he had the rugs in his arms. One was a Welsh quilt, with a design of squares and circles woven in blue, red and white on a black ground, taken from the spare bed in the minister's room. He bustled out. But on the garden path he froze. Ma had been coughing. Her sister Addy had an arm over her shoulder. Ma had a large handkerchief over her mouth.

Kate snatched the lighter rug from her father's hands. The quilt fell to the ground. Pa knelt down slowly to pick it up, while Kate ran down the path and gave the rug to her eldest brother, Ned. He spread it over his mother's knees. The cart tilted as he stood up straight and took out his watch from his waistcoat pocket.

— I think we ought to start, Pa, he said. If we want to catch the train.

His father was still kneeling on the path which was paved with slabs of pale brown stone from one of the village quarries. He seemed unable to speak or even look up. Ned looked down at his trouser-leg. Ma had reached out to tug his trousers. Her thin fingers were pulling as hard as they could. For a moment she removed the handkerchief from her mouth and told him to drive away.

JOE MILES SAT on the window-sill of the class-room occupied by Standard Two. He rubbed his chin against the darnings on the knees of his stockings. The window-sill was wide and four and a half feet above the class-room floor. His father had lifted him up to this perch and had told him to watch and wait. His father's books were spread out on the teacher's desk, but his father had gone out to refill his whisky flask from the bottle that he hid in the ruined dovecote in the Rectory Field.

The rope of the school bell dangled within his reach. From time to time he lifted his hand in order to touch the rope and make it swing. Each time he dared to do this, he looked up apprehensively to where the rope disappeared through the roof. He did not know how much action was required to make the bell ring, but each touching of the rope made it tremble all the way up. The floor space of the classroom was small, but the windows were tall and arched and the roof was vaulted like a church, no doubt because it was a church school.

Beyond his boots, Joe could see a jamjar filled with pond water. The discoloured string by which it had been carried was still tied around the neck of the jar. It had been carried to school by Ella, Pant-y-ffynon Farm,[4] who was the top of the class and sat in the front. Inside the dark water they had been told that a tadpole was changing into a frog. Joe touched the pot with the toe of his boot, tilting it away from him until only the green weed on the surface stopped the water from overflowing.

The school yard, which he could see through the window, was stony and uneven and worn by the feet of playing children. It was separated from the road to the village by a wall of dressed stone and a row of tall trees. There was an iron railing on top of the wall because of the steep drop down to the road level. The school-children were forbidden to stand on the iron railing or to climb the trees.

He saw two hands gripping the railing and then a boy with his cap on back to front pulled himself into view. This was Jac Tŷ'n y Maes, older than Joe and the fastest runner in the school. Joe could see Jac's head move cautiously from left to right before he pulled himself up higher. Jac could see Joe sitting in the window. He beckoned to him urgently. Joe hesitated. He looked down at the sunlight striking the class-room floor. He swivelled around on his bottom and when he jumped dust arose in clouds from the wooden floorboards and travelled up and down the sun-beams long after he had left the room.

AT ARGOED A complete issue of a Welsh weekly newspaper was spread over the parlour floor and over the table. The grandfather's clock lay on its side. The weights, the pendulum and the cogs had been put down carefully on the newspaper pages. Because the clock was not ticking, the house was filled with a new silence. Pa sat at the round table, examining the head of the clock, which lay face downwards. There was a strong smell of paraffin in the room. Kate stood in the doorway looking at her father. She pushed the door open a little further and sniffed.

Pa had a cleaning rag in his hands. He seemed to stare into the workings of the clock like a man in a trance. Kate put her hands behind her back and waited. He did not move. He needed a hair-cut and his grey hair protruded over the sharp edge of his collar. Kate looked over her shoulder and then tiptoed into the room. Pa's head sank forwards and Kate stood still. When she moved closer he did not see her because tears were falling from his eyes into the workings of the clock. They fell off the top of his cheeks instead of coursing down into his beard. Kate opened her mouth twice before speaking.

— Pa, she said.

He did not look up.

— Go and see where Lydia is, there's a good girl.

His voice sounded nothing like his own.

— Always . . . look . . . after her, Kate.

It trembled like an old man's voice. As he lifted the cleaning rag she saw how blue were the veins on the back of his hand. His hand too was trembling.

— Can I stay with you, Pa? Kate said.

— Go and find her, my dear. This place is so big for a child. She may be in trouble. Always remember I want you to look after your sister.

Kate nodded solemnly. She turned to leave.

— And Kate . . .

His voice was firm.

— Always remember to close the door.

Kate closed the door as quietly as she could.

THE CLASS HAD been dismissed three-quarters of an hour ago, but Joe was still in the class-room, sitting on the window-sill. Big Jones, the headmaster, had gone on his monthly trip to the Education Office to collect the teachers' wages. The money would be for himself and his staff: Miss Evans, Frondeg; Miss Parry, Infants; and Mr Miles, Standard Two, Joe's father, who at this moment sat on his high stool working at his correspondence course for an external B.A. London. With increasing frequency he opened the lid of his desk high enough to conceal the quick uncorking of a half-bottle of Irish whiskey, a rapid gulp and the squeak of the cork being replaced. Each time he closed the lid of the desk he passed his tongue over his drooping black moustache and sighed. He rubbed his hand over an empty hip pocket.

— Dad, Joe said, without turning his head.

— Yes, son?

His father licked the top of his finger before turning over a page.

— Can I read?

— Can you read? his father said.

He had a habit of repeating a question that was put to him.

— I would like you to, Joe. I would like you to. But I can't see how you can. Have you ever heard of Professor Henry Jones?[5]

— No, Dad.

— He was just an ordinary school assistant like me. But he worked. He worked, Joe, like I'm working, and from being a poor cobbler's son he rose to be Professor of Moral Philosophy at the University of Glasgow. You see what I mean, Joe?

Joe made no answer.

— How can I work if you don't watch, son? How? Have you ever heard of Seithenyn, Joe?

— Yes, Dad.

— He was the watchman on the Tower at 'Cantre'r Gwaelod'. For various reasons he neglected his duty. He stopped watching. So the tide came without warning, and the gates were opened and the whole city was drowned beneath the raging sea.[6] The price of liberty is eternal watchfulness. Yes indeed.

He began to open the lid of his desk until he saw that Joe was watching. He closed it again hurriedly.

— Joe, he said, are you watching?

— Yes, Dad.

The boy was looking at him gravely, his eyes large and unblinking.

—Through the window, boy!

Joe turned his head quickly. He could see across the stony worn patches of the school's front yard to where the wide steps descended to the village road below. From the far hill-side, the other side of the village, he could hear the noise of children shouting. There was a game of fox-and-hounds afoot and more than half the village children would be in pursuit of Jac Tŷ'n y Maes. Jac would suddenly pop up from behind a clump of gorse, just as a horde of children were making off in the wrong direction, and making his own extraordinary whooping noise, duck down again and dive down the farther side of the hill, his arms half stretched in front of him like wings, into the tall ferns while all the children wheeled around untidily, one after the other, and made for the clump of gorse which Jac had already left far behind him. After the first flush of energy the children would lose heart and the smaller ones would flop down on the hill-side, demanding a rest, declaring the whole game unfair over and over again; until suddenly over on the other side of the valley, someone would hear the call of a cuckoo and Jac would suddenly appear in full view, waving the funny cap he always wore back to front when he was running.

Near Joe's feet was a large jam-pot filled with pond water, which Ella Pant-y-ffynon had brought for the nature lesson. At the bottom of the water was a dead frog.

— Dad.

—Yes, son.

— Can I empty the jam-pot? The little frog is dead.

His father sighed.

— Can you get down? he said.

Before he had finished Joe's hob-nailed boots had landed on the desk below the window. As he left the room, Joe could hear the lid of the teacher's desk being opened.

He stood in the entrance hall of the school, which was also used as a cloakroom. It was summer, and not a single coat or cap had been left behind on the rows of iron pegs. A dark corridor with more rows of black pegs stretched down the side of the school to the path that led to the boys' privies. The door was open and Joe could see Meshach Parry, puffing hard at his pipe, carrying a bucket in each hand down the steps. Meshach's left leg was shorter than the right and he moved with great care. The buckets had to be earned across the back play-ground through the school garden and over a wall into the Priest's Field which was rented by the parson to Willy Rodgers the butcher. The contents of the buckets were emptied into a trench. Meshach made six journeys from the boys' section and eight from the girls', smoking hard all the time to keep the flies away. He saw Joe standing in the open doorway of the side corridor.

— Well, he said, limping down the path towards him a bucket in each hand, his small pipe in the corner of his mouth. Is your father still in there then?

— Yes.

Joe lifted the jam-pot.

— What shall I do with this, Meshach Parry?

— Drop it in the bucket as I pass, good boy. Mind you don't splash, though.

Joe stood waiting, holding the jam-pot ready to empty.

— Duwch just look, Meshach Parry said. That damn school garden gate has shut itself. Run and open it for me, good boy. Won't take you a wink.

Joe emptied the jam-pot into the bucket in Meshach's right hand and ran ahead of him to open the garden gate. The garden was in a flourishing condition. There were older boys who spent most of their time working in it. Big Jones liked to be there, too, as much as he could, supervising. He would ask Miss Evans Frondeg or Mr Miles Standard Two to keep an eye on his class, especially on fine afternoons, and they always obliged.

— Hear that your father's getting married again, Meshach said as he passed through the gate.

Joe was so surprised that he let the gate go and it nearly hit one of the buckets.

— Put a stone there, good boy, Meshach said. A good heavy one. It's well sprung is that gate.

Meshach limped on up the garden path, the buckets brushing the blackcurrant bushes that were planted on either side. Joe bent down very low to look for a larger stone.

— There you are. There's one. There.

Meshach was standing behind him, puffing away, smiling slightly now the buckets were empty. He shaved once a week on a Saturday night. This was Wednesday and there was a halfway white growth on his weather-beaten skin. Twenty years ago Meshach had been in the army in South Africa. A Zulu spear had gone through the calf of his leg at the battle of Ulundi,[7] and if there hadn't been a Welsh surgeon there to stitch it up on the spot Meshach said he would be walking today on one leg instead of two.

— Good for him, it will be, Meshach said. A man needs a woman. Scholar just the same as anybody else. Don't forget your jam-pot.

Joe ran back across the uneven surface of the back playground, jumped the low wall of the path that led to the boys' privy and raced down the side corridor to the entrance hall, where he saw the large front door of the school had been opened. The class-room door of Standard Two was also open. Moving closer he saw his maternal grandmother. Her black bonnet was clamped firmly on the back of her head and wagging as she spoke.

— There you are, she said.

Her eyebrows were always arched upwards and her eyelids hooded, so that her expression was always a mixture of surprise and rebuke. She was taller than his father, who was clearly afraid of her.

— There you are, John Miles. You sit there teaching in a church school,[8] and you don't deny it. Two shillings you took from my rent jug and you took it this morning, from a widow's rent jug, you took it.

— I was going to tell you …

— But you didn't, did you? And it's not the first time, either.

— It's the end of the month, Mrs Owen, he said.

— I know the date as well as you do, John Miles, she said. And I know what you took it for.

Wearily he lifted his penholder to point at Joe standing in the doorway.

— The boy's listening, John Miles said.

His grandmother turned to look at Joe.

— Tie your shoelace, she said. Do you want to fall and break your neck? Now then, John Miles, where is it? I took your flask and now you carry a bottle!

— The boy … his father said.

— I'm glad he's here. Just give it to me.

— What …

— The bottle! Hand it over.

He opened the desk and brought out the half-bottle of Irish whiskey. It was still a good third full. She snatched it from his hand.

— Come here, Joseph Trevor, she said. Joe shuffled up to her.

— Hold that jam-pot out.

She tugged the cork out of the bottle, holding it away from her as if the smell would do her damage. She tipped it into the jam-pot.

— There's been a dead frog in there, *Nain*,[9] Joe said.

— So much the better. Take it to the petty and pour it away. Joe looked at his father. He was holding his head in his hands.

— Do as I say, boy, and be quick about it.

He ran through the dark corridor again and saw the smoke from Meshach's pipe rising from the urinal. He heard the clatter of empty buckets being put back. There was a whiff of creosote in the air. He looked down at the base of the drain-pipe and poured the whiskey down the grid.

CARLO THE BLACK sheepdog was on the granary steps his tongue hanging out and his tail swinging, sweeping the dusty steps. This meant that Lydia was up there exploring. The floorboards at the far end were worm-eaten and unsafe. Pa had warned them not to play there. So had Ned. So had Dan Llew. Kate stared at the dog. The dog did not move.

— Come away, Carlo, Kate said. Come away.

She spoke as quietly as she could and the dog watched her, as if she were playing a game. Biting her lip, she moved closer.

— Come away, Carlo!

The whisper was fiercer. The dog moved his sharp head, his long tongue, curved, wet, still hung out with naked pleasure. She clenched her small fist and punched the dog as hard as she could in his soft black belly. Carlo slipped down the stone staits with a yelp of surprise. As fast as she could Kate raced up the stairs to catch Lydia under the low eaves doing something she should not be doing because Ma had gone away and there was no one about who had the time to keep her in order and make her behave as well as her elder sister.

Lydia sat reading on the granary floor, her smock spread out around her among the unswept remnants of the winter oats. When she saw Kate she jumped up and held out the old magazine. Its comers had been nibbled into a ragged curve by the mice.

— Put that down, Kate said. It isn't healthy. And look at your smock, it's all dirty. It's all dirty, isn't it?

Lydia brushed her seat and said:

— Look, Kate. Look at this. The story of this girl. She was pale and sweating. Her two little brothers had died. She couldn't sleep at night. The doctor had given her up and shaken his head. She was spitting blood. The mother was in rears. Then they were told about the New Blood Pills and she took them and in three weeks she was back in school. Look!

Kate took the magazine and held it between finger and thumb.

— It's old, she said. And it's dirty. Look at the date, 1884.

— But you can still get them, can't you? Just ask for Gwilym Flook's New Blood Pills. And there's an address rhere. Look: Apothec's Hall, Ponrypridd. Where's that Kate? South Wales?

— What for? Kate said. What do you want them for?

— For Ma, Lydia said. To make her better.

— Ma's all right, Kate said.

— No she isn't, Lydia said.

— She'll be all right when she's had a change of air.

— No she won't, Lydia said.

She screwed up her face to stop any tears coming to her eyes.

— How do you know?

— I heard Maggie Morris and Mary Parry Rice talking this morning. Mary Parry Rice said, 'The poor thing, she's gone away to die'. I heard her. Look Kate, look what it says here. '. . . These exceptional Pills strengthen the body and do not weaken it because they contain Flook's Essence, the most powerful combination the world has ever seen of the most effective herbs for purifying and strengthening the Blood...'

— It's all for selling, Kate said. It isn't true.

— How do you know?

— Well that's what it's for. For selling.

— Let's take it to Pa. Show it him.

— Pa doesn't want to be disturbed. He's got a headache. He told me. He's sitting in the parlour with the blinds down.

— I'm taking it to him. Lydia said.

She snatched the magazine from Kate and ran past her, heels clattering down the stone steps. In the yard Carlo appeared and ran behind her barking.

JOE'S GRANDMOTHER'S cottage where he and his father lived, was the nearest house in the village to the water pump, so Joe was the only boy in the village who went for water with one bucket, and his grandmother's cottage was the only house in the village without the wooden square for balancing buckets hanging on a nail near the back door.

— Joe, is that you?

His grandmother called from the kitchen. He poured the bucket of drinking water into the deep yellow glazed interior of the water pot on the slate slab and replaced the wooden lid.

— Come and get your supper then, Joe.

Joe set the empty bucket upside down on the slab. He felt the buttons of his corduroy trousers to make sure they were closed. Mrs Owen, his maternal grandmother, was entertaining Miss Dowell of Bangor, who was going to many his father. They were not using the parlour because that was where Joe's father did his studying. A small cold cheerless room, cluttered with furniture. There was a red cloth on the table on which Joe's father had once spilt ink, leaving a stain roughly the shape of the map of Africa.

There was boiled mutton for supper in honour of Miss Dowell. His grandmother and Miss Dowell had finished eating, but they still sat at the table over a cup of tea. Joe sat on the settle against the wall and his *Nain* put the plate of mutton and potatoes in front of him.

— You eat those all up now like a good boy, she said. More tea, Miss Dowell?

She seemed to close the oven door, put the oven cloth out of sight and pick up the teapot without taking her eyes off Miss Dowell. Everything in this kitchen in which they lived was at his grandmother's command, from the blackleaded grate to the gleaming plates on the old oak dresser. Even the wall clock with its broad ornate face and discrete tick seemed to have yielded to a subordinate place in her scheme of things. Outside her cottage the tall hedge which surrounded it was kept in perfect order and it was her pleasure on summer evenings to walk slowly down the garden path, a black shawl over her shoulders, and see that the rows of vegetables were in order and that the eight apple trees, with the bottom half of their trunks whitewashed, were free from any pest or blight.

— As I was saying, Miss Dowell, Joe comes with me to chapel. His father goes to church. That is the understanding we came to when poor Lilly died.

Miss Dowell nodded. She had a lot of pale yellow hair, but it was so fine that when it was dressed it all tended to slip either to one side or the other. At the moment a loose strand was suspended over her right eye and she kept on having to brush it away, with the back of her hand.

— You'll not find him easy, Miss Dowell, Mrs Owen said, taking Miss Dowell's cup to refill. There's no point at all in not facing what's got to be faced.

— I quite agree, Miss Dowell said.

— You could call him weak, but is he weak if he gets what he wants? I don't call that weak.

— No, not really. Miss Dowell sipped her tea.

— Evasive. That's what he is and that's what you'll have to look out for. Very evasive. Now my Lilly never saw this because she idolized him. But I saw it.

Miss Dowell glanced meaningfully at Joe, who was eating his way steadily through the mutton and potatoes.

— He doesn't remember her, Mrs Owen said. He's the living image of his mother and he doesn't remember a thing about her. He's very like my mother's brother, the late Reverend Joseph Hughes. He was a minister with the English in Liverpool. A very promising preacher. Only thirty-nine when he died.

— That's very sad, Miss Dowell said.

— He might have done great things, Mrs Owen said. But we must bow to the will of the Lord. Blessed be His name.

Joe looked at Miss Dowell. Miss Dowell was known to be church.

— Yes indeed, Miss Dowell said.

— He may have had the weakness when he came here, Mrs Owen said. I don't know. I don't want to judge him harshly, of course. A fresh start in a new position could make the world of difference. I'm not denying but . . .

— Little ears are listening.

Miss Dowell spoke lightly, putting up her hand to the strands of hair that hung over her eye.

— He found the bottle in the dovecote, Mrs Owen said. It's just as much of a cross for him as it is for me.

Joe bent his head as he wiped the gravy on his plate with a lump of bread.

— 'Burdens are light when borne with love,' Miss Dowell quoted. She smiled modestly when Joe's grandmother seemed to acknowledge the quotation with approval.

— It will certainly be your burden, she said. Marriage isn't all roses, so you'd be well advised to be prepared.

KATE AND LYDIA in their chapel clothes sat in the wagonette that had been sent from the castle to collect them. They were being driven by Browse, an Englishman who was Lady Glanadda's second coachman. Browse, noted for his jokes, had a cough, and even though the sun was shining he complained about the cold wind. He wore a heavy brown coachman's cloak that was tinged green with age and inside it he looked as shrivelled as an old hazelnut in its shell.

— Cor, this wind, he said to himself.

Lydia nudged Kate.

— Say something to him, Lydia whispered. He'll say something funny.

They simpered at each other and giggled. Lydia turned around to see their farm, with the house in the centre like an ancient stronghold spread over the crown of the hill. It was one of the best farms on the Glanadda estate. There was washing blowing in the orchard above the house. The farm's two biggest fields swept down below the farm to the high wall that surrounded the Great Park. Over the tree-tops below them they could see the shadows of clouds being driven across the crinkled surface of the open sea and just a glimpse of the narrow yellow margin of sand dunes.

— Go on, Lydia said, say something soft.

— Say it yourself, Kate said.

— Mr Browse, Lydia's voice lifted daringly.

Browse turned his head to look at her. There was laughter on her face already before she spoke.

— Mr Browse, say something soft, Lydia said.

He lifted his whip and cracked it around the horse's ears.

— Rice pudding and shit, he said.

The horse jerked forward so that both the girls tumbled on to the floor of the wagonette laughing helplessly. They pulled themselves back on to their seats, flushed and excited and longing to shout, as the wagonette rumbled down the remainder of the hill. The lodge children rushed out to see the wagonette swing around the corner and through the tall monumental gateway.

— Look at him, Lydia shouted. Georgie Pig! Georgie Pig!

She pointed at the eldest of the lodge children, who stood looking after them.

— Lydia! Don't shout so much.

Kate pulled her arm, but Lydia shook her arm away and looked back to put her tongue out at Georgie.

— He pulled my hair in school, Lydia shouted. Georgie Pig, that's his name and that's what he is.

Once in view of the Gothic mansion, Browse slowed up the horse.

— Look at 'im, he said without turning round.

Kate and Lydia couldn't see anybody.

— Who? Lydia said.

— Griffiths. The keeper. He's watchin'. Just waitin' for his chance to run to Her Ladyship with a tale or two. You want to watch out for him.

— Can't see him, Lydia said. Can you, Kate?

Kate shook her head.

— 'e's be'ind the big oak, Browse said. He spoke between tight lips, his head pressed back as if he were imparting a very deep secret.

— You want to watch out for 'im. Regular bloody spy.

Lydia started to giggle.

— No, Browse said. I ain't jokin'.

Lydia put her hand over her mouth, but her shoulders were still shaking.

— Fair one she is for laughin', ain't she? Browse said looking at Kate and Lydia burst out laughing again.

— Look, Lydia, look! Kate said.

She pointed to the deer peering at them from the trees on the left. As the wagonette drew nearer they scampered away.

— I've seen them before, Lydia said, from over the wall. With Ned.

— Yes, but so near, Kate said.

— Nearer than that, Lydia said. Shall we be going to the Big Doors, Mr Browse?

They were coming to the point where the main drive bore off to the right and the straight road led to the rear buildings.

— Guests for Sir Charles, Browse said. Right up to the front door.

Browse pulled a large iron ring. Lydia looked up at the doors.

— They're as big as a church, she said.

— Hush, Kate said.

A rusty grey-haired butler opened the door. He looked down at Kate and Lydia.

— Ah yes, he said.

His voice was husky and he was deaf.

— Poor Mr Jones' little girls. Follow me, my dears.

Lydia turned to see if Browse was with them but he had already started on his bow-legged way down the steps to the wagonette. Behind the butler they were compelled to walk slowly. Their heads bent upwards to look at an ornate ceiling and they both walked into the butler, who had stopped. He stretched out his arm and kept them to his side. Her Ladyship was approaching accompanied by two priests in long black cassocks. Lydia listened to their voices. Her Ladyship she had seen before, coming in and out of her carriage, and on two occasions calling at Argoed, bringing Ma and Pa presents from Rome where she had been on a pilgrimage, to see the Pope it was said, after certain struggles with nonconformist tenants concerning tithes and religious education[10]. Pa was a leader of the nonconformists. They were speaking neither English nor Welsh. It was a language the girls had never heard before. Her Ladyship stopped.

— Who have you got hiding there, Kelly, she said, pretending to peer at Lydia and Kate. Not the two Misses Jones by any chance?

She turned to say something very quickly to the two priests. The older one smiled pityingly; the younger, who was very dark, looked grave and lifted his hands to his breast. He held a small black gilt book, with his finger marking a place.

— Take them up to Sir Charles, Kelly, Lady Glanadda said.

She smiled brilliantly at the girls.

— I'll come up and see you both in a while. Shall we take tea together in the nursery, perhaps?

— Yes please, Lydia said.

The tall lady laughed throatily and bent to pat Lydia's cheek. Then she moved on and the priests followed her inclining their heads to listen carefully to what she was saying.

— Come this way now, Kelly said.

They followed him up a pitch-pine staircase which curved in such a way that it seemed to kill the noise of their footsteps.

— Are you afraid, Lydia whispered in Welsh.

Kate shook her head.

— I am, Lydia said. Will we have to do as he says?

— This is the schoolroom, Kelly said, knocking at a door and opening it.

— Good afternoon, Sir Charles. Here are two young ladies to see you.

All round the large room there was a handrail. Near the tall fireplace a boy sat at a table, writing. A fire burned brightly, but the boy had a shawl over his shoulders. He wore an Eton collar. There was a footstool under the table. In spite of the thick grey stockings and trousers buttoned below the knee, the boy had the thinnest legs they had ever seen and Kate was forced to pluck Lydia's sleeve to stop her staring at them.

— Good afternoon, dear sir, Kate said. We trust that you are better.

— Will you allow me to leave, Sir Charles, Kelly said. Her Ladyship will be wanting me.

The boy nodded.

— Go in now, girls, go closer, Kelly said. You can play some game or other I'm sure until tea. Enjoy yourselves.

Kelly went out. Suddenly the boy jumped up. The girls stared at his legs. He swayed unsteadily,

— I haven't been very well, he said.

His face was long and pale. He tried to smile. His eyes moved from one to the other. He had a hushed-rushed way of speaking the girls could barely understand. He blinked hard and pushed his thin fingers through his hair.

— I was very sorry to hear about your mother, he said.

Kate looked at Lydia apprehensively, as if she expected her to cry or misbehave in some way. Lydia's eyes were fixed on the window, although there was nothing to see except the tops of the trees that covered the slope above the park, and the clouds driven across the blue sky by the sharp wind from the south-west,

— Would you like to see my great uncle?

By some stealth the boy had changed his position completely. He was now holding on to the handrail almost alongside them. There was a stale smell about him, but his smile was very winning. Many of his teeth were bad.

They followed him down a corridor which seemed to lead to the front part of the house where the windows were even bigger. Often he put his hand against the wall to steady himself. His steps were

short and toppling. He moved like a child who had only just learnt
to walk. Outside a particular double door he stopped, lifted his eyebrows comically and raised a finger. Lydia smiled and Kate looked at
her and smiled as well.

The room was a combination of bedroom and library. Bookshelves
stretched from floor to ceiling and yet in the darkest corner there
was a wash-stand and a hip-bath. Among the books the brass and
iron bedstead seemed austere. In a high wheelchair an old man sat
looking through the window. Alongside his chair there was a reading
lectern, but the two books on it were closed. The legs of his old-
fashioned steel spectacles were folded and the spectacles lay alongside
the books.

— He never reads now, the boy said. He just sits there all day, looking through the window, until they come to put him to bed. They
have to do absolutely everything for him. He's even worse than I, if
you can believe it.

Lydia smiled again.

— Can you speak Welsh? he said to Lydia.

— Yes, Lydia said, and English.

— And you? he said politely to Kate.

— Yes, Kate said.

— I'll show you something.

He hurried across the room and dropped awkwardly to the floor.
He pulled at the doors of a long cupboard beneath the book-case.
Kate and Lydia stood beside him.

— Sit down, he said.

They both looked towards the figure that sat looking through the
window.

— It's all right, the boy said. He can't hear a thing. He never moves
all day. I spend a lot of time in this room. I know where everything
is and none of them know I come here. Look at this.

He opened a large manuscript book that had two columns of writing on either page.

— I wonder if you'd mind telling me, he said. This writing. I don't
read it at all. Is it Welsh?

Kate bent to take a closer look.

— I don't know, she said.

Lydia's head came down alongside her sister's.

— Of course it is, Lydia said.

— It's Welsh?

The boy looked at her keenly.

—Yes of course, Lydia said.

— Read me what this says.

He put his finger on a passage. Lydia saw that his finger-nails were bitten down to less than half normal size. Nail-biting was strictly forbidden at Argoed Farm. She looked at his face again. He was serious. She looked down at the ancient writing.

— It's three words anyway, isn't it? he said.

She looked at his face again. He looked impatient. She bent her head closer to the text. There was a smell like treacle toffee on his finger.

— *Rhyfel os rhyfel*, Lydia said very slowly.

—What does that mean? The boy looked at her searchingly.

— *War if war*, Lydia said.

Kate plucked at her dress. Lydia stared back at the boy.

— I see, he said at last. I see. He lowered his head thoughtfully. Suddenly he closed the book and pushed it back in the cupboard.

—Well it very well could be, couldn't it? he said.

He struggled to his feet, leaning against the bookcase.

— Would you like to see the skeleton? he said. It hangs in that closet over there.

He pointed at a door in the far corner of the room.

— It's in there, he said. It belongs to me really. If I pull a wire I can make it all rattle. Would you like to see it?

— I'm cold, Lydia said.

—You don't have to.

He lowered his arm. He sounded disappointed.

— Did you see two priests downstairs with my mother?

The girls looked at each other and then they nodded.

— They're waiting for me to die, the boy said. They want the Castle you see. They want me to leave it to them in my will so that they can turn it into a monastery. I'm the last of the line you see.

The girls said nothing. Lydia looked very pale, as if she was going to be sick.

— I don't know whether I'll live or not. Mother is always inviting the heads of different Orders. Makes a hobby of it since my father died. If I grow up I'd like to be a soldier. What would you like to be?

— I like music, Kate said. She looked anxiously at Lydia.

— What do you like? The boy looked at Lydia gravely.

— I don't know, she said.

She screwed up her face and grasped her sister's arm.

— Kate, she said, I want to go home. She shook Kate's sleeve fiercely.

— I want to go home.

—You can't go home, the boy said. You haven't had tea yet. Lydia put her hand over her mouth. The boy frowned.

— Get her out of here, he said. Go on. She's going to be sick. Get her out!

— I want to go home, Lydia said. She spoke through her fingers. Kate turned back at the door.

— Aren't you coming? she said.

He shook his head. He was very pale.

— I shall stay here, thank you, he said. Just close the door. You can tell them I don't want any tea.

JOE LAY ON his side in the big feather bed. By the chest of drawers Miss Dowell was brushing her hair. Joe looked at her shadow on the ceiling and the huge movements of her bare arm in the candlelight. His grandmother was downstairs waiting for his father to come in.

— Are you asleep, Joe?

Joe trembled under the bedclothes and moved nearer to the edge of the bed.

— No... Aunty. Miss Dowell had told him to call her Aunty.

—You're not cross with me for taking your daddy away from you, are you, Joe?

— No, Aunty.

—Villages are awful places, Miss Dowell said.

She expanded the elastic of her sleeping cap by stretching her fingers and Joe watched the strange shadow growing on the ceiling as if Miss Dowell had two heads instead of one.

— All the gossip that goes on, Miss Dowell said. It's a wonder they ever get a day's work done.

She turned suddenly and blew out the candle. Joe closed his eyes. This meant she was getting undressed. He could hear her hanging her long skirt on the foot of the iron bedstead. She had a thing with her she called a hanger. Miss Dowell worked in London House, the biggest shop in Bangor. First assistant in millinery. She got her clothes at cost price. Joe heard a strange noise. He opened his eyes. The moonlight flooded across the bed. Miss Dowell was standing in the darkness by the door, scratching herself.

— Move over, Joe! She laughed gaily, lifting the bedclothes. Joe could not move over any further: he was already on the edge.

— After tomorrow I'll be your mother, won't I?

Her hand groped towards his shoulder. Joe kept rigidly still.

— He's not an easy man to understand.

Miss Dowell heaved herself on to her back. Light as she was she had sunk low into the feather bed. She put her hands under her head.

— I think what he needs more than anything, she said, is the sympathy and guidance of a devoted woman. When he lost your dear mother, he lost more than the world can say.

Miss Dowell sighed and wriggled into the softness of the bed.

— A man of so much education and talent, she said. I always say, Joe, there's nothing in the whole wide world more important than education. I'd like you to remember, Joe, I said that.

She turned her head to study his still shape.

— Give me your hand, Joe, she said.

She stretched her hand towards him under the bedclothes. Joe gave her his hand without turning his body. She squeezed it tightly. Her hand was very hot and her engagement ring stuck into his finger.

—You are a good boy, Joe, she said, and I want you to know you can come and stay with us in Bangor any time you like.

— Thank you, Joe said.

— It's very exciting, Miss Dowell said. From our bedroom window you can see the goods yard of the station. At night you can hear the Irish Mail go roaring past. It will wake you up at first until you get used to it. When the Prince of Wales came that time — he's King now of course, as you know — we could see it all from our window. I had people from the shop in my bedroom, it was quite a party. Mr Wasser from accounts brought a bottle of port. Oh dear, oh dear, it was . . . Joe, what's that noise?

Outside the cottage gate, there was a drooling, crooning noise and men whispering, and the squeal of a single unoiled wheel, which came to a stop. Miss Dowell jumped out of bed. Joe followed her. They rushed to the window. In the moonlight they could see Hughes the policeman, with all his silver buttons shining, and two shadowy figures disagreeing over how to balance a wheelbarrow. The gate

opened and the moonlight fell on Joe's father, lying in the wheelbarrow with his legs dangling over the front. The drooping comers of
his moustache were unusually wide apart. He was smiling, something
he hardly ever did when he was sober. Suddenly, the wheelbarrow
was tipped up and he fell out in a heap in front of the little portico.
They heard the crack of his forehead against the flagstones.

Miss Dowell screamed so suddenly that Joe jumped away from
her. She rushed to the bedroom door.

— They can't leave him there, she was saying. They can't leave him
there!

And then be heard his grandmother's voice from the foot of the
stairs.

— Yes, well come along, Miss Dowell. You may as well get used to
it.

From the top of the stairs he heard the front door opening and
Miss Dowell sobbing and crying.

3

THE REMAINS OF Aunty Addy's butter-dish and the half-pound
of New Zealand butter lay in the crumpled pages of the local newspaper in the bucket that stood in the centre of the kitchen floor. Kate
stood near the gas stove. Steam was rising from the vent tin the lid
of the aluminium kettle and she bent in order to lower the gas flame.
On the draining-board, between the gas stove and the sink, was a
knitted tea-cosy, a brown teapot with its lid removed and a tea-caddy
wih oriental decorations that were still visible. She lifted the tea-cosy
to her nose. It smelt of old tea. She turned to look with clear distaste
at the bucket in the centre of the floor. It had to be disposed of. As
she picked it up, she heard the milkboy's hurried step on the concrete
outside and the rattle of bottles in the box she left just inside the
wooden door in the trellis screen that was built across the path.

It was the morning he would hammer on the door and ask to be
paid. The money was all ready in her purse near the milk jug on the
shelf. With the bucket in her hand she stood so close to the back
door she could smell the roller towel that hung behind the door.
Outside the boy had begun to whistle and to shake the money in his
leather bag. Kate lifted the bucket and looked at its contents. With

her other hand, she felt her hair and then suddenly pressed it against the socket of her missing eye. The boy knocked vigorously. The noise was like a summons. Kate stepped back, the palm of her hand covering her eye, to reach for her purse.

LIKE SOMEONE STILL uncertain whether or not to get up, J.T. peeped between the curtains of his bedroom. His flannel pyjama jacket was buttoned to the top, but he continued to clutch it around his throat. Now that the light had lost the colour of the curtains, he could see that the day was cloudy. The view from the window was dominated by the new public house. It stood in the centre of its asphalt car park as solemnly as a collegiate church in consecrated ground. Its doors and windows were arched, and edged in dressed Bath stone, and the ground-floor windows were all made of stained glass. He touched the iron catch with his finger-tips, but the day was hardly warm enough to throw the window wide open. He anchored the window at the first hole on the latch. Slowly he straightened his body and stood as upright as he could. He stretched his arms above his head and rose unsteadily to balance himself on his toes. As he exercised, he breathed rhythmically and deeply.

On the floor he placed a side mirror that had been detached many years ago from a dressing-table that Lydia had bought in a sale. He untied the cord of his pyjama trousers and let them fall. He lifted the jacket so that he could examine the small of his back in the mirror on the floor. He adjusted the position of the mirror with his feet and frowned with the effort.

When he heard the milkboy arrive at the back door he held up his head like a man pursuing an elusive line of thought. He looked down at his legs, which were long and pale and unusually hairless. He let his pyjama jacket fall and put both his hands on the small of his back. He kneaded the flesh as hard as he could with his fingers, and stretched himself to his full height, like one who is determined to keep an upright carriage as long as he is able.

WITH HER HEAD still lowered, and her hands stretched out as if to push away the air that impeded her progress, Kate struggled to arrive at the front bay window in order to catch sight of the milk-boy before the van moved further down the Avenue. The way was clearer than it would have been because she had already moved the small round table nearer to the fire, as she always did, for increased cosiness. The table had been laid for breakfast and the fire had kindled smokily in the grate.

The van was moving and the boy's head already out of sight. The windows needed cleaning. They were blurred by the damp weather and the sand that sometimes blew down the street. Rain that had fallen during the night filled the pot-holes in the unadopted road. Kate put her hand on the wooden sill of the bay window in order to lean forward so that she could see further down the Avenue. The vehicle was painted red and cream and it bounced on the road's uneven surface. The boy leapt out before it stopped, but now they were so far off, she could not read the expression on his face. He was pulling out bottles as the vehicle still moved. She looked down at the four fingers of her right hand pressed against the wood she herself had varnished brown three years ago. The wedding ring on her finger was out of all proportion, thick and heavy, and yet it could no longer be passed over the swollen knuckle. The skin of the hand was papery, but still womanly and not yet discoloured by extreme old age.

A sudden shift of light behind the clouds showed her a ghostly image of herself in the window-pane. There was an area of darkness around her eyeless socket, like a ragged hole torn in a white mask. She turned away quickly as if she were as eager not to see her image as not to have it seen. She moved to the round table near the fire and studied the objects she had lain out on the white tablecloth: two knives with blades shortened by long sharpening, two large cups, two white plates, a pot of home-made marmalade labelled with a date in her own handwriting, which tended to slope backwards.

She lifted her head to make a detailed survey of the mantelpiece. On the left there was a small bundle of birthday cards tucked behind a Staffordshire figure of young Lochinvar.[11] She moved the cards as if her glass eye were hidden by them, felt the surface of the shelf with her fingers and then looked at her finger-tips to test for dust. There was a framed postcard-size photograph of Ronnie's three children taken some years ago; the presentation clock; the lustre jug filled with cotton reels; a box of wedding-cake from Hugh's daughter in Canada; a plain brass candlestick with half a candle and behind it a box of matches.

She put her fingers to her lips and turned, frowning, to look around the room. She moved quickly to the hall and hesitated at the foot of the stairs. She climbed two steps to see if the bathroom door was open. She continued to pull herself upwards, but just as her head was about to come level with the next floor she saw J.T.'s bare feet as he hurried across the landing. She watched him as he closed the bathroom door. He was wearing a gaudy red dressing-gown that had been given to him by his eldest son.

Kate stood still on the stair, looking first down and then up as she clung to the handrail like a climber who pauses to decide whether to carry on or turn back. On the wall above the turning of the stair hung an enlarged photograph of her mother, and as she looked upwards a second time it seemed to take all her attention. She moved up to study it more closely. It was a photograph of a dark young woman taken perhaps in the eighteen-eighties. She had large eyes and high cheek-bones and her hair was piled up in curls. Kate stared at the cameo brooch on her high collar and the lips that were beginning a smile.

A spluttering sound from the bathroom made her turn her head sharply. It was the puffs and snorts of a man soaping his face vigorously and holding it close to the water to be splashed. Down in the kitchen the kettle was still boiling. In a moment he would call out for the white enamelled jug of shaving water that she always left outside the bathroom door. She hurried downstairs.

CHAINS OF BUBBLES hung from his nose and cheeks until he turned to grope for a towel along the edge of the bath and they burst in the air long before he buried his face in the towel. He rubbed his face hard and then leaned forward to inspect his image in the small mirror hung for reasons of space on the airing-cupboard door. His white hair which he always wetted when he washed stood on end and he screwed up his face as if he were examining it with some distaste. He moved closer to the mirror to examine the mole on his cheek. It was an interesting shape and not unbecoming with a square, flat healthy-looking head. A benign growth a doctor once called it and ever since it had seemed a friendly object, although strange and inviting daily inspection.

He shut his eyes and appeared to be thinking. His hands, lost in the folds of the towel, were raised in front of him and still. Before moving again, he began to hum. It was a hymn tune. His eyes opened and they were bright and full of intent. The red dressing-gown hung from the hook behind the door. From a pocket he extracted an old envelope, which he held up to examine. There were pencil scribblings on the envelope, which he could not read. He shifted closer to the window for more light on the paper which was partly crumpled.

There was a sharp tap on the bathroom door. He heard Kate's voice mutter the phrase 'Your hot water,' and he thanked her warmly in a loud voice, pressing the envelope back into the pocket of his dressing-gown. The enamelled jug was scented with shaving soap and the steam from the hot water increased the smell and spread it around. He paused as he picked up the jug to peer down the stairs, but Kate had already returned to the kitchen.

He pulled the plug out of the wash basin and set the white enamelled jug in it. The patent razor which he had had for twenty-five years was drawn back and forth several times on a leather strap before he locked the blade in the safety head and dipped the whole razor in hot water. The stick of shaving-soap was low like a candle nearly gutted, and from long use the bristles of his shaving-brush radiated from their stunted centre like an expression of surprise. He soaped his chin with the impersonal speed of a barber working on someone else's face. Stirring the hot water with his razor he moved his head to try and take in the view of the hills from the bathroom window. The narrow window could not be opened more than two inches without revealing the interior of the bathroom to anyone on the back lawn of the semi-detached house next door and therefore Kate herself had put a short thick screw in the window-frame that made it impossible to open the window more than two inches. As if to keep himself warm J.T. made trumpet-like noises with his lips. He stretched his left arm over the top of his head to pull up the skin of his right cheek, and as he lifted the razor he sang shakily — 'Your silver trumpet sound'.

4

JOE MILES SAT on the wall outside the one-storey house of the widow whose living-room was used once a fortnight for the distribution of Parish Relief.[12] On the small green which was in the centre of the village some girls were playing the square game, with one girl in the middle doing her best to race to a vacant corner as the others switched places or raised false alarms pretending to run, or calling in order to run while her back was turned. Joe watched the game, shaking pebbles loosely in his fist, moving his head occasionally, and narrowing his eyes as if looking for a target.

A tall man in black clothes and a panama hat pushed his old-fashioned bicycle up the narrow path between the green and the widow's cottage. He would need to lean his bike against the wall where Joe was sitting, and carry his black Gladstone bag[13] into the living-room where the chairs had been ranged against the wall for the poor to sit on before he called them to stand in front of the table while he questioned them, made notes in his log-book and gave them the minimum sum to cover their most urgent needs.

— Get down from there, boy, the tall man said.

He was tired and cross and late. Joe was trying to unfold his left leg, on which he had been sitting, without wriggling about disrespectfully as the Relieving Officer spoke.

— You'd be better doing a day's work instead of idling on top of a wall. Aren't you ashamed of yourself? What's your name?

— Joe Miles.

The tall man opened his mouth as if to say something even nastier. Joe saw that sweat was running down from the grey hair at his temples. And there was a faint sweat stain rising above the narrow black band of his panama hat.

— Just get down, the man said. Come on, come on.

He removed the bicycle-clips from his trouser-legs and hurried into the cottage to attend to his business. Joe stamped his left leg and studied the wheels of the big bike. Jac Tŷ'n y Maes came to stand next to Joe. He was wearing his cap with the peak in front and his hands were in his pockets to show he was relaxing. Joe was so pleased that Jac was standing next to him that he dropped the pebbles from his hand and began to blush. When Jac turned and squinted up at the sky, Joe did the same as if it were the only thing to do.

— I'd hate to have to take money from him, Jac said. That's why I'm going to learn a trade.

Joe nodded eagerly. One of the girls was pushed against Jac and then ran away giggling and protesting. Jac took no notice. After a quick glance at Jac's stern face, neither did Joe.

— Are you going to sea, Jac? Joe said.

— Good God no, Jac said. What's the use of that! I'm going to learn a trade. Fitter.

— What's a fitter? Joe said.

— I've got my indentures, Jac said. He pronounced the word 'dentures'.

— Three years with Griffiths at the Aber Forge. Then off to Birkenhead. To the shipyards.

Inside the cottage an old woman had started crying. The Relieving Officer's voice could be heard too, harsh and peremptory.

— Good God, Joe said. Listen to that. If she was my mother I'd go in and poke him one on the nose. The old horsefly.

Across the green, Joe saw his grandmother leaning on their front gate, waving to him. He prepared to excuse himself to Jac, inclining sideways in what could have been taken as a bow.

— Got to go, he said to Jac. Will there be a run tonight, Jac?

— Maybe, Jac said. We'll see.

Joe retreating from Jac's presence walked backwards.

— I expect so.

Joe jumped with delight, turned on his heel and raced across the green to his grandmother's cottage. She had a letter in her hand.

— I want you to take this to the Post Office, Joe. Are your hands clean, Joe?

He wiped his hand on the seat of his trousers and took the letter. It was addressed to his father. He put the written side of the envelope against his jacket.

— *Nain*. Joe frowned and wrinkled up his nose.

— Yes, Joe?

He looked up at the stern face and the grey hair parted so accurately down the middle.

— I want to learn a trade, Joe said. If you've got a trade you'll never be without money.

— Money isn't everything, my boy, his grandmother said. There's always work for those who aren't afraid to work.

— I want to be a fitter, Joe said. Is that all right?

— If I knew what a fitter was, she said.

— Prentice to a blacksmith first, Joe said. 'Dentures.

— Needs be very strong, his grandmother said.

— I am strong. Aren't I? Everybody says I'm strong.

— Isn't a boy in the village who gets better food than you, I know that much, she said. Hurry up now or you'll miss the post.

KATE HELD LYDIA'S hand. They both sat on a wooden trunk, staring at the rim of light coming under the door. The light spread out in the bottom corner and showed a few inches of the stones in the wall. There was no latch on the inside of the dispenser door, so they were locked in under the stairs until Pa decided they could be released.

They heard hob-nailed boots striking against the flagstones in the kitchen. Someone was looking for something. Or someone was coming to free them. Kate squeezed Lydia's hand. They both sat forward, tense with the expectation of release. The boots shuffled inconclusively. They heard a drawer open and shut. And then the boots began to ascend the stone steps from the kitchen to the churn room and fade away into the bright world out of doors.

— He'll be very sorry if we die, Lydia said.

— You musn't cry, Lydia.

Lydia pulled her hand away.

— I'm not crying.

— We shouldn't have gone to look, Kate said. And you should have said sorry to Pa straightaway. And I should have dragged you away instead of standing there with you watching.

— Everybody's got to do it, Lydia said.

— But we shouldn't have been watching.

— He should have gone to the petty in the orchard, the same as everyone else. I wish I'd given him a push. Get his soft arse in the nettles,

— Lydia! You shouldn't use that word.

— He's horrible.

— He's our cousin. He's staying here as our guest and we should be as hospitable as ... as ... Pa says.

— I'll tell Griff to twist his arm, Lydia said. And I'll pull his hair. The nasty little sneak. I'll teach him to shit in our nettles.

— Oh, Lydia. You musn't talk like that whatever you do. You really musn't. If Pa heard you he'd . . . well . . . he'd . . . please, promise. Really. Please. You musn't.

— I don't care what he does, Lydia said. He can kill me if he likes. I don't care. I'm not afraid of dying.

— Oh, Lydia, please. You musn't say that . . .

— Serve him right if they find us both in here dead. In a hundred years' time. Wrapped in cobwebs. It's all his fault.

— Lydia, please. Don't talk like that.

Kate groped about in the darkness for her sister's hand. She found it at last. Her fingers passed over her sister's fist and began to pull at one finger after the other so that she could take Lydia's open hand in hers.

JOE LAY IN bed with a smile on his face and he was still not awake. On his other side Ifan Cole turned to face the wall and belched in his sleep. Joe opened his eyes. The hammering on the small anvil below the window echoed through the yard of the smithy. It was late, because Isaac Dafydd the smith was shouting in his high-pitched impatient voice — Up, Joe boy, up, Ifan Cole! When the smith was veering towards anger he often addressed people by their full names. Joe gripped Ifan's shoulder and shook it hard, but Ifan rolled further away to the darkness where the low ceiling came down to the level of the iron bedstead.

— Ifan! Wake up! It's late!

Ifan belched again and cursed weakly. His breath smelled strongly of stale beer. Joe pulled a face and then swung his white legs out of bed to pull on his corduroy trousers, pushing down between his buttocks and the seat of his cold trousers the warm flannel shirt in which he had slept. He crouched down to catch a glimpse of the early morning mist through the low window. Isaac Dafydd had gone in again. Across the road at the open end of the smithy yard he could see the mist lying thickly on the hidden stream and clinging to the leafy branches of the alders and the willows. The two milking cows were not in the meadow. It was likely that they would be moving about in the young trees,

— Ifan! Come on. We'll get some mushrooms. I'll ask Mrs Isaac to fry them up for breakfast.

Ifan made the noise of being sick and buried his face in his pillow.

— Lovely smell from the kitchen, Joe said,

— Shurrup, will you.

Ifan's voice was muffled.

Joe bent his head as he passed through the low doorway, pulling a broken comb through his yellow hair as he ran. He bounded down the stone steps and across the yard to open the bottom half of the door of the smaller stable and let out Fly, the sheep-dog. Together they crossed the road and raced down the lane towards the river. Joe sang at the top of his voice until he stopped suddenly and put his hand on his head as if he were feeling for his cap. The dog — with a cheeky bark — plunged into the mist that clung to the ground before the trees and Joe shouted a restraining command, keeping his eyes on the wet grass. He saw a cluster of three mushrooms, the larger one a day or two older than the others and beginning to blacken and curl at the edges. Joe knelt down to pick them carefully so that earth came away with the plump stalks. He balanced them gently on his open palm, his fingers slightly crooked to hold them. He moved slowly down the meadow and his heavy boots gleamed with dew. Pursued by the over-eager dog, the two black cows lumbered out of the mist, their udders swinging. Joe shouted again to curb the dog. The cows made for the lane at their own pace. He followed them, keeping his head down, but he saw no more mushrooms.

In the yard Isaac Dafydd was again banging the anvil with a hammer. The cows stopped, intimidated by the noise. Joe ran ahead and opened the gate. The cows stepped into the mud and followed him towards the door of the shippon[14] which he had opened. He dropped the mushrooms on the dusty sill of the shippon's small window. As he tied their chains about their necks, through the wall he could hear Isaac Dafydd shouting in the yard.

— Ifan Cole! As the door turneth upon his hinges, so doth the slothful upon his bed![15]

Isaac stamped across the cobbled yard to the forge to make sure the fire was alight. The cows rattled their chains as Joe jumped over the partition into the hay bin. He opened the small door into the yard and saw Ifan Cole stretching his thin frame at the top of the outdoor stairway that led to the room in which they slept. He was very pale and his eyes were screwed up against the pain of the bright sunlight. Mrs Isaac was calling in her peculiar cooing manner that made a completely different impression from the calculating curiosity of her glance. The hot bread-and-milk stood on the table ready to be ladled into their wooden bowls. Ifan swayed unsteadily on the stone stairs. He slipped down the last four steps, the steel rims on his clogs striking sparks from the stone. He just kept his balance, then he vomited, over the small anvil. From the forge Isaac Dafydd saw it happen.

— Water, you dirty devil! he said. Joe! You too. Water from the spring. Get the cane-brush! Hurry up! No breakfast until it's all been washed away!

LYDIA HAD WASHED her hair. Still wet it spread over the towel she wore like a shawl over her shoulders. She was standing on a chair in Pa's bedroom holding the framed photograph of Ma which hung over the fire-place. There was a neat patch of unfaded wallpaper to show where the picture belonged.

—You shouldn't, Lydia.

Kate stood in the doorway in case anyone should come in the house unexpectedly.

— Ned is sure to come back for his shears, Kate said. I'm sure of it.

— I can put it back again, Lydia said.

She was prising out the board at the back of the picture with a small meat-hook.

— It won't look the same.

— Don't be such a baby, Kate.

The board split. It made a ripping noise as Lydia pulled it out. It was thin wood that split easily.

— Look what you've done! It's in four pieces! Kate said. She stamped her foot angrily.

—You're awful, she said. You're awful, Lydia.

— I can mend it.

Lydia still stood on the chair and looked at her sister calmly. She made her eyes bigger to show she was going to laugh.

— It's not funny, Kate said.

— Don't worry so much, Lydia said.

She looked at the pieces of wood on the hearth-rug. A paper fan with a floral pattern filled the blackleaded fire-place.

— I'm older than you, Kate said.

— And don't you wish you weren't.

Kate looked hurt by the quick, cheeky answer.

— I'm going anyway, she said.

— Don't be soft, Kate. You know I was only joking.

— There's nothing there, anyway.

—Yes there is.

—What?

—This.

— Mind my glass! Lydia!

The glass wobbled loosely in the frame. Kate's hands flew out.

— Hold it then.

Desperately Kate took the frame, the photograph and the glass in her arms and clasped them tightly. Lydia was studying the piece of dirty white cardboard that had kept the photograph wedged in position in the centre of the frame. She jumped down from the chair and took the cardboard to examine it in the light. She sat down on the low window-sill. Eveiything was quiet in the yard and the sun warmed the outcrop of brown and yellow stone beyond the garden gate.

— It's nothing then, is it? Kate said. There was nothing there after all, was there?

Lydia didn't answer. There were lines on the dirty white cardboard and numbers and names.

— Let's go for a walk, Lyd, Kate said. It's nice out. Just to the top of the hill behind the orchard if you like. It's nearly time for the Irish Mail.

— You go if you want, Lydia said.

— We haven't watched it for weeks, Kate said. And it's such a clear day. Come on, Lyd. Put it back. Come on, Lyd.

Lydia shook her head.

— You go if you want, she said.

Kate did not move.

— You go if you want, Lydia said. My hair's wet.

— What is it, then?

— It's a map. Map of a farm I think. The fields have got names and numbers. It's not a farm I know. The names are all strange.

— Anyway it wasn't what you thought, was it?

Clutching her burden, Kate bent her knees carefully to reach the pieces of wood on the rug.

— Well Pa was engaged, anyway. And this woman broke it off. Maggie Morris told me.

— Maggie Morris tells lies.

— This woman used to write to him. Maggie Morris told me. Even after they were married. Then she died of a broken heart. Ma found all the letters. He used to keep them in a Palethorpe's Sausage box. Ma found them in the granary. She did.

— Well her picture isn't there, is it?

— No, but it could have been.

— Well, put it back then. Pa will be back. Honestly, he told me he might be back early today.

— Don't tell fibs, Lydia said.

— Someone's sure to come. Someone is.

— I know what it is!

— What?

— This of course!

Lydia held up the rectangle of cardboard.

— He's kept it as a souvenir. This is where he used to meet her. There, see? By this clump of trees. Somebody's put a circle there in pencil. It's very faint. You can only just see it. He only had a map to look at. No picture. No photograph. Only a map. And he's kept it all these years.

— Don't be daft, Kate said.

She looked at Pa's double bed, which they both made every day. The brass bedstead was the best in the house, and the mattresses were piled so high, with the feather one on top, there was something royal about it.

— Put it back, now, will you, Kate said.

— Ma never knew. It was hidden behind her all the time. She never knew. It will be an awful shock for them both when they meet.

— Who?

— This woman and Ma. And Pa too . . . .

— Meet where?

— At the Resurrection, Lydia said.

— GIVE THE SLEDGE to Joe, Isaac Dafydd said.

He was angry. The flames from the forge lit up his dark frowning face. Ifan Cole looked at Joe who was working the bellows and holding his head down to hide his embarrassment. His hands that still gripped the sledge-hammer were trembling.

— Give the sledge to Joseph Trevor, Isaac Dafydd shouted. And be very quick about it.

He was clearly annoyed with himself for showing so much excitement, for being distracted by Ifan's condition. He shifted his feet on the cobbled smithy floor like a boxer who moves without taking his eye off his opponent, and took a fresh grip on the bent hazel rods with which he kept the grooved chisel poised above the red-hot metal of the plough-beam.

— Now! he shouted, beside himself with impatience.

Joe rushed over, grabbed the sledge-hammer out of Ifan's limp hand, and took his aim at the base of the chisel. He kept the long-handled hammer steady with his left hand, and held his right hand free to slide up and down the handle as Isaac Dafydd had shown him when teaching him to hammer a horseshoe nail of mild steel into a ring for a pig's snout in three quick heatings.

— And again! Isaac Dafydd said, encouraging him. And again!

The clanging rang through the forge and Ifan Cole stood by, watching with his mouth open.

— To the bellows! Isaac Dafydd shouted.

Ifan grabbed the bellows handle and still watched them. He had been in disgrace all day because of the trouble with his vomit. Carrying extra water from either the well or the stream took up valuable time. Ifan worked like a penitent at the bellows, and the fire at the heart of the forge glowed intensely.

— And again!

Isaac Dafydd pulled a grim face each time the sledge-hammer struck the head of the chisel.

— And another, boy! And another!

The heat from the plough-beam forced their heads back, and sweat began to pour down Joe's forehead. There was no time to wipe it away with the back of his hand. All he could do was narrow his eyes and keep his aim fixed on the hot end of the chisel. He had to go on striking until Isaac Dafydd told him to stop. His tight lips stretched with determined concentration. If necessary he would go on all afternoon.

GRIFF SAT BY the kitchen fire without saying anything. He was still wearing the brown boots he wore for school. His feet were on the hob and his hands in his pockets.

— Is the kettle boiling? Kate said, without lifting her head from the large farmhouse loaf she was busy cutting.

— How should I know, Griff said.

He did not lift his head up.

— Not yet, Lydia said quickly.

She was setting out part of Ma's best tea-service on a tray.

— Reach the cake, Kate said to Lydia.

Lydia stood on a chair and brought down the cake tin from the top of the cupboard. She pulled off the lid and smelled it. Kate glanced at her quickly.

— Is it all right, then?

— I hope it poisons him, Griff said without looking up. His hands twisted in his pockets.

— What does he teach? Lydia said.

— I told you, he said, French.

— What have you got against him, though?

— Everything.

Griff kicked the hob with his boot. Kate looked up as if she was going to reprove him. Instead she said to Lydia:

— Put a doyly on the plate first. And cut the cake. It's bad form to put an uncut cake on the table.

— Cut his throat while you're at it, Griff said.

— He's with Pa, Kate said. That's no way to talk.

Lydia went to the dresser to get a cake knife from the cutlery drawer. She paused to try and overhear the voices in the parlour. She listened intently but she could hear only the calves beginning to low at the gate that led to Cae'r Groesffordd. Soon it would be time to feed them.

— Kettle's boiling, Griff said.

— Quick, put the tea to soak, Kate said.

She sounded brisk and efficient.

— We've got to hurry. The boys will be in soon wanting their tea.

— Will you let me take it in, Kate? Lydia said.

— Pa told me to, Kate said.

The two girls faced each other across the tray. Lydia held her head on one side in a comic-begging posture.

— I know, but I'm dying to see the man, Lydia said. What did you do to him, Griff?

— If you ask me he's done something awful. Mr Nevin wouldn't have come all the way up here to see Pa if he hadn't.

Lydia made a face, imploring Kate not to upset him further as she put her hands on the tray.

— We'll take it in together, she said, smiling. The two Miss Jones of Argoed. Come on, it will be fun. It needs two anyway. You bring the teapot.

— Wait, Kate said.

It was her right to go in first, being the elder daughter. But while she was picking up the best teapot covered by an immense cosy, and the teapot stand with its lion's paw at each corner and pink tiled surface, Lydia had gone ahead with the tray. But she did not go in first.

She put her ear to the door to try and overhear what the schoolmaster was saying. She made a face at Kate to stop her opening the parlour door.

— I'm not arguing, Mr Jones, that the boy is totally depraved. Far from it, I assure you. But his behaviour towards me has bordered on the malevolent, I must confess . . .

— His voice sounds all teeth, Lydia whispered into Kate's ear.

Kate hooked a paw of the teapot stand over the little finger of the hand that held the teapot and grasped the brass door-knob with her left hand, preparing to raise her right knee to give the door the extra shove it always needed to open.

— The truth is all I want to hear, Mr Jones. That is the whole purpose of my journey. I've nothing against the boy. Nothing at all. It has always been my endeavour to . . .

— Knock! Kate whispered.

Without making too much noise, Lydia kicked the door dexterously with the toe-cap of her buttoned boot.

— Please excuse us, Kate said.

Mr Nevin jumped to his feet. He was tall and thin and he did have unusually big teeth which made him appear to be constantly smiling.

He wore a kind of summer cravat the girls had never seen before and he hastened to remove his boater from the table where Lydia plainly had decided to set down the large tray she was carrying.

Pa looked very solemn. He sat in the horsehair armchair which used to be Ma's and which figured as the Empty Chair[16] in the family photograph which had been taken the previous summer, the day before the annual preaching festival when many of the family had new clothes. The photograph, well framed and mounted, now hung on the parlour wall behind the piano, which Pa played whenever he felt in low spirits.

— Shall I pour, Pa? Kate said.

— If you please, *merch-i*,[17] if you please.

The fingers of his right hand played a quiet tattoo on the narrow arm of the chair. He was wearing the suit of dark tweed that he usually wore to go to market, and a winged collar with a black tie. His hands were pale and sensitive, unhardenend by regular manual labour. Lifting his dark eyebrows slightly, he tried to dismiss Lydia with a glance, but she continued to look intently at Kate pouring tea, and trying to prevent herself from smiling in a way that made a dimple come and go in her cheek.

— Lydia.

Pa very rarely raised his voice. He used a soft tone to exert his authority that was sometimes tinged with a widower's sadness. He stroked the underside of his beard, which was streaked with white, with a patient finger.

— The boys will be wanting their tea, will they not?

Lydia tried to attract Kate's attention, but Kate was handing Mr Nevin a cup of tea, and keeping her gaze from his exceptionally long front teeth.

— We mustn't keep them waiting, Lydia. They've got a great deal to do.

— Yes, Pa, Lydia said. She looked at Mr Nevin and said 'Please excuse me' in a firm voice.

— Close the door, *merch-i*, Pa said, just as she was passing through it.

— If you please, he added, so that she should not be tempted to bang it.

Through the door she heard him say:

— They are seven, Mr Nevin. They are seven.[18] Motherless, like the children in the poem. Five boys and two girls.

Lydia pushed her foot forward on the flagstone in the dim passage. She put her hand on the edge of the long dresser and smelt the wax polish. She raised her head. Mr Nevin was speaking, his voice a murmur, rising and falling, rapid and unintelligible.

Lydia pushed the kitchen door behind her. The top hinge had sagged and it never closed without a vigorous push. Griff had looked up quickly as she came in. She caught the look and pushed the door as hard as she could.

— I never saw anyone so hideous in all my life, she said.

Griff looked at her from the corner of his eye and looked away again.

— Honestly, Lydia said, coming closer to him to show her sympathy. He's horrible. Griff, tell me. What did you do?

— I don't want to tell anybody.

—You know I won't split. I never split.

— It's a bit childish really. I punctured the tyres of his bike with my compass. Back and front.

— Is that all?

— Well he caught me at it.

— Why though? Why did you?

— He kept on trying to make me look small in class. In front of the other fellows.

— Well he deserved it then, didn't he? Come on, help me make tea. Come on. No use sitting there brooding. Lay the table for me, Griff. Come on.

— Me?

He looked astonished.

—You may as well, Lydia said.

She winked and they both laughed.

JOE PULLED OFF his blacksmith's apron, which was made of sail-cloth, and hung it on the rusty nail that jutted out of the wall. Outside it was a warm evening. He stripped off his flannel shirt and looked around for his piece of soap. There was a great deal of sweat and coal dust and grease and iron marks to remove. He set a bucket of cold water on a stool near the open door. With an air of casual freedom he snatched the red-hot tongs from the fire and plunged them into the bucket of cold water, so that steam rose up with a great hiss and splutter. In the doorway Ifan Cole was trying to clean the clay pipe he used for smoking shag with the doubled stem of a fully-grown dog's foot. He had had some kind of a wash already, but there were still streaks of dirt visible on his neck.

— Raising spirits tonight, Ifan said.

Joe smiled at him gratefully. Ifan was good-natured and clearly bore no grudge against him. Ifan was pointing at the blacksmith's cottage. Mrs Isaac was putting a lamp in the window. The light glimmered on her round face, on the big combs she wore in her hair and on her restless eyes.

—The little green man is troubling her again, Ifan said, every time she goes into the cellar.

Joe laughed and began soaping himself lavishly. Ifan raised his voice above the splashing of the water.

— Every time she goes into the cellar, she says, he's there.

Joe nodded to show that he had heard.

—There's a special exorcisor coming from Flintshire, Ifan said.

— What's that?

— He releases the spirit so it can go away, Ifan said. Pity you don't smoke.

He put the clay pipe back in his waistcoat.

— Do you believe in it? Ifan said. That sort of thing. You know what I mean. All these children who come in here and put their hands in that water to get rid of warts. She tells them to come you know. Charge them she would, if she could.

— No I don't think so, Joe said. She hasn't had much education.

— I haven't either, Ifan said.

He put his thumb and forefinger in his waistcoat pocket and tapped them against each other, narrowing his eyes thoughtfully.

—This little green man talks to her. If she doesn't answer he bangs the cellar door in her face. She's afraid of being locked up down there, you see, and nobody hearing her. I don't like her much, but I can see her difficulty.

— Is that him coming? Joe said. The man from Flintshire?

— Duwch, no,[19] Ifan said. That's Parry Price the school. I'm going in.

— Wait for him, Joe said. He wants us to go with him to Pen-y-garn I'm sure.

Ifan did not move away. The figure had come nearer and there was no mistaking the jerky excitable walk between the hedgerows. He wore no hat and his coat was open and his heavy drooping moustache could be seen moving up and down as if he were talking to himself. He bent his elbows so that his arms worked like pistons as he forced himself along as fast as he could go. His mouth was working with the effort. His eyes bulged out of his head and he lifted his hand to fold the loose lock of hair that had flapped alongside his head as he hurried forward, over the baldness on the top of his head.

—Well, boys, he said, are we ready, are we ready? The Lord is waiting and the Lord is willing.

— I'm hungry, Ifan said.

— Run to the house, Parry Price said, pointing to the open door-way of the cottage across the cobbled smithy yard as if neither Ifan or Joe knew where it was.

— Ask the good woman for a loaf of bread, and bring it with you.

— I want butter as well, Ifan said, and I want my buttermilk. I'm hungry.

— On the cross-roads! Parry Price said.

He lifted his finger oratorically.

— Man cannot live by bread alone! It's two and a half miles to Pen-y-garn chapel. On the way I will tell you the story of my life.

— I don't know.

Ifan wiped his mouth with the back of his hand so that a smudge spread across the pallor of his newly-washed face.

Joe ran across the yard and raced up the outside steps to the granary loft where he and Ifan slept. His best suit lay in moth-balls in the bottom drawer of the battered chest of drawers that was left there for their use. As he pulled the suit out the moth-balls rattled on the thin bottom of the drawer, which he left open, sagging downwards. The suit had belonged to his Uncle Hugh, who had been a pupil teacher in South Caernarvonshire and died some years ago of tuberculosis. The material was heavy and the cut a little old-fashioned, but when he put it on it fitted him very well. He pulled on the woollen socks he had last worn on Sunday. There was no time to clean his boots. His only tie was already inside the hard collar which hung where he had left it on Sunday evening over the bottom rail at the foot of his bed.

— Can I come up, Joseph Trevor?

Parry Price stood in the low doorway, blocking the violet sky his head bent forward inquiringly,

— This is where you sleep? Not bad, not bad. I've seen much worse, you know. Does he kick?

He pointed to the impression Ifan left on the flock mattress of the unmade bed.

— He snores, Joe said, smiling.

— That's not quite as bad. Did you know you had a long nose?

As he put his jacket on Joe smelt the strong smell of carbolic soap on his hand and pressed his fingers against the side of his nose. There were one or two large blackheads there he would have liked to squeeze had there been time.

— It's not as big as all that? he said.

—That's not what I meant, Parry Price said. I was speaking in parables, my boy. What is a nose for? To breathe you may say, but I say more than that. To sniff the way, Joe Trevor, to cut a furrow down the Field of Time. A long straight furrow. Did you ever hear that one before?

— No, Joe said.

— It's mine, Parry Price said. And I've got plenty more where it came from. I'm fully equipped to climb the pulpit stairs, my friend, but I can't bring myself to do it. Did I ever tell you how I was called to read the scriptures from the pulpit at the tender age of nine?

— No, Joe said. No, you never told me.

— The famous preacher was late and the chapel was full. People were losing interest. The women were leaning over their pews and beginning to gossip. My grandfather couldn't bear it. He just couldn't bear it. So he got up and he said, pointing to me, 'Joshua Parry Price,' he said, 'will you come forward?' My mother pushed me out of my pew, and he called me again, bustling about in the big pew — he couldn't bear idleness or time being wasted. 'Up you get,' he said to me, 'and do your best. Remember whose grandson you are.' So I did my best and while I was in the middle of reading I looked up and saw the great visiting preacher standing at the back of the chapel, listening to me. It was a great experience.

— I'm ready now, Joe said.

—You'll need a bite to eat, Parry Price said, I'll wait for you down by the cross-roads. I'm expecting the son of Tanmarian and William Parry, the second carter of Taldir.[20] There will also be many others! Maybe tonight, Joe Trevor. This very night, The Great Call!

Parry Price moved down the granary steps backwards, with his hands reaching out towards the steps, as if he had no head for heights. In the doorway, buttoning his waistcoat, Joe watched him descend. He gave him time to clear and then clattered down himself at speed, and shot across the yard to the floor of the cottage. In the kitchen he filled his bowl from the cauldron hanging over the fire. Mrs Isaac stood with her fat arms folded, watching him.

— Did I see Parry Price in the yard? she said.

— That's right, Mrs Isaac.

Joe was eating as fast as he could.

—Where's Ifan Cole, Mrs Isaac?

— I've sent him with the trap to Gadlas Bach. I hear their sow has littered. He can bring two piglets back towards their shoeing bill. You watch out for him.

— Who Mrs Isaac?

— That Parry Price. As he came down the road I saw a yellow light behind his head. He used to be a drunkard.

— He never drinks now, Mrs Isaac.

— He isn't married, either. What's wrong with a man of forty earning sixty pounds a year for teaching little children that he can't be married? When you come in tonight be quiet about it. After the seance I shall be in a very delicate condition. You see to it Joseph Trevor. No hymn singing outside. If they start at the cross-roads you tell them I told them to stop, on behalf of the spirit world. Remember now!

LYDIA KICKED A path for herself through the nettles and cow parsley that grew tall against the dairy wall. This part of the kitchen garden was neglected and she had been forced to walk through Ned's rhubarb to get at it. She put down the meat sandwiches she was carrying and struggled to remove the slates that covered the iron grid that used to let daylight into the cellar where the beer barrels were stored in the old days before Ma had persuaded Pa to take up teetotalism. The slates were sharp-edged and they cut into her fingers, but she pulled at them frantically. One of them split and she pulled away the separate pieces. She lay on her belly and called her brother. For a while he did not appear. She kept on calling. The light from above her shoulder struck his white face in the gloomy interior. She asked him to come nearer. Then she saw he had been crying.

— Quick, she said. They think I've gone to the petty. Quick, take these. Take these. Is there anything else I can get?

There was a step in the cellar, on which he stood so that he could teach the hole with his hand. Lydia put the sandwiches carefully through the grid so that Griff could take each one separately.

— I'd like a drink, Griff said, clearing his throat before speaking. It was easy to tell he had been crying for some time.

— Next time I come out, Lydia said.

— Don't let Kate see you.

Griff's mouth was crammed full. His secret tears seemed to have given way to an intense hunger.

— Do you think he'll let you out soon? Lydia said. Her voice was as considerate and polite as she could make it.

— I don't care whether he does or not, Griff said.

— Did the beating hurt?

— Not much.

Griffs voice strengthened as he ate.

— That bastard Nevin sat there watching. He loved it. Never had the guts to do it himself.

— What's a bastard? Lydia said.

— I let Pa do it, Griff said. I could easily have taken the birch from his hand if I wanted to, but I let him do it.

— Is there anything else I can get, Griff?

He looked up at her.

— There aren't many lads as strong as I am who would let their fathers beat them at the age of sixteen. I could have broken that rod in two. Do you understand that?

Lydia nodded hard.

— In front of a stranger. A man like Nevin.

Lydia kept nodding.

— I know, she said.

— And I'll tell you one thing, he said.

She leaned forward to bring her ear as close as possible to whatever it was he was going to tell her. He was addressing her almost as an equal. Eagerly she watched his square determined face.

— I'll go to college, he said, if Pa wants me to. I'll pass the exams. I'll pass them all, but I'll tell you one thing. I won't become a minister.

— Griff. Griff. Would you like some tobacco? Dan Llew's got some. I saw some in his locker this morning when I was doing the beds.

He smiled at her.

— You'd better not, he said. If he caught you he'd give you an awful beating.

— I don't. . .

— Lydia!

Kate was standing behind her. Lydia scrambled to her feet. She brushed her skirt, putting out her hand so that Kate backed into the rhubarb.

— If you tell Pa, Lydia said, I'll never speak to you again. You're standing in Ned's rhubarb, you'll get a row!

Kate moved away quickly. She spoke in a hurried whisper.

— It was very wicked what he did, Kate said. He was entirely to blame. He's only getting what he deserves. Showing off all the time.

— If you say a word to Pa, Lydia said, I'll tell Ned you trod on his rhubarb.

PARRY PRICE LED the way down the steep hill from Pen-y-garn chapel. All the young men were singing. Parry Price waved his arm and sometimes turned to face them to urge them to sing with greater fervour, so that they could carry the spirit of the meeting with them into the depths of the sleeping countryside. Cattle lying the other side of the tall hedgerows heaved themselves up. Their legs and tails swished noisily through the wet grass.

In the darkness Joe could not see whose arm was linked with his own. Sometimes his feet were trodden on. His voice was hoarse with singing the words with meaningful emphasis.

> *Good Jesus Christ is on our side*
> *His blood shall wash us clean and free . . .*

When they came to the end of the hymn there was a pause when only the tramp of their footsteps and heavy breathing could be heard. In the front Parry Price began to shout.

— Don't stop, boys! Let the Holy Spirit flow like a mighty river down the torrent beds of Wales! Let us feel it, boys! Let us feel it.

In an exhausted voice he began to sing.

> *Ride, King of Hosts to victory,*
> *The sword of Death sheathed at your side . . .*

The company was tiring, but it made a great effort and the hymn rolled out. Someone tapped Joe on the shoulder. He released his arm and touched the person shuffling behind him.

— Ifan? he said. Where have you been?

— I was passing the chapel, Ifan said, on my way back from Gadlas Bach. I had two piglets under the net in the trap. Did you hear them squealing?

— No, Joe said.

He shook his head and cleared his throat to continue singing.

— It was awful being outside, Ifan said. All that rejoicing inside there. All those Hallelujahs and the chapel so full. So I thought I'd come in. I could only get as far as the porch. There were so many people standing up. You were inside, weren't you? What was it like?

— Marvellous, *Bendigedig*,[21] Joe said.

He burst forth into song.

— There you are, you see, I'm always missing things. Duw, Duw, I'm an unlucky bugger.

Joe stopped singing just long enough to say 'Don't swear, Ifan,' and carried on with the burden of the hymn.

— I lost the pigs, Ifan said. When I got back to the trap they had I pushed their way out of the net. Hadn't tied it tight enough, had I?

Joe stopped singing. He said,

— Ifan what did you do?

— It's awful, Ifan said. I'm looking everywhere for them. Every where. Down by the stepping-stones I thought I heard one of them squealing. It wasn't there. Pigs is awful animals.

— Talking!

Someone pulled Joe back into line, linking arms firmly. Joe looked back over his shoulder.

— Ifan, he said. Where's the pony and the trap, then?

Ifan made no answer. Joe stared into the darkness, but he could see nothing.

— Ifan!

He called out. The young man next to him shook his arm.

— Sing! the young man said.

Joe opened his mouth.

Not the world's nor Satan's armies
Can withstand the Saving Tide . . .

They were approaching the cross-roads. There were no lights to be seen in the smithy. It meant that Mrs Isaac and Dafydd Isaac were in bed fast asleep.

Joe shook his arm free and nudged his way through the singers who filled the narrow roadway. He came to Parry Price who stood alone in front of the group, his arms outstretched. It was not so dark at the cross-roads away from the tall hedgerows and the trees.

— Mr Price, Joe said. Excuse me. Would you mind stopping the singing?

— What did you say, my boy?

Parry Price's face was gleaming with sweat and exultation.

— Stop the singing, Joe said. Stop!

He turned around to face the young men.

— Stop! he said. Please stop!

— Hey . . . who said . . . what . . . who do you think . . . Stop? Stop? This is to go on for ever. For ever and ever!

— Yes, I know, Joe said. I'm very sorry. It's just that . . . there's misfortune at the smithy. I ask you please to observe respect.

He turned to Parry Price.

— Isn't it Mr Price, he said.

Murmurs of disagreement continued. Suddenly Parry Price lifted his hand.

— Quiet! he said. Quiet, boys!

He kept his hand raised even after the silence had fallen. It became so quiet they could hear sheep cropping the short grass on the Common.

— Less than the thickness of a silk handkerchief, Parry Price said, that's all that separates us from the world of the Spirit. Glory be to God, we can speak quietly and he can hear us. We can think and He can hear our thoughts. Thanks be to Him. Thanks be to Him. Good night, friends. Good night, and God go with you.

— Tomorrow night, Mr Price? Tomorrow night again?

— If the Lord wills it, Party Price said. If the Holy Spirit moves among us. After eight at the Wesley chapel.[22] The Spirit knows no denominational barriers. Joseph Trevor, our paths lie along the same road. I want to talk to you.

He put his arm around Joe's shoulder. Two young farm labourers fell in beside them.

— It was beautiful tonight, Parry Price said, beautiful. The Holy Spirit filled the place. I was moved as I have never been moved since my sister Nansi died. Did I ever tell you how my sister Nansi died?

— No, Joe said.

Both the farm workers listened curiously.

— My father wouldn't believe she was dying until he dreamed a dream. He saw her lying on a long white bed and at the foot of the bed two angels and at the head of the bed Jesus himself. And her face was hid from him by the wing of one of the angels. And he knew by this sign that she was going to die. I remember, you know, she used to whisper, 'When I have died once, I shall not need to die again'. She was one in a thousand, my friends. She could sing and she could pray. She was one in a thousand.

When they realized the story was finished, the farm labourers told each other it was getting late.

—You go on, my friends, Parry Price said, and God be with you.

He lifted his arm, and they went forward obediently as if they had been dismissed. The fingers of his other hand clutched spasmodically at Joe's shoulder.

— It was beautiful, Joe, he said. Very beautiful. But I tell you this, I was not called. I was not called.

— I think I ought to go in now, Mr Price, Joe said.

He looked up at the window of Mrs Isaac's bedroom. The forge was still and quiet. There was no sign of Ifan and the pony and trap. Parry Price gripped his arm tightly.

— I know why, Joseph Trevor, I know why. The sinner always knows why and I'll tell you why before I spend the night in an open ditch. And may the Lord hear me as you hear me and take pity. I try to punish myself. I don't hear the call because I prefer the flesh of the male to the flesh of the female. This is my downfall.

— Well goodnight now, Mr Price, Joe said.

— Tomorrow night. I shall call for you again tomorrow night and we shall go in search of the Spirit together again? The Holy Spirit will seek us out again, Joe.

— If it's convenient for you, Mr Price, Joe said. Goodnight.

On the inside window-sill of the outer kitchen he found his candle. He lit it. The kitchen door was not locked. Inside, above Isaac Dafydd's chair there hung a small shelf where Isaac's few books were kept: *The Bible, Pilgrim's Progress,* the old hymn book and the new hymn book, *Hygiene and Housewifery Made Plain, The Collected Works of William Pantycelyn,*[23] a *Fitter's Catalogue* for 1886, and *Dr Charles's Welsh Biblical Dictionary*. He set down his candle and took down the biblical dictionary with great care. The shelf was flimsy and the leather binding of the book was loose. He opened it under 'Y' and looked for the word *Ysbryd*. The print was very small. His fore-finger traced the words.

Of the Holy Spirit the following must be considered.

(1) The Spirit in God. (2) It is a different person from the Father and the Son. (3) That it proceeds from the Father and the Son. The Father was not begotten and did not proceed from, but the Father begot the Son and the Holy Spirit proceeded from the Father and the Son. . .

There were seven columns in the small print to be read on the subject and many of the sentences were difficult to understand. He put the book on the seat of Isaac Dafydd's high-backed chair and put the candle alongside it, and he did not close the book until his finger had moved along every line in the seven columns.

5

HIS TWO HANDS advanced to pick up the wing-tipped collar, he saw them reflected in the mirror on the chest of drawers which was tilted downwards: pale hands with fingers bunched together and narrowed like the claws of a dead goose, preparing to pick up and elevate the badge of office as far as his neck, covering the plebian band of his flannel shirt and the brass-tipped collar-stud. As he began to button his waistcoat he was drawn to the window by the roar of a heavy lorry reversing at high speed across the vast parking ground that surrounded the new public house like a parade-ground surrounding a castle. Two young men in brown overalls with leather belts jumped out of the lorry and set up a ramp down which the beer barrels would roll into the cellars at the back of the building whose shutters he could now see being opened by the yawning licensee. A woman opened a side-door to shake a duster and have a look out. A gust of wind brought the smell of beer up to his window. The barrels began to rumble down the ramp. The two men in overalls worked in silence and with speed, without shouting or joking. Abruptly he shut the window. He drew in his breath and then sighed, saying, — Behold thy gods, O Israel!

KATE BENT DOWN slowly to pick up the towel. She spread it carefully over the wooden towel rail above the bath. J.T. had also forgotten to rinse his shaving-brush and put it away. Her artificial eye was not on the bathroom window-sill. The sill was made of veined marble and she had to look closely, but the eye was not there. It was possible that it had fallen on the floor. Holding the edge of the bath, which she herself had painted green on the underside five years ago, she lowered herself to kneeling position. The bathroom floor-covering was a black and white checkered linoleum. Under the bath there was a maze of lead piping which gathered dust, a dried floorcloth which had been missing for some days, the screw-top of a bottle of pills, a spent match, but no sign of her eye. She shifted her position to survey the area around the base of the lavatory-pan and behind

the door. A small pool of liquid suggested J.T. had not been altogether accurate in his use of the water closet. She struggled to reach
the dried floorcloth with her right hand and mopped up the liquid
which was definitely urine and not water. At the wash-basin she
turned on the cold-water tap and put the floorcloth to soak. She
stirred it impatiently in the running water and then wrung it out
with both hands until her fingers seemed to swell with the effort.

THE WEATHER WAS not warm enough for J.T. to wear his black
alpaca. It hung on the hook at the back of his bedroom door. Underneath hung a clerical grey jacket that he favoured on cooler summer
days. He had more jackets than trousers. There were many of them
in his wardrobe. Some of them had belonged to Kate's brother, Ned,
who had breadth but short legs. Having more jackets than trousers
lent interest and variety to his appearance, but it also meant that they
lasted longer and the number of his trousers tended to decrease while
the number of his jackets remained constant. Carefully he removed
the grey jacket from its hanger and put it on. He looked at himself
in the wardrobe mirror from head to foot, and noted the slippers, the
wide black trousers, the black waistcoat, the winged collar, the grey
jacket. His frame was thin, but still reasonably upright. He did not
contemplate his image for long. He lowered his head and creased his
nose with the effort of thinking. He raised a finger to his lips and
lowered it again. He took out the key at the end of his watch-chain
and turned his head to consider the black tin trunk that stood
between the wardrobe and the corner of the wall. He replaced the
key in his waistcoat pocket and hurried towards his chest of drawers
to the top right-hand drawer, which he opened. Against the side of
the drawer was a small batch of diaries mostly black or brown. He
picked up his spectacles and put them on. He selected a particular
diary and began to study it with scholarly interest. It was published
by the Calvinistic Methodist Church of Wales[24] and contained the
Sundays and holidays for twenty years 1916-35. He opened it at page
thirty-four which gave the list of Sundays and holidays between April
6th and June 29th of 1924. Opposite each Sunday was the name of
the church he had preached in and the text of the sermon preached.
Luke 16.25,[25] and Habak-kuk 2.1,[26] recurred down most of the page;
Luke for the morning, Habakkuk for the evening. Out of a waistcoat
pocket he plucked a minute notebook and pulled the pencil out of

its spine. He lifted the pencil to his mouth and licked the tip of it with his tongue and then made a brisk note in fine handwriting. Gilboa, Capel Uchaf, Luke 16. 25. He put the small notebook away smiling as if he were very pleased with his own efficiency. He took out the key again and kneeled down to open the tin trunk. It was packed tight with sermons which he had written in slim green notebooks that could fit comfortably into the breast-pocket of his jacket. He delved into the trunk and extracted a handful of green notebooks. He seemed to resist a temptation to dwell over their contents. With a smile on his face he found one marked Luke 16. 25 and slipped it into his jacket pocket. He considered the red dressing-gown that lay on the bed. Once again he took out the old envelope from the pocket. He peered about for his spectacles. They lay on the chest of drawers. Without putting them on he used them to magnify the writing on the envelope. He stared hard into space as if he were trying to forge a link between two separate recollections. Then he took out the green notebook and copied in the small margin of the sermon the phrase that he had scribbled on the envelope, 'The purpose of energy is doing good.'

IN THE KITCHEN Kate grasped the kettle firmly and poured a dash of boiling water into the teapot, which she twisted twice and then tipped into the sink. Her lips pushed in and out as though with annoyance. She opened the tea-caddy which had once had a gay coloured pattern all over and dug out two and a half teaspoonfuls of tea which she dropped carefully into the pot. She turned up the gas to bring the smaller kettle once more to an energetic boil, and then poured it with a strong wrist action over the tea. She replaced the lid and wrapped the cosy around the pot, leaving her hands to rest on the cosy. She turned her head slowly so that she could survey all the kitchen's surfaces with her single eye. She did not seem to see what she was looking for. She looked up at the calendar that hung in the kitchen. It gave the days and dates for July, the days in red the dates in black. But July was over. It was now August. She lifted her hand and tore off the page, crumpling it into a ball before throwing it into the rubbish bucket she kept under the sink.

6

JUST AS THE Reverend Benjamin Davies was about to pick up his fork, Pa said

— Will you lead us in prayer, Mr Davies?

The whole family was assembled at supper after chapel. Outside, gusts of fierce wind made the windows rattle and doors bang. Benjamin Davies pushed back his chair and stood up with some difficulty. His white beard fanned out on his chest as he lowered his head.

— O Lord, he said in a muffled voice and then cleared his throat noisily, let us look out through the windows of life and watch the shadows approach and let us realize as we pull down the blinds that the night will be very long. Let us put our ears to the walls of the Universe and hear the planets thundering towards the void.

He paused as if to listen to the wind outside. Kate opened her eyes to look at the old man. All the other heads around the table were lowered. Pa's, Ned's, Dan Llew's, Griff's, Lydia's, Rowland's, Hugh's; and Mary Parry Rice stood in the doorway ready to serve and anxious to hear anything Benjamin Davies said. He was a preacher famous for his peculiar sayings, and Mary had a passion for memorizing as many as she could. She was listening so intently now she could not close her eyes and her ears were cocked like a gun-dog's.

— But glory be to Thee, it will end. Yes it will end and the Sun of Righteousness will rise in all its splendour never to set again.

He cleared his throat and shut his eyes very tightly, lifting his head so that his beard jutted forward.

— We thank thee also for this quiet assembly of one of the families of thy church. And for this food. Amen.

— I didn't get hold of that one, Mary Parry Rice said bringing in the bread basket.

Benjamin Davies looked at his plate and said nothing.

— He's very hungry, Lydia whispered to Kate.

Pa looked at her sternly and she stopped talking. The meal was carried on in silence because it was clear to everyone that Benjamin Davies had something on his mind, and sometimes the wind outside blew and cracked so loudly it made quiet talk impossible. Only the busy tapping of knives and forks on plates broke the silence of the room. Towards the end of the meal the old man lifted his eyebrows and said to Pa:

— It's this old wind. Never liked it.

Pa turned in his chair to look towards the window. The heavy curtains were blowing in the draught.

— We'll go to the parlour, Pa said, and sing hymns. It's quieter on that side of the house.

— I'm afraid it's going to be a big storm, Ned said.

He put his thumb in the armhole of his waistcoat. He leaned back in his chair. He was the eldest son and he had more right to speak than the others. He was also assistant superintendent of the Sunday School and often discussed church matters with deacons and ministers. Benjamin Davies's eyebrows shot up and down apprehensively at the word storm and he seemed to go further into his shell.

In the parlour it was colder, but a fire burnt cheerfully in the grate.

— Do you feel like singing, Mr Davies? Pa said.

— No, indeed I don't, the old man said.

Kate sat at the piano, the large hymn-book open in front of her. She turned to look at the minister. He had refused to sit too near the fire or too near the window. The wind had sent a puff of smoke into the room. The minister turned in his chair and waved the smoke away. The older boys were smiling at each other. Lydia was leaning on the piano ready to sing.

— Sing till you blow the storm out, Benjamin Davies said, and his chin sank on his chest.

They began with, 'On life's great storm-tossed sea, I sing ...'

The harmony of their voices helped to soften the metallic tone of the grand piano that suffered from weekday dampness and Kate's fondness for thumping out the notes to show how well she knew them. Pa decided the programme and the family sang best when the most volume was called for. While Kate looked for a hymn that Pa had called for without, as he usually did, giving the number, Benjamin Davies was heard to speak.

— Did you say something, Mr Davies, Pa said.

— Praise Him from whom all Blessings flow, Benjamin Davies said. Best time of your life, children, remember that. Keep together in harmony. The only way to keep the storm out.

— Very true, Mr Davies, very true, Pa said. Three four six, Kate. Let's sing that one for Mr Davies. Three four six.

JOE'S EYES WERE shut tightly and his mouth was open, but no words came out. People whose backs were bent well forward in prayer, especially the women whose curiosity was more difficult to control began to turn their heads to look at him. He was tall for his age and his wavy red hair had been brushed with unusual care. He was the only person in Engedi Vestry on his feet, the only person expected to speak. The blood had drained away from his face. He shut his mouth. He sniffed. He opened his mouth. He shifted his weight from one foot to the other, and back again. The silence grew. His last words had been 'divine help'. To stop the enveloping silence he said 'help' again, in a voice that could hardly be heard. It did nothing to diminish the silence. Joe opened one eye. The minister sat in his chair on the dais, presiding over the prayer meeting, his eyes shaded by a scholarly hand. Joe shut his eyes again, screwing up his face for a further effort.

— O Lord, he said.

But nothing more. Nothing would come, not one word. More people turned to look at him over their bowed shoulders. He kept his eyes shut. He did not move a muscle. He was transfixed.

The minister released so deep a sigh that the people in the vestry turned to look at him. Once more all their backs pointed in the same direction like stunted trees shaped by the prevailing wind. The minister seemed to be waking from a deep sleep.

— Amen, the minister said. Amen.

He sighed again and leaned forward to pick up the hymn-book on the table.

— Let us now sing, he said. Hymn number . . .

Ifan Cole who sat next to Joe, kicked him in the leg and Joe sat down noisily. The congregation rose while he was still sitting down, bathed in perspiration from head to foot, his bottom sticking to the schoolroom seat. He pulled himself up and took the place in the hymn-book from Ifan, but he was unable to sing.

Afterwards as the congregation filed out he could not lift his gaze from the floor. In the porch he saw one of the Tanmarian boys grin and pull Ifan Cole to one side and whisper in his ear.

On the gravel path outside, Joe said.

— What was he saying, Ifan?

Ifan looked at him without smiling.

— It wasn't very nice, Ifan said.

They were standing in the road outside the chapel, and Joe was studying the ditch very carefully, while the people merged into groups to greet each other briefly in loud voices before making for home.

— Well, Joe said quietly, what did he say?

— Pity to waste a good blacksmith just to make a poor preacher, Ifan said in his flat voice.

— Did he say that? Joe said fiercely. Did he say that?

— Well you asked me to tell you, Ifan said.

— How does he know? How does he know I want to be a preacher?

— Well he can see for himself can't he? All those candles you buy. Everybody knows you nearly set our bed on fire and burnt me to death in my sleep. Mrs Isaac tells everybody. You oughtn't to read so much you know, Joe. It's bad for the eyes. Where you going?

— See the minister, Joe said. I'm going to have another try next week if he'll let me.

THE DOOR FROM the churn room to the kitchen was heavy. Lydia pushed it with her elbows and it swung wide open. She remained in the doorway above the steps that led down to the kitchen. She dropped the case which she had been holding with both hands and gave a broad smile that invited Kate to look at her as an audience looks upon a figure on a stage. A few books were held together by a leather strap and tied to the handle of the case.

— Gosh! It's no joke carrying this thing all the way up the hill. She stretched her arms and touched the black doorposts with the palms of her hands.

— Come down, Dan Llew said.

He was sitting in Pa's chair, which was turned from the fire-place to the head of the table at the narrow end of the kitchen. His mouth was full of bread and butter and jam.

— Come down where we can see you.

— Where's Pa?

Lydia spoke to Kate who was cutting bread and butter. The whole dresser shook slightly with the vigour of her cutting. She looked up at Lydia, who still stood on top of the steps, smiling.

— Gone to Rhuddlan, Kate said, to the Presbytery.[27]

— Tom's got nothing to eat, Dan Llew said,

He munched and grinned and pointed to Tomi Moch who also

sat at table, on the bench between the table and the wall.

— Come in Lyd, Kate said, waving the bread knife. It gets on my nerves you standing up there.

The expression on Lydia's face changed. She picked up her case and came down the steps, saying,

— Oh if that's the way you want to be.

— I didn't mean . . . Kate said, cutting away desperately at the big loaf.

— I'll just go upstairs and change, Lydia said. There were several things I had to tell you.

Lydia pushed her way noisily upstairs.

— Miss, Tomi Moch said, his small eyes glittering as he looked up from his empty plate, you are not cutting them thick enough, see.

He wiped his narrow little red nose with the back of his finger. Tomi tended to carry the smell of the pigsties with him wherever he went. Dan Llew's shoulders shook as if Tomi had made a big joke that he would enjoy repeating. Kate lost her temper.

— You shut up, Tomi Moch!

She tipped the new supply of long slices of bread and butter on to the empty plate in the centre of the table.

— And if you want any more, Dan Llew, you can carve it yourself.

— Don't take the bread knife then!

Kate stopped at the door. Dan Llew was leaning forward in Pa's chair and laughing in his most provoking way. Kate threw the bread knife in the direction of the dresser and turned away without waiting to see if it had landed safely, or to hear what Dan Llew would have to say. She kicked off her clogs and ran upstairs.

The girls' bedroom door was closed. Kate opened it and shut it quickly, Lydia was changing, and putting away the costume she had been wearing to travel home by train from the young ladies' college at Llanelw. The books from her secretarial course, held together tightly by a leather strap, were on the floor. Kate threw herself on her bed.

— I hate that Dan Llew, she said. What right has he got to sit in Pa's chair and give orders? It's awful. And bringing Tomi Moch in with all that smell. He wouldn't wait for tea outside, just barged in giving orders.

Lydia said nothing. She had opened her case now and was sorting out her washing which she threw on the floor.

— He thinks because Pa's let him start this butchering business he can do what he likes. But what good is it going to do the family as a whole, that's what I want to know! You know how selfish he is. Thinks of nobody except himself. Look what's happening today. There's Ned having to get Isaac Hughes and our Griff and Rowland and Hugh to get the barley in and it's full of grey dust and grey thistles, and this one takes Tomi Moch to help him with the slaughtering. Prime Welsh saddles and Prime Welsh wethers indeed!

Kate looked at Lydia, but her sister was not smiling.

— I told him, Kate said, he could carve his own bread and butter! Lydia studied her washing more closely than seemed necessary and said nothing. Kate spoke again.

— I think Pa listens far too much to Dan Llew. I do honestly. Flair for business indeed! He's just sly.

Kate stopped talking and rolled on her side to watch Lydia. Her sister was bending her knees to study her own reflection in the mirror as she took pins out of her long thick hair. They were both silent. At last she caught Lydia's eye in the mirror and a smile broke on Lydia's face before she could look away.

— What's the matter with you then? Kate said, pressing her advantage.

— Well it wasn't much of a welcome home, was it?

— I'm glad you're back, Kate said. What was it like this week?

— It's a waste of time, Lydia said. Except for the book-keeping. You know what I'd like to do, Kate? I'd like to keep a shop.

— What kind of shop? Kate said,

— Oh I don't know. Any kind of a shop. So long as it was mine. Anyway I'm not going to keep this course up. I think those two old sisters are frauds I do, honestly. They don't know a thing, honestly. Do you know what Doris Humphries told me? There was a French lady staying with her cousins and she met Miss Elder, the younger sister — and she couldn't understand a word of what she was trying to say!

— Miss Elder the younger, Kate said.

Lydia collapsed on her bed with laughing. She held up a leg to watch her toes wriggling inside her stocking.

— Please miss, my leg is bleeding, Lydia said. They started to choke with laughter.

— No Lyd, you shouldn't . . .

— It's true though. That girl with a big white face what was her name . . .

— Annie.

—Yes, that's right. Think of her putting up her hand . . .

Kate began to look solemn.

—You shouldn't laugh, Kate said.

— Maldwyn Birch was on the train, Lydia said.

— Him? Where was he off to?

— Said he was coming back to the village to live. Got a job at the quarry as maintenance something.

— He's a carpenter, Kate said.

She sounded touchy.

—Well that's what he said. He asked how you were. He's still keen on you, Kate.

— Huh, Kate said.

— Remember that note he wrote to you in school. The cheek of it.

— Huh.

— He'll be round here again. You'll see. Standing in the middle of the yard. He's not afraid of Pa or anything. Do you like him?

— Me like him?

Kate sounded annoyed.

— He's only a carpenter. Pa wouldn't hear of it.

— He's awfully good looking. And he sings like a bird.

— Life isn't all singing, Kate said.

She got up and shook herself. There was a solemn expression on her face. Lydia was looking at her with respectful wonder.

—Well come along, Kate said. You'll want some tea.

THE OLD MINISTER called from his bed while Joe was still on the dark stairs.

—Who's there then?

Betsan Jones, his housekeeper, waved Joe on. Her face was fierce but friendly.

— Joseph Trefor Miles, she shouted at the top of her voice. And don't you go yelling about disestablishment[28] or you won't live to see it.

Joe saw her white dust-cap turn in the small dark hallway and float away through an open door. She had moved quietly, but the old man had heard.

— Not into the study! Don't you touch that desk, Betsan Jones!

— Touch it! I've got more respect for my fingers!

— You're in the study! Aren't you? Admit it!

— Well of course if you want the place to close up with cinders!

— There's a jackdaw in the chimney!

— Not the only place if you ask me.

— J.T.! Where are you?

Joe was standing on the short steep stairway, too polite to interrupt the argument.

— Here, Mr James, he said.

— Well come on up, John Calvin,[29] come on up!

The minister had a clear tenor voice with a bell-like note in it that seemed to carry as far as he wanted to send it. He sat up in bed with a knitted night-cap beginning to slip down rakishly over his left eye. His flannel night-gown was buttoned up to his chin and his long arms were stretched on the blanket, still holding a heavy book that he had been reading. His fluffy white side-whiskers grew below the level of his mouth.

— Are you better, Mr James? Joe said.

— I'm sixty-nine, my boy, and I can still crack nuts with my own teeth. Joe smiled and handed Mr James an ounce of shag tobacco wrapped in a neat cylinder of cream-coloured paper.

— I can't chew it or smoke it, the minister said. Thank you all the same. Keep it for me till I get better. Move those books at the bottom of the bed and sit down.

Joe picked up the books and held them in his arms while he looked around politely for somewhere to put them down. It was impossible to find a clear space on the floor of the small bedroom which was covered with books and magazines. They stood in awkward piles on the window-sill, blocking out much of the light.

— Anywhere, my boy, anywhere. Underfoot that's where they belong. They have been my downfall in this world and I sometimes fear they will cook my goose for the next.

— How's the pain in your side? Joe said. He sat down at the foot of the bed.

— Wicked, the minister said. Really wicked. Well now how did it go at Rhyd-y-fedwen?

— Fair, Joe said.

— Did you shout at all?

The minister raised his eyebrows. Joe shook his head.

— Well, never shout unless you have to. But you know, there should be occasions when you must shout. When your house is on fire you don't go out in the street and whisper the news in a neighbour's ear.

Joe shifted uncomfortably on the edge of the bed.

— I hope you didn't read every word?

— Mostly, Joe said.

— Well that's the quickest way to make every word drop dead at your feet. They are there to listen. You aim at their ears. Why didn't you learn it by heart? What was your text?

— 'What shall it profit a man if he gain the whole world?' Joe said.

— Well there you are. That's a good sermon. Very good sermon. It shows that you know what the gospel is about. You like people, don't you?

— Yes I suppose so, Joe said.

— Well there you are you see. I never did. Not really. I liked an audience. I liked a congregation. And the worse they were the better I liked them because the more chance it gave me to punish them. A great art you know, preaching. My hero was Henry Rees.[30] I heard him many times when I was your age. When he was in the pulpit the man prevailed over the Puritan. His sermons glittered with startling images and powerful appeals. He was my hero. O dear me. I'm not really ready to face my Maker. You know what the trouble with me is J.T.? I'm a very worldly man.

Joe smiled broadly.

— What are you grinning at? asked the minister.

— Worldly, Joe said. You paid for the new vestry out of your own money.

— That's not what I meant. Not at all. I did that just to be independent. To keep the deacons quiet. Keep my stock high at the Presbytery. Well there you are — my motives were entirely worldly. All the long years of my life I have rushed about from one place to the other preaching, preaching, preaching, and all the words I have used and all the meetings and sessions and synods[31] I've attended have used up all the time I should have spent getting closer to Him. Showing off, J.T., instead of getting closer to Him.

— Mr James, Joe said. The reason I want to be a preacher is because of you.

— Me? James tapped his chest with the tip of his fingers.

— I was sitting with Ifan Cole and Isaac Dafydd listening to you one Sunday morning two years ago. I don't remember what your sermon was about. There weren't many there. The sun was shining anyway. It suddenly came to me. There was nothing in life so exciting and interesting as doing good.

Mr James looked at him judicially.

—You don't remember which sermon?

— I'm afraid not, Joe said.

— The date? Do you remember the date? I could look it up in my diaries. I've never preached the same sermon at Engedi twice.

— About two years ago, Joe said. In the spring, I think.

The minister pushed his night-cap back and folded his arms.

—The young are always so thoughtless, he said. That's the difference between us, J.T.

He pointed at Joe accusingly.

—You are young, he said, I am old. Fifty years between this end of the bed and the other. There's no sense in it. I should be giving you advice. How's the Greek going?

—Very hard, Joe said. Very stiff. I was too long at the forge. Stiffened my brain.

— Nonsense, the minister said. Peg away at it! With a chisel and sledge! Hebrew too. Nothing more important. Get at the texts, J.T.! Always get at the text, It's worth all the effort you put in it now. Stand you in good stead for a lifetime.

Joe listened carefully, his eyes intent on the minister's face. He gave a small nod at intervals to show how intensely he was concentrating on what was being said.

— I tell you one thing, J.T., that worries me as I get older. I can answer all the questions. I know exactly where I stand on the drink question, on sectarianism, on disestablishment, on justification by faith, I can give you a yes or a no on every issue.[32] But as I get older I find it harder and harder to pray properly. I read somewhere — Coleridge I think — that the curse of the worldly man was the inability to pray. All these years I have been making my mind less and less accessible to the working of His controlling grace.

— Mr James, Joe said.

The minister waved him into silence.

— Prayer is the great mystery, J.T., he said. It presses itself upon me, and yet I have fought and I am still fighting to resist the aggressive generosity of God. What do you think of that?

— Well, in my opinion . . . J.T. said.

— How can you understand what I'm talking about? Fifty years like mountains of dead time between us.

The minister stared at Joe out of a dramatic expression of despair, his dark eyes unblinking.

— I do understand, Joe said urgently.

The minister lifted an accusing finger.

— I know you, he said. I know you. Your instinct is to comfort. You like people, you see. You'll be a better minister than I have ever been.

Joe shook his head vigorously.

— No indeed, he said.

— Get on your feet, boy, the minister said. I'm going to pray.

Joe stood up, balancing himself against the bed because there were books under his feet. The minister clasped his hands tightly together between his short legs, which were rigid under the bed-clothes. There was a long silence. Then the minister said,

— Teach us to pray, O Lord.

There was another long silence. Joe opened his eyes. The minister was looking at him.

— Pray, J.T., he said. Pray, will you, before my heart turns as cold as my soul!

MALDWYN BIRCH STOOD in the shelter of the coal-shed doorway, five yards from the back door of Argoed. The wind and the rain lashing at him made him turn away from the back door which was closed. From where he stood only the top shelves of the dresser could be seen through the kitchen window. Whatever was happening in the kitchen was out of sight. Moving into the rain for a moment, through the small churn-room window he caught a glimpse of Mary Parry Rice washing out the churn and hurrying in and out of the dairy, before he dashed back into the meagre shelter of the coal-shed doorway. He had given her a note for Kate more than twenty minutes ago, but there was still no sign of her coming to the door. Once Lydia had appeared in the little window of the passage that led to the boys' bedrooms. She had stood there long enough for him to see her wave and smile and then she had gone, absorbed into the endless activity of the farmhouse's warm interior. Maldwyn had begun by humming softly to himself his tenor solo in 'The Crusaders,'[33] but now his feet were getting wet and he was silent.

The back door opened suddenly. Maldwyn turned and rushed towards it, but Kate did not move aside for him to come in.

— Can I put my head under the doorway? he said. It's this wind. It keeps blowing the rain down my neck.

Kate moved backwards a pace, and he stood on the piece of wood that was meant to keep out the draught at the base of the doorway.

— Can you come? He smiled optimistically.

— Of course not, Kate said.

— I'm singing two solos, Maldwyn said. The proceeds are in aid of the Weslcyan chapel. Bring Lydia as well, then your father won't mind.

— I'm not coming, Kate said.

— Why not?

Maldwyn Birch was the best-looking boy in the village and his voice was generally admired. It was also said of him that he was a tireless worker and a skilful craftsman.

— You take a good deal for granted, Kate said. Maldwyn became red in the face.

— You mean I'm not good enough for you, he said.

— I never said that.

Kate looked beyond his left shoulder as if someone else had appeared unexpectedly under the archway that led to the farm-yard. Maldwyn did not look around.

— I can't help it if my mother drank, Maldwyn said.

— I never said you could.

— She doesn't drink any more and I never touch a drop, Maldwyn said. You ask anybody.

— I never said you did.

— Well what's the matter then . . . ?

He held out his wet hands in an appeal to reason.

— Well, for one thing I'm much too young to be talking like this. And you keep on calling round the back here. Pa won't like it.

— You're nineteen, Maldwyn said. Kate raised her head angrily.

— Who told you? Who told you?

— Never mind, you are, aren't you?

Kate's round face grew red.

— You'd better go, she said.

Her thumb clicked the latch of the back door up and down.

— Didn't you read it? Maldwyn said. Didn't you read my note?

— You'd better go, Kate said, or I'll call Pa.

— But Lydia told me last Sunday after chapel . . .

— I'm not Lydia and Lydia's not me, Kate said. Kindly let me shut this door.

Maldwyn turned and took a despairing look at the sky. The rain beat against his face. He heard the door slam behind him before he had reached the archway.

THE DOOR OF the living-room at Argoed was open and Pa sat at the table, preparing the financial statistics for the chapel annual report. He lifted an ebony ruler and he was about to draw a thick line across the page of the ledger. He contemplated the page, raised his eyebrows and gave a peaceful sigh. Lydia and Kate stood in the passage, dressed for housework. Lydia had a duster in her hand and she was screwing it around the brass door-knob of the open door. Pa looked at her over his glasses as if he were surprised that they should still be there. He said,

— Fold it up, *merch-i*.

— But Pa . . .

— We shall put it down next Saturday as we've always done in this house.

— But Pa, Lydia said, say somebody called on Wednesday or Thursday, called . . . callers . . .

— There is a door at the bottom of the stairs, Pa said, which I always require to be closed. If the door is closed no visitor will know whether there is a carpet on the stairs or not. Now don't waste any more of my time.

He looked down at his ledger, but Lydia did not move from the doorway. She said,

— There's a cupboard in the churn-room, Pa, where the boys could keep shoes or slippers or something for wearing in the house.

— Fold it up, *merch-i,* and stop wasting my time.

Lydia's mouth tightened so much the dimples appeared in her cheeks.

— But it's such a nuisance, Pa, she said, every week like this . . .

— Not another word on the subject, Lydia, he said. Not another word.

81

Lydia stepped backwards and pulled the door towards her with such speed that the slam would have shattered the frosted glass in the two upper panels, but just in time she held her hand, and closed the door quietly. The polished dresser behind her gleamed in the dimmed light. Kate had already begun to climb the stairs. She kneeled down near the top to start removing the brass stair-rods. The carpet was thick and dark, a deep red with a branching ecclesiastical pattern in solemn green.

— Come on, Lyd, Kate said. We may as well do it,

— Honestly, Lydia said, sitting on the turning of the stairs. Anyone would think this was the workhouse. Honestly they would.

— Don't raise your voice, Kate said.

She began to pass the brass rods to her sister, who sat nursing them like a bunch of long-stemmed flowers in her arms. She put her head down and murmured.

— He's a damned old fool.

— Lydia!

Kate turned her head to look down at her sister, her eyes so wide they made the rest of her face look dark and smudgy.

— I wish I was a man, Lydia said. I wouldn't be here now if I was. An unpaid skivvy. I could work in an office if only he'd let me. Just because I'm a girl.

— This is your home, isn't it? You shouldn't talk like that.

— Anyone would think we were still kids, honestly.

— Well . . . you didn't like studying, did you? You said so yourself.

— I'll tell you one thing, Lydia said, looking up at Kate. I wish I wasn't a woman, but since I have to be, I'll marry the first man who asks me.

WHEN HE SAW a group of his fellow-students having tea in the overgrown garden of the Theological College, Jacobs ran out with his box camera and kept his boater on his head with his other hand. He was a plump young man and his knock-kneed run attracted their attention. Phillips sat on the garden seat, his hat tipped forward to shade his eyes from the sun. Powell wore a boater too. Already he was straightening it at the prospect of being included in a photograph. Platt Rees, the most senior student present, sat behind a bamboo table that had several side shelves at different levels, where there were plates of sandwiches and cakes. He was filling J.T. Miles's cup from a large teapot that came from the college kitchen. Griff Jones sat in a basket chair smoking a cigarette. J.T. stretched his long arm to take his cup. Frank Morgan, who was also smoking, sat near him on the unmown grass. He was in his shirt sleeves, sitting on his jacket because he said the grass was damp. But beyond him, J.M.P. Jones lay stretched at full length with his hands behind his head, smoking a pipe with a curly stem and protected from the damp only by the thickness of his tweed trousers.

— I wonder if you wouldn't all mind moving in a little closer? Jacobs put a finger to his lips. His mannerisms were a little effeminate.

— Take us as we are, J.M.P. Jones said. Warts and all.

He spoke in a deep growl without taking his pipe out of his mouth.

— Oughtn't we to have tennis rackets or something? Frank Morgan said. Cricket bats. Anything to give us style.

He had found a comb in his waistcoat pocket and he was sitting up straight to attend to his hair.

— Why don't you pop down to the river, Morgan, and bring up the college boat?

Griff sounded sarcastic. His remark made J.M.P. Jones shake with amusement. Platt Rees smiled and folded his arms. He always wore a high collar and starched cuffs. His manner was elegant and judicial. His father and his grandfather had been ministers before him. He always expressed disapproval of vulgarity or over-excitement. Jacobs moved about on the grass so that he could make Platt Rees the centre of his picture.

— Do you suppose we shall have copies? Frank Morgan said.

— If it comes out. You're sitting in too much shade really. Jacobs kept looking up and down as he spoke. His pale cheeks were beginning to glisten and blush with his efforts in the heat of the afternoon.

— Better order several dozen for Frank, Griff said, so he can send them around the churches. Just the thing for the daughters of our more wealthy deacons.

J.M.P. Jones grunted with laughter again, but Platt Rees did not smile this time.

— Come on, Jacobs, he said. Hurry up if you're going to do it.

He glanced quickly down at his cuffs as if to see how much they were showing. One of the housekeeping staff pushed open a window overlooking the garden. She was calling out, but her weak voice did not carry very well and the afternoon was so warm her waving seemed lethargic.

— Mr Miles! Mr Miles!

— She's calling you, Joe, Griff said.

J.T. sat up. The woman raised her arm again, beckoning him into the building.

— Don't move!

Jacobs called out despairingly. For a moment J.T. kept rigidly still and stared towards the camera.

The woman raised her arm again, beckoning him into the building. When Jacobs nodded J.T. raised himself to his feet. The grass was damp. He rubbed the side of his trousers where he had lain.

— He is so much in demand, Frank Morgan said. A preaching festival in Pwllheli, mark my words. John Williams Brynsiencyn[34] indisposed. Could you please help us out at short notice?

Frank Morgan laughed energetically at his own wit, and some of the others smiled. J.T. walked towards the large red-bricked house that had been converted into a theological college, still brushing his trousers as he walked. He needed to take care of his clothes.

— Somebody by the front door, the woman said, leaning out further as J.T. got near the house. A Mr Edwards. Got a round collar. looks like church. Not chapel anyway or I'd know him, wouldn't I?

— Thank you, Mrs Proffett, J.T. said.

The front door was open and the visitor was a black figure against the afternoon light. As J.T. approached he raised his hand and because his face was so darkly shadowed it was nor possible to understand what the gesture meant. J.T. shaded his eyes from the bright light and said,

— Come in please.

The visitor stepped up and for a moment his figure seemed to swell and block out the light. He came nearer, and Joe turned to look at the serious face with large moist eyes and a row of moles on his right cheek that immediately caught Joe's attention.

— Mr J.T. Miles? he said.

His voice was long drawn out, monotonous.

— That's right, Joe said.

The visitor clasped his hands together.

—You don't know me, Mr Miles. I am the curate of St. Benedict's, of Russell Road. I'm afraid I have bad news for you.

Joe's mouth opened and he stared at the man more closely.

— Your father is dead.

Joe closed his eyes and lifted his head. The curate watched him with melancholy eyes. It seemed as if the theological student were trying to remember who his father was and that the effort gave him pain,

— It is very unpleasant to be the bearer of bad news. I offer you my condolences, Mr Miles.

Joe lowered his head.

— He took his own life. He was found early this afternoon in the gorse on the hill behind the railway station.

Joe turned to look through the open doorway. The Theological College stood on a hill outside a town which lay for the most part in a narrow valley below, with the railway yard at the farther end. Above the station a gorse-covered hill rose steeply and above it was a clump of pine trees which at that moment was being penetrated by the rays of the sun declining westward. Higher than the pine trees were the mountains that he knew by name.

— It seems he drank a bottle of Lysol. It was unlikely that he knew what he was doing. I won't distress you with details, now, Mr Miles.

The curate paused.

— We must take strength, he said, from on high. I will lift up mine eyes . . . [35]

Joe opened his mouth, and the curate paused for him to speak. There was a frog in Joe's throat when he spoke.

— But he went up there to do it, he said.

— I beg your pardon?

Joe cleared his throat vigorously.

— He went up there to do it.

The curate shook his head up and down slowly.

— Your stepmother, Mrs Miles, is in a condition of great distress. Very great distress. I wonder if you could come down with me now. I have a conveyance outside.

The curate took out a notebook and pencil from a large pocket in his black jacket.

— May I suggest you leave a note for your college authorities, he said.

Joe nodded gratefully and accepted the paper and pencil. Hesitating, his hand rotated the pencil in nervous circles over a fixed point on the blank paper. The curate leaned forward and saw that he had written nothing.

— Just say you've had bad news, the curate said.

KATE SAT IN front of the kitchen fire at Argoed. It burnt low and she had a shawl pulled tightly over her shoulders. It was nearly half-past ten and the sound of the buffeting wind outside made her sleepy. Her brothers were all in bed. Her father sat in the parlour. When she left him there with a glass of hot milk strengthened by three tea-spoonfuls of whisky, he was reading an old copy of the *Christian Companion*.

The grandfather's clock in the hall passage struck the half-hour with a hollow melancholy note.

— Kate!

Pa was calling. The parlour door was open. He was listening for every sound.

— Come here, *merch-i*.

Kate hurried to the parlour. Pa sat in the chair near the fire, still wearing his overcoat, his hat and stick still on the table.

— Is there any more hot milk, *merch-i*?

— I can heat up some more, Pa, Kate said eagerly.

— No, no.

He put down the empty glass.

— Is Lydia back yet?

— I don't think so, Pa.

Her father looked at her closely lifting his eyebrows.

— You'd better go to bed, *merch-i*.

— I don't mind waiting, Pa. I'm not sleepy.

— Bed now, he said. There's a great deal to be done tomorrow.

A sudden draught came rushing through the passage from the back of the house. Pa lifted his head. There was the distinct sound of a door being bolted.

— Lydia!

There was no answer. He listened and called again.

— Lydia! She appeared suddenly in the parlour doorway, her cheeks rosy with the fresh wind, her eyes shining, and small curls falling away under her hat. She was smiling.

— Pa, you're back, she said. Well! That's nice.

— Aren't you rather late getting home, *merch-i*.

He turned over a page of the *Christian Companion*.

— I went to send Sally Rodgers as far as Bryn Bach after Seiat. She's afraid of the dark. We got talking and before we knew where we were it was nearly ten. What time is it now?

— It's just struck half-past ten, Kate said. Do you want something to eat, Lydia?

Her father's head turned towards her as she spoke and the frown of warning disappeared quickly from Kate's face.

— Did you have a nice journey, Pa?

Lydia was drawing off her gloves. Her voice was all sweetness. Pa leaned forward to unlace his boots, but his arms dropped and he gave a little groan as he straightened himself.

— My back is very stiff, he said.

— Would you like me to take off your boots, Lydia said as she unbuttoned her coat.

— Would you, *merch-i?*

Quickly she dropped to her knees before him. She moved a low brass kettle-stand from inside the fender for him to use as a footstool.

— Put your foot on this, Pa.

Her head bent closer to the double bow on the bootlaces.

— My goodness, she said, you certainly make sure that they don't fall off.

Pa leaned forward, his elbows weighing on the chair's circular arms.

— Did you go to the Meeting, then?

Lydia did not look up.

— The Seiat? She said. Yes, Pa.

Kate stood by the table trying to catch Lydia's attention. Pa leaned back, and rolled the *Christian Companion* into a cylinder.

— Honestly, this knot, Lydia said.

— Was Joseph Jones in chapel?

— Yes, Pa.

His voice was soft, gentle, unthreatening, calm, fatherly.

— Edwards Tŷ Mawr?

— Yes, Pa.

— Caleb Morris?

— Yes, Pa,

— Did Edwards speak, *merch-i?*

— Yes, Pa. Got it.

Lydia glanced up. The knot was undone.

— What was his text, my dear?

— 'Bear ye one another's burdens.' Lydia said, grasping the back of his boot and beginning to tug at it.

Pa leaned forward slightly, lifted his left arm and brought the rolled-up *Christian Companion* down against Lydia's head. It was a short sharp blow and it sent her sprawling. She gave a shout of surprise and protest. Pa said,

— I caught an earlier train, my girl, and I was at the Meeting myself.

AS THE WIDOW moved forward to look down into the open grave the toe of her boot dislodged a lump of earth. She shivered as the muddy water splashed the side of the new coffin, dirtying one of the polished brass handles, and a lock of faded hair fell over her right eye. She pushed at it ineffectively with the back of her gloved hand. The glove was two sizes too big and she kept her fingers bent as if she were afraid they would fall off. She swayed away from the steep side of the grave and let her whole weight rest on J.T.'s arm.

Mrs Owen, J.T.'s maternal grandmother, pushed her right hand in her left sleeve and peered forward for a brief last look at the coffin. The effort of looking sketched a grimace of disapproval on her face, her eyebrows lifted even higher than ever, her firm mouth lowered. She nudged J.T. with her elbow. J.T. turned to look at her inquiringly. His stepmother was clinging tightly to his arm and it restricted his movements.

— Move on, Mrs Owen said in a whisper.

It was not easy to steer the widow safely away from the hole in the ground. Inside her glove she had a small white handkerchief which she managed to extract in order to wipe her eyes. But her glove fell to the ground. J.T. bent to pick it up. His foot began to slide towards the grave. There was a noisy fall of earth. He dug in his heel to save himself. His stepmother seemed to have lost consciousness and her weight was pushing him forward. He managed to hold her in position and slowly draw himself upright again. He looked at his grandmother. She was frowning heavily. Hastily he cast about for the best way to lead the widow away from the grave.

In the new town cemetery the grass stood high and wet after the recent rain. Over an uncompleted stone wall in front of them a cow's head hung from the next field, its dewlap just touching the wall. The widow drew back, frightened. J.T. stared at the cow chewing the cud. Once again his grandmother nudged him from behind.

— Keep to the path, she said.

On the path they encountered Mr Edwards the curate. He was wearing a cassock but no surplice. The widow revived a little and let go of J.T.'s arm to lean towards the curate and take his hand as she thanked him for everything he had done, and told him over and over again how helpless she would have been in her agony without him.

— No one will ever know, Mr Edwards, what I've suffered. The agony. And the disgrace. Unconsecrated ground.

The curate nodded gravely. He looked at J.T., and with a physical effort that showed how much the widow was weighing on him transferred her back on to J.T.'s arm. Mrs Owen stepped forward and nodded to the curate.

— We must get her back to the house, she said. She's not fit to be left.

The hired brougham was waiting at the cemetery gates, the horse's rump tight against the back of the shafts because it was pointing downhill and the brakes were too worn to keep the wheels immobile. As the vehicle began to move away the widow began to weep openly and loudly. The small white handkerchief became inadequate to absorb her tears, but she went on dabbing at her reddened eyes.

— Give her your hanky, Joe, Mrs Owen said.

She looked out of the window and studied the landscape with interest. Since she had never visited the town before, everything she saw was new and she seemed to be storing all the sights and sounds up so that when she got back to her cottage she could consider it all at her leisure.

— What's going to happen to me?

Mrs Miles wiped her thin nose with J.T.'s clean handkerchief. Mrs Owen continued to look through the window. J.T. folded his arms and wrinkled his nose as if he were working on a problem.

— Nobody cares, of course. That's the truth of it. Nobody cares at all.

Mrs Owen gave up her study of the landscape and turned to look sternly at the weeping woman who occupied the middle of the opposite seat.

— You've no right to say that, Mrs Owen said. You have been shown every consideration.

— Why did he do it?

She stared desperately at J.T.'s grandmother. Mrs Owen said nothing.

— The trains used to keep him awake. He used to have nightmares about them.

She looked at J.T.

— It's the disgrace that's killing me, she said. Is it true he'll go to Hell?

— Leave the boy alone, Mrs Owen said. He's done more than his fair share already. He's signed all the papers and that house is yours. Everything is yours. He doesn't touch a penny.

— Why though?

Mrs Miles looked sly.

— Is it contaminated? she said.

Mrs Owen sat up straight and breathed deeply.

— Kindly remember that I am paying for this funeral. He wasn't my family and I warned you enough when you took him for better or for worse.

— God is loving and merciful, J.T. said. You must bear that in mind always when you think of these things.

He spoke thoughtfully with his arms folded.

— Hell is something in our imagination, he said. Try and remember that.

— What am I going to do?

The widow spread out her hands, a handkerchief in each bulky glove.

— How can I live with the disgrace? What can I do?

— Work, Mrs Owen said. You're still young. Nothing like work. Work hard and keep your mouth shut.

— I'm alone in the world, Mrs Miles said.

— You leave that boy alone, Mrs Owen said. That's a flat condition. Or you get no more help from me.

— *Nain,* J.T. said. Be more gentle. Please.

— He's got a career in front of him, Mrs Owen said. And very hard exams to pass.

She pointed an admonishing finger at Joe, and her eyebrows were raised.

— One thing you've got to learn. Just because you're going to be a minister, she said, doesn't mean you've got to be soft.

Her body was swaying with the carriage as she continued to look at him.

— I'm afraid that's something it's going to take you a long time to learn, she said.

—You mustn't think, *Nain,* J.T. said, because the gospel is expressed in . . .

— Don't preach now, Mrs Owen said. I've got a bit of headache if the truth were known.

AROUND THE HOUSE of Argoed the wind cracked its whip. It rattled and hammered at every window and door; through the yard, around the outhouses and in the stackyard that sloped down the hill, it howled endlessly. Kate was curled up in bed in a tight ball with the clothes pulled over her head. Lydia lay on her back, her arms behind her head. She said,

— He's still there, you know.

— Shut up and go to sleep.

Kate's voice was muffled by the bedclothes. Lydia laughed before making a joke.

—Why don't you get up and make him a cup of tea?

— Shut up now, will you?

Kate turned over vigorously, curling herself up again so that her knees were almost under her chin.

— Poor old Maldwyn. Honestly Kate, you treat him like dirt. The best-looking boy in the village. I tell you if it was me he was keen on . . .

Kate put her face out of her bedclothes so that her voice could be unequivocally clear.

—You can have him, she said. You can have him.

Lydia began to giggle. She shook with amusement until her iron bedstead began to creak.

— Oh dear, she said. You are funny, Kate,

— I'm glad you think so, Kate said.

Her retort made Lydia giggle more than ever.

—Write him a note, Lydia said. I'll take it to the back door.

— I'm not writing him any more notes, Kate said. Anyway he's gone long ago. Why don't you go to sleep?

— I don't feel like sleeping.

Lydia rolled her head to one side, listening.

— He's singing, she said, controlling her giggling with difficulty. He's singing 'Crossing the Plain' to keep his spirits up. Shall I tell him to try 'Martyrs of the Arena'?[36]

—You're in a silly mood, Kate said.

Lydia weighed on her elbow and leaned towards Kate's bed.

— Kate, she said, do you remember when we were kids Pa locked us in the dispenser for watching Maelor Prys doing pee-pee into the nettles behind the pigsty?

—That's what I got for listening to you, Kate said. Go to sleep.

— He looked so funny, Lydia said, hanging it out like a little clothes-peg.

Kate began to shake with unreleased laughter.

—You are awful, Lyd, she said. Shut up now or you'll never go to sleep. You know what you're like once you get silly.

— Honestly, Lydia said, this place! It's the only way you can have a bit of fun. Anyone would think you should get a prison sentence for laughing too much.

— There could be something in that, Kate said. Laugh before breakfast, cry before supper.

— Well it's after supper now, Lydia said. Honestly, you're a proper old misery.

Kate said nothing and pulled the clothes more tightly over her head.

7

IN NUMBER EIGHT Gorse Avenue, Kate stood in the small kitchen, staring at their neighbour's cat which had presumed again to sit on the window-sill and stare in. It was a black cat with a white nose, eight months old at least. Kate's right hand felt its way under the red and brown knitted tea-cosy while she kept her one eye on the young cat. The cat yawned suddenly, with a tigerish spontaneity that seemed to open her whole head with a wedge of pink rawness guarded by spiky teeth. The yawn was over as suddenly as it began and the head was restored to its domestic smallness. The cat lifted its leg stiffly and began to wash itself. Kate smiled. Her lips twitched and then the smile broke across her face, pushing up her plump veined cheeks briefly. Then it subsided and her mouth was as firmly shut as ever. The cat looked at Kate and miaowed pathetically. Kate looked back at the cat and shook her head solemnly. The cat miaowed again.

— Don't they feed you, then, my pretty? Kate said quite suddenly as if she could keep silent no longer.

— Don't they then? Don't they then?

She moved and immediately she moved the cat jumped down from the window-sill and went to wait at the door for it to open, her head and tail up, waiting. Kate went to her pantry. It had a door as big as any in the house, but inside there was just enough room to turn from the shelves on the left to the shelves on the right. High above her head there was a small window and a hygienic ventilator of old design. She peered closely at the shelves. Outside the cat miaowed. On one saucer, covered by another saucer there was the third of the contents of a sardine tin, which she had opened the night before, to make supper with half a tomato each and a bit of lettuce.

But her attention was suddenly taken with a dish of stewed prunes. It was a large deep earthenware dish and the prunes lay in a bath of brown liquid. Looking at them closely, she saw a dull gleam of white in the brown liquid. She recognized it at once as her glass eye. Carefully she submerged her finger and thumb to pull out the eye where it rested on its side between two prunes. In some agitation, without closing the pantry door she moved to the sink, turned on the tap, and placed the eye under the cleansing jet of cold water. Her fingers rubbed the eye, inside and out many times. She turned off the tap abruptly and stopped to listen for any movements upstairs, hurried back to the pantry, and took down the dish of prunes, placing them on the wooden draining-board alongside the sink. She stirred the surface with her finger, until she seemed to see a deposit of whitish mucus in the brown liquid. Holding the prunes back with the flat of her hand she poured off the juice into the sink. Then she turned the tap on again to wash away the brown liquid until there was no trace of it left. For some time she studied the prunes, tilting the dish so that they slid from one side to the other. She lifted her head and her mouth tightened. With her head well down she opened the back door and plunged out so quickly that the cat had to jump out of her way. She whipped off the lid of the ash-can, the eddying wind pulling at her piled-up hair under its net, and she tipped the prunes in. Without pausing to look around, her head still down to one side to conceal her right eye-socket, she rushed back to the house, closing the back door behind her in the cat's face.

ON THE THIRD stair from the bottom J.T. paused to study the mat on which any letters pushed through the letter-box, or any newspapers, would fall. His hands wandered over his waistcoat pockets, giving each one a light tap. There was nothing on the mat. Kate appeared in the kitchen doorway, holding the teapot, her hands almost concealed by the cosy. She stood still in the doorway and her stillness was clearly meant to direct him by the shortest route to his chair already set before the small round table that had been moved nearer the fire for cosiness in the living-room.

— Morning, he said. How are you this morning?

She directed both her eyes at him and blinked deliberately.

—There's never anything wrong with me, is there? Kate said. Breakfast is ready.

J.T. continued to stand on the third stair. He smiled, and then opened his mouth as if he wanted to say something pleasant; but he closed his mouth and grasped the banister again for support. He looked meaningfully at the mat.

— Anything come through the post? he said.

— If there had I wouldn't leave it on the mat, would I?

— It rained all night, he said.

— Are you coming down or going up?

She looked up from the kitchen doorway impatiently.

— Down of course, he said.

He stepped down the remaining stairs and as soon as he moved she crossed into the living-room and put down the teapot on a hob in the grate made from a horseshoe by J.T. when he was an apprentice in Isaac Dafydd's smithy. Still bent, she turned to see him waiting in the doorway of the living-room. He pointed towards the kitchen.

— I'll get some prunes, he said.

She opened her mouth and drew herself erect, but before she could speak he had arrived in the kitchen and was opening the pantry door. She followed him and found him peering inside the confined space, his head swinging in unsteady amazement from one side to the other.

—There was a dishful here last night, J.T. said, squinting momentarily at the ventilator above the shelves.

— Finished, Kate said.

She turned to look at the window above the kitchen sink. The black cat with a white nose had reappeared on the window-sill. She could hear its faint miaowing and see the continual small head movements it made. She clapped her hands and made shooing noises.

— Those next-doors, she said. Three old maids with nothing to do all day and they never think of feeding that cat. Come along then. The tea will get cold.

She walked back to the living-room in a vigorous manner as if she were leading the way.

— The paper has come!

She raised her voice to an unusually cheerful pitch.

— It's in here!

J.T. stood in the doorway, rubbing his chin.

— Well there was a dishful here last night, he said. I saw them with my own eyes. I saw them.

— I had to throw some of them away, Kate said. They were bad. Without sitting down she began to pour the tea. She raised the teapot discreetly to increase the noise of the golden liquid falling into the larger cup. J.T. did not move. He stood in the doorway, frowning.

— Bad? he said. I never heard of prunes going bad before.

— Anything can go bad, Kate said. Anything.

She sat down in her place, helping herself to a piece of bread and butter and, lifting the short-bladed knife, cut it into three segments. She put down the knife and reached across the table for the marmalade pot, which stood nearer J.T.'s place. Normally she required him to begin eating first. Now he still stood in the door-way looking gloomily at the table.

— Is there any All-Bran?

— Why don't you have a look? she said.

Obediently he returned to the kitchen. Her hand trembling slightly, Kate extracted marmalade of her own making from the pot. She heard him calling from the kitchen.

— I don't see any here!

— Well that means there isn't any, doesn't it? she said.

She clasped her hands together in her lap. Her legs were apart and her hands sank as far as they could, until her dress was taut across her thighs. J.T. reappeared in the doorway of the living-room.

— I'll just pop over to the corner shop and get some, he said.

Kate lowered her head.

She heard him rattle his walking-stick against the metal frame of the hall-stand as he pulled it out.

— I shan't be long! he said.

She lifted her head to speak, but the front door slammed to and she shut her mouth firmly, making a noise through her nose. She saw him pass the window, striding out beyond the low hedge, his white hair fluttering in the breeze and a protective smile on his face. After a brief hesitation she pushed back her chair and shuffled quickly to the window. She placed her right hand on the varnished wood and leaned as far forward as she could to watch his progress.

— Ready to be nice to everybody now, she said.

She looked surprised and embarrassed at the sound of her own voice.

8

J.T. CLOSED THE PULPIT BIBLE, BUT THE TIPS OF HIS fingers remained inserted in the pages of the Acts of the Apostles. The little deacon whose mouth seemed stretched in a perpetual smile had leaned leftwards in the Big Pew[37] as if he were watching for the moment when J.T. would pull out his sermon notes and attempt to slip them as unobtrusively as possible on to the lower shelf against which he pressed his thighs to keep them steady as he attempted to deliver his peroration with great warmth.

— It was the weakling Peter who spoke! The man who betrayed Our Lord. This was the man who stood before the rulers of the Jews and spoke with inspired, fearless, eloquence. Listen to his words again . . .

J.T. opened the Bible wide enough to see the passage without relaxing his grip on the edge of the big book.

— ' . . . This is the stone which was set at nought of you builders which is become the head of the corner . . .'

J.T. lifted his head and tried to take in the whole of the congregation in his glance. His eyes shone in the rays of the setting sun, while the congregation below remained in the shadows.

— ' . . . Neither is there salvation in any other; for there is none other name under heaven given among men, whereby we must be saved.' I would like to think, J.T. said, that these words have a special, profound, meaning for young men and women of today, young people of my own age, who may be dazzled by the march of progress, the new discoveries of science, by new political ideas. I am not saying anything against these. They are all very good in themselves. What I am saying to you from this pulpit on this Sunday evening in this peaceful and beautiful countryside is that Peter's words of nineteen centuries ago are as true today as when he first uttered them. 'Neither is there salvation . . . salvation . . . in any other.'[38] For the sake of His name. Amen.

He set the Bible to one side and opened the hymn-book, giving out the number of the hymn and reading the first and last verses. The group of young men in the back who had been restive towards the end of the sermon, had risen to their feet and stretched themselves eagerly at the long note which was the signal for the congregation to rise. The uncertain notes of the harmonium were soon drowned in the powerful singing. Every pew in the small chapel was occupied and many were so full that fathers sat next to the aisle to find room for their elbows.

J.T. sat down in the shadow of the pulpit long enough to put his notes away in the inside pocket of his best suit. He put his finger inside the high stiff collar he was wearing, to ease his neck. The three deacons were facing the congregation. He levered his watch half out of his waistcoat pocket to steal a glimpse at the time.

The hymn was short and the last verse was not repeated. J.T. stepped down from the pulpit and sat modestly in the most shadowy corner of the deacon's pew. The senior deacon, a rosy-cheeked farmer with white hair, asked the children to come forward to say their verses. The children, dressed in their elaborate Sunday clothes, arose in their family pews and some hesitated so long they had to be pushed forward by their mothers, while the fathers or elder brothers who sat at the end opened the pew doors and swung their legs aside to let the children pass in ones or twos, and even threes and fours. The chapel echoed with the noise of their feet as they marched down the two aisles. In the deacon's pew they mustered into two rows, the smaller children in front, as if they were about to have their photograph taken.

When the children had finished, the senior deacon sent them back to their pews. When they had settled down, he leaned forward to grip the mahogany rail of the deacon's pew, while he addressed the congregation.

— I am sure we are all grateful to Mr Jones, our student-preacher from Bangor . . .

— Miles!

The little deacon stretched forward with his arm against the rail and whispered loudly. The senior deacon paused and frowned.

— Miles! Mr Miles. That's his name.

The little deacon nodded several times and then folded his arms and lifted up his eyes to study the empty pulpit.

— It was a most substantial sermon, the senior deacon said, and I am sure Mr. J . . . Mr Miles will be very interested to know that the late Evan Philips, the seraph of Castell Newydd Emlyn,[39] had a great sermon on the very same text, which I had the privilege of hearing on three occasions.

There was a rustle of restlessness in the rear pews and an outburst of coughing from different parts of the chapel, but the senior deacon pressed on with a summary of the late Evan Philips's sermon on Acts 4.12. When he had finished he turned first to the deacon on his left and then to the one on his right, asking them if they had anything they wished to add. Both shook their heads, the little deacon shutting his eyes tightly as he did so. The senior deacon called upon J.T. to give the Blessing, the harmonium gave the signal for a lengthy amen, and the congregation was released. They stirred about in their pews like passengers with luggage about to disembark from a crowded ship. People began to greet each other, bending down to pick up gloves and hymn-books and restraining the impatience of the smaller children. Before he could move, J.T. was confronted by the small deacon.

—Yes . . . Well . . . he said, squinting upwards.

A deformity of the spine seemed to add greater urgency to his curiosity.

— Tell me, Mr Miles, how much longer have you got in the college? Sit down a moment, Mr Miles. You are so tall you know.

J.T. moved backwards as the little deacon advanced with a small envelope in his hands. The chapel had emptied rapidly, and from the road outside came an excited noise of laughing and talking. The sun was setting and shadows were spreading inside the building. The other two deacons, the farmer and the postmaster, were absorbed in counting the collection in the fading light.

— Between you and me, the little deacon said, shifting in his seat, one thing I always like to ask students. One thing.

He leaned forward and brought his face close to J.T.'s. His breath smelt of the tobacco he chewed during the week. He held up the envelope between finger and thumb, and rubbed a corner against the end of his nose. His voice dropped to a note of even greater intimacy.

— How did you come to feel the Call, Mr Miles?

J.T. pressed his lips together, lifted his eyebrows and blinked several times. He seemed unable to speak. The little deacon moved his head sideways. His eyes narrowed as if he were giving vent to the accumulated suspicions of a lifetime. J.T. closed his eyes and lifted his eyebrows. The deacon stared at him. J.T. opened his eyes suddenly and smiled. Without speaking, he tilted sideways to feel underneath the pew for his new bowler hat. The little deacon drew himself back, dragging his left arm along the back of the pew. He lifted the envelope so that J.T. could not avoid looking at it.

— Come along.

He shook the envelope. There were coins inside. They jingled faintly.

— Take it! Take it! It's what you came for.

J.T. closed his eyes again. He lowered his head and breathed deeply. He lifted his hand to touch the wave in his red hair, and then brought finger and thumb down the sides of his nose.

— Money here is money hard earned, the little deacon was saying in an angry whisper.

The other two deacons had turned to watch them. J.T. stretched out his hand and took the envelope. His face had become very white. He stood up. The three men watched him. He lifted the envelope and tore it down the middle so that the four half-crowns fell out and rolled on the floor of the deacon's pew. The postmaster kneeled down quickly and caught one of them as it was still rolling.

— Next time you have a student, J.T. said, be sure to ask him to preach on Mark 11.15.[40]

The little deacon turned awkwardly in his seat and lifted his arm towards his colleagues.

— Witnesses! he said. You both saw what he did!

The senior deacon was nodding solemnly. The postmaster held out the half-crown in J.T.'s direction.

— Look, he said. It's yours, isn't it? It belongs to you. Come on. You ought to take it.

The postmaster sank to his knees and began to peer expertly around the dark floor for the other coins.

— That should pay my fare one way, J.T. said.

He took the half-crown. The postmaster prostrated himself further to look under the deacon's seat.

— This place was more out of the way than I thought.

— Now look here . . .

J.T. hurried out of the pew. He turned the corner too sharply and stumbled on the carpeted step.

— Look here, Miles!

The voice of the little deacon followed him down the aisle. Half a doorway oflight shone beyond the green gloom of the chapel he was passing through.

— I'll report you to the Presbytery. I'll report you to the monthly meeting! And to the College!

— Hey! Look!

The postmaster had found the other three half-crowns, and he was leaning over the pew rail, waving like a passenger left behind on an empty ship.

Outside the chapel, a group of young men in their Sunday clothes stood between J.T. and the setting sun. He stood for a moment, with his hat in his hand, the breeze animating his copper-coloured hair. He smiled, but no one seemed to want to speak to him. He studied the view, using his hat to shade his eyes. The chapel was high up on a hill-side and far below the sun was spreading a spectacular red glow over the waters of the incoming tide.

THE FIRST TIME she ever heard his voice, her hand covered with soapsuds clutched her father's drawers in a soft and slippery bunch against the washing-board. A dead spider stuck in its web that still stretched across the wash-house window, trembled in the draught that spread through the whole farm-house because the front door had been left open. Because the washerwoman, Mary Parry Rice, was ill, Kate's forearms were red with hot water, her body was warm with sweat and wet strands of hair tickled her forehead as she struggled alone with the essential washing. The wash-house was a damp room, always hidden from the sun.

She could hear three voices. Her brother Griff had brought a complete stranger into the house in the middle of a busy Monday morning. Her sister Lydia was there, probably on the stairs if the stair-carpet was still down; reasonably presentable. Her voice sounded as if she were smiling and showing her dimples.

Eager to hear, Kate leaned forward. She stared intently at the dolly[41] that leaned against the other side of the wash-tub like a wooden friend. Lydia's husky voice seemed to have an edge of excitement.

— I'm afraid Pa isn't home, she heard her sister say before her voice was drowned in Griff's loud laughter.

It sounded as if he were leaning boldly against the polished dresser in the hall, with his hands in his pockets. In order to hear more, Kate leaned too far forward and almost fell, so that to save herself one arm plunged into the water. The palm of her hand struck the bottom of the tub and the water splashed to her armpit.

She stayed rigidly still, holding her breath, while the water lapped the sides of the tub, so that if they heard, they might believe the noise was no more than the flutter of a hen's wings, disturbed in the open doorway, perhaps, by a prowling cat.

— Will you have a cup of tea now, Joe, or shall we come back later?

She heard her brother Griff's voice loud and clear. It seemed as if they were coming nearer. Swiftly she wiped the soap-suds from her arms with her sack-apron. She ran out of the wash-house into the space called the churn room, through the low back door into the back yard.

The steps on her right led up to the orchard where the first washing was already blowing on the line. An archway joined the house to a block of outbuildings. It led to the farmyard and also to the front of the house, and no doubt both the front garden gate and the front door were open and Griff and his friend standing in the hall.

Still standing in the yard, her arms cooling quickly in the fresh breeze, she studied the corner of the rain-water cistern. It stood alongside the kitchen window and it was made of great slabs of local stone, which were bound by long, rusty iron bars. She looked up from the corner of the cistern to the small window in the passage that led to her brother's bedrooms, as if she were judging the distance. She put out her hand to touch the cold stone. Moss grew in the long cracks in the slabs.

She took one foot out of a clog and then hesitated, wriggling her toes inside her black stocking. Stretching her arms she could just grasp the top edge of the cistern. She pulled and strained herself against the cold stone, rubbing her leg against the rough surface until she tore a hole in her stocking at the knee. She pulled herself up until she could see the strained reflection of her own face in the dark water of the cistern.

The slab which served to cover the cistern did not reach the edge to which she clung. To get in the house it would be necessary to balance on the edge of the side slab, hold the drain-pipe and stretch across to force the little window open. She lay panting along the edge and her hair hung down, its ends trailing in the dark water, forcing her to look downwards. She began to tremble as if she would fall in. She lowered herself down to the back yard, where she stood shaking in her stockinged feet. She turned to lean against the cistern. Opposite her was a shed where the coal was kept, where Maldwyn Birch had sheltered. Through the open back doorway of the house, she could see straight through the churn room into the wash-house, they called the Briws,[42] and the steam still rising from the great washing-tub she had deserted. Her hands, arms and clothing were stained with moss. Suddenly, as if she had heard something that suggested they were coming, Kate ran up the steps leading to the orchard and the hillock behind it. A clog fell off, but she did not stop to retrieve it. She ran towards the two-seater privy that stood in the shelter of the wall that separated the orchard from the kitchen garden. The door had sagged and as she pushed it to hide herself, it dragged across the earth floor.

IN THE CHAPEL-HOUSE students were not encouraged to read in bed. J.T. counted the five matches in the match-box and put them back unused. In the morning he brought them down in the candlestick which he put down in a conspicuous place on the table in the deacon's room. The wick of the half-candle was still white.

Half the table had been laid with his breakfast, a large pot of tea and a plate of eight pieces of bread and butter, four of which were left over from supper of the night before. The caretaker had already gone out to clean the chapel. She was related to the small deacon. When J.T. returned from a walk up the mountain the previous evening, she moved about the room clearing his supper things, filling the air with silent disapproval.

Someone knocked at the front door. J.T. munched a piece of bread and butter and tried to read the titles of the books in the glass-covered bookcase that was locked. The knocker was hammered down again. J.T. swallowed hastily and made for the front door since the caretaker was not there to open it. Griff stood outside in the bright sunshine, grinning broadly. J.T. caught a glimpse of the shadows of clouds being driven over the distant estuary.

— Doctor Livingstone, I presume? Griff said in English.

J.T. shouted and laughed. The caretaker appeared in the chapel porch, her sleeves rolled up to the top of her plump arms. J.T. rushed into the house for his Gladstone bag and his hat. Outside the chapel he shook the caretaker warmly by the hand as if they were old friends.

Griff picked up his bike from where it lay against the hedge with cow parsley thrusting through the spokes. J.T. walked away from the chapel still waving to the caretaker, who did not wave back.

— What a place! he said to Griff. What a place!

— Did Jac Brain ask you how you came to feel the Call?

J.T. nodded and Griff bent over the handlebars of his bike, overcome with laughter. They walked down the steep white road that had been hewn out of the hill-side.

— Two factions in there, Griff said. The majority that work in the lead mines, and the men who go down to the Black Parlour.[43] You can see them coming up this road three o'clock any afternoon. Up to twenty-five of them, so black their own wives can't tell one from the other. All members at Soar. Jac Brain is a foreman carter at the lead mines. He runs the place. The other two deacons are afraid of him. I can't think why.

— I'm afraid I didn't behave too well, J.T. said.

Griff was hanging J.T.'s Gladstone bag on the lamp bracket in front of the handlebars of his tall black bicycle.

— Put your hands on my shoulders, Griff said.

He was in the saddle, one foot on the ground the other on the pedal.

— What shall I do with this hat? J.T. said.

— Stick it between your teeth, Griff said. Or leave it in the Set Fawr with compliments to Jac Brain!

He pushed off, unsteady with laughter, while J.T. with the brim of his hat between his teeth, stumbled after the wobbling bike, getting his left foot on the hub-step and his right knee on the iron carrier.

— I suppose it's lack of education, J.T. said.

He spoke loudly into Griff's ear.

— Hold tight! Griff said. This hill is one in six.

J.T. gripped Griff's shoulders, keeping his head down and narrowing his eyes against the stream of air that flattened his hair down first on one side and then the other. The bicycle bumped up and down on the uneven surface of the road which was scarred with the ruts of the heavy wagons that travelled back and forth from the lead mines above the village to the nearest railway station on the coastal plain five miles away. Further down the road passed through a wood and the trees grew high on either side so that hardly any sunlight broke through. Turning a sharp corner, they saw two great horses straining to pull a heavy wagon up the hill. Behind these were two more pulling a second wagon. Griff squeezed on his brakes with all his strength. They had no effect. He steered the bike into the ditch that ran on the left of the narrow road. J.T. pitched forward without time to lift his hands to protect his face. His left knee gave way in the soft earth, his hat flew away and his forehead sank into a bed of nettles. While they both lay in the ditch, the straining horses were being urged on by the carters, who were furious at having the impetus of their ascent impeded. The wagon wheels rattled and thundered past their heads. With a sudden access of strength, Griff pulled his bike over himself out of the wagon's path. Through the noise and the dust they could hear the carters cursing them. One voice J.T. had heard before. Before the cavalcade had turned the corner, they caught a glimpse of the crab-like walk of the small deacon, wearing a blue linen jacket, heavy boots and velveteen trousers hitched with 'Lon-don-Yorks', leather straps just below the knee, but still unmistakable. Between the damning and the blasting they heard quite distinctly — 'a damned tuppenny ha'penny 'prentice preacher chucking half-crowns all over the Big Pew. I'd like to know what the world's coming to!'

KATE EMPTIED THE slops of her wash-basin into the bucket on the rush mat. Her sister Lydia's bed was by the window that overlooked the wall that divided the orchard and the kitchen garden. When she lay down she saw the clouds racing across the sky beyond the tops of the trees in the orchard.

— I'd like to know why they were laughing so much, Kate said.

Determinedly she pulled on her second best skirt over her freshly-ironed calico drawers.

— You've got soap in your ear, Lydia said.

— It's a good job Pa isn't here, anyway, that's all I can say.

— Do you think I should change?

— Of course you should. Don't ask such soft questions.

— Griff likes him, Lydia said. I can tell.

— I don't see why he should laugh so loudly in a strange house, Kate said. Whoever he is. It's not becoming.

Lydia swung out her legs, stretched herself as she rose from the bed and sauntered to the dark closet in the wall where they kept their clothes; Kate's on the right, Lydia's on the left and hat boxes on the floor.

— Did you tell them I was doing the washing?

Kate was trying to sound casual.

— Didn't mention you at all, Lydia said.

She turned her head for a moment, moving her eyes provocatively, and then she peered into the closet. She spoke again, but her voice was muffled by the hanging clothes. Kate watched her, anxiously holding her breath. Lydia stepped back holding up a long green skirt with six black buttons down the side, to examine it in the light. Kate turned away hastily, picking up her hairbrush. She worked determinedly at her long hair, first one way and then the other. Her hair was straight, and as strong as Lydia   s but not so dark and wavy.

— I do think Griff takes a lot for granted, Kate said. Bringing a total stranger without any warning. I don't know what Pa will say.

— He won't be back until after tea, Lydia said. Mr Miles will be gone by then.

— He might come back early, Kate said.

— You'll see him coming through the road gate when they let the cows out after milking. Is this all right, Kate?

Kate looked at her sister's reflection in the small mirror on their dressing-table. There were hair pins in her mouth.

— Um, she said, nodding.

— Wish we had a decent mirror, Lydia said. Can't even tell whether my hat's on straight in that old thing.

— Where did you go, Kate?

Kate frowned and mumbled.

— To hide? I was thinking to myself while they were standing in the hall, I bet old Kate's disappeared. Can I have some of your eau-de-Cologne?

— Bringing a complete stranger into the house on a Monday morning, Kate said. And taking Pa's gun. That's the limit, I must say.

— Hadn't he got nice hair? Lydia said. Beautiful colour. Auburn. Wavy.

—Well I didn't see him, did I? If you ask me, Griff had no business at all to give him Pa's gun.

— There's something funny about him though. It must be those big blue eyes.

— Soft you mean? Kate said. Like a rice pudding?

They both burst out laughing.

— I shouldn't be surprised that he fancies himself with the girls, Lydia said. Although I don't know either. There's something shy about him. Unless it was the rash.

— Rash?

— Nettle rash on his forehead. Lydia pulled a naughty face.

— Don't know where he'd been I'm sure.

Kate held her lips together tightly to prevent herself from giggling.

—You're getting silly, now, she said. Hurry up. If he's coming back for dinner there's a lot to do.

GRIFF HELD UP his father's gun, expecting J.T. to take it. J.T. was holding his bowler hat, his other hand on his forehead where the lumps of the netdc stings were beginning to itch. Lydia stood on the stairs, smiling as the sole of her left foot rubbed gently at the pile of the stair-carpet.

— Dock leaves, Lydia was saying.

—We'll pick them as we go along, Griff said. Hang on to this, J.T.

J.T. held out his bowler hat and swung it around nervously. He was looking at Lydia.

— Put it on the hallstand, Griff said. Then the dogs won't eat it. They all laughed. J.T. took the gun.

— Hang on a minute, Griff said.

He slipped a game bag over J.T.'s shoulder.

— Turn your hat upside down and we'll ask every deacon that passes to drop in a half-crown! The J.T. Miles Fund we'll call it. Society for the Promotion of Putting your Foot in it.

Lydia laughed so much she almost lost her balance.

— Come on! Griff called from the garden.

J.T. rushed out after him.

The garden gate swung behind them. They crossed the yard, J.T.'s fox-coloured hair waving in the breeze. Lydia waved to them from the front door. Griff marched on unheeding towards the stackyard and J.T. lifted his arm hesitantly to wave back.

— Rabbits are a pest on the bottom there, Griff was saying.

J.T. hurried along to keep up with him, although Griff's legs were so much shorter than his.

— But I tell you what . . .

Griff paused to close the stackyard gate. J.T. hurried into the field as if he were apologizing for being late.

— There's a covert. Right at the bottom. Full of pheasants. It's a bit early I know. But if I see one . . .

He winked at J.T.

— I missed a rabbit and hit a pheasant, and that's all there is to it.

J.T. was looking at the view westwards. The coast swelled out into the sea and in the distant sand-dunes there was a tall light-house painted in black and white circles. J.T. shaded his eyes with his hand.

— Where's that then, he said, half pointing with the gun he was holding.

Already Griff was out of earshot, racing down the sloping field as if he were going into battle. J.T. took a deep breath and plunged down after his friend, his best boots skimming over the tufted grass, Pa's gun held in the air over his head, and the empty game bag bumping on his buttocks. Because it tilted down a broad slope the field which was eleven acres seemed much bigger. Griff was already crossing a stile around which dock leaves grew to an exceptional height. J.T., out of breath after racing down the slope grasped a handful of dock leaves and pressed them to his burning forehead.

— What's that wall? he said to Griff, pointing with a bunch of dock leaves at a high wall that ran along the bottom of the long field to the left.

— That's the wall of the Glanadda Park, Griff said.

— Who lives there?

J.T. could see tall chimneys far away among the trees.

— The last of the family died a few years ago, Griff said. The people said he had too much brains and not enough legs. They had handrails everywhere so that he could walk about. He was sixteen.

— Who is there now?

Nuns, Griff said. Dozens of them. It's like a Rookery. They were R.C.s,[44] the family. Boy left it to this new Order in his will, under the influence of his mother. That's what they say anyway. The estate was sold, that was when my father bought Argoed. Last big landlords you know in this part of the world.

— Is the mother still alive?

— Oh yes. She lives in Italy. She's got some kind of rheumatism. She can't open her hands. Pa writes to her twice a year, News and high thoughts. Come on now.

They walked across the level field, climbed over an iron gate, and skirted a field with a tall crop of oats still green. Griff stood stock still. Rabbits were playing on the gentle slopes beyond the oats where the hay had been cut and carried. J.T. lifted his gun to his shoulder and tried to look down the sights. Griff pushed the barrel aside with his left hand.

— Not worth it, he said very quietly.

The rabbits looked up as if they had heard him. He walked on. They scampered for their burrows in the soft bank of the hedgerow alongside which they were walking. They reached the top of the rise and Griff pointed to a thick wood that ran downhill from the bottom of the hayfield.

— That's full of pheasants, he said.

Between the hayfield and the wood there was a wide ditch and a rusty wire fence which would have been difficult for J.T. to cross if Griff had not been there to help him. Inside the wood the ground became softer as they penetrated further in. J.T. tried to tread warily, but the evenness of the mossy surface deceived him, and his Sunday boots were soon covered with mud. Griff was looking up into the light that filtered through the thick branches. Twice he lifted his gun to take aim and lowered it again. They came to firmer ground where the trees grew taller. Griff lifted his hand. He turned to look at J.T., pointing to his eyes and lifting the gun, suggesting he should prepare to take aim. There was a rustle in the branches and Griff fired and the whole wood seemed to spring into a new and more urgent existence. Griff pushed J.T.'s shoulder roughly and pointed.

— Look, he said. Over there! Shoot!

A cock pheasant was rising with a heavy whirring of wings from a low branch less than twenty-five yards away on J.T.'s left. It seemed to stay poised in mid-air for a second that was never going to pass.

— Go on, Griff had time to say again.

J.T. took aim with flustered inaccuracy. The gun sat uneasily on his shoulder. The report echoed through the wood.

— And again! Over there!

Griff, who usually made so much of being calm, was getting very excited.

— Fire again! It's a double barrel, you idiot. Over there!

J.T. could see nothing to fire at, but as if anxious to oblige he fired at a patch of blue sky he could see between the branches.

— Didn't you see it? Griff said beside himself. It was so near you. Another one. You could have pushed it over.

J.T. turned to look up, his neck stretched and his gaze searching the tops of the trees. Suddenly he realized Griff was laughing.

— What's the matter ? J.T. said.

— You, Griff said. Do you expect him to leave his name and address?

J.T.'s face flushed.

— Well *you* didn't hit anything either, he said. Griff slapped him on the back.

— That's true, he said. It's a good job Frank Morgan isn't with us or we'd never hear the end of it. There'd be a notice in the vestry of every chapel from here to Aberdaron: 'These men cannot shoot straight!'

— Old Frank's not so bad, J.T. said.

They walked to the left where the trees stood further apart and there was no longer any need to avoid the low branches.

— That's what you think, Griff said. There's a bridle path down here that leads up to the park wall. If we go that way we might catch some rabbits on the quarry bank. It doesn't matter anyway if we don't. You're not all that keen on shooting, are you?

— I'm enjoying it very much, J.T. said.

Griff held up his hand. J.T. tried to make his footsteps as quiet as he could. He stepped on a broken branch half hidden by last year's leaves and its crack echoed under the tall branches. Griff made a face of disapproval and warning. J.T. looked apologetic. Walking with stealth was slow and tiring and his hands on the gun had begun to sweat. The mud on his best boots had begun to dry. He shifted the empty game bag on his shoulder. Suddenly, before he could stop himself taking his next step, Griff had taken aim again and had fired at something. J.T. could not see. Whatever it was he missed.

— Why the devil can't you keep still, Griff said. J.T. was too close behind him and he stepped back.

— I'm sorry, Griff, he said.

There were no rabbits on the quarry bank. The last gunshot had sent them into hiding. But it was a warm place, sheltered from the wind and Griff threw himself on the ground to rest. J.T. followed more carefully, sitting down on an outcrop of stone. The quarry itself was small and overgrown with brambles.

— We should have brought a dog, Griff said, rolling over on his belly to be able to look up to where J.T. was sitting.

— Sent him in there. That quarry is teeming with game.

J.T. nodded and searched his pockets for a handkerchief to wipe the sweat off his face.

— You look like a crowned bard,[45] sitting up there. Griff said.

— I'm afraid there's no poetry in me, J.T. said. I wish there was. The truth is I can no more write a verse than shoot a pheasant. I feel the loss, I do really.

— Far too many poets in Wales, anyway, Griff said. Look at our Col. Regular tommy-rot factory.

— J.T. smiled and scratched his head.

— In every respect, Griff said.

He fell silent, pulling at a long stem of grass as if he could say more and preferred not to.

— What do you mean?

J.T. leaned towards him to catch what he might murmur.

— I don't believe any of it, Griff said.

He kept his gaze fixed steadily on J.T.'s face gauging the effect of his words.

— Not one word, he said.

J.T. said nothing. The hum of the wild bees in the brambles on the edge of the quarry nearest to where they sat seemed to grow louder in the silence. At last J.T. cleared his throat.

— Do you mean, he said hoarsely, do you mean you've lost your faith?

— If that's the way you want to put it, Griff said. I just can't go on swallowing it all any more.

— Swallowing what? J.T. said.

— Talking about God as if he were the Moderator of the Free Church Council, Griff said. As though our denomination owned him and kept him in a box under the pulpit and stood on it every Sunday. As if he went over the accounts of every chapel with the two other members of the Trinity and signed them with 'examined and found correct'.

Griff made a gesture with the stem of grass as if it were a pen and he was signing a document with a flourish.

— I admit there is too much emphasis on organization in our Connexion,[46] J.T. said slowly. There is too much talk about collections and funds and . . .

— Listen, Griff said. I'm not arguing. I'm confessing. I don't believe a single word of any of it.

J.T. lifted his gun with his hand as if he were about to say something.

— Is that gun loaded? Griff said.

J.T. slipped the catch and opened the gun.

— No, he said, looking up at Griff, who laughed.

— Thought you wanted to shoot me, Griff said.

— Good heavens. . .

— Promise you won't say anything?

Griff took the grass stem from his mouth and pointed it at J.T., who looked as if a cloak of misery had suddenly been clamped over his shoulders.

— Promise?

J.T. nodded gloomily.

— Well for goodness sake, J.T., what's it all for? Have you ever asked yourself that?

— How can you be a candidate for the ministry, J.T. said, if that's the way . . .

— Well I'm not, Griff said, sitting up suddenly, a look of triumph on his face. I'm not you see.

— At the Theo Col. I mean you must. . .

— The moment I've got my degree, Griff said, the very next day I'll be back home, here in the parlour, with my father, and I shall tell him, 'Pa I'm going to be a lawyer'.

J.T. looked puzzled.

— A lawyer? he said.

— It was the only way I could ever ger near a college. You are thinking I've deceived him, raised his hopes and all that. All right, well I have. But hasn't he treated us all as if we were his private property? Things to dispose of just as he fancied. He'd control our actions and our thoughts if he could. Have our minds out on the table for inspection every morning. Haven't you noticed the way he runs the place? Everybody his allotted job, every minute of the day. Ned with the horses, Dan Llew with the cattle, Rowland and Tomi Moch with the pigs, himself and Hugh with the sheep, the girls in the house . . .

— You all look very happy as far as I can see, J.T. said.

— Happy! Do you know those two girls have to go to the privy at the same time to get a moment to themselves?

J.T. looked away as if Griff were being indelicate. Griff jumped to his feet.

— You know something, J.T., he said. We are on the threshold of an absolutely new kind of world. I want to be part of that. Something that free men carve out for themselves, something new, something the world has never seen before. Think of what we shall be able to do soon — fly, go under the sea, move about at great speed, join up the ends of the earth . . .

Griff paused, his arms outstretched.

— What's the matter? he said. Why are you looking so miserable?

— The things you are saying, J.T. said. You make me feel so old-fashioned.

— Well, do you think I want to spend my life dealing with people like those awful deacons you chucked the half-crowns at last night?

— They are an exception, Griff, J.T. said.

— What does religion do? Griff said. Organize the world as though it were a damn great sheep farm, preparing everyone for the next world. You know what I think? I don't think there is a next world. No hell. No heaven. Nothing.

— 'I am a stranger in this world,' J.T. quoted a well-known hymn. 'My home is outside time.'

— Tommy-rot, Griff said. Who said so? How does he know? We live and we die. And that's the end of it. And a good job too.

J.T. began to clear his throat excitedly.

— That's just crude materialism, he said.

His voice had begun to tremble.

— All right, Griff said. All right. Let's start from there. A new start. I refuse to go down suffocated by the past. Honestly, I do.

J.T. began to lift his arms, the gun resting across his knees.

— Now let's be consistent, he said excitedly. Let's be consistent shall we? What did the Greek philosopher say? He who says he owes nothing to the past is still a child. Something like that.

— You've still got that little notebook then? For copying out apt and elevating quotations?

— Let's be serious, Griff.

J.T. stretched his neck and ran his hand through his hair.

— All of what we are is the past, isn't it? Come on now let's examine the evidence. Admit it! Come on now.

— Good old J.T., Griff said, stooping to pick up his gun.

— Well come on now, let's argue it out.

Griff shook his head.

— No use, he said. Arguing is no use at all. You know what I think life is for, J.T. It's a test. You've got to carve something out of it.

Griff made a gesture with his fist of tearing something tangible out of the air around him. He began to move forward up the slope,

— Now wait a minute, J.T. said. You just said it was a test. There I agree with you. There we are on common ground . . .

Griff turned to look down at him.

— J.T., he said. Don't tell them anything at the house, will you? About what I've told you.

— Of course not, J.T. said. Why should I?

Griff put his arm on J.T.'s shoulder as he came level with his knees.

— I've never told anybody, Griff said.

J.T. came level with him and Griff's arm was lifted upwards by the movement.

— You'll change your mind, J.T. said. You'll see. Things will change.

— Good old J.T., Griff said, shaking his shoulder.

He slapped his back and then let his arm fall so that he could again lead the way to the top of the slope.

9

FOR A WEEK-NIGHT service, the chapel was unusually full. Kate sat at the harmonium, her handkerchief a tight ball between her hands, which she wiped from time to time, looking down for a long time and lifting her head as slowly as she could so that no one in the congregation behind her could notice she had moved. Pa sat in his usual seat in the corner of the Big Pew, his arms folded, his gaze fixed on the lamp-bracket on the right of the empty pulpit. Lydia sat with her brothers in the family pew that ran below the window to the left of the Big Pew, at right-angles to the other pews in the chapel. The new minister, who had not long occupied the manse near the sister church in the next village, stood near the communion table, his fingers inserted at two places in a slim black book, his mouth firmly shut, a twitching clearly visible in both his pale cheeks. Three of the deacons sat in attitudes of neutral piety, but a fourth, Caleb Morris, kneeled by his seat in silent prayer, his tightly-clasped hands half buried by his beard. The minister began to turn his head in the old man's direction, and the eyes of the congregation could no longer withhold from doing the same thing. His lips were moving urgently, but no one could hear what he was saying. Kate's neck began to ache with the effort of not turning to look at her sister, who sat in the centre of their family pew between Dan Llew and Rowland. There were no children present and the loudest noise was the buzzing of a bluebottle in the glazed window-pane that let in the sun from the west.

At last Caleb Morris stirred. His hand groped towards a pocket inside his jacket and extracted a large coloured handkerchief. He wiped his eyes, blew his nose and weighing heavily on the pew took his seat once more, nodding in the direction of the minister without raising his head. Quickly the minister turned to the congregation and said:

— I shall read from the tenth article of our Confession of Faith.

He opened the book, cleared his throat and began to read rapidly and clearly.

— 'For as much as man, when God first created him, was able to obey and keep God's laws yet did he disobey and break the covenant God had created. The serpent deceived Eve and Adam harkened to his wife and voluntarily broke the commandment of his creator by eating of the forbidden fruit. Thus did he break the covenant with God and thereby lose the right to life and entered into the shadow of Death that the prohibition threatened. As this same Adam was the root and representative of the human race, his sin is theirs, and his corruption inherited by all his seed, since in nature all men are descended from him. Wherefore, through this natural corruption the human race is helplessly inclined away from good, and always tending towards evil.'

The minister paused, and then looked at two persons sitting in a pew behind Kate. He opened his slim book at another place. He said:

— I shall also read the thirty-first rule of discipline laid down for members of our religious society. 'Let no one who has been disciplined be received back into full communion and membership without satisfactory signs acceptable to the church assembled of true and full repentance of his or her fault or faults. "Take heed to yourselves: If thy brother trespass against thee, rebuke him; and if he repent, forgive him. And if he trespass against thee seven times a day, and seven times in a day turn again to thee saying, I repent: thou shalt forgive him." Luke chapter seventeen, verses three and four.'

He looked up again, in the direction of the pew behind Kate. Kate bent her head as if the seat of the harmonium should have been lowered for this occasion.

— Mary Morfydd Williams, formerly Morris, and Robert John Williams, if you repent fully of your transgressions and wish to be received back into the bosom of this religious society, will you signify this by standing?

There was a pause that seemed long, before Kate heard behind her the rustle of a stiff dress and the sudden determined shuffle of a man's heavily-shod feet. Caleb Morris turned slightly in the Big Pew to look at his daughter and his new son-in-law. He could be seen to swallow and to shake his head slightly as he turned away again.

— If it is the wish of this church assembled to welcome back this brother and sister into full communion, will you indicate this by a few moment's prayerful silence?

Kate's head plunged low on her breast. Under half-closed eyelids she kept the keyboard of the harmonium in view and rubbed her hands again with the ball of handkerchief. Her hymn-book in old notation was already open at the prearranged place. The minister's voice would be the signal to open her eyes, raise her head, place her feet on the pedals and prepare to play.

— Let us now sing, the minister said. Kate's head jerked up.

— Hymn number five hundred and fifty four. Five, five, four.

Let my heart be Thine own Temple,
Let my spirit be Thy Nest,
And within this lowly dwelling,
Holy Spirit, come to rest . . .

Her hands trembled at the first chord struck, and the music dragged as if her control over each finger was incomplete. Lydia looked up anxiously from her book. Pa stirred uneasily in his corner. But Kate lowered her head and shoulders and carried on until the apparatus of sound came fully under her control. The congregation rose and sang with great power and energy as if everyone wanted to drive out the oppressive silence that had governed the whole space inside the chapel walls.

Let all my senses, like brave singers,
Work their fingers upon strings
That with gladness eversounding
Praise the Holy King of Kings.

Kate's feet worked faster to increase the volume of sound from the harmonium to match the whole-hearted effort of the congregation. She glanced from the music to the family pew and saw Lydia's mouth in a round O of full-throated praise. Ned, as was his habit, was holding his head slightly to one side as if it eased the flow of music from his head. Pa, like the other deacons, had turned to face the congregation for the singing, and he was beating the air with his open hymn-book in a determined effort to preserve a strict tempo and prevent some of the older members of the congregation from dragging.

The hymn was over. In accordance with denominational custom, no Amen was sung. Briefly, almost inaudibly, the minister pronounced the Blessing, and with much shuffling and whispering the congregation began to file out, while Kate played a simple voluntary. Lydia as she passed down the aisle tried to catch her eye and give her an encouraging smile, but Kate was concentrating too hard on the unfamiliar music to notice. Wrong notes were not so noticeable as people collected their belongings, began quiet conversations and moved towards the doors with their attention taken up with the fresh view they took of each other after their hour-long pew imprisonment, so that Kate could give free rein to a vigorous and occasionally impressive rendering.

The voluntary was short and, having repeated it once, Kate came to a quick end as a singer ceases to sing when no one is listening. She closed the stops, pulled down the lid of the harmonium, put the large hymn-book away and picked up her gloves that lay on the seat beside her. She turned to see who remained in the pews behind and saw Mary Morfydd and Robert John still seated in their places as if they were waiting for the service to begin. Robert John was frowning, but Mary Mor-fydd's sharp knowing face was serene and composed, her head as always held slightly to one side and her thin mouth stretched in the opposite direction, as if she questioned everything she saw.

Kate had to pass their pew. She hesitated and tried to keep her eyes from looking at Mary Morfydd's body above where her hard-working hands were folded placidly in her dark lap. They had been forgiven formally and perhaps they were waiting for some fellow-member to give a smile and a kind word. Kate smiled.

— Hello Mary, Kate said, shyly.

Mary's eyes moved to examine the young woman who stood in the aisle, wearing a new pair of gloves and ready to sympathize. She was four years older than Kate. Together ten years ago they had watched a stallion urinating forcefully in a green field and Mary Morfydd had rebuked Kate and Lydia very sternly for giggling. Now she looked at Kate as if her authority over her was still unshaken.

The deacons and the minister stood conferring in the Big Pew, their backs in a semicircle beneath the pulpit.

— We're not the first and we won't be the last, Katie fach.

Mary Morfydd spoke quietly and calmly. Kate nodded and then blushed hotly. Mary's eyes returned to the contemplation of the empty pulpit and Robert John, stiff in his heavy suit, folded his arms, parted his lips and involuntarily puffed a sigh out through his drooping moustache.

IT WAS A WARM evening in August and the small station platform was crowded with men and women in their Saturday clothes. J.T., Griff, and Frank Morgan were on their way to their Sunday engagements. Each of them wore a dark Sunday suit and carried a small Gladstone bag.

— Splendid place, Bodadda, Frank Morgan said. Very good rough shooting.

Griff winked at J.T.

— I hear they have three unmarried daughters, Griff said. Did you know that, Frank?

— No, Frank said. I didn't know.

He put up his foot on an empty luggage trolley.

— I have no idea at all. I've only met the father and the eldest son. The father is a county councillor. Both of them are deacons.

— I know, Griff said. I've been there. Never got a second invitation, though. I can't think why. Everybody knows what a splendid preacher I am.

J.T. stirred uneasily and looked up the line to see if there were any sign of the local train pulling up the incline.

— Let's hope Miss Alice Rosser doesn't get to hear about it, Griff said.

— About what? Frank said aggressively.

— About the three unmarried daughters, Griff said, and the rough shooting. If you work on his land for nothing for fourteen years, Frank, he might give you a pair of them with the rough shooting thrown in.[47]

— Steady on, Frank said. Remember where we are. There may be somebody listening.

— Such a lot of people here tonight, J.T. said. Is there something special going to happen?

An increase of noise and the tread of heavy feet came from the wooden-floored waiting-room. It sounded as if there were more people pressing in than the ticket collector could deal with. The station-master was collecting the tickets and he had complained to them when they greeted him that he was forced to do everything himself at the busiest time of the week because the porter's wife had just had her tenth child that afternoon. There were louder shouts and laughter, and members of the quarryman's brass band began to appear one by one, carrying their instruments, some in frill uniform, others with only peak caps and red jackets and others, as if called at short notice, still in their Saturday-afternoon clothes. Self-consciously they clung to their instruments, but as their number grew they began to assert their importance and look around the platform deciding where best to place themselves. Frank Morgan raised his hat and addressed two young ladies who were standing in front of him.

— Pardon me, he said. Could you tell us what the excitement is about?

When they turned to look at him, he saw they were both much younger than the manner of their dress, and they bent towards each other in a suppressed giggle and turned away again.

— Of course! J.T. snapped his fingers. I remember. I know what it is. It's the crowned bard coming back from the Eisteddfod. From the National at Wrexham. That's what it is. He lives near here. He's won for the second time. Brilliant chap I believe.

The train was sighted. A rustle of excitement swept through the crowd. Women leaned on the arms of their escorts to stand on tiptoe and crane their necks to see the oncoming train. J.T., taller than the average, had little need to change his position. The band hastily started to tune their instruments and puff and blow themselves into a state of readiness. There was an elephantine ripeness about the euphonium and the bassoon that stood out boldly against the clatter and excitement. The small train drew in slowly, people leaning out of the carriage windows, puzzled and excited by the unexpected welcome.

— What was the subject?

Frank Morgan raised his voice to make himself heard in J.T.'s ear.

— Subject? J.T. said.

— Of the Ode.[48] At the Eisteddfod this year. What was the subject?

— Oh. *The Holy Grail.*

Frank nodded vigorously. The engine began to hiss fiercely and clouds of steam billowed out between the gleaming wheels as they ground slowly to a halt.

— That's it. I remember now. Thought of having a go at it myself when the List of Subjects came out. Wish I had now. This chap is still at college.

— Do you know him?

— Oh yes.

J.T. turned to look Frank Morgan in the eyes and Frank nodded again as if to dispel all doubt. Two men, followed by the station-master who now had a green flag tucked underneath his arm, rushed up and down the carriages. They forced open doors excitedly and one even got inside and looked underneath the seat. Someone said: 'He's not on it'. The word went around the people on the platform and there was an audible groan of disappointment. The bandsmen put the heavier instruments down at their feet. The conductor who had arrived late frowned, folded his arms and thrust forward one leg in an attitude of disapproval.

— He's very shy, Frank Morgan said.

— *Poeta abscotidus,*[49] Griff said.

He put his hands in his pockets and grinned.

— I wish I'd had a go, Frank Morgan said wistfully. After all, its a perfect subject. Purity. High ideals. Knightly love.

— And a bit of rough shooting, Griff said. Come on, J.T. All on board. This is the last train. Think of tomorrow, my boy. You mustn't disappoint the saints at Abergorlan.

KATE WAS UPSTAIRS making the beds when she saw the postman pushing his bike over the uneven surface of the farmyard. He leant his red bicycle against the mounting-stone and shuffled as fast as he could, close to the garden wall to the back of the house. At the archway he saw the back door was open. Behind him a dog barked savagely. He rushed into the house and closed the back door.

Kate hurried down the bare stairs, pushed her feet into her working clogs and ran up the kitchen steps to the churn room, but Lydia was already there, complaining about the lack of light and opening the back door. The postman was sitting on the slate slab alongside the upturned milk-buckets, holding his sack open, his glossy rimmed oval helmet pushed back and his nose almost inside the sack. Lydia watched him, her hands on her hips, leaning forward to see as much of the interior of the bag as she could.

— It's a good job I'm not a postman, William Edward Jones, or I'd open the lot every day.

She spoke very loudly and he looked up at her through his steel-rimmed spectacles, as if he had just been able to catch what she was saying.

— It's a position of trust, he said.

His voice squeaked as though he did not use it often. Lydia nodded encouragingly.

—You are just the man for the job, William Edward, she said. How are the birds?

He smiled wistfully. His hobby of an evening was to sit in his garden, which he never dug, feeding the birds.

— They are fine, he said, just fine.

He pulled out a letter from the bag. His hand had been on it for some time. He looked at Kate and then lifted the letter to examine the name and address.

— For you, he said.

He looked at Kate as he spoke and she lifted her arm at once. He put the letter in her hand. He took off his spectacles and folded them judicially.

— From South Wales, he said.

Kate pushed the letter into the pocket of her apron. Lydia looked at her and lifted her eyebrows as high as she could.

— Give William Edward Jones a glass of buttermilk, Kate said. I've got to finish upstairs.

She nodded to the postman and bustled back down the kitchen steps.

— Right away, your worship, Lydia said. And then maybe he'll bring *me* a letter next time.

William Edward lifted his helmet, creasing his forehead as he looked up inside it.

—You know what I tell all the young girls, Lydia Jones? he said. Lydia was in the dairy filling a mug from the buttermilk churn with a long-handled ladle.

— 'Don't lie in the wood, till you've kneeled in the church', Lydia said.

Her voice echoed loudly in the whitewashed dairy and she dropped the ladle into the metal churn with a cheerful clatter. William Edward clapped his helmet back on his head and took the mug of buttermilk from Lydia.

— Who told you then? he said. His mouth was open with surprise.

—You did, Lydia said, last year. And the year before.

William Edward held the mug in front of him and shook his head.

— *Duw, Duw,*[50] he said. I must be getting old.

As soon as he had gone, Lydia ran upstairs. She found Kate standing by Pa's bed still reading the letter.

— What does he say? Lydia said.

She smiled carefully as if to show warm interest and give no offence. Kate did not look pleased,

— Nothing much. He'll be preaching at Afongoch the Sunday after next. Wants to know if he can call.

Kate threw the letter on Pa's bed. Lydia picked it up and read it aloud.

— 'Dear Miss Jones,' she read, 'it was most kind of you to send me the photo of your sister and yourself and I hasten to acknowledge the receipt of same. It is a very beautiful photo if I may say so. I am preaching twice this week in this very busy town. It is not for me to say how well for self-praise is no recommendation, The people here look as if they are doing well. The chapels are well attended, but the public houses are also very full I am afraid. I think perhaps the young ladies are more forward in these parts. Last night I attended a lecture at the Welfare Hall, given by Mr O.M. Edwards, the Chief Inspector of Schools for Wales.[51] On my way out I saw four young women lighting cigarettes and acting in a very frivolous manner considering the gravity of the lecture they had just heard. Mr O.M. Edwards is a very fine man in my opinion. His ideals for Wales are far higher and more elevated than those of more popular men like D.LL. George for example.[52] This is only my opinion.

'You will be glad to hear I saw your brother Griff last week and that he was in excellent health. I shall be preaching in your vicinity the Sunday after next at Afongoch chapel. I wonder if it would be convenient for "Mr So and So" to call. (Griff told me about your sister's name for me. I think it is very amusing.) Perhaps on Monday if it is no trouble. I am afraid this is not an interesting letter.

'With kind regards to your sister and yourself, and all the Argoed family. Your sincere friend, J.T. Miles.'

— Umm.

Lydia hummed wisely and nodded her head.

— What's the matter? Kate said sharply.

— 'Your sincere friend,' Lydia said. Not 'yours truly' or 'yours sincerely'. 'Your sincere friend.'

She looked at her sister meaningfully.

— Don't talk soft, Kate said. Come on. We've got work to do. Pa will be back at twelve and he'll want his dinner on the table.

— He's got nice hair, Lydia said. Very nice.

— You're always saying that, Kate said. You don't buy a horse by the colour of his tail.

— Honestly. You're so choosy with men . . .

Kate went downstairs. Lydia followed her.

— He's so slow though, Lydia said. Got no 'go' in him, has he? He's so serious. I'm not saying he doesn't laugh. He laughs a lot. But he's always thinking of principles, that's what I mean.

— I thought you were going down to the village, Kate said. We are very short of sugar, you know.

— Of course, as Griff says, he's had a very hard life. Fancy his father killing himself. Awful, isn't it? Gosh I'd never kill myself, would you Kate?

— No. I don't suppose I would, Kate said.

— Kate?

— Umm?

— Do you like him?

Lydia almost whispered the question, smiling as sweetly as she could.

— If you don't hurry you'll not be back before Pa comes, Kate said and turned away towards the kitchen oven so that Lydia could not see her face.

A SUDDEN BURST of flame from the furnaces of the ironworks three miles away down the coast lit up the road as it wound past the open quarry to the top of Argoed hill. Kate saw the light gleaming on the highly polished leggings worn by Archie Griffiths, Bodafon Hall. He had walked ahead and he was standing on the edge of the quarry looking eastwards, his hands behind his back and one leg in front of another like a portrait of a commander above a battlefield.

— There's no fence here, Archie said. It's hardly good enough.

— That's what I've been saying for years, Kate said.

Her voice was higher pitched than usual. There was hardly any wind and yet she talked as if there were some invisible obstacle her voice had to overcome. Dan Llew nudged his brother Ned — they were both walking behind her. Ned drew himself up and ignored the nudge. The flames from the furnace died down and Archie Griffiths became a shadow further up the road against the moonlit sky. Ned took longer strides and caught up with him before Kate and Dan Llew.

— I've been saying it for years, he said, on the Parish Council. There ought to be a wall there. A high wall. Children could easily fall over.

— Especially at night, Kate said.

— They shouldn't be out at night, should they? Dan Llew was in a frivolous mood.

— In the winter I mean, Kate said. You know very well.

— In my mother's day, Ned said, there was a good fence here. A good strong fence.

— Flames from the furnace every five minutes, Dan Llew said. Better than street-lighting and it costs nothing at all.

— Mind the edge, Miss Jones.

Archie Griffiths took Kate's arm. She came so close to him she caught the scent of his hair pomade mixed with the smell of tobacco that clung to the thick surface of his jacket. Ned and Dan Llew walked ahead, and Archie did not let go Kate's arm. Kate bent her head passively. She said nothing. She heard the crunch of her brother's boots on the uneven surface of the road in front. She heard Dan Llew say,

— I sacked him anyway. I said, 'I'm not having anyone in my shop who can't cut meat properly.' And that was that.

— Do you think that was wise, Dan? Ned was saying in his most judicious manner.

— Your brother Dan is doing very well, Miss Jones, Archie said in a low voice. Very well indeed.

— He has been fortunate, Kate said.

She felt the pressure of his hand in her arm tighten.

— He has a very acute business brain, Archie Griffiths said. He saw his chance and he took it.

— Well as Pa says, Kate said, he prefers the ringing of a till to the ringing of a bell. Dan Llew's heart is more in the world than in the church.

— Come now, Miss Jones, Archie said, with a courtly laugh. Isn't that a little old-fashioned?

Kate pulled her arm free from his grasp.

— It may well be, Kate said. It may very well be.

— I would be the last person to speak lightly of religion, Archie Griffiths said.

He spoke swiftly and anxiously, touching her arm again.

— I never told you this before, but my mother always wanted me to go in for the church. She had an elder brother you know, who died. He was a curate at Llangollen for many years.

Kate nodded politely.

— But of course my father wanted his only son to carry on Bodafon Hall, so that was the end of it.

— We'd better hurry, Kate said, or we'll be left behind.

He had taken firm hold of her arm again.

— I've been anxious to talk to you all evening, he said.

— What is there to talk about, Mr Griffiths?

The furnace flames lit the sky again and the glow gave his face unusual animation and only his wax moustache appeared to be still. He had taken off his cap and his carefully dressed hair, which was parted in the middle, seemed to be looking nearer. The gateway to Argoed was not more than thirty yards away. Her brothers had already left the road and she could no longer hear their voices.

— All sorts of things, Kate. All sorts of things.

She felt his waxed moustache against the side of her nose. It tickled her. She moved her head. She wanted to sneeze.

— We really must go in, she said.

The furnaces were closed and in the dark his arm arrived around her waist and he was pulling her towards him. His lips pushed out and his eyes were large. His breath smelt of stale cheese.

— Kate, he said, Kate.

She shook her head and felt the end of his moustache bending against her cheek.

— No. Really. Please.

He released his grip.

— I'm sorry, he said. I should have spoken first. Kate, Kate, will you marry me?

Kate turned around to look down the hill. The countryside was so silent, it seemed that either up in the farm or down in the village, his words had been overheard. All the way up the hill they had had their backs to the estuary, and they had not seen the moonlight on the distant incoming tide.

— I know my mother and father are still alive and I've got two sisters at home, Kate, but the whole place will be mine one day. And another thing when my Uncle Pentir[53] dies I'll inherit Bodawen as well and that will make nearly four hundred and fifty acres in all. I

got five hundred after my great-aunty Polly you know. I bought con-
sols with it. They're very good.

Kate turned away from looking at the moonlight on the open sea.

— You'll have to ask Pa, she said.

J.T. HAD PUT his Gladstone bag on the luggage rack above his head
and under it his new Burberry mac neatly folded. The man who sat
opposite him was about his own age, but had begun to lose his hair.
He was winking at J.T. The wink creased the collier's blue scar on
the bridge of his nose, which was twisted and broken in a way that
made his face appear to be always smiling. He waved an unlit cigarette
between his thick fingers. He held an unlit safety match delicately
between finger and thumb of the same hand, and almost hidden in
the tough palm of the other a box of matches which he shook from
time to time as if he were playing a tambourine.

— Science, he said to J.T. That's the thing, boy. That's the coming
thing. Uplift the whole bloomin' human race. And that's a fact.

He shook his match-box and winked. The compartment was a
non-smoker. In the window corner a small fierce looking white-
bearded gentleman with a large Roman nose was reading a book
through pince-nez. His eyes strayed every so often to the unlit match
in the collier's hand.

— Where you from then?

The young collier tapped his teeth with the match.

— I'm from North Wales, J.T. said.

— Down 'ere on a visit?

J.T. cleared his throat and clasped his hands together tightly. He
pressed his back into the upholstery behind him.

— Preaching, J.T. said.

The collier nodded sympathetically.

— Lot of preachers in North Wales, aren't there?

He smiled encouragingly. J.T. smiled back.

— Makes you think sometimes who does the work.

J.T. was prepared to go on smiling, but the man in the corner put
down his book and took off his pince-nez. Two oval red marks were
engraved at the top of his nose. He held his head down as if he were
still peering over the top of the spectacles he had taken off and which
he now raised with a flourish in the direction of the collier.

— Look here, he said. Look here. I can't help overhearing your talk. Have some respect, young man. Show some respect.

The collier leaned back and put the unlit cigarette in the corner of his mouth.

— Well, well, he said. Who are you then?

— Never you mind who I am.

His beard moved as he shut his mouth firmly, replaced his pince-nez and resumed his reading. The collier leaned forward, swaying a little with the movement of the train.

— What you readin' then?

The bearded man lifted the book nearer to his face. The collier let his body sink slowly forward along the empty seat until he could read the title of the book on the spine of the jacket.

— 'The Principles and Faith of the Social Reformer,' by P. T. Hansford.

He levered himself back into an upright position, the unlit cigarette still in his mouth, the match still poised between finger and thumb.

— Oh very nice, he said, very nice indeed.

His fingers covered the lower half of his face as he took the cigarette out of his mouth. He leaned forward to tap the older man gently on the knee with the same hand that held the cigarette. The reader lowered his book and pressed his thin knees, away from his hand, against the door of the compartment with a curiously feminine raising of the heels. The leather window strap lay across his kneecaps like the fringe of a skirt.

— Sorry, the collier said, drawing himself away. I was goin' to ask you. You know Keir 'ardie?

— No, the reader said, angrily. I'm happy to say I don't. And I might also add it is a sad sight to see a young man of your age the worse for drink so early in the morning.

— Hold on!

The collier stretched out a long arm, pointing a crooked finger at the man in the corner.

— Hold on, now.

J.T. leaned forward as if to restrain the collier. The long arm dropped. J.T. sank back.

— Nip of rum with the morning tea. Healthy habit. Especially on holidays. My sister Ed gettin' married see. This mornin', Down in the Vale there.[54] A farmer's boy. Stupid clod really. Never thinks. But I know he'll be nice to her and she can look after herself. So I don't worry.

The collier smiled at J.T. and then at the man in the other corner, who turned his book face downwards on his knees and took to studying the landscape through the window. There was a shallow river running alongside the track and the low backs of terrace houses with very brief back gardens. The collier let his head fall back and looked through the window on his side where the mountain made abrupt ascent and hardy sheep cropped the short grass.

— Doesn't look so bad in the sunshine, does it? he said.

Absently he put the cigarette in his mouth again and lifted the matchbox to use the striking side. The rattle of the matches in the box brought the white beard around. They stared at each other and J.T. tried to look from one to the other without moving his head. The older man folded his arms. His book almost slipped off his knees. He released a hand to catch it, raised his knees, folded his arms again, without taking his eyes off the match in the collier's hand. Suddenly, the collier flung the match away, pulled the cigarette out of his mouth and put it back behind his ear.

— Oh damn, he said. Why didn't I get into another bloody compartment?

— Language, the older man said, shaping the word so fully that saliva could be seen glistening on his gums inside his dull beard.

The collier looked at J.T.

— Sorry I'm sure, he said. But I ask you, what a way to start a wedding day.

J.T. seemed to nod sympathetically, frown and search his mind for something amiable to say. The bearded man picked up his book again. The collier winked at J.T. and lifted his hand to his forehead, separating his index finger narrowly from his thumb. J.T. looked puzzled so he repeated the sign, nodding in the direction of the other man, who lifting his eyes suddenly, caught the collier emphasizing his meaning by rotating his forehead against the extended finger and thumb.

— I presume you are trying to suggest that I am narrow minded, he said quickly without putting down his book. Well let me tell you something. The laws of the State are made to be obeyed. They are put there for the protection of the individual and the well-being of the community and the sooner you and your kind realize that the better it will be for all of us.

The collier seemed to cheer up. He shook his head very slowly like a practised debater about to make a telling point.

— No, he said. No. my friend. You are wrong. I can read just as well as you can. And my old father he learnt to read when he was over fifty in our Sunday School. I'll tell you what the laws are for my friend. To protect the rich against the risin' poor. That's what they're for. To protect capitalism everywhere. I can read, see. I can read. But they are out of date and I'll tell you why they are out of date. Because the workers can read. All of them. And they can think. And they can see a new world comin'. That's what I was trying to tell you, see.

He turned to look intensely at J.T.

— Science and socialism, brother, he said. That's the remedy. Aye, aye.

He nodded vigorously in agreement with himself, as if that was all there was to be said on the matter. When the man in the corner leaned forward and pointed the tip of his beard at him, he looked surprised.

— Let me tell you something. My name is Professor Temple Morgan. I have just been up to Mr Keir Hardie's constituency.[55] I have just been giving your fellow countryman two lectures on the meaning of citizenship. It's a pity you weren't present. You might have learnt something.

— *Duw, Duw,* the collier said.

His open face appeared to show wonder and admiration.

— Shall I tell you something else?

— Aye, go on.

— I am myself the son of an ironworker from Pontypool. Unlike your father, my father died without learning to read or write. I worked in the ironworks and studied at night. I was one of the first students to enrol at the new University of South Wales and Monmouthshire at Cardiff.[56] My father lived to see me on the same platform as the late King Edward. I was there on that platform when he was installed as Chancellor of the University of Wales on June 26, 1896. I am telling you this because I want you to know that I struggled hard to climb out of the pit of ignorance by education and effort. That is the way the best citizens are made. That is what has made this country great and will make it greater.

The collier nodded in the most friendly way.

— And let me add just one thing more. Your Mr Hardie is aggravating labour difficulties and trying to teach the working man the greed and aggression that used to be the monopoly of the landowners. As the son of a working man I am sorry to have to say this. But it is exactly what I've been saying in Merthyr Tydfil, and I'm glad to have the opportunity of saying it to you. I hope you will remember my words as long as you live, my friend, because I mean every word.

— Aye, well. You've gone over, haven't you? the collier said.

— What?

The pince-nez fell from the professor's nose.

— I can argue, see. I can read.

The collier leaned forward to look eagerly from J.T. to the professor.

— You're on the side of the bosses, mun, and the pity of it is you don't know it. Have you read Marx? Now I've read Marx. Have you read Marx? Have you studied him?

J.T. looked at the professor. For some reason he was hesitant to give an answer.

— Would you mind adopting a less aggressive tone. Marx is not to be taken seriously either as a philosopher or an economist.

— Aye, but have you read him? *Das Kapital.* That's what I'm askin'. Straight.

— He is not considered by the best authorities to be . . .

— Aye, well, you 'aven't, 'ave you? I 'ave, the collier said. And it makes 'istory very clear to me. Makes it all as clear as daylight.

The train passed a narrow signal-box, its wheels clanking as it crossed the points.

— I think we're coming into Caerphilly, J.T. said pleasantly.

The collier laughed, snatched the cigarette out from behind his ear and pointed it at J.T. before putting it in his mouth.

— Iesu o'r North,[57] he said. Morris Evans Oil for troubled waters. Get a smoke here anyway. And a paper.

He heaved himself up to his feet, pulling the window strap roughly until the window fell and he could put his head and wide shoulders out. He opened the door from the outside and jumped out while the train was still moving, landing rather unsteadily and calling as he ran forward.

— Don't go away. I'll be back. Bit more education.

The professor looked at J.T. It was difficult to tell whether or not he was blushing because the hair of his beard grew high on his checks.

— Agitators like Hardie do a great deal of harm, he said. You see what they're like. No humility. Mark my words, if they go on like this Christianity won't be able to touch them. They'll harden you see. Are you a Baptist?

— No, J.T. said. I'm a Calvinist Methodist as a matter of fact.

The professor nodded abruptly as if he were regaining confidence.

— All these denominational differences have got to be sunk, he said. They're in the way you know. They're in the way.

— Yes, I quite agree, J.T. said.

Unlike the rapid eloquence of the other two, J.T.'s North Wales speech was slow and overmeditated. At the moment when he seemed at last to be prepared to put his point of view, the collier re-appeared in the open carriage doorway. Standing on the platform, his physical size was greatly reduced, and J.T. and the professor were able to look at him without raising their heads at all, as when he had stood in the compartment and dominated the confined space.

— Good God, he said. Just look at this.

The long newspaper was open and he held it up so that they could read the headline in thick black type across the top of seven columns. Then he turned to hold up the paper against the sunlight and read it himself.

— 'Germany at war with two Great Powers,' he read. 'War declared on Russia.'

He lifted the newspaper higher to study the sketch map at the bottom of the page.

— 'Germany's strikes against France. Map showing Luxemburg.'

— You'd better come in, J.T. said. The train is due out.

The professor took out his watch from his waistcoat pocket. A small gold medal dangled on the middle of the chain. The collier climbed in and slumped into his corner, still reading.

— 'An appeal to our people. Patriotism, in the face of the ominous facts which now press themselves upon the attention of the public, is not a sentiment: it is a duty.'

He put the paper down to look at J.T.

— Well it's nice to know that, isn't it? he said. Marvellous, isn't it, the way they help us to think.

He picked up the paper again. The professor leaned towards J.T.

— Do you think, sir, you are so much younger, could I ask you to purchase a daily paper on my behalf?

He raised his eyebrows and smiled ingratiatingly. The door of the compartment was still open. From a waistcoat pocket the professor extracted a penny which he held up delicately between finger and thumb. J.T. nodded vigorously as if he were very pleased to have something to do, but a porter suddenly marched past, pushing the door of the compartment to with a loud bang.

— 'The patriotism of the Welsh collier.'

The young collier read in a tone of heavy irony, from a leading article, snorting with contempt from time to time. The professor stared longingly at the newspaper. The engine made up steam and the train began to move.

— It's a very delicate situation, the professor said to J.T. Very delicate.

— 'Coal for the navy,' the collier said, putting down the paper. 'Forgo the two days' holiday. Do not let the nation down in its hour of peril.'

— I don't envy the Foreign Secretary his job at this moment, the professor said. I don't at all.

— 'One great blast on the horn of patriotism!'

The collier threw down the paper over the seat alongside him and the professor leaned forward eagerly to take a closer look.

— Blast the word, he said, staring sternly at J.T. Blast the bloody lot of them. For whose benefit, I ask you?[58]

He fell silent and the train began to climb slowly through the wooded hill-side. The professor made no attempt to conceal the fact that he was reading and even ventured to stretch his hand out and lift the corner of a page. At last he leaned back into his corner, took off his pincc-ncx and turned to claim J.T.'s attention.

— I think I've formed my view, he said. The collier's eyes lifted to study J.T.'s face.

— On a nice day like this, he said.

—Yes, the professor said. There is only one answer. The sooner we enter the lists the better. It stirs the blood I must say. I wish I were twenty years younger.

10

THE WIND SENT a curtain of rain curving through the empty yard and half a dozen hens crouched broodily in the dust underneath Archie Griffiths's horse and trap in the open cart-house. The horse pulled at the hay in the rack, shaking its head with the effort and making its harness rattle. Tomi Moch, crossing the yard with a thick sack folded high over his shoulders, stopped to study the horse and cart, his mouth open with curiosity. He spat untidily like a child imitating an adult and moved side-ways to peer beyond the garden gate. The gate leaned unlatched on the stone path. It had to be lifted before it would close. Tomi put down the empty bucket he was carrying and walked slowly up to the gate. Kate, who stood in the shelter of the portico with Archie Griffiths pulled her hand away from his and turned sideways so that she was looking at the brass doorknocker that was a point of gleaming brightness in the general dullness of the afternoon. Tomi stretched his lips and nodded at Archie Griffiths, who nodded stiffly back.

— Got to close it, Tomi said. Cattle passing come in sometimes.

He stiffened his small hand to make a gesture representing cattle passing. With both hands he lifted the gate and then latched it dexterously with the index finger of his left hand, which he then lifted to push a rain drop off the end of his nose. Instead of moving away, he stared at Kate and Archie, who were unable to say anything to each other while Tomi stood watching them.

— Are you going to make a soldier, Archie?

— Say Mr Griffiths, Kate said.

— Archie I always call him, Tomi said. I was telling Dan Llew what to do with these Germans. I was saying, 'like the bullocks,' I said. Tie them one by one to the iron ring in the wall and smack 'em hard on the forehead with the pole-axe. For him to do, I mean. You've seen him Archie with the bullocks. He never misses.

— Haven't you got any work to do? Kate said.

Tomi smiled and the saliva dribbled out of the corners of his mouth thicker than the rain on his face. His shoulders shook with the amusement he was feeling.

— Oh aye, he said. Always plenty of that at Argoed. 'Head in the wind and feet in the mud.' That's what they say about Argoed. Always say that. Long before your father and mother come here. Aye indeed.

Hard place to work.

His small eyes settled on Archie's body and examined the details of his dress.

— Look good like a soldier, Tomi said. Officer's clothes. Lovely. Good waist you've got there Archie. For a belt for polishing like.

— Mr Griffiths is engaged in work of national importance, Kate said.

— Well *diwc,* aye, Tomi said, picking up his bucket, so am I. Pigs must eat, same as anybody else or they won't be worth killing. Get nothing for them. Is your father in there?

— He'll be out any minute, Kate said.

Tomi began to shake again with amusement, his head lowered against the wet wind.

— Never comes out in this rain, Tomi said. Don't blame him neither, I wouldn't if I was him, but I'm not, am I? More's the pity.

Tomi moved down the yard, the heels of his boots striking the rocky surface first, and the empty bucket swinging.

— Cheeky thing, Kate said. Archie frowned.

— Honestly, Kate, he said, I can't see how your father could have heard.

— Well Dan Llew talks so loudly, Kate said. He's so full of his own importance he doesn't care about anybody else.

— I wasn't laughing at him, you know, Archie said. I swear I wasn't.

— Well maybe you weren't, Kate said, but that's what he'll think. Pa's very sensitive, Archie. He hates being laughed at.

— Dan said this silly thing about him hiding in the cellar in a thunderstorm and it sounded so funny the way he said it.

— Dan thinks he's so clever.

— If he was playing the piano how could he hear?

— He stopped playing. He heard all the laughing in the kitchen and he stopped playing. He doesn't like people laughing.

— Is that why he won't see me?

Archie's forehead was creased in a deep frown.

— He's got a bad headache. He gets them sometimes. Awful they are. I know. I get them too. There's nothing to do but go to bed and draw the blinds. It is awful.

Archie stared at the roof of the coach-house that could be seen above the garden wall. Clumps of soft moss grew here and there on the wet slates. He made a wide gesture with his arm and Kate looked at him.

— What's the matter? she said.

— He's against me, Archie said.

— No he isn't.

Kate spoke with great emphasis.

— I mean this is the second time. I may as well not have called.

Kate clasped her hands together and said nothing.

— Mother will think it very funny. After all she knew I was calling this afternoon.

He paused abruptly, turning to stare up at the narrow gap between the front door and the lintel. He seemed to expect someone to be listening the other side of the door, but there was no sound inside the house.

— After all there is a great deal to do in Bodafon these days, I mean...

— Well, if it's all too much trouble, Kate said, you'd better hurry back.

She pushed at the door violently with the back of her arm and stepped inside the house.

— Go on, she said. Go on.

Her face was flushed and she put her hand to her cheek.

— Just because we laughed, Archie said.

— There's laughing and laughing, Kate said. Don't let me keep you. Bodafon Hall is waiting.

Archie moved his head from one side to the other as if he were trapped between the grey walls of the portico and could think of nothing to say. The door closed in his face, and as he looked up the bulging brass-knocker touched his nose.

Kate stood in the hall. The doors of the rooms on either side were open to display their polished order. She saw the hard chair in the parlour where he had sat while she had gone upstairs to ask her father to see him. It stood in its accustomed place. From where she stood she could read the date carved into its back: A.D. 1702. It bore no trace of use, gleaming like a museum piece. She remained standing in the hall, surrounded by the silence of the cleaned and polished house.

THE PRINCIPAL SAT back in his chair, his white head almost touching the carved wood behind it. On his desk were the galley proofs of his new book and, surrounded by open books, a cup and saucer still half filled with tea gone cold. His pale face was round and clean shaven, but his skin was covered with a network of small lines. His eyes were large and reproachful like an old sheepdog's. They moved slowly about the room as he listened to J.T., as if he found the halting recital of the young man's difficulties intolerable to listen to. J.T. sat in the position of interview, across the desk, but his chair was pushed back and his hands rested with wrists out on his thighs and his face was flushed with the effort of argument. There was a letter lying open on the edge of the large desk nearest to him. He continued to struggle to speak, but when the Principal raised his hand, with a nod of respect he stopped talking in the middle of a sentence.

— Mr Miles, your arguments are not new to me. I don't have to tell you I'm sure that for years I have been using what little influence I possess to secure international arbitration, goodwill with Germany, and the possibility of a general disarmament.

The Principal leaned forward, his finger-tips meeting over the proofs of his book, and his eyes downcast as if he were about to read a few lines aloud.

— Let me be quite honest with you, Miles. I don't mind confessing to you when on August 5th I learned we had declared war on Germany, the fabric of my life seemed to crack. You know how much I loved Germany for her intellectual leadership. My books are evidence. My lectures are evidence. But Germany sinned, Mr Miles. Germany has sinned against world civilization, by barbaric violation of Belgian neutrality. Germany must be beaten, whatever the cost.[59]

— Christianity, J.T. said, clearing his throat with the effort of speaking.

— Do not, pray, assume that Christianity and war are incompatible. This is not so. I would not like to think of one of my most hard-working and conscientious senior students taking refuge in such a softened version of his religion, just at a time when history calls out the man of God — as it once called out Abraham and Jephtha[60] — to sacrifice the very thing he treasures most.

The Principal shut his eyes suddenly and J.T. looked up to see on the high mantelpiece the photograph of the Principal's eldest son in uniform.

— The spirit of sacrifice, Mr Miles, is at the heart of the Christian religion. The nation is calling in its hour of need and it is the best and bravest of our young men who are answering the call. To my own knowledge it is the finest flower of our youth who are the very first to offer themselves to death.

— But the way of peace does not call for wholesale slaughter, sir, J.T. said.

— Sacrifices have to be made, Miles.

The Principal clenched his fists tightly.

— There is no other way. And I'll tell you something else. I see three great truths reaffirmed in this dark sky. Three great truths. The belief in the immortality of the soul is immeasurably strengthened. Do you think these brave boys could face death so stout-heartedly without a sure and certain hope in a better resurrection? That is the first truth. And the second is this, the ability to make sacrifices is an ennobling thing and will elevate our nation to a new standard of morality. I am certain of this. Vice will become intolerable to a people who have felt the divine power of sacrifice. And that brings me to my third truth. A deeper and more thoughtful sense of the eternal will take possession of the nation in a way it has never done before.

J.T. cleared his throat again and the noise reverberated in the further corner of the room in a way that made the Principal frown with irritation.

— Thou shalt not kill, J.T. said.

— Mr Miles, I have taken my stand, the Principal said. If you have come to me for advice, I have given it to you. If you have presumed to come to me and reason with me, I must tell you that you are presuming too much on the affection I have always tried to show towards my senior students.

J.T. lowered his head and looked miserable. The Principal pushed back his chair and rose to his feet with slow dignity. He was not wearing his gown, but he was enveloped in authority. His clean-shaven chin sank into the white collar and stock that was just visible above the insert in the high waistcoat whose black silk buttons climbed up the Principal's thin torso almost to his neck.

— My dear Miles, he said. If you feel as you do, take my advice and join the Royal Army Medical Corps.

J.T. picked up the letter on the edge of the desk in front of him. There the Principal had laid it down at the beginning of the interview to keep it well apart from his own books and papers. Once again J.T. read the letter through slowly as if he were memorizing the contents. It was written on lined notepaper in a spidery uncertain copper-plate.

Dear Mr Miles,

I have been instructed by the Pastoral Committee to inform you that several members of this church are very disturbed by your attitude to the war as expressed in the sermons you preached in Bethania on the second Sunday in July. The committee would like to feel that the call given to you was unanimous. Therefore, in view of this serious difficulty, the committee feels that it would be better for all concerned if you would consider the call as withdrawn. They also feel it would be wiser for you not to attend the Presbytery meeting at Horeb next month and request you not to attend, I remain, yours faithfully,

John Oswald Williams, Secretary, Pastoral Committee,

Bethania CM.[61] Church.

J.T. lifted his head slowly and looked at the Principal, whose chin was still sunk on his chest.

— What shall I do about this? J,T. said, lifting the letter.

The Principal did not look at the object that was held up for his inspection.

— My dear Miles, he said. I have already told you. There is nothing you can do. You have chosen to say certain things publicly. Voices have been raised against you. You must take the consequences. My advice is, it would be foolish in the extreme for you to appear in the Presbytery and demand a further hearing. It would also be undignified and embarrass the church at Bethania quite unnecessarily.

J.T. nodded slowly.

— That's it then, he said.

The Principal raised his eyebrows and his eyes grew large and moist in the papery pallor of his face. The letter in J.T.'s big hands fell into its well-creased folds at the touch of his fingers. He felt in his pocket for the envelope.

— Why should so many men slaughter each other? J.T. said. That's what I want to know. Why?

— We must go through with this, Miles, the Principal said.

He leaned forward across the desk and lifted his voice as if he were prepared to address an unseen public.

— All the way through the fire and the furnace until the Germans are taught a lesson they will never forget. Never.

J.T. licked his lips nervously and had to clear his throat yet again before he could speak.

— What lesson? he said.

— What lesson? What lesson? The Principal lifted his finger in a warning gesture.

— Not to cut the hands of little children off, he said. Not to bully little nations. Not to be beasts.

— How can you teach them a lesson if they are dead? J.T. said. What can you teach the dead?

— You don't seem to have heard me, Miles.

The Principal's voice rose angrily.

— Have you no sense of honour? Little Belgian children with their hands severed at the wrists!

He struck his wrist several times with his stiffened index finger.

— Promises broken. Villages burnt. Old men shot. Young women raped. Germany is a mad dog, Miles. It must be put down. There is nothing else to say.

The Principal was waving his arm.

— Nothing, he said. Nothing.

J.T. spread his hand across his eyes and pulled at the skin of his temples.

— That's it then, he said again.

— Yes, Miles, the Principal said. That is it.

PLATT REES'S WALKING-stick sank into the sandy soil. They had reached the foreshore and he wanted to sit on his stick as if it were a shooting stick, but it sank too low in the sand. He was elegantly dressed. His jacket was open and it hung neatly on his slim figure. He tugged the stick out and he saw that Lydia was smiling. Frank Morgan, wearing a mackintosh, jumped on a tufted hillock and pointed at the shore dramatically.

— Come unto these yellow sands!

He tried to capture the attention of both Lydia and Kate. Lydia had let go of Kate's arm and she was shading her eyes to stare at a mansion in the woods across the wide bay.

— Kate, she said. It's such a pity. We should have brought Ned's binoculars.

Kate did not answer. She was disturbed by a button that hung loose at the side of her boot, The fingers of her hand stretched down in a vain attempt to touch it without bending.

Platt Rees had decided to smoke a pipe. With his stick over his arm, his hands were busy with the task of filling his briar pipe from his new tobacco pouch. Lydia was trying not to stare at him. He wore rimless glasses and around his neck a new clerical collar. Frank Morgan made another bid for the girl's attention.

— The tide is turning. The turning of the tide!

He pointed towards the sea. Shadows of the moving cloud darkened both the smooth sand and the blue water.

— I want to be a nursing sister, Lydia said. Pa won't let me go.

— Oh I can understand that.

Frank spoke quickly, without thinking, as it appeared, in case anyone else spoke first. Platt Rees put his loaded pipe between his teeth,

— Why not? Lydia said.

She looked fierce. Kate looked at the loose button on her boot.

— Well . . . Frank said.

— Go on, tell me. Do you think I'm not capable? Or not to be trusted?

— Well the farms are important you know, Frank said. We must feed the island fortress. There's sense in that, isn't there?

— Pa was livid with Griff for joining up. Lydia's eyes shone with excitement.

— Absolutely livid. Especially the Flying Corps.

— Did I tell you about my vow? Yes, mine.

Frank looked mischievous and pointed at himself. Platt Rees lit his pipe.

— I'm not going to smoke or drink until the war is won!

— Well that will be a big help, Lydia said.

She plucked the hat pin from her white hat, swept it off by its wide brim and plunged the pin back into the material.

— What's happened to J.T. Miles?

Kate passed her tongue over her lips and turned to look back up the rough track by which they had taken their slow walk to the sea.

— Doesn't he live with his grandmother?

Platt Rees took out his pipe and held it in front of his face with the stem pointing upwards.

— Didn't she bring him up?

— She died, Kate said.

She spoke without turning around.

— Really?

Platt Rees raised his eyebrows.

— I hadn't heard.

— We hear, don't we Kate? Lydia said.

Kate took no notice. Frank Morgan came closer to them.

— He had the most fearful row with Prinny, he said. The day after his B.D. results.

— Is he a B.D.? Lydia said. We didn't know that, did we Kate?

— By the skin of his teeth I was told.

Frank was pleased now to have all their attention.

— Someone wrote a letter last week to the local paper and called him Heimrath von Miles. The man who wants the Germans to win. He'll get himself into awful trouble. They've withdrawn the call from Bethania, Rhos.

— He's got integrity, you know, Platt Rees said. He spoke very slowly, with judicious care.

— Somebody sent him a white feather.

— Serve him right, Lydia said.

Kate looked at her.

— Well he's got to be taught a lesson, hasn't he?

Platt Rees pointed the stem of his pipe at Frank Morgan.

— How did you know? About Bethania?

Frank smiled and winked.

— I have my spies, he said.

— No, seriously, Lydia said. At a time like this when a country's very life is in danger . . .

— Listen!

Kate spoke sharply.

— What's the matter?

— ''Tis the breath of summer, sweet on the morning air . . .'

Frank Morgan intoned poetically.

— Seriously! Listen!

— In the sky somewhere, Lydia said.

She swung around making two holes in the sand with her heels.

The quiet sky was suddenly alive with a noise they had never heard before. They all looked up, shading their eyes, but there was no telling from which direction it came, until a biplane suddenly appeared over the wooded headland to the north of the long beach. It was losing height as it flew into the wind.

— He's going to land!

Lydia jumped up and down with excitement.

— It's Griff! I'm sure it is.

The aeroplane sank lower in stages and as it drifted nearer, Lydia began to run forward, waving.

She ran as fast as she could, her long skirt flapping against her legs, her hair falling from her head in bunches and blowing around her shoulders. The big hat she carried was folded back by her running. The aeroplane on its stalky legs was bouncing to a stand-still along the wet sand near the sea, its engine still spluttering. Kate had run after Lydia. She was followed by Frank Morgan in his mackintosh and lastly came Platt Rees who ran unwillingly. As the flying machine taxied into the wind and turned to face the way he had come there were four figures at varying distances moving towards it across the empty beach.

Kate suddenly stopped running. Her stockings were slipping down her legs. Overcome with embarrassment she sank down into the sand. Frank Morgan hesitated as he caught up with her. She rose up to wave him on. Patches of damp sand clung to her navy blue skirt. Platt Rees paused and offered his arm, even bowing slightly.

— Look after Lydia, she said.

In the aeroplane the pilot pushed up his goggles to rest on the tight leather helmet he wore. He had a big face. He had a smile like Mr Punch that curved upwards and showed two top teeth missing. He had switched the engine off and the machine was still. The long wooden propeller was made of polished mahogany. Lydia stopped in her tracks when she realized the pilot wasn't her brother. She was near enough to inspect the machine closely. She looked down at her boots that were covered with wet sand, and her hand felt blindly at the condition of her hair.

— How'd you like a ride!

He was a very large young man. The open cockpit seemed too small for him. Lydia walked nearer.

—Where are you from? she said.

— Toronto.

He grinned delightedly.

— No. Now I mean.

— That would be telling.

— What is this?

Lydia pointed boldly at the aeroplane.

— This is a Harry Tate!

The pilot slapped the edge of the cockpit with his gloved hand.

— A short cut to heaven. How about a ride?

— My brother's in the Flying Corps, Lydia said.

— Is he now? What's his name?

— Griff Jones.

The pilot pulled a face and shook his head. Then he held out his hand.

— Pleased to meet you, Miss Jones, he said.

Politely Lydia took his hand. Her hand was lost in his thick leather glove. He did not let go.

— Comin' up? he said.

He tugged at her arm and Lydia tried not to smile. Frank Morgan moved nearer, as if to show he was watching. He looked back at the others. Kate was limping forward, leaning on Platt Rees's arm.

— I think Kate's twisted her ankle, he said.

The pilot still held Lydia's hand.

— I can only take one, he said. Kate stood at some distance away. She refused to come any closer.

— Lydia!

— My sister's calling, Lydia said.

— How about a rendezvous, the pilot said. I get so damned bored on this island.

— Where are you stationed?

Frank Morgan tried to make his voice sound official. The pilot let go of Lydia's hand. She moved away from the machine. The pilot was struggling out of the cockpit. He stretched his arms as he stood on the sand. In his heavy flying coat, with puttees on his long legs, he looked top heavy.

— You lot live here?

— Not really, Frank Morgan said. Where are you stationed ?

— Ever see such a goddamned hole? Don't you go mad with nothing to do? Out of sheer boredom?

Lydia moved backwards and turned to examine the laminations of the polished propeller.

— Are you in any difficulty?

Platt Rees clasped the lapel of his jacket and spoke soberly. The pilot regarded his clerical collar closely.

— Not really, he said. I get so fed up with this island. Ah well. I'll be on my way.

He saw Lydia touching the propeller.

— Unless you fancy a ride, lady.

Lydia smiled.

— Shall I go, Kate?

— Of course not!

Kate was pale, exhausted with embarrassment and unexpected exertion.

— Ah well. Stand back then, lady.

He switched on the engine and kicked wet sand against the wheels of the undercarriage.

— Ah well, he said again. Maybe one day I'll find a landing beach inhabited by one solitary beautiful woman.

He gave Lydia a final wink and swung his propeller. The engine functioned. He clambered into the cockpit. They watched him with wide-eyed wonder. He waved and before they could lift their hands he had taxied off down the wind. As the aeroplane turned in the distance, Lydia ran sideways until her feet splashed the margin of the sea. The flying machine lifted itself from the ground miraculously, gaining height as it passed over their heads and flew on above the white mansion in the woods. It kept their entire attention until it had flown out of sight and hearing,

— Amazing! Frank Morgan said.

Lydia was looking at the empty sky.

— The marvels of modern science. Isn't it amazing?

Lydia ran back to Kate.

— I thought it was Griff, she said. Did you like him?

— No, I didn't.

Platt Rees and Frank Morgan stood listening to them.

— Didn't you hear what he said? About this island? I thought it was very insulting. It's our land he was talking about. What right has he got to come here?

— But Kate, he was only joking. Wasn't he?

She turned to the two men. They looked at each other grave and judicial.

— He had no right to talk like that, Platt Rees said. It will be a sad day for the world if that type ever got the upper hand.

ISAAC DAFYDD SAT wedged in his chair. J.T. stared at the old black-smith's hands which were swollen with arthritis and lay on the curved arms of his chair like inanimate objects. Outside it was raining and smoke twisted up thickly from the wet coal that Mrs Isaac had just tossed neatly on the fire from a small shovel so that only her thick arm came momentarily between her husband's field of vision and the unexpected visitor who sat sideways in the chair opposite.

— Where will you live then?

Isaac used the second person singular as if J.T. were still the young improver who had lived for more than two years under his supervision and under his roof. The arthritis gripped his head in a vice of stillness. His eyes, also, were still and glazed like a drunkard's. When he blinked, the action seemed exaggerated and the effort of speaking gave the false impression around his blue lips of the beginning of a smile.

J.T. shook his head.

— I don't know yet, he said.

— How much did you get for the cottage? Isaac Dafydd said.

— It wasn't any use to me, J.T. said, as if he were making an excuse. Dora Evans was very good to my grandmother. Always very loyal to her.

— What about the garden and the two-acre field behind it?

Mrs Isaac's voice had deepened with the passage of time. She stood with her arms folded and her feet apart by the table, in the very centre of the kitchen. Salted hams hung from the beam above her head. The shelf of books above Isaac's head seemed poised at the same angle as eleven years ago. Nothing in the kitchen had changed. Not even the smell.

— Dora's brother Ned has the field, J.T. said. Keeps stores there. Does a little buying and selling I think. Can't work very hard, you see, because of his heart.

— *Diawch!*

Isaac pushed himself up his chair and pulled a face with the effort.

— You got nothing then? he said. His voice was harsh.

— They're very badly off, J.T. said.

— Did you give them the deeds? Isaac Dafydd said,

— I don't think there were any. I never saw any, I know that.

Isaac Dafydd closed his eyes.

— No method, he said. No order. Thank God you never became a blacksmith.

— Don't forget I won the Poor Apprentice Prize, J.T. said with a smile, as if he were anxious both to cheer up Isaac Dafydd and change the subject.

— If you don't learn to look after yourself, the old smith said, you'll end up by being a public nuisance.

His lips were stretched tight with pain and irritation. He continued to mutter 'on your own . . . bankrupt in twelve months . . .' Then he looked straight at J.T. and said:

— Have you had a Call?

J.T.'s face grew red. Shifting his eyes to see if Mrs Isaac was watching, their glances met and she did not look away. J.T. breathed deeply.

— It was withdrawn, J.T. said. Because of my attitude to the war.

—You've become a politician then as well, Isaac Dafydd said.

— No. It's not that, J.T. said. War is unchristian. That's what I've been saying. It's not the christian way of settling things.

— *Diawch,* you are an innocent, Joe Miles, you really are.

Unexpectedly, Isaac Dafydd lifted his left arm and all his outstretched fingers pointed at J.T.

— If I were fit now, I'd make a fortune. A fortune. They're going to open a big munition factory at the Junction. That's a fact for you. And if a skilled man like me could get there, I'd earn a fortune. And beat the Germans as well. Kill two birds with one stone. Instead of that, I sit here like a waxworks. Without a fire in my own forge.

—What's happened to Ifan Cole? J.T. asked.

— Camel Lairds,[62] Isaac Dafydd said. They'll take anything there now. I should have gone there in 1889 when I had the chance. I'd have been a rich man by now. No doubt about it.

J.T. smiled and sat more comfortably in his chair.

—Why didn't you go then? J.T. said.

— Didn't fancy living in those dark streets, Isaac Dafydd said.

—Well there you are you see! J.T. made a light-hearted gesture.

—There you are, what?

J.T. let the palm of his hand fall on his knee with a quiet slap.

— If everyone did that the world would be a better place. Give up the glitter of gold for the quiet of the countryside. That's the answer.

— Don't talk rot! Isaac Dafydd said.

His voice touched falsetto under the pressure of his irritation.

— The trouble with you is you don't know what you're talking about, my boy, and you have the impudence from somewhere, I don't know where — I knew your grandmother and your mother and they were modest people — to set yourself up as a minor prophet. Go away now before I lose my temper and say things I'll be sorry for. Go on. Go away.

J.T.'s mouth fell open and he bent forward as if someone had poked a stick into his stomach. Mrs. Isaac unfolded her arms and touched him on the shoulder.

—You'd better go, she said.

J.T. rose stiffly to his feet. He had to lower his head to avoid the hanging ham. Mrs Isaac hadn't offered him a cup of tea. He was no longer welcome.

— Go now or you'll upset him, she said.

J.T. looked down into her face. Her voice had been full of reproach. Her forehead was creased into a frown that glistened because of the oily quality of her skin, and under her thick eyebrows her eyes were fixed on his collar and tie.

— Come to the door, she said.

She led the way. Outside the rain had stopped and the cobbled yard had many small puddles. The main door of the forge was half-shut as if the top hinge had bent, and inside all was dark and quiet. J.T. looked back into the kitchen. Isaac Dafydd's head was still fixed in the direction of the chair in which he had been sitting and his swollen hands were curved over the ends of his chair-arms.

— I came to see how he was, J.T. said.

— He gets very irritable in the afternoon, she said. She looked up into his face.

—Why don't you wear a clerical collar?

She made a gesture with her fingers around her own neck.

— I don't believe in them, J.T. said, to tell you the truth.

— Very nice, I think.

She nodded in agreement with what she herself had just said.

— Pity. He'd have liked to have seen you wearing one. Isaac always had great respect for the cloth.

J.T. looked at the stone steps leading to the loft, above the stable where he and Ifan Cole once slept. The door was shut. Discoloured wood was visible in streaks beneath a coat of paint that had once been dark red and in the bottom right-hand corner rats had chewed away a hole. Against the steps a cart-wheel rotted inside the tight clasp of its rusting iron rim. The spokes had once been painted the same dark red as the door.

— Do you hear anything of Parry Price the school man? J.T. said.

— I did indeed, Mrs Isaac said. He moved from one school to another in the south and went into a decline.

J.T. shook his head sadly but Mrs Isaac folded her arms and gazed ahead of her as one framed in the low doorway of her own home, entitled to make a judgment.

— The drink, she said.

THE EISTEDDFOD TENT was packed. The daylight filtered through the gently flapping canvas roof. In the audience there were eight thousand people. The bards in their robes occupied a steep bank of seats at the back of the wide platform. The chaired bard, who was a small man, leaned sideways in one half of the ceremonial chair. He listened intently to the white-haired orator in a frock-coat, who stood alone in front of his vast, attentive audience. At intervals there were doorways in the semicircular canvas wall and large policemen stood in these areas of bright daylight to keep back the crowds outside in the Eisteddfod field who were straining forward to catch what they could of the orators' words. The policemen's helmets had polished crests and silver buttons gleamed down the dark bulk of their uniform. With one hand holding the lapel of his coat and the other free to make gestures, the orator pitched his voice accurately to reach the furthest rows of the assembly where they were accepted eagerly as much for the effort and skill that went into their sending as for what they said.

Lydia leaned forward so that she could look first down the row beyond Kate's attentive face and then to her left beyond her brother Griff, who was on leave and whose arms were folded high on his chest, partly obscuring her view. Lydia gave Kate a nudge, but Kate frowned and continued to listen intently to the orator.

— I say again to this assembly of the eisteddfodwyr of Wales, this war is a crusade in the defence of little nations . . .

— Don't, Kate said.

Her lips barely moved as she stared intently at the man on the platform.

— J.T.! Lydia said. J.T. Miles. I saw him.

Kate's head remained tilted and her attention never wavered.

— The greatest art of the world was the work of little nations . . . The orator's voice lifted at the end of each statement as if it carried with it the sum of the emotion of all the people present, so that when the orator released the key word from his lips the hands now resting motionless in laps would begin clapping and create a rainstorm of applause.

— The most enduring literature of the world came from the little nations. The heroic deeds that thrill humanity through generations were the very deeds of little nations fighting for their freedom!

The applause broke. Lydia had not been as attentive as others and she was a little late in beginning to clap her hands. She made up for this in extra vigour which also enabled her to turn her head to where J.T. Miles sat away to her right in the row behind them.

— He's not clapping, Lydia said excitedly in Kate's ear. He's not clapping you know. He's not clapping.

Griff touched her arm. She smiled at him. He smiled back and held up a finger to indicate there was another sentence coming.

— Ah yes. Ah yes. . .

The applause died away into complete silence.

— Ah yes, and the salvation of mankind came through a small nation.

A wave of sighing spread around the audience, and many nodded and muttered approval as if they were in chapel. Griff winked at Lydia as if to say he had told her it was coming.

— Let me . . . let me . . . the orator said, stuttering, interrupting himself, and at the same time shifting his weight from one foot to the other so that the movement brought him nearer to his audience and in more intimate contact with them.

— Let me tell you of a sheltered valley I know of in my native country, farther than the harps of our bards from the horrid shriek of shot and shell! A beautiful valley, snug, peaceful, comfortable, sheltered from all the bitter blasts. Comfortable, my friends, but sometimes enervating. All the bolder boys would love to climb the hill above the village and glimpse the great mountains in the distance.

The orator paused. A quick gesture showed a lesson was to be drawn. He began again on a note of greater intimacy.

— We, all of us, you and I, have been living in a sheltered valley for generations. Now, out of our selfish comfort the stern hand of war drives us up the slopes to see the peaks of duty and honour and patriotism clad in glittering white. And highest of all . . .

He lifted his arm and looked upwards.

— . . . The peak of sacrifice pointing like a rugged finger to heaven.

His arm came down slowly, the index finger still erect. He bent his wrist until the same finger was pointing at the audience. Then he opened his arms wide as if to embrace the long ranks of listeners who sat below him.

— Fellow eisteddfodwyr, young men of Wales, this little nation, your country calls and I know and you know it will not call in vain.

Heads suddenly began to turn in irritated consternation. Another voice was calling. An intruder was speaking. J.T. Miles, an angular young man with untidy red hair had risen to his feet and was stretching out a hand that clutched a programme of the day's events towards the platform, in an appeal to the orator.

— But there is another way, sir. There is another way, sir, is there not?

His voice wobbled and trembled with nervous emotion so that at first neither Lydia nor Kate recognized it. He was pushing a finger down his collar as if to give himself more voice. Griff turned to look over his shoulder without unfolding his arms. His eyebrows were raised and his forehead furrowed. Kate and Lydia looked at each other anxiously, Kate growing pale and Lydia disapproving and indignant.

After the shocked silence, a buzz of disquiet began to build up, which was pierced by angry shouts that came with increasing power.

— Sit down!

— Shut up!

— Sit down!

— Throw him out!

— Shame on him!

— Sit down!

J.T. lifted his arm again. A man sitting next to him plucked away at the bottom of his jacket; but J.T. gripped firmly at the seat in front of him which was occupied by a stout lady in black. She blushed furiously as her chair twitched under her and at seeing so many faces turned towards her. Her husband in a sudden rage hammered at J.T.'s knuckles with a folded newspaper until shreds of its pages fell away.

On the platform, the orator quickly recovered. He raised his hand dramatically.

— My friends!

The ringing voice topped the growing disturbance and once again could be heard clearly at the back of the Pavilion.

— As long as the men and women of this noble generation last, they will persecute this righteous war, this war for the weak against the strong, this war of Good against Evil, this war for the honour of this ancient country, until the summit of glorious victory is finally conquered!

As at a symphony concert a storm of applause broke out as he finished and Kate allowed herself to release a pent-up sigh of relief. Her shoulders, which had been rigid since the moment J.T. first called out, sagged and she bent forward, breathing heavily. This made it easier for Lydia to try and catch J.T.'s eye, so that she could show all her disapproval, but J.T. was still on his feet, looking despairingly towards the platform where the orator had already sat down in the vacant chair near that of the chaired bard. The orator lowered his head as the archdruid conferred with him, and then nodded, giving his blessing to what was being suggested to him. The chaired bard dried his hands on the arms of his chair and lifted his eyes modestly to the roof. He was prepared to be over-looked. The whole canvas pavilion seethed and hummed like a hive that had been disturbed. The archdruid pushed the white folds of his headdress over his shoulder, lifted his hand, and called upon the assembly to stand up and sing the Welsh national anthem. An experienced conductor in bardic robes stepped forward at an urgent gesture from the archdruid and with hand and voice induced the audience to sing, at first unsteadily and then, as the melodic line struck home to every inattentive ear, with confident harmony and swelling power. The orator himself rose to his feet and with the freedom of a man who has discharged a heavy task turned first to one side and then the other, willingly submerging his own voice in the united effort, an equal among equals to be seen sharing the pleasure of communal sound.

As the singing was in progress, J.T. suddenly decided to get out. With uncharacteristic carelessness he pushed his way down the row to the aisle where sawdust had been scattered on the grass to keep it dry. His neighbours backed away from him as if he carried an infectious disease. He hurried out with his head down, his mac over one arm and the programme still clutched in his right hand. At the entrance a stout policeman, who was not singing, suddenly took him by the shoulder while his head was still bent and twisted him around so that he was facing the way he had come. He turned to look up at the policeman with a look of protest, but before he could open his mouth, the policeman, without changing the expression on his face, jerked his knee hard into the base of J.T.'s spine so that he stumbled forward. For the remainder of the anthem he stood isolated in the gangway. He turned once as if to make a fresh attempt to get out. The policeman raised a warning finger on a level with the lowest silver button on his uniform. J.T. lowered his head and rubbed dust out of his eye with the back of his finger. When the singing came to an end and the bards were filing out in ceremonial exit, J.T. turned again and this time the policeman clenched his fist, so low down however that no one except J.T. appeared to see it.

On their way out people who were aware that J.T. had caused the disturbance at the end of the orator's speech hurried past him, as if knowing who he was gave them added reason for getting out quickly before the gangways became too full of people for easy movement.

Wedged between strangers in the narrow exit he felt the policeman's hand on his shoulder. The policeman's face with the eyes in the shadow of the helmet, was lightly pockmarked and the ends of his moustache touched the helmet strap that rested on his chin.

— All right then, he said.

J.T. saw him pass his tongue along the edge of his moustache and then nod. J.T. tried to stand and talk, but the increased pressure of the crowd was pushing him forward.

— I beg your pardon?

Now J.T. had to turn his head to ask the question. Other faces, pale and empty with fatigue, turned to look at J.T.'s effort to converse with the policeman.

— Down there. By the rest tent. Wait there.

The policeman lifted his arm and with his wrist bent downwards pointed to an empty tent some twenty yards away, beyond the muddy path along which people were now hurrying. There was a general effort to get to the railway station in order to make sure of a seat in the limited number of special trains that had been arranged for the eisteddfod. In the officials' enclosure, a large motor-car was waiting to drive the orator to a country house on Anglesey where he would be spending the week-end.

Uncertain whether to leave or stay, J.T. stood by a guy-rope near the entrance of the empty rest tent. A stiff breeze blew from the sea and he shivered with cold like a man recovering from shock. Then the sun suddenly broke through the clouds and he screwed up his face to protect his eyes from the dazzle. People hurried past where he stood and he could smell the stuffy human sweat of people wearing many clothes because of the uncertain weather. He opened his eyes and thought he saw someone he knew, the placid features of Jack Jacobs of Welshpool, who had been called to an English-language church far away in Monmouthshire. Jacobs who had a box camera at the Theological College. J.T. called out his name but Jacobs passed on without appearing to hear.

— In there!

A small man stood in front of J.T. and pointed towards the entrance of the rest tent where a grinning fisherman held back the tent-flap and motioned J.T. to enter. He spoke in a high-pitched voice.

— Are you talking to me? J.T. said.

His voice sounded polite but puzzled.

— Yes, you. Bloody pro-German.

Someone pushed him hard from behind so that he stumbled over the guy-rope. The fisherman caught his arm and steered him around to face the tent entrance. As he turned he caught a glimpse of the policeman again, this time accompanied by a colleague, strolling down from the Pavilion, but a push from yet another unseen hand sent him staggering into the interior of the tent.

— What do you want? J.T. said.

Now there were five of them standing closely around him. For a moment they were absolutely still as if each one of them wanted to hear him breathing. The little man who had spoken to him first jerked his head inside his stiff collar and said.

— We thought you wanted to make a speech, didn't we boys?

His head jerked again in a nervous tic. J.T. had seen him before. He was an assistant in a chemist's shop in the High Street. He usually stood between tall-necked bottles full of coloured water and behind him innumerable square drawers with chemical names printed in heavy black letters on white porcelain plates. He had also seen his face at singing festivals and shouting at local football matches.

—Should I know you? J.T. said politely.

— Yes indeed you should, Mister Heimrath von Miles. Pity for you there aren't any Germans here now, isn't it? Pity we haven't got a bayonet, boys, for a little practice. We could cut his heart out and send it to France!

J.T. lifted his elbow and charged towards the entrance so that the mackintosh on his arm covered the little man's face. The suddenness of his movement gave him a moment's advantage and he reached the tent entrance just as one of the policemen was lifting the flap to look inside. Once again J.T. found himself watching the pockmarked policeman licking the fringe of his moustache.

— Trouble? the policeman said mildly.

Some of the men hesitated. The chemist's assistant pointed at J.T. and said,

— It's all right boys. They know he's a pro-German.

— Well now, the policeman said, stooping down to step inside the tent. My colleague here will keep guard outside and I shall see that justice is done inside.

He straightened himself, tugged at his helmet strap, smiled and folded his arms.

— Look, J.T. said, trying to keep his voice steady. I don't want to fight. Not anyone. I believe in peace. Peace between all men.

— He's afraid, the chemist's assistant said.

— I'm not!

The chemist's assistant strutted up to J.T., exaggerating his own height in a way that made his friends laugh.

— Watch! he said.

He turned around and lifted a finger as if he were about to give a demonstration of manual dexterity that had to be followed vety closely. He stiffened a forefinger and poked J.T. in the waistcoat hard enough to make him step back.

— The Kaiser's friend! he said.

He poked again, and this time J.T. raised his hand and tried to brush the finger away. The little man removed his hand and after an exaggerated wave ripped open J.T.'s fly buttons. As J.T. bent forward to protect himself with both arms, the fisherman rushed up behind him and hit him so hard on the back of the neck that he tumbled in a heap on the ground, at the same time opening his mouth in an effort to shout.

— Laugh, boys! the chemist's assistant said. Laugh now! He's telling us lovely jokes.

Imitating the style of a popular footballer taking a penalty, he aimed a kick at J.T.'s crutch. One of J.T.'s legs shot out with unexpected fierceness and caught the chemist's assistant's leg with a crack that sent the little man spinning into the empty folding chairs. He lay on the ground moaning and cursing, covered by chairs.

— Kill him, boys! he said. Kill the bastard! He's broken my bloody leg. Throttle him, Tommy! Throttle him, d'you hear me?

Lying on the ground, J.T. heard Griff's voice outside the tent. He was talking to the policeman. He heard Griff say 'Yes but tell me, by what authority?' and then he shouted.

— Griff! Griff! In here. In here, Griff. They're trying to kill me. Griff stooped down low to get past the second policeman, who stood by the tent pole that divided the entrance. The left side of his uniform jacket buttoned over to the right shoulder and it bulged out as he bent down and his forage cap fell off. He picked it up and straightened his uniform jacket which reached a third of the way down his thigh. His manner was purposeful and authoritative, as he studied the scene. Short as he was, he stood back a pace to address the policeman.

— Have you been given authority to let this happen?

His voice was firm and under control. J.T. crouched on the ground his back turned to conceal the doing up of the buttons of his fly. There was a green stain on his face. He looked so pale, it seemed at any moment he might vomit. The chemist's assistant pushed aside the chairs and pulled up his trouser to examine the kick on his leg. The policeman licked the ends of his moustache.

— You do realize, don't you, Griff said, that you were standing inside the tent while your friend outside attempted to prevent my entry? You do realize, don't you, the seriousness of the case?

The policeman's face grew red so that the pockmarks became a white rash. J.T. struggled to his feet, his right hand rubbing the back of his neck and his face screwed up with pain.

— He's a pro-German!

The chemist's assistant gasped out his protest and lifted an arm in J.T.'s direction. The other men stood in the centre of the tent looking lost in the watery gloom, exchanging glances and anxious to be gone.

— How do you know? Griff said.

When he turned to speak to the chemist's assistant the group began to whisper among themselves. There was uncertainty and recrimination already in their voices.

— How? Just tell me how? Griff said. I would be interested to know. I know this man. We were in college together. He's a preacher as a matter of fact. This man you attacked.

— Griff, J.T. said, clearing his throat.

Griff took no notice.

— If you want to fight, Griff said, tugging at the long skirt of his jacket, there's plenty of fighting going on in France. Plenty.

— Griff, J.T. said. Let's go, shall we?

— I mean, Griff said, if each and every one of you would care to give me his name and address I dare say I could put you in touch with the nearest recruiting office. One doesn't want to see all this fighting spirit go to waste, does one. Now you, for example.

He pointed at the fisherman.

— The Royal Navy could do with men like you, I dare say.

J.T. moved towards the exit, the policeman stood to one side and held back the flap of the tent. He nodded at J.T. encouragingly, and smiled in a most friendly way.

— Come on, Griff, J.T. said. Let's just leave them, please.

— What's your name?

Griff was still addressing the fisherman, who muttered under his breath.

— Speak up please. I can't hear you.

— Griff. Will you come now? I'm in a bit of a hurry.

Griff looked at his friend, who was still rubbing his neck

— Please come, J.T. said.

Outside they stood in the mud while people still hurried along the narrow causeway of railway-sleepers. J.T. had begun to talk excitedly. Griff listened.

— If you've got your motor-bike, Griff, if you gave me a lift on the pillion, we could go there now. Get there before him and I could deliver it to him by hand.

— What?

— My petition.

Griff smiled.

— Have you written a petition? he said.

— The Plas Coch people are good Methodists. They'll let me talk to him, Griff. In our language. It could make a difference.

— You really believe that?

— Well, in the end, the dialogue is between man and man. He stopped talking because of the expression on Griff's face.

— What's the matter?

— There can't be anything more defenceless. Not even a chicken in a cracked egg.

— Will you give me a lift?

— A chapel-bred Welsh poet, Griff said. A chicken in a cracked egg.

— I'm not a poet.

— You should have been.

— Will you give me a lift? Yes or no?

Griff lifted his hand in mock alarm.

— Right, he said. I hope I've got enough petrol. Just think a cupful of petrol could stop the war. Come on.

11

STILL CHEWING, Kate rose from her chair at the small round table and moved to the window. She lifted her right hand as if to push the air in front of her, until it came to rest on the varnished sill and she was able to lean forward and see as far as the end of the unadopted road. She held her head forward until the veins in her neck stood out. Traffic flashed by along the coast road, but her eye was focused on the turning where J.T. should have appeared, carrying a packet of cereal under his arm.

A family car made the turning into Gorse Avenue and it bounced forward, throwing up the tightly-packed occupants until the driver, realizing the condition of the road, pressed the sole of his shoe on the brake. He was late pushing down the clutch pedal with his left foot, and he tugged the gear lever into second with a grinding noise that made Kate jump, and then straighten herself to make her own equilibrium more secure.

The car came to a halt between two houses opposite so that it was impossible to tell which neighbour was about to receive visitors before nine o'clock in the morning. The driver, having opened his door, seemed to fall out. He stamped his feet several times and stretched himself so that slowly he became taller and broader and Kate could see the horizontal creases in the back of his blue coat expanding. Putting his hands on the seat he had just vacated, he put his head back in the interior of the car. There were at least two grown-ups, two children, and a woman with a baby on her lap inside the car. The driver, who had springy black hair and a pale gleaming face, emerged once again from the interior and went around to open the boot. He was joined by the woman with the baby in her arms. The white woollen shawl was stained with regurgitated food and fragments of melted chocolate. The baby was asleep. The woman swung her burden to one side to point at a bag she needed that was buried in the luggage in the boot. The driver began to pull out large cases in order to get at it. They had to be put down carefully on the driest parts of the pavement. The far-side rear door of the car opened and two little girls stood on the pavement. They began to shiver in their thin summer dresses. Inside the car an elderly woman heaved her chest and spread herself out on the back seat. She seemed in no hurry to emerge. Also in the rear there was a shrivelled man in an open-necked shirt who might have been her husband and possibly the children's grandfather. He was smiling. Kate could see his teeth glistening in the gloom of the car's interior. A small boy emerged unexpectedly. He ran up and down on the road, jumping over the rainwater in the puddles. The woman with the sleeping baby on her right arm called out to restrain the boy, but he took no notice. For a time neither at No. 6 nor at No. 10 was there any sign of a front door opening. The door of No. 8 was painted green and had a heavy black knocker as well as the mouth of a letter-box painted the same colour. The windows of No. 6 had curtains of white nylon that were cross-hung and were taken down for washing once every month. The door of No. 10 was painted brick-brown. There was no knocker; instead, in the doorpost an illuminated button was inserted that shone very conveniently in the night and when pushed rang a brief chime in the hallway of the house. Occasionally in the front window of No. 10 a narrow card was inserted which read 'BED AND BREAK-FAST'. It was the door of No. 10 that opened, and Mrs Box stepped out into the breeze and folded her arms. Her face was flushed, probably from sitting too near the electric fire. She was a woman who often complained of the cold.

Kate bent forward to take another look at the mouth of the Avenue. There was no sign of J.T. returning. Briefly she watched the encounter between Mrs Box and the newly-arrived family. There were handshakes taking place. The driver hurried back to help the elderly woman out of the car. She had waved the small man in an open-necked shirt aside, but she seemed relieved when the strongly-built driver gave her his arm to weigh on.

Kate turned to look in on her own living-room. She had the house to herself. She had eaten as much breakfast as she wanted. But J.T.'s breakfast was untouched and the place that was laid for him undisturbed. She stood still, as if deciding what to do. Only the clock ticked in the silent house. Suddenly animated, she crossed to the small table and put her cup and saucer on top of her plate. She lifted the pile of her breakfast things, keeping the knife in place by covering it with the thumb of her right hand and holding down the spoon in her saucer with the index finger of her left hand. She paused to survey the small table. There was nothing else she could remove until J.T. had eaten.

In the kitchen, she bent down stiffly on one knee to extract an earthenware pudding dish from the bottom of her kitchen cabinet. She placed the dish on the marble top of the old wash-stand. In the pantry, half a dozen eggs lay on a switch of hay in a cracked dish. Kate took one, together with a jug of milk which was covered by a piece of muslin weighted around the edges with coloured beads. She put these down on the working surface. From a shelf above this she reached for a bowl for beating the egg. With her other hand she opened a drawer and took out a fork. Pressing her teeth into her lower lip, she cracked the egg on the rim of the bowl, opened the shell and allowed the contents to slide into the bottom of the bowl. She picked up the bowl with thumb and finger and, tilting it towards the light, began to beat the egg vigorously with the fork. The sudden clatter made the cat jump from the window-sill outside. She put the bowl down for a moment and stretched her arm up so that she could take a pinch of salt from the old stone jar on the shelf without taking it down. She added the salt to the beaten egg. She also reached down a small saucepan into which she poured half a pint of milk. For the sugar, she returned to the pantry for a packet that had already been opened. The cat reappeared on the window-sill outside, but Kate paid no attention to her. She peered closely into the open drawer for a dessert spoon. The one she chose was worn thin with long use and was discoloured. With a safety match she lit the gas-ring and also the oven. She held the saucepan over a low flame while she stirred in the dessertspoonful of sugar. She hurried back to the marble-topped table, beat the egg again half a dozen times and almost skipped back to snatch the saucepan away from the flame. With a steady hand she poured the milk into the bowl and resumed beating the mixture with the fork until the surface was covered with air bubbles. As she poured the mixture into the small pudding bowl, she continued to stir it with the fork, scraping the surface so that nothing was left behind and wasted. From the pantry she fetched a piece of nutmeg. The grater hung on a nail above her head. With tight lips she grated nutmeg over the surface of the pudding. She bent down to put the pudding dish in the oven and turn down the heat regulator. She slammed the oven door with a heavy hand. When she stood up again she appeared out of breath. Lowering her head, she leaned against the table, and her eye was fixed on the bowl, the saucepan, the fork, the dessert spoon, the broken shell, the packet of sugar, the nutmeg grater, the nutmeg, as if she were calculating the strength she would need to wash up and clear away.

J.T. HAD THE packet of All-Bran safely tucked under his arm. Mr Wilson of Blue Corner Stores was squinting at the till, working out the change. Mr Wilson wore a loosely-knitted fawn pullover that was zip-fastened up to his neck where his Adam's apple rose and fell as he muttered the amount to himself. He had shaved. His pallid cheeks glistened and there were still traces of soap in his ears, but part of a pyjama jacket could be seen riding above the floppy collar of his pullover.

— Not so nice today, is it? Mr Wilson said. Eightpence change. His voice trembled slightly as he spoke and his glance tended to wander around the shelves, as if he were haunted by some secret fear about the future of his stores.

— It suits me, J.T. said, smiling cheerfully.

Mr Wilson hastened to agree with him.

— It is very healthy, of course, he said.

They nodded to each other. J.T. hesitated.

— Mrs Wilson keeping well? J.T. said.

Mr. Wilson drew a deep breath, and exhaled as he answered, so that his Manchester accent trembled with even deeper concern than ever.

— She's as well as can be expected, he said.

The door-bell of the shop pinged. While J.T. was still nodding his head in sympathy with Mr Wilson over his wife's condition, a new-comer was greeting him heartily. The voice was commanding and incisive, but still excited and friendly.

— J.T. Miles! the very man I wanted to see. The very one!

A small man stood beaming comfortably in the doorway. Wilson coughed, smiled, nodded.

— Morning Mr Wilson! Feeling the draught?

He shut the door quickly without changing his expression of keen delight or taking his attention from J.T. He wore the jacket and waist-coat of a faded brown suit, grey flannels that flapped above his ankles and black boots very similar to the boots J.T. was wearing. He stepped forward with his short right arm stretched as far as it would go. On the wrist of the other arm hung a copious black shopping-bag.

— *Bachgen, bachgen,*[63] he said. I am glad to see you!

He squeezed J.T.'s hand, holding his elbow with his left hand so that the shopping-bag swung between them. Without letting go, he turned to speak to Mr Wilson whose finger-tips were spread on the empty counter.

— We were in college together! he said.

His small face beamed so much his eyes, magnified by the gold-rimmed glasses he was wearing, were surrounded by countless creases. The grey moustache under the wide nostrils was stained brown at the edges by tobacco smoke. His mouth was open and his lower lip pushed out slightly to indicate he intended to continue talking and giving information of great interest.

— He was the captain of our cricket team, Mr Wilson! The captain!

He pumped J.T.'s hand several times and did not let it go. J.T. looked modest.

— That was nice, Mr Ellis, Mr Wilson said.

— Now I wasn't a Theological, Mr Ellis said.

He dropped his voice and lowered his head as if to take Mr Wilson further into his confidence and released J.T.'s elbow to tap himself on the chest.

— But they were always a couple of men short and I used to turnout as wicket-keeper. Didn't I, J.T.?

— Oh yes. Yes indeed.

J.T. nodded amiably. Mr Ellis let go his hand and pushed his own knuckles into his lips.

— I heard you were about, you see, and I was going to call.

— Have you come here to live? J.T. said.

— Indeed I have. My daughter lives in number four, Winston Drive.

Mr Ellis swung his arm to indicate in which direction Winston Drive lay. J.T. nodded attentively.

— She's a Mrs Tibbot now, of course. Her husband is a P.T. inspector for the county. Not H.M.I. Not yet. He's a very good fellow. Welsh speaking. I've got five grandchildren, J.T., and they're all Welsh speaking, thank God. Mari, my other daughter, she married a solicitor. Mari Williams she is now, not Mari Ellis. Well it is nice to see you after all these years.

Mr Ellis turned to address Mr Wilson again.

— Do you know . . .

He stepped nearer the counter, paused to think more deeply and lifted his head again.

— Do you know, this gentleman and I haven't met for forty years. Just think of that. Not for forty years.

Mr Wilson folded his arms high on his chest and shook his head. He smiled slowly and his hollow cheeks folded back with wonder.

— And here you are, Mr Wilson said.

— Yes indeed, said Mr Ellis. Here we are alive and kicking as the saying goes.

— Yes indeed.

Mr Wilson shook his head slowly as if to prevent his amazement evaporating with indecent haste.

— We did meet once, J.T. said.

He seemed reluctant to spoil the effect and yet compelled to state the facts.

— You're right!

Ellis lifted a finger.

— You are quite right. We met at the Cardiff Eisteddfod, 1938. Correct?

J.T. opened his mouth widely to indicate polite disagreement.

— No, he said. I wasn't there I'm afraid. I missed that one.

— Wrexham? 1933?

— No. I'm afraid I haven't been much of an eisteddfodwr[64] over the years.

—Where was it then?

Mr Ellis pulled out a folded piece of paper from his waistcoat pocket, opened it with the same hand and then handed it silently to Mr Wilson, who took it eagerly, murmuring his thanks, and spread it out flat on the counter with a business-like pressure of the side of his hand.

— I'll get on with this then, shall I? he said in a very quiet voice.

Mr Ellis nodded rather imperiously and continued to stare at J.T.

—Where? he said.

— In London, J.T. said. On the steps of the British Museum. I think you were in charge of a school trip. Only a few minutes. You had to go inside after the boys.

Mr Ellis lowered his head and stared at the floor. He lifted his head.

— Do you know, he said, I've no recollection. No recollection at all.

—You were pretty busy at the time, J.T. said.

— Can you remember what year it was?

— Before the war of course, J.T. said. In the 'thirties I should think.

— The bacon, Mr Wilson said, interrupting hesitantly. It's best back Mrs Tibbot usually has . . .

Mr Ellis showed the palm of his hand in histrionic warning.

—You know what these women are like, he said. Same as usual.

Mr Wilson snorted with amusement. Mr Ellis put his hands back in his pockets. Mr Wilson began to hum as he stood back and studied his shelves. He planted the tins, packets and bottles with a cheerful bang on the counter.

— Well, J.T. said.

He took a step in the direction of the door.

— I'm very glad you have settled in the neighbourhood, he said. We shall talk again.

—Wait two seconds, Mr Ellis said. Just two seconds.

He suddenly became animated and visibly friendly.

— I'll walk up the road with you. I wanted to ask you something. I'll call back, Wilson. I'll call back for the order.

He pointed at Mr Wilson, nodding to induce agreement, as he grasped J.T.'s arm at the elbow.

— Leave your bag, Mr Ellis, Wilson said. I'll fill it for you and it will be here waiting on the chair.

He bent over the counter to point at the empty chair, where stout elderly ladies often sat to recover their breath. Mr Ellis hurried across and put the shopping-bag in Mr Wilson's out-stretched hand. He and J.T. hesitated politely at the door.

— After you, Mr Ellis said, and pushed J.T. in front of him.

Outside, Mr Ellis looked up and down the coast road. He pointed at the heavy white gates of the holiday camp two hundred yards away to the East. The camp occupied twenty acres between the coast road and the sand dunes. At the height of the season it accommodated 6,000 people.

— I had a shock when I saw that, Mr Ellis said.

— It's been there a long time, J.T. said. During the war it was an army camp. R.A.S.C.[65] it was.

—Yes, well you see I don't think I'd been here since the 'twenties. I came here on holiday in 1924 with my first wife. Nice quiet place it was then. The things that have happened in our time, J.T. The things that have happened. Which way?

J.T. pointed the way back. Mr Ellis took his arm and steered him forward, at the same time stretching his neck to be able to speak confidentially into J.T.'s ear. His tone of voice had become soft, musical and expressive.

— Thought you might know, when are they burying J.M. Jones?

— I hadn't heard . . . J.T. said.

— Saw it in the paper the day before yesterday, Mr Ellis said. Thought you might know. I was very fond of old J.M. Do you remember what he said to old Prof. Arnold? 'Sir, unlike Lord Beaconsfield,[66] I was reared in a bookless home.'

Mr Ellis chuckled. J.T. smiled and then began to frown.

— Did J.M. say that? he said. I always thought it was . . .

— I was there when he said it, Mr Ellis said emphatically. Sitting there right behind him.

— Dear me, J.T. said.

He flicked his fingers twice across his eyebrows.

— Do you remember that pipe of his? I'd never seen anything like it before. He bought it in Heidelberg. I remember once it set his pocket on fire. Brilliant fellow.

Mr Ellis sighed deeply.

— We are getting fewer of course, Mr Ellis said. First thing I look at every day when I open the paper. The columns. Did I tell you I've got five grandchildren, J.T.? Last was born in October '61. Might be more of course. Mari's only got one. Brilliant little fellow. Always got his head in a book. I tell her straight out sometimes I'd like her to have another. Alban his name is. Deric Alban Williams. Thinks a lot of his grandfather. Doesn't show it of course. That's how they are now. Self-sufficient. Have you noticed? Like pets in a cage. I often say, you know, what is a house now except a blown-up toy cupboard. Gadgets, toys everywhere.

Mr Ellis's attention was taken by an approaching car. He wheeled around as it shot past.

— Wasn't that Doctor Armstrong?

He turned to watch the car disappearing westwards towards the centre of the town.

— I think it was you know. Who's your doctor J.T.?

— Dr Armstrong.

— Good, isn't he?

— Yes he is, J.T. said. He is very good.

— He's been wonderful with Megan and the four children you know. Nothing's too much trouble. Nothing at all. Of course he and Gilbert are very pally. They play golf together. Gilbert Tibbot, my son-in-law.

J.T. nodded to show that he had understood. They had reached the turning into Gorse Avenue.

— I live down here, J.T. said. Number eight.

Mr Ellis turned and inspected the Avenue. He seemed to make a particular note of the unadopted road.

— Very nice, he said. Nice to be near the sea. That's what I told Megan and Gilbert. They're farther from the sea. But it's a very quiet neighbourhood.

He looked at the new public house. It dominated the corner, and the asphalt car park that surrounded it reached to the back-garden walls of the houses on J.T.'s side of Gorse Avenue.

— Pity about that, Mr Ellis said.

— It's too big to move, J.T. said.

Mr Ellis looked up at J.T.'s face to see if he was smiling.

— It's like a cross between a castle and a cathedral, Mr Ellis said. He was very pleased with his simile.

— Isn't it though? Just exactly that? Stained-glass windows and everything. And the entrances vaulted. Like a bank.

— The House of Baal,[67] J.T. said grimly.

— Times have changed, Mr Ellis said. This isn't the place I used to know. But there we are. My daughter lives here. And my grandchildren.

— I fought against it, J.T. said. The land down here belonged to my wife's family.

— Is she still with you? Mr Ellis said quickly.

— She died, J.T. said. I share a house with my sister-in-law. It's her house really. She makes a home for me.

— I had a nice little house in Leominster. I bought it when I retired. Very small you know, but comfortable. Just the thing really. But my girls were worried I'd be lonely. They persuaded me to sell it. So I spend three months with Megan and three months with Mair. Every other. Alternately. Keeps me young you know. Works out very well really.

J.T. nodded politely.

— We must keep in touch now, Mr Ellis said. We must talk again. Are you on the phone?

— No, I'm afraid not, J.T. said.

— Which chapel do you go to?

— Libanus. I preach once or twice every month.

Mr Ellis looked at him closely as if he were trying to recall something he had once heard about J.T. and had forgotten. Each had a foot extended in an opposite direction and they seemed to remain connected now only by the last thread of Mr Ellis's curiosity.

— Two wars, he said. Two world wars since you and I were in college together. Do you know J.T. I'd like to rake up preaching again. I would really. I had a Sunday School class at Leominster for twenty-five years. With the English of course.

J.T. took the packet of All-Bran and put it under his other arm. He looked anxiously down the Avenue. The exterior of No. 6 looked calm and permanent. There was no sign of any one in the front window. There was a car outside No. 10. Its heavy tyres had splashed out the dark water in the potholes of the Avenue.

— Well I won't keep you.

Mr Ellis sounded huffy. J.T. suddenly became animated.

— I was so surprised to see you, he said. It's my sister-in-law actually. She's being taken out by a niece of ours for a drive you see, and she wants to get her work finished. It's quite natural. She does everything herself. An amazingly competent person really. Only Doctor Armstrong wants her to take it easy. Rather worrying really. She does so much.

J.T. stopped abruptly. They were silent for a few seconds. But when J.T. saw that Ellis was about to speak again, he said,

—We must talk. Very pleased to see you. Come over one evening perhaps. I'll speak to my sister-in-law. It's her house of course. I must go now.

He took Ellis's hand and shook it warmly.

—Very glad to see you, he said. We shall talk again.

12

THE DESK WAS SO PLACED that when he raised her head Lydia could see, above the curved gold letters, 'W. H. Bayliss, Estate Agent and Valuer', the window of her brother's butcher's shop across the wide street. By pressing against the desk and turning her head she could also see the lower steps of the covered footbridge that spanned the railway station, and a corner of the white gates of the level-crossing. Sometimes the view of the bottom of the footbridge would be blocked by the polished wheels of an old trap lodged in the gutter, when a train was due to arrive.

Lydia wore black half-sleeves to protect the arms of her freshly-ironed white blouse. Her dark hair was gathered into a high bun with a few curls allowed to fall on her forehead. Between her desk and the door there was a long table that served as a counter when people came to pay their rents. Kate was leaning against this. She wore a grey costume with a low belt and some of her hair showed under the brim of her Henry Heath hat.

—What on earth is she doing? Kate said.

With her head on one side, she was listening to Mrs Bayliss in the loft of the shed outside in the yard. Furniture was being pushed about. A bedstead dropped with an echoing clatter. Then came the grating reverberation of a hob-nailed boot going through the springs of a bed.

—Who's that? Kate said.

— Charlie, I expect, Lydia said. He's had some beer and he's in a bad temper. Half an excuse and he'll put his foot through anything.

Kate stared at her sister.

— Do they put up with it? she said.

— What else can they do? Lydia said. Men are scarce. He's the only one that knows where everything is.

Lydia pulled a face of comical despair. Kate made a critical survey of what was described on the door in black letters as *General Office, Enquire Within*. The dark walls were covered with calendars given away by manufacturers, and posters of varying sizes announcing auctions and sales. Most of them were old. One, half-hidden by the open door, announced a farm auction for a day in June 1913. There was no means of telling the original colour of the wall-paper behind them. Kate took off a glove and passed the tip of a finger over a corner of the mahogany table and, glancing down, took notice of the amount of dust.

— Don't they ever clean this place? Kate said. Lydia tilted her penholder towards the backyard.

— You know what she said this morning?

— Mrs B?

— She said, 'I know it's daft, but it's the only pleasure left to me in life.' She says there's a chest of drawers in the back of the loft behind the double wardrobes and the bedsteads. Charlie says there isn't. She wants it for her house.

— She's rather vulgar, Kate said.

She drew on her glove and frowned disapprovingly.

— She's very nice to me, Lydia said. Much nicer than he is. He's so suspicious. And so mean.

— I don't know what Pa would say, Kate said.

— Say what?

— If he knew what this place was really like.

— What's wrong with it?

— Well it's hardly clean, is it? And as for estate agent, it looks more like a pawnshop to me.

— It's a very good business, Lydia said. And I like it here, so don't you go carrying tales and stories. You just can't bear it that I'm enjoying myself, can you?

— Don't be silly, Kate said.

— If I can't go nursing, I'd rather this than staying at home. I told

Pa that to his face.

— I do think you're a bit hard on him, Kate said. He's only doing what's best for us all. Ever since Ma died he's carried it all on his own shoulders.

— I'm not so sure, Lydia said.

— What do you mean?

— Look at all the free labour he's had for a start. Ned, Dan Llew, you and I, Griff, and now Rowland and Hugh, working like a herd of donkeys for next to nothing. I can't think why Rowland doesn't join up. Dan Llew was saying yesterday he's the best fighter in our family. That's praise coming from him.

Outside on the wooden steps that led down from the loft of the long shed a heavy piece of furniture was being bumped down from one step to another, and there were loud shrieks of protest from a woman. Lydia put down her pen and jumped off her high stool.

— This is worth watching, Lydia said.

There was just enough room for her to pass between the table and the wall.

— I must be going, Kate said.

— Don't go, Lydia said. Archie Griffiths said he'd call.

— Oh him, Kate said impatiently.

— He was here first thing. Ned must have told him you were coming down.

— Ned had no business, Kate said. Mrs Bayliss's voice came from the yard,

— Lydia love, just come over here and give us a hand will you?

— Really, Kate said.

— It doesn't matter. I like doing it, Lydia said.

She lifted her finger in mock warning.

— Now you wait, Katie Jones. Don't move from here. Coming Mrs Bayliss! Now you just wait here.

Kate restrained herself from stepping into the corridor, where it was possible that Mrs Bayliss would see her from the yard. Across the corridor, the door to Mr Bayliss's room, which was marked Private, was ajar, but not wide enough for Kate to be able to see inside. Mr Bayliss only came in when business appointments demanded it. He suffered from chronic bronchitis and rarely went out from the red-brick house that stood among half-grown trees just off the road that led to the new golf course.

On the pavement outside the window she heard the clatter of

heavy boots and a bicycle being set to lean against the wall. There was a knock on the street door, which was already open, the sound of feet on the linoleum in the corridor and J.T. appeared. He wore the clothes of a farm labourer; a linen jacket and corduroy trousers. The two top buttons of his flannel shirt were open and he wore no collar. When he saw Kate he tried to tidy his hair hurriedly with his open hand. Kate raised her eyebrows and pressed her lips together severely.

— Hello, J.T. said.

— Good morning, Kate said.

She blushed suddenly and looked desperately around the office for something that could legitimately take her attention.

— I'm sorry, J.T. said.

— Sorry for what?

Out in the yard there was a crash and the muffled noise of a man swearing. Mrs Bayliss was shouting.

— Did you ever see such a God-awful stupid man!

J.T. looked startled. Kate made no sign of having heard. J.T. breathed deeply and made an effort to speak, forcing himself to look directly at Kate.

— I understand that you don't approve of me living in Brynbach cottage. I didn't realize, I mean when Griff suggested . . .

— Really, Mr Miles, Kate said. It's nothing to do with me.

— Isn't it?

J.T.'s voice sounded unusually loud. Kate turned to face him as if he were threatening her. She spoke with nervous speed.

— No, indeed it isn't. Indeed it isn't. But if anyone asked my opinion I would say it was very odd for a minister, well a preacher anyway, to be walking around looking like a farm labourer and living by himself in an empty cottage. And if you must be a farm labourer, why are you coming to town in the middle of the morning dressed like that and coming to an estate agent's office? People will start saying all sorts of things.

— People, J.T. said.

He sighed heavily.

— Well people are people, Kate said. And people will always talk. You can't change that any more than you can change people.

J.T. pulled at the skin of his cheek with finger and thumb and then pushed his finger over to his mouth so that he could nibble the side of his finger-nail. Kate stared at this disapprovingly and when he became aware of her stare he dropped his hand and clasped it quickly with his other hand as if he were trying to conceal it.

— If you'll excuse me, Kate said, I'm going across to the shop.

J.T. moved aside.

— Perhaps you'll tell Lydia I've gone across.

Kate hurried out while J.T. was still nodding. He stretched his neck to watch Kate crossing the road, her hand raised to stop her hat blowing off. From the yard behind the office came the rumble of a hand-cart being pushed over uneven cobbles. He heard Mrs Bayliss call out in her loud cheerful voice, and in a moment Lydia ran in laughing and wiping her hands.

— Oh, hello.

She stopped smiling.

— Where's Kate?

Lydia passed to the further side of the table.

— She's gone across to your brother's shop. She asked me to tell you.

They looked at each other in silence.

— I heard from Griff, J.T. said.

— When?

Lydia was excited.

— This morning. I brought the letter. I thought you'd like to see it at Argoed, so I brought it here.

He handed her an envelope. Lydia glanced at the postmark.

— He's still in England, she said.

— Well it was posted in England anyhow, he said.

She took the letter out eagerly and J.T. watched her reading it. Intent as she was on reading the letter and even silently speaking the sentence at the bottom of the page before turning it and continuing to follow its sense along the top line overleaf, she seemed to grow more conscious, in the silence, of his presence, and more than once her left hand slowly felt around the back of her hair. She brought the letter closer to her face.

— Terribly small, this writing, Lydia said.

— He does that so he can get more on a page, J.T. said.

Lydia read on and then suddenly smiled so that her cheeks showed her dimples.

— Oh gosh, she said. Pa had better nor see this.

— What?

She held the letter out, pointing at a particular sentence. J.T. moved closer to inspect it.

— No indeed, he said. I'm glad you pointed that out. I hadn't thought at all,

— Well there you are, Lydia said.

Her voice was playful and friendly. J.T. smiled as if the sun had shone for the first time for weeks.

— He likes you, doesn't he? Lydia said.

— He's a fine fellow, J.T. said. The best friend I ever had. He says extreme things about religion I mean, but I honestly believe he is a Christian at heart. I honestly do.

— Pa hasn't forgiven him, Lydia said. Not really. He's proud of him in public, but you know when he came home on leave they avoided each other. It was quite comic sometimes. Or it would be if it weren't so sad. Griff spent as much time as he could with Ned. That was funny because he and Ned had never had all that much to say to each other. Ned was hedging and Griff said he wanted to learn to do it properly. Training hedges!

— Did you see what he said about the Old Testament? J.T. said.

— Where?

Lydia looked puzzled.

— In his letter.

J.T. pointed gingerly at a sentence. Lydia lifted the letter closer for him to see. Their hands touched momentarily and they both withdrew with a speed that would have been guilty had they not suddenly smiled at each other.

— There it is, J.T. said.

Lydia read it.

— 'I tell you, Joe, this is an Old Testament world we are living in. Anyone would think the New Testament had never been written. That's your job I suppose if you believe in it. To stick up for it, I mean. I wish I could — but there we are. I think I'm a fatalist. Men are fools. Always were, and always will be. I wish I'd been born an Englishman. They seem to take this basic fact for granted. Here they do anyway. No fervid Cymric idealism allowed here. All that sort of thing left to the P.M. . . .'[68]

Lydia was frowning. She stopped reading.

— I don't understand it, she said. It's too clever for me.

— He's a Christian really, J.T. said.

He smiled contentedly as he put the letter back in its envelope.

— Well he doesn't seem to think so himself, does he?

J.T. pressed his lips together and nodded wisely.

— I think I'm right, he said. I hope so anyway.

— You didn't show it to Kate? Lydia said. The letter.

— She didn't give me a chance, J.T. said.

This made Lydia laugh. She began by giggling and the effort of making herself stop caused her to crow suddenly, and at this sound she could restrain herself no longer. J.T.'s face broke into a wide smile and his shoulders shook. Lydia watched him and, as she sobered, she pointed at him and said.

— You know what Pa said about you? I heard him say it. When you first came to Argoed with Griff.

— Something awful, I'm sure, J.T. said.

He wiped the tears of laughter from his eyes with his knuckles.

— 'That one will never make a good minister,' Lydia said. 'He laughs too much.'

KATE PUSHED OPEN her father's bedroom door with her knee. The bedroom window was closed and she wrinkled up her nose. Pa had sunk under the bedclothes and his night-cap lay on the pillow.

— Come on now, Pa, Kate said. Move these things so that I can put your tray down.

He pushed his arm out like a swimmer striking out of a sea of bed clothes. He opened one eye, saw Kate standing at his bedside with a breakfast tray on which a boiled egg occupied a central position, and then let out a groan. He pulled himself up on his pillows with great difficulty and began to mount a coughing fit, tapping his chest weakly with his fist.

— This ... old ... dry ... cough, Pa said in a low constricted voice.

— Move these things please, Pa, Kate said.

He rolled over and picked up the magazines and papers on the bedside table and held them up, letting his head fall back.

— Where shall I put them? he said.

Kate put the breakfast tray down and without answering took the magazines and papers from his outstretched hands.

— You ought to have the window open, Pa, Kate said.

Pa stretched out a hand as if to ward off a blow.

— No indeed, he said. Not when I'm like this.

— I thought you were feeling better last night, Kate said.

— Hardly slept a wink all night. This cough . . . Pa tapped his chest.

— Well, Kate said, don't forget there's the Presbytery meeting at Flint tomorrow. You want to get better for that, don't you?

She picked up a pair of heavy socks, a shirt, and much-repaired long woollen underpants.

— Can I take these to the wash? she said, looking around the room for any other garments that could be lying on the floor.

Pa scratched the bald top of his head. He picked up his night-cap and put it on. Eyeing Kate closely, he combed his beard with his fingers.

— Pass me my teeth, he said.

When Kate handed him the set of upper teeth he clamped them firmly in his mouth and his face at once looked sterner.

— He was after money, Pa said, inaudibly, putting his weight on one elbow and staring mournfully at the breakfast tray. Kate contrived to scrutinize the bedroom, moving about with the clothes in her arms.

— Pour me a cup, *merch-i,* Pa said.

Kate gripped the washing with one arm and leaned away as she poured tea into the large cup that was used by Pa alone.

— You must never believe men like that *merch-i.*

Pa shook his head wisely.

— I've seen so many of them, I can tell you. I'm sorry to say the world is full of them.

— I don't quite know what you are talking about, Pa, Kate said sharply.

When she put the teapot down, unexpectedly he reached out and grasped her hand in his, very tightly.

— Archie Griffiths, Bodafon Hall, Pa said. Nothing in him, Kate. Nothing at all. He was after your money. Nothing more or less.

— What money have I got, Pa?

— You're my daughter, aren't you?

Pa smiled and squeezed Kate's hand and shook it.

— Insensitive fellow, Pa said.

He let go Kate's hand and his chin sank on his chest. His melancholy eyes studied the sky outside and then turned slowly to look at his daughter's face.

— You're not holding it against me, are you Kate? he said.

Kate smiled and shook her head.

— I never liked him anyway, she said.

Pa frowned.

— Never liked him? he said. Never liked him?

— No, not really.

— Well, really.

Pa lifted a helpless arm and let it fall back on the feather mattress.

— Well. It's just as well I am ill sometimes, isn't it? Or I'd never find out anything. I used to worry a lot about it you know. It isn't pleasant for a father to think he is depriving his daughter of something she deeply wants. You know I've always tried to give you everything you really want, don't you Kate?

— Yes, Pa, Kate said.

— I often think . . . Pa said, I don't know either . . . .

He paused and picked up his teacup without passing his finger through the handle. He brought his other hand underneath the cup so that the steam rose up and warmed his nostrils. He began to hum 'What a friend we have in Jesus'.

— What's the weather like, *merch-i?* Pa said. Perhaps I ought to get up to dinner.

— Looks as if it's going to pour, Kate said.

She bent her knees at the low window to look up at the sky.

— Pa . . . Kate said.

— Yes, *merch-i?*

— Nant-y-Wrach and Engedi are looking for a minister, aren't they?

Pa sipped his tea noisily.

— They may have to wait some time, Pa said. Ministers are not so easily come by these days. In fact there is a letter from the Ministry of War, which we shall be discussing tomorrow, asking us to urge our younger men to serve as army chaplains. Nant-y-Wrach may have to wait if the country calls.

— I was thinking, Kate said, you might bring J.T. Miles to their notice.

— That one!

Pa sounded indignant.

— Griff writes to him. Griff says he's very sincere. He did ask us particularly to treat him kindly.

Pa put down his cup.

— I don't like people seeing him come here so often, he said.

— Give him his due, Pa, he never comes here. It was only when Griff was home on leave, just once, that's all.

— He's not well thought of, you know, not at all. In the Connexion I mean, apart from anything else. His views . . . apart from anything else . . .

— Well, said Kate, if the shortage of ministers is all that great, I don't see why he couldn't be given a call.

A sock dropped from the pile of washing she clutched. She bent down quickly to pick it up and her face grew red with the sudden exertion.

— It wouldn't be much trouble for you to mention it, Pa. Hughes Pant Mawr is always saying how much he respects your judgment . . .

Pa waved her to silence.

— My dear girl, the first thing that would cross their minds would be why I should be so concerned about him.

They looked at each other in silence. It was possible to hear Pa's watch ticking under his pillow. Neither seemed prepared to speak. It was as if each having more to conceal than to reveal at the same time struggled by the silent exercise of will to compel the other to acknowledge an obligation to speak. Pa looked away and said:

— My dear girl, he's very lucky not to be in prison. He's very lucky not to be shot.

Kate wrapped the washing she was holding into a tight bundle and pressed it against her stomach.

— I dare say he will be soon enough, she said.

THE INCESSANT RAIN had carved contours into the softer parts of the lane's surface. As he trudged back to Brynbach cottage, the overgrown hedges dripped rainwater into the wet sack that covered J.T.'s bowed head. The loaded leaves of a hazel branch tipped a sudden cascade over the lid of the milk-can he was carrying. Voices made him look up and he saw little Moore the Irishman and his invalid son Louis kneeling in the lane alongside a pram which was filled with firewood and provisions that were half-covered by a sack. A wheel had come off. Moore was holding the pram and Louis looked up grinning when J.T. stopped to ask if he could help.

— A short prayer, Moore said. Ask them to turn the rain off.

J.T. put his milkcan down and kneeled to examine Louis's efforts.

— Would you like me to have a go? he said.

Moore shook his head. He was short of breath, but as he looked down he went on speaking.

— We'll manage I think . . . Was there ever such a waste of mechanical talent. A man like me mending prams . . . Would you believe . . . I was born with a spanner in each hand?

Louis lifted his pale face to look at J.T., and said,

— It doesn't belong to this pram by rights. These wheels, two different sizes.

— Mechanical triumph that it goes at all, Moore said.

He began to chuckle so that the pram shook and his son had to tell him quite sharply to keep still. Moore adjusted the sack on the pram to cover the corner of a large loaf.

— Tell you what I would like, he said. A drop of milk if you could spare it. We've been to the village you know, and it does seem a long way to the farm. And it's getting dark and it's so wet . . .

— Of course, J.T. said. You're welcome.

— I'll send Louis up the lane with a jug, after, Moore said. Such a relief. Thank you very much. Have you got it on, boy?

— It's you won't keep still, Louis said.

— Hang on, Moore said. Mr Miles, would you mind holding this corner a few seconds?

— I can do it, Dad, Louis said.

— I know it, Moore said. Don't I know it. But I'm the engineer aren't I, Mr Miles? Was ever a man more needed in a locality to speed up the war effort? Come on, boy.

J.T. took the weight of the pram. Louis scrambled awkwardly to his feet. He was fifteen at least, but only four-foot-ten. He stood with his hands on his hips, watching his father closely, the rain running down his narrow cheeks, his mouth open and his fleshy lower lip hanging down in the way that gave his face an expression of perpetual discontent. Moore gave the wheel a shake.

— Come on you square peg in a round hole! he said. That's it . . . Now Louis, where's that nut, for Jesus' sake.

He glanced up quickly at J.T.

— Not to mind the language, he said. You can let go now.

Louis bent down to examine the wet ground more closely. Where the pram stood there was a patch of grass, but about their feet there was dark sand and small stones.

— Get your nose down before it gets too dark, Moore said. Louis was now on his hands and knees.

—You had it Dad, he said complaining

Moore squinted up at the low cloud.

— This is more discomfort than the human race should have to bear, he said.

He got to his feet and looked at his hands. He was a short fat man and the coat he wore was too big for him. A piece of binder twine was wrapped twice around his middle. He had large feet and the toes of his boots turned up.

— Awful, he said.

His bulging pale blue eyes swivelled up to look into J.T.'s face.

—To be brought to this state by an extravagant woman. May God forgive her. Have you found it yet then?

— No, Louis said. And I never will if you don't come down and help me.

J.T. knelt hastily.

—What does it look like? he said.

— I'm not to bend again today, Moore said, standing between them, his feet apart. Or my back will never straighten. And all the machines I've got to spend the day under tomorrow.

— It's just a square nut, Louis said.

—To lose a nut in the rain, Moore said. If the Kaiser could see me now. I told you, didn't I, how I drove him back to the hotel in Baden-Baden in nineteen-nine?

— There's nobody you haven't told, Louis said.

— Beautiful English he had, Moore said. I told you that, didn't I? He had one arm you know inches shorter than the other. I couldn't say this to everybody round here, as you know, but in my opinion he was a very decent man indeed. And he took a very intelligent interest in motor engines. He really did. We got quite pally. If I'd have known how much trouble that extravagant bitch I married would have brought me to, I'd have put in for a pension on the spot. And he would have given me one too. We got on very well together.

— Here it is, Dad, Louis said triumphantly. I've got it!

— Aye well, put it on, there's a good boy, and let's get home. Ten to one that blessed fire's gone out. As true as I'm standing here I'd be the best mechanic in Welsh Wales, if only I could find a woman to look after that fire.

He grinned at his son, but the boy scowled back. J.T. stretched out for the milk-can and Moore watched his hand as it closed around the handle.

— And by the by, he said. You know I think I saw a light in your cottage as we were passing. I could have sworn I did. Hello, I said to myself, Mr Miles is come home early. That's why I was so surprised, when I saw you coming round the corner.

— Oh ... I ... wonder ... J.T. said,

Moore looked at him as if he wanted a full explanation.

— Come on, Dad, Louis said.

He wore mittens on his hands and J.T. watched his wet fingers take hold of the pram handle from underneath, as if he were going to lift it up.

— Come on, Dad, I'm cold. My knees are wet,

— Yes well, we'd better be going. Louis will come over for a drop of milk, or I'll come myself, Moore said.

Louis had already pushed the pram around the corner. With an awkward wave of the hand, Moore waddled after him. J.T. looked up the lane thoughtfully and suddenly broke into a run. The milk in the can spilt down the sides and he stopped to lift it up and examine the tricklings. Then he walked steadily forward, holding the can further away from his side and looking at it often to make sure no more was spilled.

There was a bridge of two long flagstones across the ditch to the cottage gate, which hung rotting on its permanently open hinges. The small garden was full of dank weeds and nettles grown shoulder high and run to seed. An oil-lamp without a shade stood burning a low flame in the kitchen window. Firelight made the austere kitchen seem inviting. He scraped his boots noisily on the iron sunk into the ground alongside the door, and he continued to scrape when the boots were tolerably clean as if he hoped someone inside, at the sound of his feet, would come and open the door. He undid the knot of the string that had kept the sack secure over his shoulders. He hung the wet sack on a nail driven in the wooden panel erected just inside the door to exclude draughts. He shifted his shoulders as if they had to be exercised after removing the dampness of the sacking and began to unbutton the old over-coat he was wearing. He saw Lydia by the fire, holding a saucepan containing a steaming stew that smelt so good it brought saliva to the corners of his mouth. Lydia was wearing a pinafore. She had laid the table ready for him. There was freshly baked bread somewhere in the dim room. The two-roomed cottage was warm, almost dry, and homely with the smell of good food. J.T. moved back to the open door to take off his overcoat and conceal himself from Lydia. He hung the coat on a nail and pressed his face into his left hand as if he were praying. He heard Lydia speak while his hand was still clutching his face.

— Well, she said, smiling. Aren't you going to say anything? He moved towards her, nodding and blinking.

— Did anyone see you coming? he said.

— Four ministers, fifteen deacons and about twenty-five cows, she said. Are you going to wash your hands? Look over there.

He turned to look behind him. There was a new white enamel basin on the window-sill near his bed, and half a bar of soap alongside it, and on his bed, which had been made, there was a towel he had not seen before. While he washed his hands and face, Lydia poured the stew into the tin pudding plate that he used. Then she put the saucepan on the hob to keep it warm and poured hot water from the iron kettle into the teapot. When he came to the table, she was already standing there, ready to pour tea.

As he stood nearer her, he moved his hand so that it touched hers. They both looked down as if they were observing their hands, and without any power to control them. They appeared childishly shy, unable to look at one another and each able to hear the other's heart beating in the evening silence. Outside the rain had stopped and there was the beginning of a watery sunset. Somewhere in the overgrown hedge a solitary thrush was singing. He lifted his hand to touch her face. He wanted to look at her. But the movement was awkward and his hand brushed against her breast. He felt the softness beneath his hand. Lydia looked up, her eyes catching the light, big and puzzled.

— Lydia, he said. Oh Lydia.

He let his hands rest on her shoulder and moved nearer to her so that their bodies touched. When they kissed, he held her so tightly that she cried out for breath.

— Oh I'm sorry, Lydia, he said. I'm sorry. And my clothes are so dirty . . .

— No, she said. It's all right. It's all right, Joe, really. I'm all right. Come and eat now, Joe.

— Oh Lydia . . .

He sank to his knees, his arms around her waist, and pressed his face against her belly. She held on to his shoulders nervously. He sank lower and his hands were fastened on to the back of her skirt so heavily that she bent forward.

— Joe she said. Don't weigh on my skirt, Joe. You'll pull it off. Please.

— Oh Lydia, I'm sorry.

He sat back on his heels his hands in his lap, his face wet with tears.

— So much kindness, he said. I was so tired coming up the lane and so utterly alone. I never expected this.

— Come and eat, Lydia said, and then you'll feel better.

The chair he sat in had a broken back, kept reasonably firm with binder twine. He ate the stew with an old tin spoon. Lydia stood watching him eat. He stretched out his hand and she took it. He drew her hand to his lips and kissed it.

— You'll have to let go, she said, to eat properly.

— I keep on trembling, J.T. said. I love you so much.

— Shall I cut some more bread and butter? Lydia said.

J.T. nodded and turned in his chair to watch her. She took the lamp from the window-sill and set it on the small draining board where she was cutting bread and butter. The lamplight suffused her face and breast as she worked. He called her name and she lifted the bread knife in a motherly way, telling him to stay in his chair.

— I've never seen anything as beautiful as you, he said.

Lydia looked mock-reproving, but as she cut the loaf her foot tapped the beaten earth floor of the cottage as if she wanted to dance.

— You're like an angel, Lydia, J.T. said. A real angel.

She carried three slices of bread and butter to the table on the lid of a biscuit tin.

— You didn't used to notice me, Lydia said. I was just a silly schoolgirl, wasn't I?

She dropped the bread and butter on to his plate. He pushed his chair back.

Where are you going? she said.

— There's another chair, he said. For you. The best chair. I keep my best suit on it.

He threw the suit on the bed and brought the chair over to the table.

— Put it by the fire, Lydia said.

— Don't you want something to eat?

Lydia shook her head. She put her feet on the fender and leaned forward to watch the flames leaping in the fire. J.T. went on eating.

— It all looks so different, he said, swallowing a great mouthful of food.

— This is how people should live, he said. In peace. With love.

— You wouldn't find many people willing to live in a shack like this, Lydia said.

She was looking dreamily into the fire.

— An earth floor, she said. A rusty grate. Damp higher than the windows.

— It's better than the trenches, J.T. said.

Lydia looked at him. He had stopped eating and was breaking a thick piece of bread and butter into small pieces.

— You never stop thinking about it, do you? she said.

— I want to stop it, J.T. said. That's all. Just to stop it.

— What's the use of talking, Lydia said. It's so silly really. There's nothing you can do.

— The slaughter, J.T. said. The awful slaughter. It will go on and on. I pray to God to stop it, Lydia. Every hour of the day. Men are doing this to Him. Every bullet that finds flesh, every piece of shrapnel that tears through a body — every time it's a new nail being hammered into the palm of His hand, a new sword being thrust into His side.

J.T. stood up and began to pace up and down the confined kitchen.

— You know what the worst temptation is? he said. The worst temptation of all?

Lydia sighed, and got up to clear the table.

— To stop believing.

J.T. lifted his arm and lowered his head, searching for the word he wanted.

— To cut, he said, to cut away the moorings. No connection with humanity, no connection with God. Outside the plan. To hold on to your little bit of life like the man who buried his one talent, and not to care about anyone or anything else. That's the temptation. To hug your own little bit of life to yourself, and fondle it and hide it and nurse it like a miser with his savings, paying out days like pennies and feeling safe, knowing that you've got thousands more to come.

Lydia leaned against the draining-board and clasped her hands together in front of her.

— If only you could preach like that in the pulpit, she said. He was standing in the middle of the room.

— It doesn't come to me easily. Not in the pulpit, he said. I'm tied to my notes because I keep on seeing faces that put me off. It's funny, they grow big in the pew. These faces that put me off I mean. My throat tightens when I see them, and I start coughing. It's self-indulgence really.

— Does my face put you off?

She was smiling at him. He put out his arms towards her.

— Lydia, he said. God sent you to me. To care about you. To love you. I don't know what I'm saying.

He put his arms around her gently.

— I love you, he said. You are the whole world to me. I want to spend my life staring at you. You make me want to talk so much Lydia . . . Do I sound like a fool?

— Shush.

She put her finger on his lips and he became quiet. She stroked down the hair on his eyebrow which grew out at the corner and gave him a startled air. Her hands joined behind his neck and their thighs pressed together as they stared into each other's eyes.

— God sent you to me, J.T. whispered.

She put her head on his chest and listened to his heart beating. His hands pressed down her back and touched her buttocks. She closed her eyes and lifted her head, her lips apart. He kissed her. Her mouth was open and his tongue slipped gently between her lips until it touched hers. They drew apart and looked at each other as if they were sharing a new discovery that made them both tremble.

— Marry me, J.T said. Please marry me. Lydia nodded.

— On the bed. Now, he said.

Clumsily, still holding each other they shuffled towards the bed. Lydia shivered.

— I feel cold she said. Hold me for a minute, Joe. Hold me.

He breathed shallowly as he held her, as if he were afraid to move. He stood back in surprise when he felt her forearm against his chest, pushing him away.

She sat on the edge of the bed. He stepped nearer her. She lifted her hand to touch his trousers and then let her hand run down his leg, taking hold of his calf.

— Not now, she said. Not here.

J.T. kneeled alongside the bed. He stretched out an arm and laid his head in her lap. He tried to speak, but his voice was muffled in her pinafore and skirt. She stroked the back of his head heavily, pushing up the hair that needed cutting.

— Always liked the colour of your hair, Joe, she said. And your neck. A boy's neck.

He lifted his head and said:

— How can we marry, Lydia? How?

— We'll manage.

She spoke in a comforting voice and kept on stroking the hair on the back of his neck upwards as if she was enjoying the hair brushing against the tips of her fingers.

They were silent together when they heard Moore the Irish man's voice calling outside in the lane at some distance. They jumped to their feet. Lydia was agitated,

— What's the matter? she said. Who's calling?

— It's the Irishman. Outside Moore shouted again.

— Mr Miles! Mr Miles! Will you come quickly, please?

J.T. rushed to open the door. He met Moore by the gate. The little man stood in the lane gesticulating. As always he wore several layers of clothes as if it were just as cold inside his cottage as outside. But he had no cap on and thick grey curls fell around his ears. From the weak lamplight through the open door J.T. could see that the crown of his head was as black and as greasy as the lining of an old cap.

— At my place! Moore said, waving his arms.

He seemed to be distracting J.T.'s attention from the top of his head.

— It's serious, he said. Miss Jones Argoed. She's damaged her eye, you know. I think a thorn got into it or something like that. Will you come now? She's got her handkerchief against it and won't let me see it at all. She said her sister would be calling to bring you some food, since she couldn't bring it herself.

— Her sister's here, J.T. said, pointing to the doorway behind him.

— Well, come along now, will you?

Moore waved his arms. Lydia appeared in the doorway. To J.T's surprise she was wearing a scarf and a long coat and carrying a deep basket.

— Don't tell her, Joe.

As she whispered, Lydia kept her eye on Moore to see if he were listening.

— Don't tell her. About us. Not yet.

Moore led the way down the lane.

— It's a terrible thing to happen, he said. She could lose her eye for ever, and that's a lot worse, isn't it, for a woman. I don't quite know how it happened. It was a thorn, she said. But how it happened I don't know. In my life this has happened twice before. This will be the third time if... What I mean ...

Moore spoke quickly as he walked quickly. J.T. kept alongside him. Lydia had waved him in front.

— And it's all happened in these parts too over the last seven years. There was William Williams Rhoscath. A heifer did it as he was trying to tie her up.

Moore dropped his voice so that Lydia should not hear.

— Sharp end of the horn in his eye. The thing was he kept on expecting it to mend and he'd get his sight back. 'When the cuckoo comes,' he used to say to me. 'When the cuckoo comes, Mr Moore.' Well the cuckoo never came. It can only mean one thing you know, some of these farmers are too mean and lazy to cut their hedges. I mean I've seen it myself, a briar hanging out eight feet into this lane ...

Lydia began to run. He stopped suddenly as she shot past them. The empty basket bounced on her arm. J.T. called her name and then he began running. Moore trotted behind them, rolling from side to side as though taking care not to let one large foot trip over the other.

The door of Moore's cottage was open and Louis his son was standing there. He wore a yellow jersey that reached to his knees, and without a cap his hair fell about his ears in a manner that seemed an exact replica of his father's. His lower lip hung down further than usual. He was ready to speak as soon as the running figures were both still and waiting to hear what he had to say.

— She's gone, he said. She'd left her bike in the Mill. She wouldn't wait. She wouldn't wait.

He said 'she wouldn't wait, Dad,' again when his father arrived, puffing heavily and stretching out a hand in anticipation of leaning on the gate.

13

J.T.'S ARM WAS still raised in farewell as Mr Ellis marched briskly back to the Blue Corner Stores to collect his shopping. The breeze was to J.T.'s back and it blew his trousers in the same direction as his waving, strongly enough, as it appeared, to bend his knees. He brought down his arm so that his hand rested on his head and his hair fluttered around his fingers.

— Good morning, Mr Miles!

Miss Pickering stood behind him, her blue eyes and her dentures gleaming, and her hearing-aid already in position. In her hands she held tightly a rolled-up exercise book.

— I saw you passing, Mr Miles, she said, and I said to myself 'Mr Miles won't mind,' but now I'm not so sure.

— Oh good morning, good morning.

J.T. nodded and smiled.

— It's not my business I know, Miss Pickering said, but should you be out in this wind without a hat? I don't think so.

— How is your mother, Miss Pickering? J.T. said.

He raised his voice and spoke slowly and distinctly. Miss Pickering smiled to show that she had heard.

— She's keeping nothing down, she said. They say they don't know what she's living on. They've X-rayed her four times this week. I told them not to tire her. At the hospital. After all she's ninety-three.

— Is she really?

— I know this sounds wicked, but I can't say that I miss her. For the last eighteen months she'd got this habit of humming. She used to hum all day. It must have been very loud because I used to hear it even with this thing switched off. And when I go to see her now she thinks I'm Phoebe. Well Phoebe's been dead for thirty years. You'd think she'd remember me. As you know, I've looked after her since Father died in 1938.

—Yes, of course, J.T. said.

He looked serious and sympathetic, but suddenly Miss Pickering burst out laughing,

— It's all right provided you keep your sense of humour.

J.T. looked down at her admiringly. Her little face had a waxy surface that corresponded strangely to the cameo brooch in her pink blouse.

— I was wondering, Mr Miles, if you'd check it for me.

Miss Pickering held up the exercise book.

— Your Welsh is so good, she said, so pure.

— There's nothing wrong with yours, Miss Pickering. I'd say it was excellent.

J.T. bent down a little to speak more directly to the microphone of her hearing-aid. Miss Pickering gave a giggle of pleasure.

— Oh indeed it isn't, she said. My mutations are awful, sometimes. They really are. Mother was the trouble you see. She came from Oswestry and her Welsh was never any good really. Anyway if you wouldn't mind looking at it. Alter anything you like. I know it isn't good, so I won't be offended.

J.T. took the exercise book, opened it, glanced at Miss Pickering's bold round handwriting and closed it again.

— Haven't got my reading spectacles, he said.

— It's a free adaptation of Shelley's 'Ode to a Skylark', Miss Pickering said. You know.

We look before and after

And pine for what is not. . .

— 'And our sincerest laughter with deepest grief is fraught,' J.T. said.

— Well no, Miss Pickering said.

— Was that wrong?

J.T. raised his eyebrows. Miss Pickering laughed delightedly. She plucked the exercise book out of J.T.'s hands. J.T. looked down to see what had happened. He brought his hands together and drew the palms against each other. He looked puzzled.

— Our sincerest laughter, with *some pain* is fraught,' Miss Pickering said. It isn't as bad as all that, you see. *Some pain* not deepest grief.

— Very good, J.T. said. Very good. I'd like to read it.

He held out his hand for the exercise book. Miss Pickering shook her head.

— Not now, Miss Pickering said. I can see you've got something on your mind.

— Bring it over this afternoon, J.T. said.

— I don't think so, Miss Pickering said. Your sister-in-law wouldn't like it.

— Let me take it with me, he said. You wanted me to see it after all.

— It means a lot to me, Miss Pickering said. I would have had to give up teaching anyway you see, apart from Mother. My hearing was going. Not that I'm missing all that much. People don't say all that much when they talk, do they?

Miss Pickering clutched at her cardigan and turned suddenly to get inside her garden gate which was not more than three paces from where she was standing. She closed the gate carefully and turned to wave once more, before going into her corner house. The window of her living-room, where her mother used to sit wrapped in blankets, was open as usual. The noise of the traffic never worried either of them. She used to be seen sitting with her mother, lost in her reading while the old woman's eyes moved ceaselessly as she watched cars, buses, lorries and pedestrians, endlessly passing by.

AS KATE STOOPED slowly to pick up the letters on the doormat, she hiccuped and her mouth filled with vomit. She lifted her head in an attempt to swallow and the force of her effort swung her bent body to the right so that her buttocks landed heavily on the tiled floor, and the top half of her body fell helplessly against the door. It became dark. With a grunt of pain the vomit was swallowed. Her mouth fell open and she gasped for air like someone who had been too long submerged under water. Her head struck the panel of the door so hard that the door-bell reverberated and there seemed to be some connection between the sound waves expanding above her head and the hair that fell on to her shoulder out of the broken hair-net.

She continued to sit propped up against the door. Had there been more letters or another paper to come they would have fallen past her head and the flap of the letter-box would have clattered like gun-fire in her ear. She blinked and the stairs reappeared dimly in their accustomed place. Light fell from the window in the wall at the top of the stairs on the glazing that covered Ma's photograph. The kitchen door was open and the cat was inside. She had left the back door open when she heard the flap of the letter-box clatter smartly from the vigorous thrust the busy postman gave to it as he pushed the letters through. The cat stood lengthwise in the kitchen doorway, its tail aloft, staring at the human figure that sat with her back to the front door. The cat and the woman seemed frozen in their attitudes, as still as stone figures.

The fingers of her left hand stirred among the sharp bristles of the doormat. Without moving the rest of her body or taking her gaze away from the cat, she began to rub her wedding ring with her thumb until she felt the bristles pressing hard into the tips of her fingers. This upset her balance and her body slid slowly to the right, pushing her elbow sideways until it served as a prop for her whole weight, and the movement stopped.

She was in this position when the door-bell rang. The ringing was loud, fierce, insistent, filling the small hall. The cat disappeared. Kate frowned and a groan escaped from her lips that was drowned by the noise pressed on by the urgent finger on the other side of the door. She bent her knees and struggled to her feet, clawing at the small area of wall between the frame of the door and the hallstand. For a second her face was buried in the folds of J.T.'s second best overcoat. It smelt like an old hymn-book. The ringing stopped. The person outside had perhaps seen her shape blurred through the frosted glass. Kate's hair fell from her shoulder. She made an effort to lift it and then gave up. She opened the door a few inches and peered out.

Mrs Box of No. 10 was outside. She too stood sideways as if her visit did not involve any attempt to invite herself in. Her arms were folded, and as usual her face was flushed with the heat of the electric fire. Her eyes were apologetically large.

— I am sorry to disturb you, Mrs Bannister, I really am.

She paused as if she hoped Kate would speak. But Kate hung on to the metal knob of the Yale lock and said nothing.

— It's these people have come, Mrs Bannister, and they're one more than they said in the letter. I've not room for them all you see. As it is our Lawrence is sleeping on a mattress on the floor. I was wondering if you could take one of the girls perhaps, or the old lady if you like. They'll pay of course, and so they should, of course, coming all like that without a word of warning. Do you think you could, Mrs Bannister? It would be just the bed of course, no meals or anything. They are very nice people. The father's the manager of a shop in Chorley. The wife told me she was an infants teacher before she got married. It's still infants, isn't it, I said and she didn't mind my joke at all. Good sport she is . . .

Mrs Box stopped because Kate had begun to shake her head.

— I couldn't manage, Kate said.

She coughed carefully to clear her throat, without opening the door any wider.

— Well of course you know best, Mrs Box said. But they'd be no trouble at all.

— No, Kate said.

Her head was aching and she couldn't prevent herself from frowning as Mrs Box was staring at her.

— It is a way of supplementing the income of course, Mrs Box said, if the room is there. Everybody does it now. Even the best people, like lords and things. I mean when I was young I wouldn't have dreamt of it. My mother was very strict. But it isn't a bad thing at all because it makes people more friendly. Makes them mix . . .

— I want to close the door, Kate said. I'm not very well.

— Oh my goodness, Mrs Box said. You do look a bit seedy now I come to look. Shall I send for the doctor?

Kate shook her head.

— Well I can you know, quite easily. Our Lawrence could phone or he could get you something from the chemist. . . ?

Kate shook her head and shut the door. She moved carefully to the foot of the stairs, where she sat down. She placed her elbow on her knee in order to support her head, and stared at the three letters that still lay on the doormat.

J.T. FUMBLED FIRST in one trouser pocket and then the other for the door key. He pushed it carefully into the lock, stretching his mouth because the key turned stiffly. He pushed the door forward, and with his hand still on the key, and his head lowered he saw the letters lying on the door mat. He pulled hard at the key to get it out of the lock and slipped it back into his trouser pocket as he kneeled to pick up the letters. He frowned as he stared at the names and addresses on the envelopes. A groan made him look up quickly. He saw Kate sitting at the bottom of the stairs, her arm over the banister and her forehead against the wooden sphere that surmounted the bottom post. Clutching the letters, he walked towards her and then stopped as if he were afraid of approaching too near.

— What's the matter? he said.

She raised her arm to point at the door he had left open.

— Shut it, she said.

With anxious haste he obeyed her.

— What's the matter, Kate? he said.

— It's nothing. Just a turn. I'm all right now. See what that cat's up to.

— Which cat?

— Which cat! Next door's cat of course. The pantry door is open. Go and see.

The colour was beginning to return to her cheeks. She moved her arm and spread her fingers wide over the polished ball on the end of the banisters as if she were preparing to pull herself to her feet. She heard J.T. making a warlike scattering noise as he shooed out the cat. Her mouth was threatened with a smile. Her hand slackened its grip on the polished wood. J.T. reappeared. The packet of All Bran was still wedged under his arm.

— Eaten every one of the sardines left over from supper, he said. And look at this letter!

He held up one of the letters, and his forearms stuck out from his body like a toy making a gesture of mechanical greeting. A corner of the letter was soaked in sardine oil.

— What shall I do with it? he said.

His voice was agitated,

— You can always throw it away, Kate said.

— Seriously. What shall I do?

— Wipe it with the dishcloth, Kate said.

He nodded intelligently and made for the sink to carry out her suggestion. It took him a little time to find the dishcloth. He paused for a moment as if he were about to ask her for further guidance. Then he sighed and shook his head. He lifted the plastic bowl in the sink and saw the dishcloth. He touched it with his finger. It was full of water. He hesitated. The letters were still in his hand. As one who had settled on a course of action, he put the letters down on the draining-board and with the packet still under his arm squeezed the dishcloth with both hands, wiped the corner of the letter with tender care, dropping the dishcloth back in the sink and holding the letter away to examine the result of his work, and then putting it down with the other two as if to compare them.

— Who are they from then?

Kate had shuffled as far as the kitchen doorway.

— Are you better?

J.T. stared at her anxiously. Kate nodded and her finger began to grope in her fallen hair, preparing to restore it to order.

— We ought to have a phone in the house, J.T. said.

— Well if you think you can afford it, Kate said. I know I can't.

— Suppose we wanted the doctor . . .

— I don't want the doctor.

— No, but suppose we did?

— There's a kiosk on the Beach Corner. Not more than a hundred yards away.

— Ronnie and Thea have offered . . .

— It's my house, Kate said, and I don't want it.

He stood by the sink and she stood by the door. She pointed at the letters on the draining-board.

— Take them away from there, Kate said, and go and eat your breakfast. The bread and butter will be like bricks. It goes hard with waiting. You took long enough to get that stuff. You'd better go and eat it.

She stood to one side to let him pass.

— I'll have to make fresh tea as it is, she said. J.T. stopped in the doorway.

— I'll do it, he said.

Unexpectedly she pushed him in the small of his back.

— The old tea will do anyway, J.T. said.

— Bring the pot in here, she said.

She seemed cheered at having pushed him as if her strength was flowing back. She turned up the gas under the kettle, reached for the tea caddy and gave it a slight shake to calculate the contents. A measuring spoon rattled inside.

— The less there is inside the less there is to spill, she said.

— What?

J.T. called from the other room.

— Hurry up with the pot, Kate said.

— I saw Ellis Maentwrog in the shop, J.T. said, returning with the teapot.

— Who's he then? Kate said.

She concentrated on making tea as quickly as she could and also listening to what J.T. had to say.

— We were in Col. together, J.T. said. He used to play for the Theo Col. cricket team. He's been an acting headmaster in Leominster I think he said. For years.

— What's an acting headmaster? Kate said.

The steam rose in clouds as she poured the hot water into the teapot and she turned away her face to avoid it.

— An acting head, J.T. said.

— Oh.

Kate put down the kettle noisily and thrust the lid on to the teapot.

— There you are, she said. Who were the letters from?

— One from Thea, I think. From Italy.

He stood holding the teapot with both hands and smiling at Kate who avoided his gaze.

— Oh, she said. What does she say?

— I haven't opened it yet.

She turned her back on him and began to tidy the sink. J.T. hurried back to the breakfast table. He put down the teapot carefully, and opened the letter. It was written on thin paper in a rapid scrawling hand that tended to join words together by long loops. J.T. examined it very closely. He lifted his head to call out.

— Her writing doesn't get any better.

Kate came in the living-room and opened the drawer of the mahogany sideboard. It was tight and she had to shake it first one side and then the other, until it opened smoothly. The drawer was fall of folded tablecloths and shallow boxes of various sizes. Kate extracted a narrow box that had the fading picture of a hair-clipper of German make on its lid. A piece of twisted elastic kept the lid on. As she pulled off the elastic Kate said,

— Mrs Box, Number Ten wanted us to let a room. She's taken more than she can find room for. I told her I wasn't well.

J.T. looked up sharply.

— We should get the doctor, he said quickly.

— I had to get rid of her somehow.

— What's that for?

J.T. pointed at the hair-clippers. Kate was exercising the steel arms between her thumb and index finger.

— I promised Mrs Hobley I'd give the old man a trim.

— When?

— This morning. They'll be here before ten. That's why I want to get this place dear. I want to put a chair over by the window and some newspaper on the floor to catch the hair.

— Shall I read it? It isn't very long,

J.T. held the letter up for Kate to see. She gave a brief nod.

— 'Dear Dada and Aunty Kate,' he said. I don't know who owes who a letter but here goes. David and I are coming to England on September 7th. David has business in London, making arrangements for a new film, and he says I can come with him. Now he suggests I hire a car in London and drive over to see you, stay perhaps for a few days if it doesn't put you out and then bring you back, both of you. He says there is no reason at all why you don't come to San Tarenzo for as long as you like. Well let's be practical and say six weeks? It looks as if we shall have to go to Egypt late in December. Anyhow that's all by the way. The main thing is we want you to come and stay at the villa. There's lots of room and in any case you don't have to leave just because we'll be off to Egypt. Why not decide to winter here? It would do you both the world of good. Noel, David's boy, goes back to school on 22nd of September so he'll be coming with us on the 7th. He's growing so fast it will be two or three days' work fitting him out. He's getting to look very like David and he's very sweet. Had a letter from Ronnie's wife a few weeks ago. Ronnie wants to take his leave in February next year and Sheila was wondering if they could rent part of the villa. Of course David said they could have it any time and no question of rent. Wouldn't it be nice if we could have a family reunion on the shores of the Mediterranean? I'm sure this is where the Celts all came from originally. I feel so much at home. Do, do, do think seriously of coming, It's a wonderful plan. Looking forward so much to seeing you soon, Thea.'

— She never asks how we are, Kate said.

— What?

— I said she never asks how we are.

— What do you mean?

— What I say. Pour your tea. And what about that stuff?

J.T. opened the cereal packet and shook some on to his plate. He added milk and sugar and began to eat thoughtfully. Kate went to the kitchen to fetch a chair. On her way back, holding the chair against one leg bent in front of the other, she said,

— What are the others about?

J.T. munched his cereal and moved his head to examine the other two envelopes. He swallowed the cereal. Kate waited for him to speak without putting down the chair.

— Do you think we ought to go? he said.

— Where? Kate said.

— To Italy.

Kate pushed the chair in front of her and set it down with a bump by the window.

— Out of the question, she said.

— Why? J.T. said turning to look at her.

— For one thing, she stole another woman's husband, Kate said. And he's been divorced twice before. I don't want to see him ever, let alone stay in his house. Villa or no villa.

— She's my daughter, isn't she?

J.T. turned back and ate as if he had suddenly been attacked by hunger.

— We're supposed to forgive, he said.

— There's a difference between forgive and condone, Kate said. You know as well as I do. She doesn't like me. She never did like me. But that doesn't stop me making her welcome whenever she comes here.

— Once a year, J.T. said.

His mouth was full. She did not appear to hear him.

— Everyone wants to think they are nice, Kate said. It's all false really.

— I'd like to see where she lives, J.T. said.

— We'd all like things, wouldn't we? she said.

She sat down heavily on the chair she had carried in. Her face was pale. She put her hand over her eyes. J.T. had his back to her.

— What if we all just lived for ourselves, Kate said.

14

THE FOUR GERMAN prisoners ate in the sunless room where Mary Parry Rice did the washing on Mondays and Thursdays; the room where Kate had once been caught at the wash-tub when Griff brought Joe Miles to Argoed for the first time. They sat at the trestle-table that Ned had knocked together long before the war for the annual Sunday School tea which was given at Argoed. Under Rowland's supervision, the small one called Putzi came as far as the top of the kitchen steps to collect their midday stew. He knew more English than the others and he was eager to make jokes. Rowland would look down and smile sometimes and perhaps say to Ned in his laconic Welsh — the little weasel was too small to shoot!

Sometimes Pa would eat a little earlier in order to pass the wash-house door and stand for a moment with his hands under his overcoat tails, watching them eating. He would stare with uncontrolled curiosity, his lips falling apart and a frown of concentration on his face, until one of them would look up and bow and smile and say something polite in German that Pa could not understand. Pa took no notice. He would seem to be saying to himself that a master observes as of right the behaviour of slaves without any obligation to display a desire to communicate. He looked around the room as if he were taking an inventory of its contents rather than counting the number of prisoners. Then he would suddenly move away, calling for his dogs.

When the telegram was brought to the back door, the prisoners were in the middle of their meal. The postmistress's son Edwin tapped nervously at the open back door. In the kitchen where Pa's chair was vacant, Rowland was laughing because Hugh had just drunk tea from a cup which Kate, Ned and he himself had in turn taken to be a slop-basin. Each had poured the dregs of their own first cup of tea in it. Hugh had come last to the table, talking excitedly about the tractor he had seen working that morning on a neighbouring farm. He reached out to the point on the table where his cup usually stood. It took some time for each one of them to appreciate what had happened. Lydia who had left the table to cut more bread and butter was the last to have the event described to her. They were able to laugh more freely because Pa was not in the room.

Outside the postmistress's son knocked more loudly. In the wash-house Putzi pushed the trestle-table aside and got to his feet. The boy jumped when he saw the small foreigner in the unfamiliar uniform. Putzi noticed his reaction and smiled and winked.

— Small soldat, he said, trying hard to be funny. No gun.

The boy held up the telegram. Putzi offered to take it. The boy shook his head. Lydia put her foot on the first of the three steps leading up from the kitchen.

— What is it? she said to Putzi in English.

— Post, he said, pointing at the boy who stood outside out of Lydia's vision.

She called out in Welsh and the boy came in timidly, taking off his cap. Lydia saw the telegram.

— Kate! Kate!

Her sister swallowed a mouthful of bread and butter. She looked at the table hastily as if there were things on it that should not be seen there. Ned, Rowland and Hugh stopped eating. The boy held out the telegram, but Lydia did not take it.

— What's the matter? Kate said.

She sounded cross. The muscles around her false eye twitched. She lowered her head when she saw the telegram. She took it and opened it. She moved back to the table and suddenly seemed out of breath. For some reason she pointed at Hugh.

— What is it? he said.

— That's Griff's place, she said.

Ned picked up the telegram. He began to read it in the voice he used in chapel for making announcements. He had a soft comforting voice and people liked to hear him giving out information about coming events. Last winter he had been elected a deacon at the early age of thirty and it was remarked at the time he was the youngest deacon the church had ever elected, and how pleasing it was to see both father and son sitting in the Big Pew. After 'killed in action' his voice trailed off and he bent his head. Rowland picked up the telegram and stared at it.

— Griff, he said. Griff.

— The devils, Lydia said. I'll kill them. I'll kill them.

She turned to the sideboard and picked up the bread knife. Putzi was still standing near the open door. Edwin the postmistress's son had disappeared. It was as if he wore special shoes for delivering telegrams, so that no one should hear him coming or going.

— My brother is dead!

Lydia shouted at Putzi, pointing the knife.

— My brother! You killed my brother!

— Mister! Putzi said. *Cameraden!*

His mouth seemed to be too full of saliva to speak. He put out a hand with the palm turned outwards to protect himself.

— Mister!

Rowland pushed Hugh against the wall and stretched across his legs. In his haste he overturned the cup that had been used as a slop basin and the cold tea spread over the tablecloth. He caught Lydia by the elbow just as she was on the steps. He slipped his hand along her forearm and gripped her wrist. She slipped and clutched at the floor with her other hand.

— I'll kill them, she said. I'll kill them all.

Rowland pulled her to her feet. He held her arms firmly. She began to struggle again.

— Look here, Ned said to Kate. Take her upstairs. Take her up for goodness' sake.

Kate tried to put her arm around Lydia's shoulder. Lydia shook her off.

— Take her, Ned said angrily.

He was in charge, but there was still no decent semblance of order.

— You!

Ned pointed to Putzi.

— Go to the fields of Marian Mawr and fetch Pastor Miles.

— Marian Mawr?

Putzi opened his mouth and nodded eager to obey.

— Go!

Ned walked up the steps, urgently communicating with hands and voice.

— Bring Pastor. Pastor, savvy? Quick.

Putzi nodded eagerly.

— Snell! he said. Very quick.

— He can't go, Rowland said. He can't go wandering off by himself. He's under supervision. Hold her. I'll go.

— Now come, Lyd, there's a good girl. Come on now.

Ned used his softest voice. It was the way he coaxed animals. The sound of a master who is without fear and yet full of infinite sympathy and pity. At this sound Lydia broke down. Her body was convulsed with weeping and she rested her forehead on Ned's shoulder.

— There's a good girl, Ned said. Good girl. Good old girl.

He led her to the foot of the stairs, Kate opened the door. There was no carpet on the stairs.

— I'll take my boots off, Lydia said,

— Never mind, Ned said. Come on now. Upstairs. There's a good girl.

At the sound of 'there's', which he elongated caressingly, Lydia burst into another fit of weeping. She tried to sit on the stairs. Firmly and gently Ned urged her on. She nodded as if she were anxious to obey him and slowly made her way upstairs.

WITH FEET APART, each to his row the three men tugged at the base of the leaves of each mangold in turn. The leaves were heavy with rainwater. With their long knives they sliced away at the roots. Then they balanced the mangold on the palm in order to first slice the leaves off at one stroke and then toss the trimmed object over the side of the muddy cart.

The mole-catcher led the way. When he judged the cart was full, he flourished his knife and yelled in his high-pitched voice and the carter would grin, but hurry to obey. The mole-catcher was his uncle and famous for his bad temper. When he spat, he seemed to judge the wind so that the tobacco-stained spit floated in an upward curve before landing in the mud.

Woods the Englishman followed close behind the mole-catcher. He worked silently all day as if being unable to speak Welsh were a kind of dumbness. His feet were unusually big and his heels dug deep between the rows. He always seemed to be smiling gently to himself.

However hard he worked J.T. never caught up with the other two. In the early afternoon his back ached so much it was clear that he was relieved when it started to rain and they made for the hedge to collect their sacks. Woods put his sack over his head and looked like a monk in a cowl. He also wrapped one around his middle like a skirt. The mole-catcher fussed about with his string and when he had tied the sack over his shoulders to his own satisfaction he glanced at the open gap at the far end of the field.

— Look at that bastard! he said to Woods in English.

He lifted his blade and pointed at the carter already on his way back with an empty cart.

— Doesn't give us a chance, the mole-catcher said. Ought to be called up, that one.

The row of trimmed mangolds had hardly begun to grow. The rain began to fall more heavily.

— Come on, the mole-catcher said. Before he gets here.

— There's somebody with him, Woods said.

It was just as surprising to hear him speak as to hear what he was saying. He nodded towards the cart in the distance.

— Who the devil is it? the mole-catcher said.

He led the way back to the rows, moving briskly for a man of his age.

— Somebody on the 'spec I bet, he said.

He spoke to J.T., but did not expect a reply. He pulled at a mangold, spat and swung his knife. J.T. hurried to his place and worked as fast as he could until he heard the mole-catcher's voice again. He glanced up and saw the other two watching the cart come nearer. The mole-catcher had his free hand on the small of his back.

— Rowland Argoed, he said. What can he be wanting?

As he spoke, Rowland jumped from the cart and ran forward through the fresh earth where the mangolds had already been harvested. He ignored the mole-catcher and Woods the Englishman, and stood in front of J.T. breathless, his legs apart. His face was flushed with bewilderment and alarm.

— Come home, he said. My brother Griff has been killed. Come home.

The mole-catcher stepped back through the rows.

— What's the matter, Rowland? he said. Rowland turned his head, wildly.

— It's my brother Griff, he said. He's been killed.

J.T. dropped his knife. It was a section of old scythe blade. It sank into the damp soil. The carter came nearer and leaned forward acutely when he sat on the front of the cart.

— Come on then, Rowland said to J.T. Ned wants you. Pa's away. Will you come now?

WHEN ROWLAND AND J.T. arrived at the yard they saw the four German prisoners in the cart-house, sheltering from the rain. Tomi Moch was also taking shelter, but as far as he could from the prisoners of war.

— Bloody Germans, he said.

His small eyes were redder than usual. He had been crying.

— Don't swear Tomi, Rowland said absently.

— Hugh has gone on Lydia's bike to the monthly meeting. To get your father like. He changed. Put a collar and tie on.

Tomi pointed at one of the upstairs windows.

— I saw him. Quick wash. Ned will make the arrangements, he said.

He tilted his head on his short neck to look at J.T. in the face.

— He should have been an undertaker, Ned you know, he said. Speaks nice. Good at arranging. And he always liked woodwork, didn't he Rowland? Always a good carpenter, Ned.

— Come to the house, Rowland said.

They hurried across the yard. Rowland's legs seemed more bowed than ever as they crossed the outcrop of rock that made the uneven surface of the yard near the side of the house. Ned appeared in the archway in his shirt-sleeves. He called Tomi and waved. Tomi hurried across, stumbling over the outcrop in his haste.

— Take the Germans to the Old House, Ned said, and set them on the potato-sorting. I'll come there later in the afternoon.

— Awful news, Tomi said, screwing up his face. I don't know what I'll do.

Ned shook his head, smiled sadly and patted Tomi on the shoulder.

In the churn room Ned put up his finger and lowered his head, and Rowland and J.T. stopped to listen to him,

— Dan Llew's got to know, Ned said. Could you go down to the town on your bike, Rowland? I think perhaps you could send a telegram to Aunty Addy of Denbigh asking her to inform the Clynnog side of the family.

— I'll go and change, Rowland said.

— Come into the parlour, Ned said to J.T. Lydia has taken it badly. As you know they were always very close.

They both sat down in silence. Each sat on the edge of a chair, aware of his working clothes and looking surreptitiously at his boots to make sure there were no lumps of mud that had missed their attention outside the back door. Ned sat near the table and he stretched his arm along it, tapping the polished surface with his finger-tips. After a long silence he spoke.

— I thought perhaps . . .

J.T. nodded hastily. He knelt on the carpet placing his elbows on the solid seat of the chair.

— O Lord, he said, clearing his throat. Look down in mercy on this family in their hour of bitter sorrow and tribulation. The Angel of Death has found us out and has taken away our beloved brother. We thank Thee for him and for all the wisdom and happiness he shared with us.

Ned's heavy breathing broke into sobs.

— I remember when Ma died, he said. I was only a lad . . . I remember it so well . . . Griff took Hugh for a ride in her old wheel-chair. . .

They both looked up suddenly. They heard feet clattering down the carpetless stairs, and Kate's voice calling. They waited motionless and somehow guilty like two thieves caught in the act, knowing it was too late to make any attempt to escape. Lydia opened the door. Her face was blotched with her tears. J.T. got to his feet.

— What are you doing here? Lydia said.

— Now then, my dear . . . Ned said in his most soothing way. This time his voice had no effect on her.

— Well, what are you doing?

— Praying, Ned said. Just praying. What else can we do?

— You could go out there and help, Lydia said.

She glared unreasonably at both of them.

— That's what you could do, she said.

She let go of the door-knob to point at J.T.

— You with your principles. You stay home and let them all die. All of them. Griff was fighting for you. And what do you do? What do you do?

Her voice was rising to the verge of a scream.

— Lydia, J.T. said.

He stepped towards her. She stepped away, pressing her back against the dresser in the narrow hall.

— Don't come near me. I never want to see you again as long as you live unless I see you in khaki. I mean it. I mean it.

Kate was standing at the bottom of the stairs. Nervously she touched her eyelid as if she wanted to stop it twitching.

— It's no use screaming, she said. Screaming won't bring him back.

15

J.T. HELD THE small bible over the side of the bunk to catch as much light as he could from the dim bulb. His bunk was fourth in a layer of five. Above him was Private Moses Katz. Below him Private Cynwal Elis, who had the gift of being able to sleep under most conditions. An Indian regiment slept in the bunks on the other side of the narrow passage. The men kept their blankets tight under their chins, and had no difficulty in sleeping. When his elbow became numb, J.T. lay on his back and his other arm touched a seam of rivets which vibrated endlessly as the troopship ploughed its way forward. As he lay still the sweat rolled down his face. The faint currents of air were not enough to dispel the rancid smells in the hold. His lips moved as he recited as much as he could remember of the chapter of Paul's Epistle to the Romans,[69] which he had been trying to read. His nostrils had become accustomed to the smell, but occasionally a loud groan or cry from a sleeping soldier would make him move his head and look up and down the hold, wondering from where among the hundreds of dim sleeping figures the sharp cry had come. On the top bunk above him Katz once again turned over.

— Taff.

J.T. heard the whisper just above his head.

— You asleep, Taff?

J.T.'s head rolled sideways and he saw Katz's haggard face looking down over the edge of his bunk. The whites of his eyes were large in his dark face, and his wiry black hair stood on end as a result of his tossing and turning. The small mouth under the heavy black moustache, except when he smiled, was turned down in a curve of permanent despair.

— I've been thinking, Katz said. All of us you know, all of us. We is victims.

— We are, J.T. said.

He lifted his arms slowly and put them under his head. The small Bible lay open, balanced on his stomach. Only stillness could defeat the heat. Absolute stillness and silent prayer that perhaps went on even when his lips were not moving. Katz leaned over further to study J.T.

— You are, Katz said, intelligent man and yet sometime I think you understand nothing.

He sniffed hard.

— You want to go to the latrines?

J.T. shook his head.

— I tell you I can't stand going there by myself. Suppose I fainted. I faint very easy.

— It's better if you keep still, J.T. said.

— You don't know nothing, Katz said, I tell you there will be such a revolution the world has never seen anything like. History will never be the same again and you will read on your little Welsh Bible and you will not know it happens! What is this you talk about God is Love? Who says this? Who knows? Because he don't come down and shoot all the naughty men? Why bother? All the naughty men are shooting each other.

Katz clasped his hands together and shook them urgently.

— Oh Taff, I must live to see it. I never forgive History if some Turkish man shoot me dead over there.

He leaned further over to wag his finger.

— And you. You take your nose out of that Bible and you'll see it. You'll see a new world being born.

— 'Heaven and Earth shall pass away,' J.T. said, 'but my words shall not pass away.'

— Now what does that mean? Katz said. Just tell me. I would very much like to know.

J.T. made no attempt to answer.

— Just tell me, that's all.

— I'm sleepy, J.T. said. Very sleepy.

— You don't damn well know.

Katz grunted and lay back on his bunk. J.T. heard him scrape his heels backwards and forwards on the tough canvas above his head. He drew them up slowly, paused for an unequal period and then shot them back so that his body was rigid from head to toe. It was a relief when he decided to talk again.

— You heard of Combat Police?

— No.

— I heard. In France I heard. At the clearing station. Men shot in the head for not going over the top. It is a fact.

J.T. sighed deeply and shuddered.

— When they say 'stretcher-bearers forward' I go quick. I don't want my brains spread all over the sandbags. You'll see. Heaven and earth and all.

J.T. heard him snort with amusement. It was a peculiar sound which he produced by constricting the throat and blowing air through the thick hair in his nostrils, with his lips pressed tightly together.

— Now I say quite clearly to this lieutenant who is a Jew like me, I was an Austrian. I have brothers in Austrian army, and cousins. What if I shoot my brother? I cannot carry arms. 'Right,' he says. 'I sympathize. I get you transfer to another theatre of war.' Good. Palestine. Good. I go home I say. But my problem is the same. There are Austrians there. Why should I shoot them?

—We are not expected to bear arms, J.T. said. That has been stated categorically.

— But this Sa'-Major Roberts. You heard him. He says terrible things.

— I don't think he means them, J.T. said.

Katz started wagging his finger again.

—You know the trouble with you, Taff? You know? You led the sheltered life. That's true. You look at the faces of men and you see men like yourself. You think this Roberts is Welsh like you. He is a cruel bastard. He is so cruel. He would crucify me just for a laugh.

— You shouldn't say that, J.T. said. I know for a fact he goes to chapel in Wrexham . . .

— Ach!

Katz fell back on his bunk.

—What's the matter? J.T. said. Are you feeling ill?

—You, he heard Katz say. You. You make me sick.

Once again he began scraping his heels against the canvas. Suddenly J.T. raised his fist and knocked the underside with his knuckle.

— Stop it please, he said.

Katz rubbed his nose silently and then shot them down. He waited a moment and then brought them up again with a deliberate rasping sound.

— Don't be childish, J.T. said.

Cynwal Elis woke up. He put out his thick arm, grasped the bar above him and pulled the top half of his body level with the fourth bunk.

— Is he at it again? he said to J.T. in Welsh.

— He is rather, J.T. said.

Cynwal raised his voice.

— Katz, he said with his guttural North Wales accent.

—Well?

Katz sounded sulky.

—You keep still, Katz, or I'll pommel you.

— Huh, Katz said.

— Huh what ?

Cynwal brought the fist of his free arm into Katz's view.

— Call yourself a pacifist! Katz sounded indignant.

— Chastisement, Cynwal said. Good for you.

Other men began to wake up. There were shouts and curses. Even the Indians were disturbed. The corporal appeared suddenly, swaying under the dim light.

—What's up then? he said. What's up?

He was a small man whose voice had become permanendy hoarse through a consistent effort to sound fierce.

— It's hot, corporal, Cynwal said.

The Corporal looked at him suspiciously, as if he were uncertain how to take the monotonous statement. The way Cynwal spoke English, it was impossible to place his tone. It could be indifference. It could be complaint. It could be insolence.

— Hot! I know it's bloody hot, the corporal said. You don't have to wake up the whole ship to tell us. Get you head down or I'll have you on a charge.

—And you, he said to J.T.

—And you!

He looked up to the top bunk where Katz lay almost out of sight.

— I can hear you in my sleep, Katz. You're like a bee in a bloody bottle!

LYDIA SAT ON the mounting stone. Kate had both her hands on the garden wall. Her eyes followed a grasshopper that tried to conceal itself against the yellow stone. Between her fingers she had a sprig of lavender which she had plucked from the bush that grew outside the front door of the house. It was a Saturday evening and she wore a duck-egg blue knitted jumper outside her skirt with a loose tasselled girdle of the same material. Lydia wore a belted mac that was shorter than her skirt and a pair of shoes designed like a man's brogues. Her green Sunbeam bike with its corded back mudguard had slipped down from the wall and lay almost flat on the grass verge. Tomi Moch had been burning weeds in the garden all afternoon and the smell of smoke still hung on the air. He gave up the work reluctantly when Ned called him to take the milking herd down the leafy lane to the stream that ran in a narrow valley on the landward side of Argoed farm. Because of its exposed position on the crown of the hill, Argoed quickly ran out of water in dry weather.

—You should see the way he half closes his eyes when he takes a puff on his cigarette. You know, he bends his head back like this.

Lydia gave a demonstration and Kate watched her closely.

—You've been smoking, Kate said.

Lydia nodded.

I like it, she said. Mrs B smokes too.

— She shouldn't, Kate said. And you shouldn't either.

— Why not?

Lydia leaned back until her head touched the wall. She tapped the bun of hair gently against the wall and waited for her sister to explain. The setting sun made her turn her head sideways and screw up her eyes.

— It's unbecoming, Kate said.

— Oh that, Lydia said.

She bent her head and rubbed her chin on the lapel of her mac.

— He must be very clever, she said. The way his eyes wander about. He's thinking all the time.

— Who isn't? Kate said.

— He came in twice today, Lydia said. Each time he gave me a salute. Mrs B says his father is a bishop in Africa somewhere. Honestly I don't see why we can't have him here to tea.

— Pa wouldn't like it, Kate said.

— But his father's a bishop, Lydia said.

— Anyway you shouldn't flirt, Kate said.

— What about you!

— I'm not engaged, am I?

— Who said I was?

— Lydia!

— He never bought me a ring, Lydia said.

She picked up her bike and stood holding the handlebars almost as if she were having her photograph taken.

— But you . . .

Kate shook her arms as she urged the right words to come to her lips. She began to tremble and blush.

— We didn't do it, Lydia said, if that's what you mean.

— I didn't mean anything of the sort!

Kate's voice was loud on the stillness of the evening air, and when she had spoken she looked quickly towards the road gate. Even though it was some fifty yards away someone could have been passing.

— Say what you mean then.

— You know very well what I mean.

— No I don't.

— At least you could be true to him.

— Well I am true.

Lydia's mouth began to tremble. She dropped her bike and thrust her hands in her mac pockets.

— Fine way you have of showing it, Kate said.

Lydia sank to her knees and placed her arms on the mounting stone.

— He might never come back. So many of them don't come back.

Kate bent forward.

— Well you did your best to send him, didn't you?

Lydia looked into her sister's face as if her attack was a complete surprise. Then she buried her head in her arms and started crying.

THE DRESSING STATION was sheltered from the west by a rugged escarpment. Because of the danger of drawing shell fire, no smoke or fires out of doors were allowed, that night. Shadowy figures stood outside the dispensary where it was reported tea was being brewed. J.T. made no effort to join the crowd. The night was cold. He lay wrapped in his waterproofed sheet, with his back resting against a boulder. In the far distance, outside the village they had passed the previous day, wild dogs were howling. When he rested his head on the rock and looked up at the stars they seemed to be wheeling by at a tremendous speed. He closed his eyes wearily.

— Miles! Miles! Are you sleeping then?

J.T. shifted his head and he saw Fred Salmon's loose upper lip trembling over his long teeth. Fred had one knee on the ground and one arm against the boulder and the back of his hand under his chin.

— This is it, Fred Salmon said.

His eyes were fixed on J.T.'s face, waiting for any sign of feeling. J.T. nodded slowly. Salmon shifted about. He picked up a handful of pebbles and rattled them in his hand.

— This place reminds me of the country between Salt Lake and Chocolate Hill,[70] Salmon said.

He made himself more comfortable and leaned against the boulder, folding his arms.

— I'll never forget crossing that lake, he said. It wasn't a bloomin' lake anyway. Just a mile and a half of slime and a thin crust of salt on top. Half a pint of warm water and an Oxo cube, that's what we had, and not enough time for the cube to melt. We started out all right, all nice and tidy, and just as the sun was coming up the shelling started. Came straight at us between the hills and the rising sun. We lost the path and I got up to my knees in the mud. We were a perfect target. As we got to the edge the machine-guns started. I thought I was hit, but I wasn't.

Salmon stopped talking.

— Where's Cynwal? J.T. said.

— Scrounging for tea, I expect.

Salmon glanced at J.T. and bared his teeth. They shone in the moonlight.

— It wasn't the worst though. By midday we got as far as what was left of a wall at the foot of the hill. The Turks couldn't have been more than fifty yards away. I was lying where two battalions joined sort of thing, and right by my nose there were two colonels arguing the toss. One was for digging in and the other for advancing.[71]

J.T. turned his head to look at the hundred-foot high cliff behind him. Dark lumps against the sky seemed to puzzle him. Were they men or guns? Were they moving or still? Because his head was turned Fred Salmon's voice sounded far away.

— Just imagine me lying there under their feet, hearing the lot. Anyway it was 'ten rounds rapid' and then 'fix bayonets' and we were off. I saw the colonel go down less than ten yards from the wall. The one who wanted to dig in. We crossed this field anyway, and the Turks fell back up through the trees on the slope. We thought we were doing fine. Six of us got to the top of the rise. We got stuck on the far side of a huge boulder. Ten times as big as this one. We could see the other side of the Dardanelles.[72] The thing was we were stuck. There was a sergeant with us. Not our sergeant, he was dead in the Lake. This sergeant was a Geordie. Will Richards from Pwllheli was hit in the neck and bleeding like a pig. There was another chap lying there dying. We didn't know him. We had to leave him anyway. We bandaged Will up and we put him to sit on a rifle between the sergeant and me. We started back, down the hill only more to the left this time, through the shrub. Dead everywhere, more British than Turks. And the wounded squirming around, looking for somewhere to put their heads in the shade. Very like here the countty was, only more of a slope. We nearly fell into a trench held by what was left of some Lancashire Fusiliers. Somehow we got across and we shambled over to an oak tree. There were wounded there already. We propped him up against the trunk so that he was protected from shrapnel except his legs. The Turks were counter-attacking. The sarj and I jumped into the trench. But the worst thing of all happened next. The scrub caught fire. The heat and the shells. I don't know. Every man still alive out on that slope was burnt to death.

— What about this man from Pwllheli? J.T. said.

— Will? He died before the morning. We buried him there. Under the oak tree.

J.T.'s chin sank on his chest and his eyes closed.

— Funny sort of war that was.

Fred could not stop speaking. The low tone of his voice with its Cardiff drawl would imply that he was thinking aloud, and yet he kept glancing at J.T. to see if his words were taking effect.

— Old-fashioned I suppose. Everything so primitive. I don't know. Hard to tell really whether it's getting better or worse. Very hard to tell. . .

— Listen! Listen, Fred.

— What's the matter! What's up?

Salmon turned his head from one side to the other and the whites of his eyes glimmered.

— Over there!

J.T. scrambled to his feet, holding the waterproof groundsheet around his neck.

It's singing, he said. Welsh singing. That's where Cynwal is. Are you coming?

— I can't sing, Salmon said.

— Never mind, J.T. said. Come on.

Reluctantly Salmon got to his feet. Before being transferred to the R.A.M.C.[73] as a motor ambulance driver, Salmon had spent eight months in various hospitals with enteric fever and the thinness of his frame emphasized the exceptional length of his face. They hurried past a large ammunition dump in an olive grove, anxious to arrive at the singing before it was stopped for one reason or another. They found the men crowded into the patio of a deserted farm-house. Many of them were in full kit, carrying their rifles, waiting orders to move. They sang softly hymns in the minor key, *Cwm Rhondda, Diadem, Crug-y-bar, Aberystwyth,* They sang from memory, powerfully, with feeling, and yet controlled so that the volume of sound belied the numbers of men assembled. Starting to sing words that were so familiar to him, J.T. moved about among the men smiling to himself. When he paused to see if there was anyone near whom he knew, he saw Fred Salmon's lips part, ready to join in the singing whenever he could.

— I'm Wesleyan, Salmon said. Roath Park.[74] I used to be in the choir. The moon shone on J.T.'s upturned face. A small man stood alongside him and gripped his arm tightly.

— I know you, the small man said. J.T. Miles, isn't it? You don't remember me. Armon. My father was caretaker at Theo Col. Remember the fuss when Miss Crimp was locked in and had to get out through the window?

They shook hands warmly. J.T.'s ground-sheet fell open and Armon pointed to the Red Cross armband.

— 'If I come through this desert . . .'

He smiled as he quoted the hymn and J.T. squeezed his hand again sympathetically. They stood side by side as if they were singing in a chapel service. At the end of a hymn, while the echo of the music was dying away, a single shot rang out loudly. After a second's pause when every head in the yard had turned towards the olive grove, there came the first human scream which tapered off into a wail. No one moved. There were more shots. This time a little further away. Hoarse shouts in English from an N.C.O. The sound of running feet and a low branch broken, coming in their direction on the open side of the yard. No one seemed to breathe. A short silence pressed in on them. The thud of a bayonet being driven into flesh and a scream that was so near that J.T. could not prevent himself shivering from head to foot.

There was no more singing. The men stood talking in groups until they were called back to their platoons. They dispersed quickly and quietly. Armon was gone before J.T. could speak to him again. The farmyard was emptying rapidly. The place was being restored to its own loneliness. The voices giving orders were moving away. Cynwal saw J.T. and hurried to join him.

— Mostly new these chaps, he said. Some of them wanted to sing again tomorrow night. They haven't any idea . . .

— I think they know, J.T. said. Deep down they know.

Cynwal shook his head. Fred Salmon joined them, out of breath and pale.

— It was a Turkish patrol. In the olive grove. As near as that. We could have trodden on them as we came along. Honest. There were five of them. All dead, thank God. I spoke to one of the sentries. He said they must have stopped to listen to the singing.[75]

KATE WAS HAVING tea with Dan Llew's wife, Annie Grace, in the drawing-room of the large house he had bought, a mile and a half outside the town. Around the house were fifteen acres of good grazing where he kept stores so that he was registered as a farmer as well as a butcher, engaged on work of national importance. The windows of the house were shaped in Bath stone and the hard red brick was partially covered with Virginia creeper. Through the drawing-room window there was a view of a well-kept drive, a lawn and a fringe of ornamental shrubs backed by young trees that hid the house from the road.

Annie Grace was good-looking except for the reddening at the end of her nose and her plaintive manner. She sounded tearful when she offered Kate a cake. Even when she smiled her expression resembled that of a clown who expects any minute to have a bucket of water poured over his head.

— These are very nice, Kate said.

The cake was small, but Kate made it last by taking small bites.

— I made them myself, Kate fach,[76] Annie Grace said. Let me give you some more tea.

She held out her hand. Her long white fingers tilted downwards. Annie Grace had been to a boarding-school. She had a reputation of being artistic. Kate handed over her empty cup.

— Dan is working hard, Kate said.

She wiped a crumb from the skirt of her costume.

— Far too hard, Annie Grace said.

She stared at the cup she was filling.

— You've known him longer than I have, she said. Was he always so keen on money?

— It's Pa's fault really, I suppose, Kate said. He encouraged him.

— More than the others?

They sat close together, the tea trolley in front of them, preparing to go as far as each thought wise and appropriate in discussing the family.

— Well really, Kate said. I thought Ned was never going to get married. Pa was so keen to have him in charge at home you see.

— Dan was saying . . . Annie Grace hesitated.

—Yes?

Kate sounded prepared for criticism.

— That Ned wouldn't perhaps fare so well on his own. Nothing against Ned, because as you know Dan thinks the world of him. But he feels he's lacking in business experience. Your father really made him into an excellent foreman. A working foreman, he said. Of course Bessie being a little older will help.

— She's certainly very sure of herself, Kate said. I was there last week and Ned asked me to show her how I made *bara brith*.[77] She didn't like it one bit.

Annie Grace gave one of her sad smiles.

— Well it wasn't very tactful of him, was it?

Their conversation lapsed. Dan Llew's two boys suddenly dashed across the drive outside, kicking the gravel as one tried to avoid being caught by the other. They were dressed in knickerbockers. John Arnold, the eldest child, was six and he attended St Hilda's Private Preparatory School for Boys. Kate looked at her sister-in law as if she expected her to take her children in hand, but Annie Grace leaned back in her armchair and contemplated her out-stretched hand.

— There were so many of you, she said. I've told Dan we shan't have any more. In this world as it is you can't bring up more than two properly.

— I think we were very happy really, Kate said.

She sounded defensive.

— Each of us had his or her job to do. Each of us had a place. Griff will never come back of course.

— Poor Griff, Annie Grace said. I wish I had known him better. He was the brain of the family.

— Ned at Tir Coch. Dan here. Hugh in the army. Rowland is determined to get married this year . . .

—Young men must marry, Annie Grace said. She smiled understanding.

— I meant to ask you . . .

She placed her hand lightly on Kate's arm.

—What happened to Luther Parry?

Kate blushed and put down her cup. Annie Grace said:

— I thought he was very nice. He came here to supper when he was preaching in town. He took a great interest in my sketching. Dan liked him too. What happened, dear?

— Nothing really, Kate said.

— He was quite gone on you, I thought. Talking about you all he time. Paragon of all the virtues.

Annie Grace smiled again and waited for Kate to answer.

— I don't think he was sincere, Kate said.

Annie Grace suddenly popped a whole cake into her mouth. She pushed a crumb from the corner of her mouth between her lips with the tip of her finger. She swallowed the cake.

— What makes you say that? she said. He's not a Methodist of course and that would count a lot with your father . . .

— It's not that, Kate said.

— What then?

— I don't think I would trust him . . ., Kate said.

She seemed to summon up all her strength. She looked Annie Grace in the eye,

— With women, she said.

— O dear, I am sorry to hear that, Annie Grace said.

She dabbed the corners of her mouth with her finger and eyed another cake.

— How do you know?

— What I see and what I hear, Kate said. Putting two and two together. Lydia was saying only last week, in the carriage he put his hand on her knee.

— Well . . .

— And it wasn't the first time.

Annie Grace shook her head sympathetically.

— Lydia's very free of course, she said. I know it's her way but it does lead on to — well you know what I mean.

— She's my sister, Kate said. She wouldn't lie to me. Or make things up. She's my sister.

— I'm not suggesting that, Katie fach. I'm just saying her manner, you know what I mean. And she seems to say just whatever comes into her head.

— I keep on telling her, Kate said. Over and over again. She says I nag her.

— Well it's for her own good, Annie Grace said. It certainly is. And I'll tell you something else in confidence. I'll tell you because it will concern Lydia. But don't breathe a word. Not even at home.

Because it's all at a very delicate stage.

Kate nodded and prepared to listen carefully.

— Dan is taking over Bayliss, Estate Agent and Valuers.

Kate's mouth opened.

— I don't know the details. Bayliss's health is bad of course. He wants to give up. And Dan lent him some money two years ago. They've settled on a price and they're on good terms.

— What's the trouble then? Kate said.

She had recovered from her surprise and her head was bent as if in deep thought.

— Mrs Bayliss, Annie Grace said. She doesn't want to let go. As you know she's a very noisy woman and if she can make it difficult she will. You can correct me if I'm wrong, Katie fach, but isn't your sister Lydia very pally with her?

— I'm afraid so, Kate said.

— Well there you are.

— What's Dan going to do about it?

— I wish I knew my dear. It's money, money, money, all the way with him.

Kate got up.

— It's time I went Annie Grace, she said. My train. It'll take me a good forty minutes to walk to the station.

— Well if you wait, Katie, I think one of the Trojan vans are coming by five o'clock.

— Mustn't miss the five-fifteen, Kate said. Pa will be expecting me. There's a lot to do.

— Well lovely to see you anyway.

Annie Grace stood up. She was taller than Kate. They seemed to consider shaking hands. Annie Grace bent to kiss her sister-in-law.

— Come again soon, she said. And keep it to yourself won't you. About Bayliss.

CYNWAL GRIPPED HIS arm so tightly he couldn't move. For some reason the shelling had stopped, so that the groaning of the wounded and the dying could be clearly heard.

— Keep down, man, Cynwal said. They're sweeping.

Beyond the shallow depression where they lay was a flat barren field, an open track and beyond the track a cactus hedge around a shattered garden. The house was a heap of rubble, flattened by shell-fire. Through the hole where the house had stood there was a view of orange groves that for some reason appeared untouched by the battle.

— Listen! J.T. said.

— They're Turks. By the cactus hedge.

Cynwal held on to his arm.

— No. Nearer. Didn't see him. Listen!

A weak voice was cursing and groaning.

— Oh . . . bearers! Why don't the bastards come!

— We're falling back, Cynwal said. The aid-post has been hit. We've been ordered back, man. Don't you understand?

Cynwal shook his arm impatiently.

— We can't cross that field anyway. They're sweeping. The last spasm lasted four minutes.

As if he felt his argument had gone home, Cynwal relaxed his grip.

— We'll get him in, J.T. said.

His face was flushed with excitement.

— Not over that field, Cynwal said. It's too risky. In any case I've told you we've got to report back . . .

— We could leave him here.

J.T. pointed to the bottom of the hollow.

— Make him comfortable and come back.

— You're not fit to be a soldier, Cynwal said. You don't know how to obey orders. You look so damn quiet, and every now and then you behave like a raving madman.

— Come on!

J.T. picked up the stretcher and crawled over the top of the nullah. For a first time he had a clear view of the wounded man who was calling. He was sitting in the middle of the track, his legs stretched in front of him, looking down at a pool of his own blood. His rifle still hung by a strap from his neck. His fair head was close cropped. His mouth was open and in his bewilderment he looked like a child.

Cynwal had crept alongside him.

— He's too far gone, he whispered in J.T.'s ear. We can't do anything for him.

— There's another one. In the ditch.

J.T. pointed.

— It's a Turk, Cynwal said. No it isn't. It's a Jerry. It's a Jerry officer.

I'm not going to risk my life collecting one of those. What do you think I am?

— Where are they then?

The young soldier sitting in the road was crying. They could see the tears streaming down his face.

— Where are they then? Christ, where are the bastards?

As soon as J.T. stood up the machine-gun began firing. He ran forward. A bullet splintered the stretcher-pole and the impact almost threw him off his balance. He had almost reached the boy, who was looking up, his mouth open, like a child watching an acrobat at a circus, when J.T. fell as if his legs had been swept from under him by the relentless flailing of an invisible sledge-hammer. His head struck a stone and for a few moments he lost consciousness.

When he opened his eyes his head was facing the way he had come. He saw Cynwal on his hands and knees, his mouth hanging open and blood oozing darkly from a hole in his forehead. It had hardly begun to pour down his face before he toppled over and lay still.

Dragging the leaden weight of his legs, J.T. crawled towards the track. When the machine-gun stopped he heard his own voice repeating the phrase 'most merciful father' over and over again.

— Here!

The wounded boy was twenty yards further down the track and could not turn around.

— Here, the boy kept saying. Bearers over here!

Near the cactus hedge J.T. saw the German officer more clearly. He was a man in his late thirties, with a waxed moustache. He was still staring glassy-eyed at his shattered leg as if some terrible mistake had occurred. Near him was a dead Turk lying face downward with his hands clawed into the earth. Slowly he dragged himself towards the shade of the cactus hedge. When the boot of his right foot began to fill with blood as if he had stepped in a puddle he began to study his own condition. He looked down and saw blood welling up from a wound in the muscles of his left thigh.

With care he set himself against the cool earth of the bank below the cactus hedge. He seemed to study his own body as if it belonged to someone else. Slowly, with sweat pouring down his face, he removed the boot on his right foot, murmuring under his breath fragments of first-aid treatment such as 'elevate the limb and expose it' and *'look at the colour of the blood'*. He extracted a clean dressing from his pack and applied it gingerly to the wound in his foot. His breathing came with greater difficulty as he bandaged the pad as tightly as he could. He felt dizzy and sick. His head dropped back against the bank. There was also the thigh wound to attend to. He filled his left hand with a pad and clamped it over the hole in his trousers hoping to staunch the flow of blood.

MRS BAYLISS STOOD with her back to the office fire, large and unyielding, her hands clasped behind her back and a cigarette hanging out of the corner of her mouth. Her eyes were hooded against the smoke and from where Lydia sat on the high stool, her elbows on her desk, it appeared that she was looking down her nose.

— If you want to go, you don't have to stay, Mrs Bayliss said.

She took the cigarette out of her mouth, tapped the ash into the fire-place, and replaced it in her mouth.

— That sounds like double-Dutch, but you know what I mean.

— I don't want to go to tell you the truth, Lydia said. I honestly don't.

— This place is in a mess and it always will be a mess I suppose. That brother of yours is bound to win in the end, but he didn't win this time.

— I daren't say anything, Lydia said. Pa's only got his version of the story and in any case he'll never listen to me. But I'm ashamed of him Mrs Bayliss, I really am.

— He isn't exactly a good advertisement for Welsh non-conformity, is he?

— A bit of human kindness would be better than chapel four times a week, that's what I think!

Mrs Bayliss's shoulders shook with a growling masculine laugh. Then she coughed without removing her cigarette.

— A bit of honesty wouldn't be bad, Mrs Bayliss said, just to be getting on with.

Lydia blushed. She looked down at her hands and then turned to examine the letters and account books that were on her desk.

Mr Bayliss appeared in the doorway. He was wheezing badly. Lydia stared at the pulse in his scraggy neck. He weighed on the door knob, pressing the back of his other hand into his ribs. An open copy of the *Liverpool Daily Post* dangled between two white fingers.

— War news better, he said, struggling for breath. Americans in.

— What d'you say?

Mrs Bayliss straightened her back as though demonstrating to her husband how he should stand.

— The way you mumble. How can you expect people to understand you?

— The Americans ...

He bared his yellow teeth with the effort of speaking distinctly.

— ... are in.

He turned to smile at Lydia. Her head had tilted to one side and her big eyes were watching him sympathetically.

— Sorry you're going, my dear. Never mind.

He lifted the newspaper for her to see, and lowered it again.

— He'll be back soon. Then you'll get married.

— Huh! Married!

Mrs Bayliss raised her voice.

— She's not going to get married, are you love? Make yourself a slave to some man for the rest of your life. She's not so daft.

— Service ... 'perfect freedom', Mr Bayliss muttered.

He turned carefully in the doorway, preparing to cross the passage to his own office.

— What d'you say?

Mrs Bayliss raised her voice. Her husband ignored her questions.

— What did he say? she asked Lydia. Did you catch what he said?

Lydia shook her head.

— Does it on purpose, she said. He knows it annoys me. Men!

— He didn't look well, Lydia said in a sympathetic voice.

— Didn't he? Looked the same as usual to me. See people everyday you never notice.

There was a noise in the yard.

— Is that Charlie?

Mrs Bayliss listened carefully. She nodded and threw her cigarette into the fire.

— Lazy so-and-so, she said. Wait till I get at him. He knows I've been waiting here all morning to shift that Plas Gwilym stuff. Lovely stuff. You can't really see it piled up in the shed. Your brother was there you know. At the sale.

— Dan?

Lydia looked surprised.

— There was a lot of stuff there he would have liked. I could tell. He was just too mean to bid.

Mrs Bayliss rolled her eyes. She seemed to be making an effort to make Lydia smile.

— Well here goes, she said. Back into the fray.

OUTSIDE IN THE brilliant sunshine beyond the lowered blind a tram that seemed to shudder and groan under its load of passengers, clanked its way around the hospital corner. It trundled off towards the centre of the city and once more the ward was left to the fitful silence of the siesta. Most of the wounded men were sleeping, but in the bed next to J.T. Lance-Corporal Hotchkis rested on his elbow. He was smoking a Woodbine[78] and glancing down from time to time at the stump of his amputated leg. His lips moved as if he were engaged in a prolonged calculation. He blinked often. His eyelashes were noticeably long. His sallow cheeks were hollow and hungry. He drew hard and long on his cigarette, until there was little left to stub out on the sea-shell on his locker. When he came to the end of his cigarette his frown showed he was no nearer an answer to his problem. He extracted another cigarette from the packet by his pillow, lit a match and held it to one side to see if the bloodstain on the bandaging of his stump had grown any bigger. At the sound of the match being struck J.T. moved his head.

— You awake?

Hotchkis applied the flame to the new cigarette. He had seen J.T. move his head. J.T. opened his eyes and sighed.

— Why don't you lie down and get some rest, he said.

Hotchkis grinned.

— Got to watch it, he said, or it won't get better.

He pointed the wet end of his cigarette at J.T.

— I know what you're thinking, he said. Watched kettle never boils. Well this bastard don't stop boiling.

— You should lie still, J.T. said. You don't lie still long enough.

As though he were content now that he had engaged J.T.'s attention, Hotchkis began to look around the ward. He did not seem pleased with what he saw.

— Cor, he said. Look at 'em. What a mob!

— What's the matter? J.T. said.

— The matter?

He drew heavily on his cigarette. He moved his head and saw a patient in blue tunic and red tie standing at the entrance to the ward. The visitor moved with the slow gait of a man walking in a dream. He was studying the cards that hung above each bed and he thrust his legs forward as if the air were breaking like water against his knees. Hotchkis released the smoke he held in his mouth.

— Nosey Parker, he said.

He watched his approach with critical interest. The visitor's body was a thin frame inside his blue tunic and slacks. His face was alert as if he were listening to significant sounds from any direction. He paused to read the card above J.T.'s bed and then lifted his hand offering it to be shaken. The smile on his round face was motherly.

— Friend! he said in Welsh.

Hotchkis pulled a face and J.T. struggled up to take the offered hand which waited motionless as he mumbled an apology for his delay in taking it.

— J.T. Miles! I am so glad I've found you. I was talking to the chaplain. I heard you were here. Do you remember staying on my grandfather's little farm at the foot of the Black Mountains? Do you remember my cousins, Elsie and Sally?

J.T. was smiling with the effort of remembering.

— How can you? Why should you? Your preaching tour in the South. Summer 1914.

J.T. nodded eagerly.

— Of course I remember.

He began to laugh.

— They sewed up the sleeves of my new raincoat. I didn't find out until I got to the train. Sally and Elsie Griffiths. Terrible practical jokers. They sang duets.

— There you are!

They laughed triumphany. Again Hotchkis grimaced. J.T. caught a glimpse of this, and the visitor saw Hotchkis's reaction mirrored in J.T.'s face.

— You must excuse us, he said to Hotchkis in jovial English.

— You are lying next to a well-known preacher!

Hotchkis raised his eyebrows and drew on his cigarette.

— Well that's marvellous, isn't it? he said.

The visitor continued to beam at him.

— Are you getting better? he said.

— So they say.

Hotchkis pointed at his stump with the hand that held his cigarette.

— Never get that back though, will I?

The visitor breathed in deeply and shook his head.

— Got a pack of cards? Hotchkis said.

— I'm sorry . . .

— I get bloody fed up you know, lying here.

— Can I get you some books . . . Magazines . . .

— Get me some crumpet. Wog or white. Anything will do. Bring'er in on a trolley an' a bottle of beer 'anging from her fanny.

The visitor grew pale and swallowed hastily. He put out his hand to steady himself on the edge of J.T.'s bed.

— That's no way to talk, the visitor said.

— Fuck off then.

The visitor looked at J.T. and moved around to the other side of the bed. Hotchkis watched him. Then he blinked and bent to look at his bandages.

— Don't take any notice of him, J.T. said in Welsh. He's full of bitterness. What's your name?

— James Foster Jones.

He breathed deeply, closing his eyes.

— I want to dedicate myself to Jesus Christ,

— There's a stool under the bed, J.T. said. Why don't you sit down?

— It's not ambition, James Foster said. My soul has made a choice. I want to talk to somebody who understands. I had a piece of shrapnel in my skull as big as a half-crown. Bits there still I think. I was lying out there for two days. No shade from the sun. Soaking wet at night. I saw him, Mr Miles. He came to me. Like a green shadow he was. He bent over me. The first thing I saw on the ground when they found me was a torn page from Mark.[79] As if somebody had left it there on purpose. Come unto me . . . Now this is my problem. To what am I called? I'll tell you an experience I had. Here in this hospital. On a Sunday morning, in the ward, there was a service and Communion for those who wanted it. And this padre, he looked at my card and he said it was an Anglican Communion. He saw on my card I was Welsh Calvin so he said he couldn't give it to me. Now I know Jesus wasn't like that. I can read. Anybody can see what he was like. It wants changing, Mr Miles. It all wants changing.

Sweat had broken out on his pale face. It balanced in the curve of his upper lip like water at the bottom of a spoon.

— I ask myself, what am I to do? There are three courses open to me. The lay ministry. Go back to my old job in the tinworks. Bear witness. As I try to do now. As soon as you're better, Mr Miles, will you come and address our group in The Soldiers Home? We've got eight or nine theologicals from the R.A.M.C. I'm sure you know some of them. Fellowship. Bible Class. Week-night service. Then again, the second course is aiming for Oxford. I always dreamed of going there. Work hard. Become fully equipped. Train for the ministry. Take care of a church. Or the third course. The best course I think. Take a degree and go back and work alongside my old mates. One of them. But bearing witness to a new way in the world.

A spasm of pain passed over his face and he bent forward, clutching his belly.

— We don't want no smells in here, Hotchkis said.

He had been watching James Foster for some time. As he rushed out of the ward, Hotchkis smiled and turned to wink at J.T.

— Don't wink at me!

J.T.'s voice trembled.

— What's up with you, for God's sake?

— Don't wink at me!

Hotchkis twisted his fag-end into the shell.

— Blimey. The bloody Welsh, he said.

16

KATE FOLDED HER arms. On the kitchen chair, set in isolation for the light from the bay window, she sat like an ageing fighter in the corner of a ring, stooping, arms folded, her legs apart.

— What's in the others? she said. If you don't open them soon they'll go bad.

J.T. laughed and shook his head appreciatively. Kate put a hand over her eyes. He picked up a letter and took yet another look at the handwriting. He picked up a knife.

— I've no idea who this is from, he said.

— There's some butter on that knife, Kate said. He made an apprehensive grimace and put the knife down.

— Do it with the handle of your teaspoon, she said impatiently.

— It's somebody old, anyway, he said. He thrust the handle of the teaspoon under the flap of the flimsy envelope, and extracted a single sheet of lined notepaper. He examined the object with care, turning it over. There was no writing on the back. He cleared his throat and began reading.

— 'Dear Sir, I am writing to tell you that old freind Ifan Cole passed away this morning.'

— Oh dear. Dear me. Poor old Ifan.

J.T. lowered the letter. A dear old friend.

— Who was he then? Kate said.

— An old friend, J.T. said, lifting the letter. A dear old friend.

— Well, I'm sure I never heard of him.

He continued in a sadder voice.

He was seventy-eight and very poorly for some time. We were great friends and we played bowls when he was fit, and he told me how he used to work with you in the forge many years ago but you got on well and he said he was always lazy. He always said he would like you to have his watch. It is the same watch he had in the forge. It has stopped, but it is a good watch. It is here for you if you come for it the Matron said.

> Trusting you are in good health,
> I am,
> Yours faithfully,
> Owen Williams (aged 82 years)

— Dear me. Dear me.

J.T. shook his head and swallowed.

— Poor old Ifan. Poor old Ifan.

— Who was he? Kate said.

— Owen Williams? Somebody in the next bed I expect.

— No. The man who died.

She waited impatiently as he shook out his handkerchief before blowing his nose very loudly.

— Ifan? J.T. said. Ifan? One of the kindest. One of the kindest. Never harmed anybody except himself. Used to drink too much sometimes.

He turned to look at Kate and smile in a peaceful way. His eyes were filled with tears.

— He wanted me to have his watch, he said. After all these years.

— Who was he? Kate said.

— Well you heard, didn't you? In the letter. He used to work with me in Isaac Dafydd's forge.

He spoke defiantly as if Kate were showing disapproval of his having ever worked in a smithy.

— Why didn't you say so then?

— Best days of my life, J. T. said. With old Isaac, and Ifan. Working from morning till night. Learning my craft. Not a care in the world. Those were the days.

— What's the other one?

— It's an appeal.

— Honestly, Kate said. They're for everlasting asking for money.

— They're doing their best, Kate. You've got to struggle to save the best . . .

Kate put her hands on her knees and got up.

— I've got work to do, she said. I told you old Hobley's coming to have his hair cut. And Gwyneth is coming. Taking me over the Denbigh Moors. It's not raining either. I've put an egg custard for you in the oven. And there's cold ham and tomatoes.

J.T. piled up the breakfast dishes he had used.

— You mustn't over-excite yourself, he said.

— Over-excite!

Kate spoke so sharply the dishes rattled in his hands.

— If there's one thing I never do, she said, it's over-excite myself. Put those down. You'll only break them.

— What shall I do then?

— Go and read the paper, Kate said. If it's one thing I can't bear it's a man getting in the way in the kitchen.

— I'd better write to this place, he said, picking up the letter signed by Owen Williams. I'd like to go to the funeral really. Poor old Ifan. It's in Anglesey this place. A sort of hospital I expect . . . Kate!

— What is it? Kate answered from the kitchen.

— Do you think that Gwyneth would take us there today. I mean, it would be a trip for you, wouldn't it? And we'd kill two birds with one stone.

He stood listening for her answer. He heard her slam a cupboard door. He frowned thoughtfully. His heel twisted uncertainly in the worn carpet. He made his way to the kitchen.

—What do you think?

As soon as he had spoken, Kate, carrying a tray, was on her way back to the living-room, so that he addressed the question towards the gap between the gas stove and the sink, and turned to the doorway to wait for an answer. His mouth opened expectantly as he moved back to the living-room.

— Um?

—You'll have to ask Gwyneth, won't you? You'd better take these.

She had scooped up the letters and she held them out in such a disordered way that he hurried to retrieve them.

— Go and write in the other room, she said. It isn't cold.

His hand trembled a little as he put the letters back in their envelopes.

—Yes, he said. I'll do that right away. I ought to take my collars to the laundry some time this morning.

— If you wore clerical collars you wouldn't have to go so often, Kate said.

J.T. smiled and shook his head as if he were enjoying an old joke. The smile faded. He looked at the letters.

—What shall I say? he said.

— Say? Say? How do I know what you should say?

As she picked up the tray, the door-bell rang.

— I'll go, J.T. said,

— They've come too soon, Kate said.

She seemed agitated by the noise of the bell and she set the tray down before changing her mind and starting off for the kitchen with it.

— I'll go, J.T. said.

— No. Wait!

She spoke over her shoulder sharply. In the kitchen she put down the tray on the draining-board and fumbled at the knot of grey tape that held her pinafore tightly around her. The bell rang again.

— Shall I answer it? J.T. said.

He swayed forward to ask the question from the doorway of the living-room. The letters were still in his hand. Kate stared hostilely at the blurred image of a woman's head beyond the frosted glass. She shook her head in answer to J.T.'s question and murmured under her breath,

— That's not Mrs Hobley.

She opened the door and J.T. heard Miss Pickering's voice.

— Oh, hello Mrs Bannister. I'm sorry to disturb you.

Kate nodded unhelpfully.

— I thought you ought to know. I just saw your brother, Mr D.L. Jones, getting off the bus. He looked rather strange, so I came out to see which way he went. I thought he might be visiting you. But he went up the hill. I went to the corner beyond the new public house and I could see him going up the old road. He was walking very fast for a man of his age, I must say.

— J.T!

She turned her head, plucking nervously at the cameo brooch at the throat of her loose-fitting dark blue dress.

— Yes, Kate?

She opened the door a little wider.

— It's Dan Llew. He's started walking to Argoed again.

J.T. nodded a hasty greeting to Miss Pickering.

— Is there anything I can do? she said.

— Thank you very much . . . J.T. said gratefully.

— We'll have to phone for a taxi, Kate said.

She looked at J.T. as she spoke as if she wanted to share her thoughts with him alone.

— Well I'll be getting back, Miss Pickering said.

She stepped back towards the open garden gate. J.T. strode past Kate.

— It was very good of you, Miss Pickering.

Miss Pickering made a self-disparaging gesture with her hand and pointed to No. 10.

— Haven't they got a phone at Mrs Box's? she said.

Kate took a step forward into the narrow porch.

— No. Not there, she said.

— Well I'll have to go down to the call-box at the mouth of Beach Road, J.T. said.

— The sooner the better, Kate said. I'll go and get my coat on.

— There's no need . . .

J.T. held out his hand in an attitude of restraint. Miss Pickering passed through the gate he held open and turned on the pavement to wait for him.

— You don't have to come out, J.T. said. Kate stared at him.

— He won't recognize you, she said.

She continued to keep him under the surveillance of her eye until it was clear he had grasped her point.

— Have you got four pennies? she said.

She waited impatiently in the porch while he stood in the open gateway, fumbling in his trouser pockets. He examined the coins on his extended palm and then looked up at her.

— Have you got a penny?

Kate pressed her lips together, turned and made for the sitting-room. There was a mahogany bureau there and inside the lid there was a decorated cardboard box which had once contained half-a-dozen handkerchiefs. A Christmas gift from her sister. In it she liked to keep a permanent store of loose change to be used for petty charges outside the normal expense of housekeeping. At the bottom of the box were a few photographs, some of which had been snipped with scissors into odd shapes either to fit into small frames or to exclude a person from a group.

Outside Miss Pickering was saying:

— It's very worrying for her.

She wrapped her grey cardigan more tightly around her pink blouse against the fresh breeze.

— I'd rather she didn't come you know, J.T. said. She won't admit it but it upsets her.

— They're changing all the names, Miss Pickering said. I do think that's wicked. Fancy calling it the Greenhill Estate.

— I believe there is a petition organized by Ffoulkes, the Wesleyan minister up there, against changing the names, J.T. said.

— I should think so too, Miss Pickering said. I shouldn't tell you I know but I've been trying to write a poem about it for weeks. It's called 'The Birthright'. It's so difficult to say something new. For me anyway. I just haven't the talent. Still I'm not doing any harm, am I?

J.T. was looking down at her sympathetically as if he were searching for words of comfort and encouragement when Kate called from the edge of the porch.

— Here you are!

She held out a penny. She was in her slippers and did not want to step out on the path or expose herself more than necessary to the public gaze. J.T. hurried to take the penny.

— The Hobleys, Kate muttered.

— Eh?

He had not understood. She stared uncertainly at the elderly couple in plastic macs coming up Gorse Avenue. Mrs Hobley, who guided her shuffling husband, lifted the arm that held her handbag in jolly greeting. Kate lifted her hand briefly.

— They're coming, she said.

— Poor chap, he said.

J.T. turned and Miss Pickering turned to watch the Hobleys approach. She did not know them well and nodded shyly. Mrs Hobley bent her head to give a particularly sweet smile and Mr Hobley lifted the peak of his cap which balanced on the top of his head as if someone other than himself had set it there. They paused outside the open gate.

— Well, Mrs Hobley said, smiling bravely. Here we are.

She turned to look at her husband. His stroke had given a sardonic twist to his mouth.

— He doesn't look too bad, does he?

— Come in, come in, J.T. said.

Kate stood to one side and brushed the air into the house.

Mrs Hobley smiled prettily and stepped forward delicately, her husband shuffling alongside her. She paused again on the porch

— Well what do you think of him? she said.

— He looks very well, J.T. said.

He now stood on the path.

— Vitamins, Mrs Hobley said. Massive doses.

She looked at Kate closely.

— You could do with some, she said.

— She's had a bit of an upset, J.T. said, moving nearer.

Mr Hobley had now seen him and his eyes lit up.

— Padre! he said.

Mr Hobley was the former owner of the Gwalia Men's Wear and under his plastic mac, worn because of the uncertain weather, he was dressed in a smart navy-blue blazer with chromed buttons. The thick legs of his spectacles pushed out his ears and he spoke in a hoarse blurred whisper. Miss Pickering began to venture back towards the gate. She had her hand on her lips like a person about to make a suggestion.

— It's my brother, Kate said.

— Hush a minute, Bob, Mrs Hobley said to her husband.

— He's been walking up the old road, J.T. said. Miss Pickering saw him.

— He's going up to Argoed, Kate said. I'll have to go and stop him. Mrs Hobley was taken aback.

— Oh, she said.

She looked at J.T. and Kate in turn.

— Oh, she said. Should we . . . do you think . . .

Miss Pickering had crept forward on tiptoe. She stood behind Mrs Hobley, who turned quickly when she heard her speak, her mouth still round with uncertainty and perturbation.

— I'd like to suggest something, Miss Pickering said.

Mrs Hobley, stared at her eagerly. Her husband was still smiling at J.T., a sardonic smile that suggested that as men among women they had to be tolerant and patient and wait a long time for their turn to

— Why don't Mr and Mrs Hobley come and wait at my place until you get back?

Mrs Hobley looked relieved. She turned to test Kate's reaction to the suggestion and looked back at Miss Pickering again.

— Well, she said.

A smile was growing on her face.

— We could make a cup of tea or something.

Mr Hobley swayed on the porch step. His wife stepped off as if to prop him up and he followed her, laughing, Kate was left alone on the porch step.

— Please yourself, Kate said.

Mr Hobley suddenly grasped Miss Pickering's arm.

— A soldier's cup of tea, he said.

He straightened himself and stood back a little without letting go of her arm.

— Do you know what a soldier's cup of tea is? he said.

Something of his old strength seemed to be returning to him. He turned his head to look at J.T. and wink, and the houses of the end of the Avenue were reflected in the large lens of his spectacles.

— Shall I tell them, Padre?

He looked at each of the women in turn as if he were about to give a performance. He did not let go of Miss Pickering's arm.

— You get a mug, he said. Not an ugly mug. But the biggest mug you can find. Am I right, Padre?

J.T. nodded and tightened his grip on the fourpence in his hand.

Mrs Hobley looked anxious.

— Well as I was saying, Mr Hobley said, giving Miss Pickering's arm a slight shake, you put the tea straight in the mug. No messing. As much as you like. And pour the boiling water on top. And plenty of sugar. Sugar for shock, isn't it Padre? And that's a soldier's cup of tea.

He let go Miss Pickering's arm. His wife looked relieved. Kate spoke to J.T.

— You'd better go and phone, she said. I'll go and get my coat.

Kate went in. At the gate there was some confusion. Miss Pickering said that Mr Miles should go first. Mrs Hobley agreed. Mr Hobley did not understand and he stood in the gateway until his wife, failing to pull him back with an apologetic smile, pushed him on.

— Well, J.T. said.

He hurried up the uneven pavement, watching out for puddles. He glanced at the sky. The rain clouds seemed to be driven on by the freshening wind and blue patches were appearing. He did not notice a beige-coloured Standard Eight drawing unsteadily across the road until it drew up ahead of him. The woman driver put out her head and called out cheerfully.

— Uncle! Where are you off to?

— Gwyneth!

J.T. stood still. It was clear from his face that he was thinking hard. He lifted his hand with the index finger extended and turned to see if Kate was in view. He was overtaken by Miss Pickering and Mr and Mrs Hobley. They paused. He smiled hastily and spoke loudly.

— This is Miss Gwyneth Roberts, senior French mistress at Cilgwyn Grammar School. My wife's cousin's youngest daughter. We are very proud of her.

Gwyneth was holding the wheel of her car tightly. Her face was plump and laughing hid her eyes completely, especially since she pressed her head back, but her teeth were excellent and her broad smile seemed to cheer them all up. Mr Hobley stood back to improve his line of vision and gave a very broad smile too.

— This is Miss Pickering, Gwyneth. She is a very good poet. Very good.

— Mr Miles you shouldn't say such a thing.

Gwyneth had poked a hand over the car window which was not completely wound down.

— This blessed old window is stuck, Gwyneth said. It'll go up, but it won't go down.

— Mr and Mrs Hobley of course you've met before, haven't you? Mrs Hobley flexed her knees to smile.

— How are you, my dear? she said. No. Don't get out now.

— Well, Miss Roberts couldn't have come at a better time, could she? Miss Pickering said.

She looked up at J.T. in the attitude of a loyal supporter, presuming to remind the leader of the task in hand.

— I'm taking Mr and Mrs Hobley over to my place for a cup of tea, she said to Gwyneth, bending down.

— A soldier's cup of tea, Mr Hobley said, saluting.

His wife took his arm, Gwyneth continued to smile, and looked at her uncle, waiting for an explanation,

— It's your uncle, Dan Llew, J.T. said. He's gone off. Gone off up the old road. He's done it before you know. He thinks he's going back to Argoed.

— We'll move on then, Miss Pickering said.

Mrs Hobley bent down for a final smile, at the same time pushing her husband on by steady pressure on his arm. Gwyneth lifted her hand in farewell, turning her head to catch the eye of her uncle who was standing too close to the car.

— Where's Aunty? she said.

— Move your car forward, will you Gwyneth? Outside the house.

He started walking backwards as he was speaking, and turned to look up at the bedroom windows of No. 8. His head surveyed first one side and then the other of the Avenue as if it were filling up with invisible bus-loads of Sunday scholars all in his charge for the hazardous annual outing. He pointed helpfully to the spot opposite the garden gate of No. 8 where he thought Gwyneth could park. She lifted her hand and nodded cheerfully as her car bumped slowly forward on the wrong side of the road. Kate appeared wearing a loose overcoat that was too big for her and a hat with a brim that shaded her face and prevented her looking sideways without turning her head.

— Taxi! J.T. said jovially,

Kate walked past him. The hat gave her a purposeful forward-looking air. Gwyneth unlocked the door on the passenger side and Kate got inside.

— How are you, Aunty?

They kissed and Kate held on to her niece's hand.

— I've got such a lot to tell you, she said. Can't say anything now.

She bent forward to call out at J.T.

— Get in, she said.

— Shall I close this gate?

J.T. had his right hand on the garden gate.

— He's quite helpless, Kate said under her breath.

She raised her voice.

—Yes of course!

Gwyneth opened the door behind her for her uncle to get in.

He fell back in the hard seat and pulled the door to with a big sigh and a laugh.

— I suppose the quickest way, he said, would be . . .

— I'll tell Gwyneth the way, Kate said. You'll have to turn first.

As the car turned all their heads turned. They seemed to be willing it to function in response to their united gestures, as it shuttled back and forth executing a three-point turn over the rough surface of the unadopted road.

— Turn left here, Kate said, lifting her left hand at an angle from her body.

She swallowed and frowned as they waited for a stream of traffic to pass, Gwyneth bending as far forward as she could and peering left and right and left again. Kate looked at her.

— When you've a moment to look, she said. Is my eye straight?

Gwyneth looked at her and smiled and a smile seemed to twitch at the corner of Kate's mouth as she turned her face right for inspection.

—You look fine, Aunty.

— Is it straight?

—Yes it is. Turn left again?

— That's right.

Kate nodded contentedly. J.T. leaned forward as if to say something and then sank back again.

— That awful public house, she said.

— The House of Baal, J.T. said loudly, folding his hands in his lap.

The car climbed up towards the bridge over the railway. From the top they could see the point almost half a mile ahead where the road forked. To the left the old road ran through a stretch of high hedges, to the right a new road took the traffic inland.

— There are more going up, Kate said.

She was looking at the new housing estates that branched out on either side of the new road.

— All fields twelve years ago, she said.

She made a gesture with her hand.

— Up the old road, she said. It's uphill. I expect we'll find him sitting by Cae Melyn Pond. There's a bench there. He'll be taking a rest. And then he'll start taking the top road to Argoed. He was always a great walker. He had a lot of faults but there was never anything lazy about him.

— That's one for me, J.T. said.

He sat back and laughed cheerfully.

— I wasn't thinking of you, Kate said, without turning round. It's going to clear up, Gwyneth. The weather's going to clear up.

— How's old Hughes?

J.T. spoke up in a chatty voice from the back seat. He was looking about him with evident pleasure, enjoying the ride very much.

— Oh he's terrible, Uncle, he really is. You may as well say he's given up teaching. Just sits in the staff-room all day playing chess. Thinks of nothing else.

— His brother was a brilliant man, J.T. said. A mathematician. Very brilliant. He had T.B. you know. They put the poor fellow on minesweepers you know in the first war. He wasn't very strong. Seasick every day he spent at sea. Never got over it. They made him a lecturer but he didn't last a term. I used to go and visit him at the sanatorium. He just wasted away, poor fellow. This younger brother of course was after my time. A good old family though. Very staunch at Sardis Penywaun. Their father was the grandson, no, wait a minute now . . .

— Straight on, Kate said. We're bound to see him now. Around the next corner I shouldn't wonder. She's not fit to look after him you know, she really isn't. She's too busy worrying about her own health. I told him. I said, 'Look here, Dan, you want a house-keeper sound in mind and limb. I mean, this woman is a creaking gate . . .'

— Fair play, J.T. said.

— I know her better than you do, Kate said. I've seen her put margarine on sandwiches before today, and our Dan worth sixty thousand if he's worth a penny. What's she saving it for?

— Now look . . . J.T. said.

It was difficult sitting in the back to gauge Gwyneth's reaction to what Kate was saying.

— He's my own brother, Kate said. The only one of us left apart from me and I should think I had a right to speak my mind if anyone has. You know I'm the last to waste words when words are not worth wasting . . . There he is!

A white-haired man in a grey suit was crossing the road, from the bench on the green bank where he had been resting. His course was set for the top road where the old landmarks could guide him.

— Drive past him, Kate said.

Her voice trembled with excitement.

— Don't try and attract his attention whatever you do.

As the car passed him he stood still in the road, a frown on his face, his white hair blown about. His mouth was open and he peered at the car over the top of his bifocal spectacles. His pale face was flushed with the unaccustomed exertion out of doors. He clasped his hands behind his back, glanced at his brown boots and resumed his walking.

— Last time, Kate said, I met him by the new cemetery, I told the taxi man to draw up on the lay-by by the cemetery gates. Now the thing is, Gwyneth, I'll get out and walk down the road to meet him. I'll talk to him. You keep behind us and when I lift my hand like this you overtake us and I'll say, 'Oh look, here's Gwyneth, Alice Glanaber's daughter, she'll give us a lift home. Isn't that lucky' or something like that.

Kate spoke more rapidly than usual and as Gwyneth reversed the car down a lane, she gripped the top of the dashboard as if she was eager for action. She got out as quickly as she could and gave the car door a great slam. In the road she looked back and made a sign to indicate that Gwyneth should wait there until she saw Dan Llew coming into sight.

He came around the corner quite suddenly, almost at a trot. Kate pointed at him so that Gwyneth could understand she had seen him. She put her hands behind her back and walked slowly to meet him. She walked near the crown of the road. Gwyneth nosed her car slowly out of the lane, looking both ways with great care and shooting forward rather too quickly, bringing the car to a sudden stop on the other side of the road, so that J.T. was jerked forward and had to put up his hand against the back of Gwyneth's seat to prevent himself falling forward.

— Hello Dan, Kate said in a calm voice.

They were still too far apart. He had not heard her. They drew closer to each other.

— Hello Dan, Kate said again. Where are you going?

He stopped suddenly. He seemed to accept her as a familiar part of the landscape.

— I'm going up to see Pa, he said. Where are you going?

— I'm going down to the new shop, Kate said. Why don't you come with me?

— Well, I can't, can I, if I'm going up to see Pa?

His voice had the old familiar note of impatience.

— It's that fool Tomi Moch, he hasn't half boiled the swill. We've got to get rid of him. There's nothing else for it. I can't lose a herd of pedigree pigs just because a half-wit doesn't do his job properly.

He stared at Kate as if he were angry with her.

— Tomi's dead, Kate said.

— Dead? Dead? Who said he was dead?

— He died soon after the war, Kate said. He was living with his half-sister in Holywell. She was very good to him. He got run over in the High street and then developed pneumonia. You went to his funeral.

Dan Llew frowned and turned towards the hedge. He seemed to be staring at the roots of the grass on the bank that had just been cut.

— Is Pa dead too?

He spoke in a whisper as if it were dangerous to speak too loudly. Kate lifted her hand and Gwyneth saw her signal. Dan Llew turned to look at his sister, unconsciously smoothing his hair down with his right hand.

— I was more worried about Ma you know. Much more. When Ned and I picked her up to put her in the governess cart she was as light as a feather.

His voice was becoming firmer and more lucid.

— Do you remember Ma, Kate? She was a good woman you know. A very good woman.

Kate took his arm and turned him to face the way he had come.

— She used to make gravy like you, Dan Llew said. Annie Grace never got the hang of it.

The beige Standard Eight glided past. Going downhill, Gwyneth had not bothered to switch on the engine.

— Well, Kate said, look who's here.

Dan Llew lifted his head abruptly so that the loose skin under his chin was stretched tight.

— It's Gwyneth, Alice Glanaber's daughter. She'll give us a lift home. Isn't that lucky?

Dan Llew nodded obediently. Kate spoke without any surprise in her voice and he seemed to react to the tone rather than to what she said.

— Sit in the back with J.T., Kate said. You can have a chat on the way home.

— Hello Uncle, Gwyneth said cheerily.

— Hello Dan, J.T. said, moving into his corner to make as much room as he could.

— All on board, J.T. said.

Dan Llew kept his lips firmly together. He tried to keep his face expressionless, but his eyes moved about so much it seemed his mind was teeming with suspicious thoughts. No one knew what to say to him. With his mouth so firmly shut he kept them all silent.

17

PA ROUNDED THE corner on the stairs, keeping his elbow up against the inside wall to prevent himself placing a foot on the narrow end of the treads.

— It would be much safer if the carpet was up, he said.

Kate was in the kitchen making pastry on a corner of the big table. In the churn room there was the noise of someone rinsing the milking buckets.

— Mind the kittens, Kate called out.

Pa was in his stockinged feet. He wore thick grey socks that were knitted for him by the old widow who kept the post office. Every year this woman knitted him three new pairs of the same weight from the same wool and re-footed two old pairs. Three kittens tumbled over each other on the mat at the bottom of the stairs, one all black, one with white feet, white nose and a white tip to the tail and the third a tortoiseshell. Pets. Their mother stood between Kate and the fire-place, watching the kittens carefully, her tail erect and swaying gently.

— Where are they?

Pa raised his voice sharply as if it were less trouble to shout than to look. He paused, his hand on the wall, to belch and wait for an answer. His beard was untrimmed and he was not wearing his false teeth.

— At the bottom of the stairs, Kate said. On the mat.

— *Merch-i,* Pa said. I can't for the life of me find my teeth. Do you know where they are?

— How on earth should I know? You mean you want me to look for them?

— Never was anybody to touch you for finding things, Kate bach. Gingerly he continued to descend the stairs.

— In that respect you are even better than your mother was. I don't like all these cats in the house.

He looked down disapprovingly at the heaving heap of kittens at his feet.

— They should have been drowned at birth, Pa said. You'll never get rid of them now. You should have told Tomi to drown them.

— There's a letter from Lydia, Kate said. It's on the mantelpiece. She passed the glass rolling-pin between finger and thumb to remove the fragments of pastry that were stuck to it.

— I left my spectacles upstairs, Pa said.

— I see you left the tray up there as well, Kate said.

— What does she say?

— Ronnie's teething, Kate said.

— Ronnie, Pa said. Why do they give him a name like that?

— Ronald Griffith Miles, Kate said. Very nice name, I should say. Why ask me? She just liked it, that's all.

— Something she's picked up in the South there. He could have had Nant-y-Wrach and Engedi!

He stood on the mat in his stockinged feet, frowning down at the kittens. He seemed anxious not to meet Kate's stare.

— They would have lived near here then. But they weren't good enough for him. Not big enough. He had to have a big church in the South. I can't think what kind of a minister he makes, currying favour with the working classes.

He paused as if to think of something more biting that would make Kate speak. But she said nothing. His toe twitched inside his stocking as he pushed it as near as he could to the kittens without kicking them. The cat looked up at him apprehensively.

— There's a new type of minister coming into fashion, Pa said. I was talking to Hughes Pant Mawr about it at the Presbytery. I told him I didn't like the smell of them, let alone the sound of them. He agreed with me.

She stood aside to allow him to pass unhindered to his chair in the narrow end of the kitchen. Pets darted under the table. He sat down heavily in the high-backed wooden chair. He jerked his thumb in the direction of the recess in the wall beyond his right shoulder.

— I'd like a small window there, he said. It would be very useful. Give me a view of the yard. See what's going on without going outside. Where are my boots?

Kate released one hand from the rolling-pin and pointed to the steel fender against which the boots were balanced. Pa stooped to put them on, stamping each foot in turn on the flagstoned floor. He paused with his hands on his knees, both boots unlaced. He passed his hand over his mouth.

— I want my teeth, he said.

— Mrs Teck!

The noise in the churn room stopped.

— Were you calling, love?

— Would you mind popping upstairs and getting Mr Jones's teeth? I expect he's left them under his pillow ...

Pa shook his head, but Kate did not seem to notice. She sifted more dry flour through her fingers on the roll of pastry. Pa lifted his hand and shook it, and lowered it quickly when Mrs Teck came down the three steps into the kitchen and stood for a moment to wipe her wet hands on her apron.

— Good morning, sir, Mrs Teck said.

— Good morning, Pa said.

He peered at the floor as if he had lost something.

— I'll run up and get them then, Mrs Teck said.

— If you would, Kate said. Mind the kittens. Oh, bring the breakfast tray too, will you?

Mrs Teck nodded, and then paused with her hand against the wall to look down at the kittens at her feet.

— Bless my soul, they are pretty, she said. I'd love to have one, Miss Jones, I really would. But they make my George sneeze. Isn't it a shame?

Mrs Teck ran upstairs. She was a small fat woman who always appeared slightly dazed.

— My George, Pa said. Drunken sot.

He tugged vigorously at his long bootlaces.

— She's at it too, Pa said. You mark my words. I've seen her groping along the ditch coming up from the village. Disgusting.

— She's got a lot to put up with, Kate said.

— It's up to us to set a good example in these difficult days, Pa said.

— I was fond of old Mary Parry Rice, Kate said, but quite honestly, Pa, this woman gets through the work in half the time. And she doesn't steal candles or sugar.

— Old Mary never stole a thing in her life!

— Don't you remember Lydia seeing them sticking out of the long pocket in that old skirt of hers. The candles, when she was bending over? Don't you remember?

— Hush, Pa said.

Mrs Teck returned, holding out the set of upper dentures above the tray she was carrying. She held them delicately between her finger and thumb. She smiled and blinked.

— Here you are, sir, she said. My hands are quite clean.

Pa hesitated, looking at her hands for a second. Then he took the teeth, turned his head away and slipped them in his mouth.

THE SCHOOLMASTER'S WIFE tapped lightly on the back door and lifted the latch. When she spoke, she pitched up her voice.

— It's Jenny Leyshon here. Can I come in?

She paused, and as soon as she heard Lydia's voice answered herself.

— Of course I can. That's what I like about it. Are you in the snug, Lydia?

The room she called 'the snug' was a tiny kitchen at the back of the manse where everyday meals were eaten. There was a table against the window, with room for four — one at each end and two facing the window. And there was a Welsh dresser and enough room to pass easily between the table and the dresser when the two chairs were pushed in. The table was laid for a cold supper.

— My dear . . . do you mind?

Jenny held up a hymn-book in her gloved hand. Lydia sat on a low chair by the fire with her baby sucking at her breast. She turned slightly so that her pale breast was not so fully exposed to Jenny's eager gaze. She looked over her shoulder to return Jenny's smile.

— Come and sit down, she said.

Jenny tiptoed forward and sat down neatly in the chair that fitted tightly between the Welsh dresser and the grate. She stretched her neck to look at the baby.

— Isn't he wonderful! she said. Sucking away. Eyes closed. Ecstasy!

— It was a long session this evening, Lydia said.

— Four new members having their letters read. Takes a bit of time, Jenny said. Bless him. Wonderful little boy. Where's Ronnie?

— Ronnie wouldn't go to sleep, Lydia said. He could hear the singing from the chapel.

— Marvellous sermon, Jenny said, lifting her ungloved hand. Against the madness of war. And the childishness of it. And the pointlessness. It settles nothing. One war sows the seeds of another. He's got a following, Lydia. The whole church is behind him. And the church is growing.

Lydia moved to make herself more comfortable and her nipple slipped out of the baby's lips. His face quickly reddened with anger, but deftly with two fingers guiding it, Lydia put her nipple back on his lips. His mouth pulled at it greedily. Jenny watched fascinated. She wriggled her shoulders and looked into Lydia's face.

—Wonderful nipples you've got, Lydia, she said.

Lydia looked down blushing and yet smiling so that the dimples showed in her cheeks.

— It's something people don't think of, isn't it, when they talk about beauty?

She held her head to one side as she spoke as if she were canvassing support for her statement.

— My sister 'Melia had a lovely figure, she still has, but you know her nipples were so small she couldn't breast-feed. I think that's an awful shame. I mean it is one of the pleasures of motherhood, isn't it?

— It can be an awful nuisance, Lydia said.

— Yes but all these middle-class women buying tinned milk to keep their figures. I mean, I do believe that is wrong, I really do.

—Well this is certainly cheaper.

— And better! Of course it's better, I mean, I studied biology, my dear, so I know.

Lydia pulled a face half in pain and half smiling.

— Ooh, the little blighter!

— What's the matter?

Jenny looked puzzled and stretched forward to watch the baby more closely. He was kicking against the open palm of Lydia's hand.

— Ooh! Lydia said, wincing.

— What is it?

— He's biting me!

They both laughed happily. Lydia did not bother to conceal any of her breast any more. She began to play with the baby's bare feet. She shifted in her chair and let her head rest against the wall.

— I'm exhausted, she said. I couldn't get Ronnie to sleep. And this one was beginning to cry. Could you hear him in the chapel?

— Good heavens, no, Jenny said. He's not all that strong. Across the street . . .

— Gosh, I haven't put the kettle on. Joe will be in any minute. And look at the fire.

Jenny put her gloves and hymn-book on the dresser. She lifted the iron kettle.

— Does it need filling? she said. It's so heavy I can't tell.

— Don't you bother, Lydia said. You've got your new costume on . . .

— Good gracious, girl, what does that matter . . .

She held the kettle well out in front of her and made for the back kitchen.

— Goodness, it's dark in here, she called out.

— Don't look at the mess, Lydia said.

— This tap is stiff!

— I'll be in there all day tomorrow, Lydia said. Washing day!

— You ought to get help.

— I would if we could afford it, Lydia said. Look at my hands.

She held them both out, the baby resting on the crook of her arm, his feet still pushing, although the palm of her hand was no longer there. Jenny put the kettle carefully on the fire in the narrow grate and its weight made the ash fall noisily.

— My dear, I don't know how you manage.

She sat down and picked up a brass-handled poker to clean more ash away from the bottom of the fire. She put down the poker and said,

— No. I think I do really.

— I get so worn out, Lydia said. I fall asleep every evening.

— There are plenty who would change places with you.

— With me?

— They all think you're marvellous of course. I didn't mean that though. He always looks at you so lovingly.

Lydia laughed.

— He can't help that. He's always looked like that.

— It's so romantic somehow. He's like one of those film actors you know. All that fair hair and the serious way he looks. You know what I'm like. I always say what I think. It must be wonderful.

— Joe's all right.

Lydia slipped her breast back inside her bodice and lifted the baby up against her shoulder so that she could rub his back.

— It's wonderful, isn't it?

Jenny smiled and nodded eagerly. She had an unusually sharp nose and together with her habit of opening her eyes wide and lifting her eyebrows it gave particular emphasis to her expressions.

— That's where it is, you see. That's where the heart of the business lies from a woman's point of view. She must be deeply satisfied sexually.

Lydia pressed her burning cheek against the baby's shawl.

— I think friends should be able to speak openly and frankly about these things, Jenny said. I really do.

Lydia patted the baby's back and listened carefully, her head lowered as if she were prepared both to learn and to defend herself.

— I mean I don't know what your parents were like, Lydia, but mine brought me up as if I were a walking coat-hanger. You know, all wood from the neck down.

Lydia smiled as if it gave her pleasure to hear Jenny laughing. She widened her knees and laid the baby across them, his head pillowed against her thigh.

— I'm going to change him, Lydia said.

— They brought us up to feel guilty if we thought about it, let alone talked about it. You know my poor mother, I couldn't tell you what she thought was going to happen to her when she got married. She was literally terrified, and if you knew what she thought was going to happen to her in bed with a man you'd understand why. A shopkeeper's daughter from Swansea you see marrying a gentle enough young mate on a ship . . . You must have had some idea mustn't you — brought up on a farm.

— I suppose so, Lydia said. Could you open that cupboard please and pass me the jar of vaseline? And underneath there are some dry nappies.

Jenny reached everything that Lydia needed. She held the white nappy up to the fire to warm it. Lydia put two safety-pins in her mouth. As she did so she looked down with pleasure at the baby's buttocks.

— Isn't he sweet? Jenny said. She lifted the nappy and tried it against her cheek.

— I enjoy watching him, she said. It's strange really. You'd think I'd be jealous. A barren woman. That's me.

Lydia held out her hand for the nappy.

— Oh Jenny! You're young yet. You can't tell.

— I'm older than you are, Jenny said.

She sat down again, clasping her hands together and straightening her back.

— In a year I'll be thirty. We've been married six years you know, Morris and I.

She paused and her eyes, enlarged by the lens of her spectacles, seemed to take in every detail of the room and her gaze finally settled intently on Lydia's face.

— How often do you do it? she said.

Lydia looked down quickly at the point of the safety-pin passing through the bunched corner of the nappy. Her face became red.

— I know it's a thing I shouldn't ask, Jenny said, but you are my best friend, my only real friend in this place. In any case it's oftener than once a month. Isn't it?

Lydia nodded. She still appeared unable to look at Jenny's anxious face.

— Well that's what I get if I'm lucky, Jenny said. And never any satisfaction. Never.

Lydia lifted the baby to her shoulder again and began to rub his back. On the fire the water in the heavy kettle began to hum.

— Do you think I can get him to talk about it?

Jenny's lips tightened and her head shook sadly.

— An educated man you'd think. No more selfish than other men. He loves his politics of course. Loves debating. Fancies himself as a bit of a debater. But he never discusses it. Discusses anything. But not that.

Jenny raised her hand in a gesture of forbidding,

— Never.

The front door of the manse opened. They could hear J.T. inviting someone in as he turned up the wick of the small lamp that stood on the window-sill alongside the front door. The women looked at each other. Lydia looked guilty. Hastily she adjusted her bodice and buttoned up her blouse. Jenny held out her hands offering to hold the baby, but Lydia did not let him go.

— Here they are you see!

J.T. held back the draught-excluding curtain so that Morris Leyshon, who stood beside him, could see inside. He pushed his head forward. He had a round cheerful face of ruddy complexion He looked over the top of his spectacles to create a comic effect.

— Mrs Miles! How are you this evening? Both of you. Vernon Joseph and his mother.

His manner of speech was oratorial. He looked at J.T. seeking approval.

— You were in there longer than usual, Lydia said.

She smiled and invited Mr Leyshon to be seated.

— Thank you, no, he said. We shan't stay. Mr Miles will be needing a rest.

He looked at J.T. again.

— I'm fine, J.T. said.

— Marvellous sermon, tonight, Mr Leyshon said. Great! First class! 'And the Lord said unto Cain, Where is Abel thy brother? And he said, I know not. Am I my brother's keeper?' There's a text for you. A marvellous sermon.

— It was splendid, Mr Miles, Jenny Leyshon said.

She rose to her feet and picked up her hymn-book and gloves.

— It really was.

— Ronnie wouldn't go to sleep, Lydia said, looking intently at Joe. He could hear the singing in chapel.

— Why don't you two stay and have a bite with us, J.T. said.

His arm was still outstretched holding up the heavy curtain. He looked first at Morris and then at Jenny, who smiled very gratefully and shook her head.

— We'll leave you in peace, Mr Miles, she said.

— There's only cold meat and pickles, Lydia said. I haven't had time to make anything else.

— Thank you very much, no, Morris said. Come along, Jenny Leyshon. We are holding things up.

— No indeed, J.T. said, lifting the curtain higher as Jenny bent to pass under his arm. You know we are always very glad to see you.

Lydia rose to her feet and patted her baby's back gently, shifting her weight from one foot to the other as she rocked him to and fro.

— A SUMMER'S DAY! Pa said. A summer's day!

The sunlight glistened on his white beard. He lifted his stick to point out a ship far out at sea. But Ronnie had begun to run down the slope. He allowed his knees to give way and he lay on the thick grass, looking up at his grandfather's shape against the sky. He saw a head crowned with a hard hat and a stick with a silver collar pointing out to sea. His grandfather stood on the rise above the orchard that gave a clear view of more than ten miles of the coastal plain, of an eastern corner of Anglesey, of the Wirral, and on a clear day such as this one the most westerly curve of Lancashire and even the highest point of the Isle of Man. In the orchard, thick with apple blossom, Aunty Kate stood with a scarf wrapped around her head. She was waving to attract her father's attention, but the breeze blew her voice away and he did not turn. The sunlight glistened on the rich grass that was already long enough to be blown in one direction.

— Pa, she cried as she walked carefully upwards.

There were treacherous rabbit holes and purposeless hollows hidden by the fast-growing grass. At last he turned.

— Where's the boy? she said. I asked you not to let him out of your sight.

Pa smiled innocently and pointed down the slope with his stick.

— There he is, he said.

Kate came forward until she could see where Ronnie lay, his feet pointing upwards, his head lolling backwards.

— Get up at once! she cried. Ronnie! Get up! The grass is very damp.

Ronnie raised his legs and rolled head over heels. He sat up and blinked. Kate beckoned. He began to crawl up the slope.

— Dan Llew is here, Kate said.

Her father turned eastwards to look at the ironworks.

— The furnaces are out, he said.

He shook his head.

— They'll be hungry soon. And dangerous.

— He wants to borrow money, Pa. I can tell.

—They all buy newspapers on Sunday, Pa said. They want electric light and hot and cold water and indoor lavatories. They want heaven on earth. That's what it amounts to.

— He wants to buy more property in the High Street. Annie Grace told me — she never could keep anything to herself. Now listen, Pa. He's not to have it.

— He's got an eye for business, Pa said.

— It's all he thinks about, Kate said.

— Doesn't bury his talent in the ground, Pa said.

Ronnie gripped the bottom of his aunt's skirt. She leaned sideways to pull his hand away, finger by finger and then hold it firmly in her own. Slowly the three of them started walking back to the house. Pa paused to point at the old house that stood alone now in the field beyond the L-shaped outhouses.

—When I was a boy, he said to Ronnie, I was trapped in there by a big black bull.

Ronnie looked up at his grandfather. He turned his head slowly to look at the old house. It had no windows or doors, but at a distance its sixteenth-century form seemed well preserved. In the front doorway, standing on a ramp of mixed dung, straw and old hay, a young heifer stood chewing the cud.

— Is that a bull? Ronnie said.

His grandfather laughed.

— Is it, Aunty?

— No, Ronnie. It isn't.

— Timorous, isn't he? Pa said.

Kate gave him a warning look.

— Clever but timorous. Takes after his father. I must say one thing for his mother, never was afraid of anything. She should have been a boy.

— Not even thunder, Kate said.

Her father frowned. He stood still for a moment as if searching for a quick answer that would explain away his fear of thunder and accuse her of disloyalty in mentioning it. No words came, only a cross look. He tried to quicken his pace, but they had arrived at the steps that led down from the orchard to the back yard and he had to move with care.

Dan Llew's motor-car was parked as near as he could get it to the front garden gate. It seemed bigger because of the sharp angle at which it was parked, the wheels turned by the outcropping rock and the hood so much larger than the body.

— Ned's here too! Kate said.

She pointed to a pony and trap that had been placed in the coachhouse. Pa seemed to make an effort to suppress any excitement. He stood still at the foot of the orchard steps, looked upwards and narrowed his eyes to examine the roof of the house, lifting his stick to where he imagined he could see a loose slate.

Ned and Dan Llew were standing in the kitchen. Ned wore his second-best overcoat and a bowler hat. He was frowning as Kate came in. He gave her a quick smile and a nod. Dan Llew was more at ease. He had a soft hat with the brim turned down all round and wore a long belted trench-coat.

— Who's this then? he said looking at Ronnie. Is this Lydia's boy?

They could hear Pa stamping his feet outside the back door as he always did.

— Take your hats off, Kate said quietly. You don't want to set him a bad example.

Her brothers sighed and removed their hats.

— I shan't be staying, Ned said.

He sounded as if he were making a statement of policy.

— It's all good building land anyway, Dan Llew said, turning the palm of his hand to the low fire in the grate.

He appeared to be concluding a conversation.

— Well boys, Pa said, making his way carefully down the three steps to the kitchen.

They both asked him how he was.

— Haven't been at all well. Have I, Kate?

Kate was helping him out of his overcoat. His sons moved aside hastily to make his way clear to the high-backed chair by the fire.

— Any news of Hugh?

He sat down heavily, lifting his eyes first to one son and then the other.

— I saw him last week, Dan Llew said. At the Abergele mart. He asked after everybody.

Pa looked at the fire and tightened his lips.

— He's only got to come and see me, he said. You can tell him that if you see him again.

— There's another kid on the way I believe, Dan Llew said.

— Dan . . ., Kate said in a warning voice.

She shot a glance at Ronnie, who stood listening, his mouth wide open and his eyes intent on catching the exact tone of each remark as it was made.

— He should never have married her, Ned said. A Catholic.

— Would you like to take a look at Uncle Dan's motor car?

Kate spoke to Ronnie. He nodded eagerly, watching his uncle's face, waiting for permission to run out and climb in the tourer.

— Don't touch anything, there's a good boy. You'd better go with him, Kate. I should think he's strong enough to release the brake. How old are you, boy?

— Five and a half, Uncle, Ronnie said.

— Time flies, Ned said.

— I thought I'd make you some tea, Kate said.

She tried to catch her father's eye, but he continued to stare at the fire in a melancholy way.

— Take him out, Ned said meaningfully. Just for a short while. I'll explain later.

— Would you like to go and play the piano, Ronnie? Kate said. Just for a short while.

— I want to see the motor, Ronnie said.

— Yes all right. You play the piano for a while and then I'll take you to see the motor.

She put her hand on the little boy's shoulder and guided him through the door.

— Play your little tune, Kate said. The one I taught you and we can hear from the kitchen. See! I'll leave the door open.

Ronnie nodded gravely and climbed up on the piano stool. As she came back to the kitchen, Ned was extracting a denominational weekly newspaper from his coat pocket. He unfolded it carefully as if he were looking at a speech he had prepared. Then he folded it up and put it back in his pocket.

— Is it true? Dan Llew said.

He nodded in the direction of the parlour. Kate stood in the door-way. Ronnie was knocking out the first notes on the damp piano.

— What?

Kate closed the door quietly.

— J.T. giving up three months' salary!

— Who told you?

Dan Llew looked at Ned.

— T. Machno Jones, Ystrad, Ned said.

He always enunciated ministers' names with relish.

— He'd seen Reese Blaenwaen at the Cardigan Presbytery, and he told him.

— Most of his congregation are colliers, Kate said.

— Sometimes I think he's not all there, Dan Llew said.

— He has principles, Kate said. He tries to live up to them.

— Make some tea, *merch-i,* Pa said. My throat is quite parched.

— You'll be telling me next he's a socialist, Dan Llew said. I mean to say his first duty is to his wife and children. Like any other man. He always wants to be different. I shouldn't say it because he's married to my sister, but I've never met a man who got on my nerves so much. Never.

Pa leaned forward and stirred the fire under the heavy kettle.

— I'd like a window there, he said as he leaned back in his chair.

He was pointing to the alcove over his right shoulder.

— Give me a chance to keep an eye on the yard without going outside. If either of you should see Wynne Bannister . . .

— Not him, Ned said. He charges the earth. He won't roll up his own sleeves. He's all pipe and trilby. That council-house conn-act has gone to his head. A craftsman should never give up working with his hands.

— I mean, what are they going to live on? Air?

Dan Llew snetched out his hand as if asking for an answer.

— This boy's up here. Living on you.

— We don't mind, Kate said quickly. We like having him, don't we, Pa?

— I'm not saying that. Then Lydia will be up here and the other child. The little one. Vernon is it? And they'll be here for two or three months. Mark my words. And you know what the next thing will be. They'll want a church near here. She won't stick it down there. The weather's good now. But just you wait. It will be hell on earth down there and she won't stick it. Then what happens?

— No use crossing your bridges until you come to them, Kate said.

— He's a modernist, you know, Ned said.

Once more he took the folded newspaper out of his pocket and took a peep at it. It was clear there was an article in it on which he wished to comment.

— Whatever that means, Dan Llew said.

— Reason before faith, that's what it means. Isn't that so Pa?

Pa nodded solemnly. He began to drum the arm of his chair with the tips of his fingers.

— A watched kettle never boils, he said.

— It's much worse in the South, Dan Llew said. They are on the very edge of revolution there, you know. On the edge. It would be just like that silly fool to get mixed up in it.

— Well, Kate said.

— He's a modernist, Ned said. There's no doubt about that.

— His first duty is to his wife and children. Isn't that so, Pa? His first Christian duty.

— They could stay with us, Ned said. We've got plenty of room at Cefn. Bessie and I would be glad to . . .

— Aunty! Aunty!

Ronnie was screaming in the parlour. Kate rushed out and Ned followed close behind her. They found Ronnie kneeling on the floor between the piano and the piano stool. His elbows rested on the stool. His hands were pressed together and his eyes distended.

—What's the matter?

Kate spoke sharply.

Ronnie pointed to the window and Kate turned to look. There was no one there.

— I saw a ghost, Ronnie said. A big ghost. It filled the window. The room went dark and I turned and saw it.

— What's the matter with him?

Dan Llew appeared in the doorway.

— I want my mam, Ronnie said.

His face was crumbling and tears bulged on the ends of his eyelashes.

— There you are, you see, Dan Llew said, looking at Kate.

Ned opened the front door.

— Look, he said, there was somebody there. The gate is open.

— Was it Tomi, do you think? Dan Llew said.

— It can't be Tomi, Ned said. I saw him down in Cae Pant as I was coming. He saw my cart. He waved to me.

— Come on then . . .

Kate sat in an armchair and tried to coax Ronnie on to her knee. He made himself heavy to lift.

— A white face, he said, and a white beard . . .

Ned and Dan Llew were outside in the front garden. Kate turned the chair in order to see through the window. Ronnie pushed his head under her arm so as not to look.

— There's Uncle Dan's car, Kate said. Look. You can see it. Nobody's touched it. Isn't it a nice colour? Do you like it? Shall we go and see it?

Ronnie went on shaking his head. Ned came back in the house.

—Tell Dan to come in and shut the door, Kate said.

— Kate!

Pa was calling from the kitchen.

Kate taised her voice impatiently.

—What is it, Pa?

— It's Jesse Hopkin. At the back door. What's all that crying about?

Pa appeared in the passage. Dan Llew closed the front door and wiped his feet on the mat.

— Be a man now, Pa said

— Boys don't cry, Dan Llew said. Take you in the car in a minute.

— Jesse Hopkin! Kate said. That's who he saw. Ronnie, did you hear that, love? Jesse Hopkin you saw. Pressing his dirty old nose at the window. Did he put his tongue out? Did he?

Ronnie nodded unwillingly.

— Comfort the poor and the homeless, Pa said in a pious voice.

— Never done a day's work in his life, Kate said.

—Your mother was always kind to him, Pa said. She was a very kind woman. Every spring he'd call. Like the cuckoo. Did you ever read *The Scholar-Gipsy* by Matthew Arnold?[80]

— I remember you reading it, Pa, when we were boys, Dan Llew said. About an old shepherd, wasn't it?

Pa frowned and lifted his finger.

—You never listened, he said.

They heard a series of loud knocks on the back door.

Listen to the cheek of him, Kate said. Knocking our door like that.

— Be charitable, Pa said. This man was in school with Sir Elis Gruffydd.[81]

— He's a lazy old liar, Kate said.

But Pa had hurried away to give the old tramp a formal welcome.

— He'll sit in the barn all day, listening to him, Kate said. And tomorrow he'll be sniffing with cold and complaining. Mark my words.

LYDIA WAS AT the front door of the terrace house, steering out the pram. She tipped it back to pass the front wheels over the strip of wood that kept out the draughts, and Vernon, well wrapped up for the walk, let his eyes roll back in order to see his mother's face. Out on the pavement Lizzie Williams, a fourteen-year-old, clasped her thin hands together in front of her and shook her bobbed hair out of her eyes after telling Beryl her younger sister to stand still.

— Don't let go, will you? Lydia said as she tucked the rug more tightly around Vernon. It hasn't any brakes you see. Which way are you going?

— Past the old Works we thought, Mrs Miles, Lizzie said. And along the path by Cwm Wood. Our Beryl can collect bluebells.

— Don't let go then, will you?

Jones, Pant Dairies, made a clicking noise and his horse shifted a few feet nearer as he worked his way down the terrace. Lydia turned to pick up a jug from the hallstand. She drew her cardigan more tightly around her and stepped into the street.

— A quart today please, Mr Jones, she said.

Mr Jones's left foot was in a surgical boot and he limped heavily as he moved around his milk float. The body was painted brown and the mudguards above the tall wheels were scrolled in yellow. He tipped the polished churn forward so that the milk poured more quickly into the jug and built a head of foam. The floor of the float was grey and damp with a mixture of mud from Mr Jones's boots and spilt milk.

— Nothing for the horse today, I'm afraid, Lydia said.

She handed Mr Jones two pennies and he dropped them into the pocket of his brown overall. Then he lifted his hand and scratched the stubble on his scrawny neck above the narrow white collar he wore without a tie.

— Saw Mr Miles's name in the *Western Mail* this morning, he said. Headlines. That report of his is making a stir. They are awful too, those houses in Big Street. I was just telling Mrs Protheroe, number ten, they ought to call it Pig Street.

— There are over a hundred families living there, Lydia said, they were all in favour of my husband's report, except Mrs Abel Elias.

— The Pentecostal,[82] Mr Jones said.

He was listening eagerly.

— Except her, Lydia said. 'Houses are things of this world, Mr Miles,' she said. 'When the Lord comes I shall dwell in his mansion for ever and ever.'

— What did Mr Miles say?

Mr Jones smiled and pushed his hand under his soft hat to scratch his head, so that the hat tilted over his nose.

— 'All right, Mrs Elias', he said, 'but what about the sick child next door?'

Mr Jones nodded approvingly.

— That was very good, he said.

Lydia retired into the house, balancing the jug carefully and closed the front door with her heel. She stood still at the foot of the stairs, listening. Then she walked through to her kitchen and stood the milk jug in an enamelled bowl of water on the tiled pantry floor.

The fire needed attention. She moved the tall fireguard carefully so that the small garments folded over it for airing should not fall off. She raked out the fire vigorously with a long steel poker. She lifted the iron handle of the oven door to examine the pie and the rice pudding cooking inside. She closed the door quickly and put more coal on the fire.

Again she paused. The door leading to the passage was open. She looked towards it as if she were expecting someone to appear.

She rinsed her hands in the bowl of water that stood in the sink and dried them on the roller-towel behind the back door. On her way upstairs she took off her cardigan. At the top of the stairs she paused and stared at the closed door of the back bedroom that J.T. used as a study. She turned and made for the front bedroom where she and her husband slept. As she was throwing back the bedclothes over the brass and iron rails at the foot of the bed, J.T. came in. He stretched himself and smiled, running his hand through the tousled waves of his hair. He went through the motions of simple drill but Lydia did not look at him.

— Can I help? he said. I feel like some exercise.

Lydia shook a pillow.

— Plenty of wood in the back, she said. I had to chop my own sticks this morning again.

— Yes, I'm very sorry about that.

J.T. put his hands in his pockets.

— Shall I turn the mattress? he said.

— I can manage, Lydia said.

He grasped the feather mattress, pulled it towards him and threw it right over. Then he bent down and began to thump it with his fists.

— All right, Lydia said, trying not to smile. Save some of your energy.

— Come on then, J.T. said. Let's hurry and we can take Vernon out for a walk.

— He's gone already, Lydia said. Lizzie Williams has taken him.

— Well let's go together then, J.T. said. We can do a little visiting at the same time.

He came around the bed to stand near her. She stooped to pick up from the floor a magazine she had been reading in bed the previous night. As she rose he put his arms around her and pulled her to him. He stroked her hair. She stood quite still as if to show she was patiently waiting for him to let her go.

— I like your hair short, he said.

— Do you? she said.

— It makes you look so young.

He put his hand on her breast and began to stroke it gendy. She pushed his hand away.

— There's a time for everything, she said.

— Last night, he said, you kept pushing my hand away. What's the matter?

— If you don't know there isn't any point in my trying to tell you, is there? Lydia said.

— I love you so much, J.T. said.

He gripped her shoulders strongly and forced her to face him. He tried to kiss her on the lips. She moved her head.

— You must tell me what's the matter, J.T. said. You keep pushing me away. I get obsessed with the things I've taken on. Is that what's the matter? I've got to do it, Lydia. All the suffering that goes unnoticed.

— Yes, Lydia said.

Her voice was toneless. She looked at his chest as she spoke and not at his eyes.

— You've made a man of me, he said, trying to be light-hearted and make her smile. I was never any good at preaching until I married you.

His hands were caressing her. She shook her head stubbornly. He whispered with his lips on her ear:

— You know how much I want you. I need you, Lydia. This very minute I need you and you know I need you.

— I'm not just a fancy woman, Lydia said.

J.T. let her go. She marched out of the room. He rushed after her.

— What do you mean? he said. I don't understand you. What do you mean?

— I don't understand you either, Lydia said.

She was in the boy's room, throwing the bedclothes off Vernon's cot.

— What is it, Lydia? he said. What's the matter?

— On Saturday I'll be gone, Lydia said. Vernon and I will be on the way north to Argoed and you can have the place to yourself.

— Why are you talking like this?

— That's what you want. So that everybody will say 'Look at the sacrifice he's making! Forgoing his salary for another two months. Wonderful man. lives for his church. Lives for the miners. Won't touch the money contributed by the owners'.

— Lydia.

— Doesn't matter about us, does it? We don't count.

She made a gesture that included the cot and Ronnie's bed.

— It's nearly seven weeks since I've seen my boy, Lydia said. My own boy . . .

She sat down on Ronnie's bed. J.T. struggled to speak. He sat down beside her. He took her in his arms awkwardly. She pulled herself away and buried her face in Ronnie's pillow. Her shoulders shook, and the pillow muffled her crying. J.T. lay beside her, determined to soothe her. He stroked her body and rubbed her back and when at last she turned her warm tear-stained face towards his, he kissed her lips.

— As we always were, he whispered. As we always were.

When he began to undress her, she held his wrist in her hands.

— Not now, she said. No. Someone might call. No. Not now.

— Yes, he said. Now. It must be now.

Her head lay on the pillow, watching him, her eyes wide as if they were exploring mysteries in his face and as if she were trying not to listen to the continuous murmur of his voice caressing the idea of her as tenderly as his body was treating hers. Then her eyelids closed. Her brow furrowed in response to what he was doing and her lips parted so that her quickened breathing could develop in a moan and a quiet cry that in turn compelled him to increase the power of his thrust until a sweat born of effort and restraint broke out over his face, which sank closer to hers. Their lips found each other again. Their breath and their tears mingled.

They lay still and silent alongside each other, her hand held tightly in his. In the street there was the noise of argument between a trades-man and a group of strikers setting out for walk on the mountain-side with their greyhounds.

— Why can't they go back to work? Lydia said.

J.T. rolled over towards her and lifted his hand to stroke her hair.

— There's no excuse for not working, Lydia said. I work hard enough. Why shouldn't they?

— It's not as simple as that, J.T. said.

He spoke as gently as he could.

— For less pay and for longer hours, J.T. said. These are free men not slaves. A free man must have a fair price for his labour. Especially when it's all he's got.

— What about me? Lydia said. Am I free or am I a slave? My hus-band works longer hours for no pay. Now just tell me what I am. Am I free or am I a slave? A slave to all these people.

— What we do, J.T. said patiently, we do voluntarily — of our own choice.

— My choice! Lydia said.

She sat up.

— I like that, she said.

— No, wait a minute. Wait a minute, my sweet.

J.T. tried to pull her down, but she resisted. He sat up alongside her.

— They have no choice, he said. They are being driven. Being driven like animals. They've got to stick up for themselves. And I've got to be with them, Lyd. On their side.

Lydia jumped off the bed. Angrily she began to put her clothes back.

— A man like you has no business to get married, she said.

J.T. pushed his fingers through his hair and smiled.

— You think I'm joking, don't you? she said. Well I'm not. And I'm right. Look at you now ten o'clock on a Monday morning.

J.T. got up to pull on his trousers.

— You're supposed to be a minster, Lydia said. And you've got no shame. No shame at all . . .

There was a knock at the front door.

— There you are, she whispered fiercely. What did I tell you . . .

— I'll go, J.T. said.

— I could hit you, Lydia said. I could really. I could hit you.

18

GWYNETH PRESSED HER foot down on the brake. The temporary traffic light was red. A row of cars waited their turn to cross the bridge. It was paved with wooden planks that rattled noisily as each car crossed it. On the right a bulldozer worked up and down the foundation of the new road that was being built up to a higher level with the soft stone of a nearby quarry. Dan Llew stared at the machine as it jerked its way forward on its caterpillar tracks, a wave of stones dancing in front of its wide steel jaw.

— I should have gone the other way, Aunty, Gwyneth said.

Kate nodded and stretched her fingers inside her gloves.

— It doesn't matter, she said.

— So many cars on the road now, Gwyneth said. Whatever way you go. It's all going to grind to a halt soon.

Gwyneth turned her head to smile at J.T. and Dan Llew who sat in the back.

— A chap on our staff has written a play about it, she said.

— Is that so? In Welsh I hope?

J.T. grasped the back of Kate's seat and drew himself upright to demonstrate interest.

— Oh yes. The idea is that petrol loses its inflammability. Won't burn any more. Because of cosmic rays, or something. So cars are stranded all over the place. And horses become very valuable. It's a good idea, isn't it? He was telling me about it last week. It's going to be broadcast.

J.T, was smiling as he listened.

—Very original, he said.

— Far-fetched, I'd say, Kate said.

She stared gloomily through the windscreen at the back of the car in front. It was a broad saloon and a woman with a beehive hair-do on the bench seat in front leaned her head very carefully on the driver's shoulder. Fumes escaped from the exhaust as the engine was still running. Kate lifted a gloved hand to point.

—Why doesn't he switch off? she said.

— I was going to suggest, Gwyneth, J.T. said, when we got back. A very dear old friend of mine has died in Anglesey . . .

— Old friend? Kate said. You said yourself you'd only seen him twice in the last fifty years.

—Very old friend, J.T. said determinedly.

Dan Llew tapped Gwyneth's shoulder.

— Turn off down there.

He smiled widely for the first time since they had persuaded him to get in the car. He nodded encouragingly in the direction of a muddy lane that led to a quarry in the hill-side. Gwyneth looked at her aunt.

— There's a grab working in there, Dan Llew said.

He made a gesture of grabbing so that they could all clearly understand what he meant.

—You never saw anything like it. Like a crane, you know, with a stiff neck, and it takes great bite out of the hill-side. Great bites and drops them straight into a big lorry and they just drive it down the lane there and tip it straight on the road. You never saw anything like it. I went in to see it last time I was up here. I worked it out you know . . .

He seemed dissatisfied with the quality of attention that Kate and Gwyneth were paying him and he turned to address J.T. as the only other man present.

— In my father's day it would have taken six men ten hours to do what that thing does in ten minutes.

J.T. opened his mouth while Dan Llew stared intently at his face as if to measure the degree of his wonder. He turned to Gwyneth and tapped her on the shoulder again.

— It would be worth your while seeing it. An education. Nobody's too old to learn.

— It's a private road I think, Uncle . . .

— Private road nothing. It belongs to Will Hanks. I lent him two hundred to buy a second-hand lorry. I started him off, girl, and look at him now. He'll end up a millionaire you know.

Kate gave Gwyneth a warning look.

— I like to see things for myself, Dan Llew said. Remember during the war, Kate, when the Jerries were bombing Liverpool. I used to watch it all night from the roof of the old house. Won't take a minute.

— The lights have changed, Kate said,

She gave Gwyneth a nudge followed by a quick nod. The car jerked forward.

— Gwyneth's got to go to Ruthin, Dan, Kate said.

She lifted her voice without turning her head.

— Urgent business, she said. Isn't it, Gwyneth?

— Yes, Aunty.

Gwyneth nodded and steered her car after the broad saloon over the bridge. When they had crossed the bridge Dan Llew sat back frowning, his mouth open, his relaxed body jerked first one way and then the other by the uneven surface of the track. Unlike J.T. he made no attempt to hold the passenger strap that hung from the column between the door and the side window. Instead his hands hung limply between his legs.

— It's all based on appetites, J.T. said.

He pointed at the garish hoardings that had been erected at intervals on the grass banks around the roundabout.

— Seems dangerous to me, Gwyneth said. Taking people's attention from the road.

— He's asleep, J.T. said.

Dan Llew's eyes had closed and his mouth hung open.

— Best thing for him, Kate said.

She shook her head sadly.

— It's a shame to see him like this. It's very sad you know, Gwyneth, to be the last one of a large family left with all your senses.

— Best of the bunch, isn't she, Uncle? Gwyneth said.

She half turned to address J.T., who smiled, nodded sagely and shook the strap he was holding with his left hand in one handed applause.

— Look out! Kate said sharply.

Gwyneth swerved left and the driver of the car approaching them blew his horn angrily as he passed. The road was narrow with a high wall and a fringe of trees beyond the ditch.

— Sorry, Aunty, Gwyneth said.

— I'm not afraid of dying, Kate said, but I don't see why I should have to take you as well.

Kate turned her head so that the rim of her hat should not prevent her examining the view through the door window.

— Look at that wall, she said.

A section of the high wall had recently fallen and the stones still lay in a mound that was blocking the ditch. Gwyneth drove her car slowly along the narrow road.

— It's years since I've been along here, Gwyneth said. That's Bodafon Hall, isn't it?

— Can't see anything like that without wanting to get out and clean it up, Kate said. Pa was the same. Except he always got somebody else to do it, of course.

— It's a training place for boxers or something, isn't it? Gwyneth said.

Kate turned around to look at Dan Llew and J.T.; Dan Llew had opened his eyes again. The word 'boxers' seemed to have caught his interest.

— My sister Kate nearly married Archie Griffiths, Bodafon Hall, he said to J.T. Pity she didn't really. He was a bit of a fool, but she'd have had the lot. He went bankrupt you know in 1931[83] and he shot himself. Put the gun in his mouth.

Gwyneth pulled a face.

— Oh Uncle, she said. *Ych a fi.*

— Funny thing, Dan Llew said, both my sisters married fools. What's the date today, Alice?

— The date? Gwyneth said.

She licked her lips and stared at the road as if she were too embarrassed to look at her aunt.

— August the twenty-second, isn't it? Gwyneth said.

— Um.

Dan Llew's jaw fell as if he were trying hard to remember something.

— Somebody's birthday I suppose, he said.

They were all silent. The rhythm of the car's motion seemed to impose silence upon them. It made steady progress now down the straight coast road, moving in the inside lane and frequently overtaken.

To their right lay the golf links, the sand dunes and the sea. Dan Llew lived in a new bungalow he had built in the best residential area of the next town.

—There were ten of us you know, really, Kate said suddenly. There was one before Ned. He died of convulsions. People didn't understand things in those days. Fool of an old doctor we had. Then there was Richard. Between Dan Llew and Rowland. I can't remember him. Meningitis he had. And there was a baby after Lydia. Only lived for three weeks. Wasn't even christened. Ma was so poorly.

Gwyneth glanced up into her driving-mirror. She saw her Uncle Dan Llew's eyes were closed. She leaned towards Kate.

— Did you hear him call me by my mother's name? she said.

— He wants to go back all the time, Kate said. It's very embarrasing sometimes. This housekeeper of his, Mrs Wilson, she keeps on talking English to him all the time. You know what he said to me last week, 'Kate,' he said, 'there's a strange woman keeps on coming into my bedroom, I want you to get her out of here.' . . . 'She's your housekeeper, Dan,' I said, 'Mrs Wilson. She's been with you since 1952.'. . . 'I don't like the look of her,' he said. 'Get her out of here.'

— Perhaps we should have gone up to Argoed, Gwyneth said. Taken him up, I mean, just for the ride.

— Can't bear to see the place, Kate said. Houses on both sides of the road. The orchard gone. The Old House pulled down. Think of that! Standing there all that time. Just knocked it down. Said it wasn't safe. And that John Arnold, he never thinks of coming to see his father. Only when he wants money. Norman is a much nicer boy. Mind you John Arnold is the favourite. He cheats his father every day that God sends, but he's still the favourite. And there's poor Norman with all his troubles never fails to visit his father every day and Dan hardly gives him a thank-you.

Kate stopped talking. Gwyneth treated her silence with respect. J.T. looked through the window, studying the view with what appeared to be interest and pleasure.

— I know business is business, Kate said. But I can't forgive John Arnold selling Argoed the way he did. I can't think how he ever got round his father. Greed, I suppose. Dan never could resist money.

— It must be awful for you, Aunty, to see the place.

— I never go near there, Kate said. I never think of it. What's past is past. That's what I say.

— Still, Gwyneth said, looking nostalgically at the road ahead. The old days. The old style. There was a lot to be said for it.

— We all had our jobs of course. Kate spoke in a business-like tone. Every Tuesday Ned took the wagon down to the Black Parlour for a load of coal. He used to tip it any old how against the coal-house wall on the orchard side and poor Lydia and I used to shovel it in. Hard work for girls, you know. Rowland was the chief cow-man. He always named the cows. Lady this or lady that every one of them. Lady Smith, Lady Somerset, Lady Bannerman, Lady Fach and Lady Fawr. John Henry's very like his father in that.

— How do you mean, Aunty?

Gwyneth leaned her head to one side without taking her eyes off the road.

— Always naming things. He gave everything a name.

Gwyneth looked into the driving-mirror. Dan Llew had snorted. He was still asleep.

— I thought he'd woken up for a minute. I expect he's tired out after walking.

— Dan did the killing in the Old House. I remember one winter when Tomi Moch was ill I had to hold the candle for him. Sticking sheep he was. Very fast worker. The blood pouring into an old bucket always looked black. Ned and Isaac Parry did the ploughing until Hugh was old enough. He was very keen. I started butter-making when I was twelve. Mary Parry Rice's hands. She had eczema and Pa didn't fancy it. Griff liked being with the horses until he went to college. He was a good worker, Griff. Used to show off he was so strong. Dan Llew had his own hens you know in the orchard. Sold the eggs and kept the money. Very tight he was in those days. Mad about money. I don't know what Pa did really. He just told everybody else what to do. He was very particular. Like a woman in the house. Couldn't bear dust and dirt. Poor Lyd and I, we worked very hard really. The whole place shone, you know, and when the windows were open in summer and the garden was in good trim — Ned liked the garden — the whole place smelled very sweet. I used to like the smell.

— Think of them changing the name, J.T. said, bearing his weight on the strap as he leaned forward.

— Name's got nothing to do with it, Kate said abruptly.

She seemed to resent the fact that J.T. had joined in the conversation.

— Well it has, you know, he said.

He pulled on the strap so that his back straightened.

— All the past is in a name, he said. What else is there left? Names. They're very important. Words. *Argoed, Argoed, y mannau dirgel . . .*[84] The man who wrote the first history of the Tudor family was born in that old house.[85] Elis Gruffydd his name was. He lived through the siege of Calais.[86]

— In the Old House? Kate said.

— There's every reason to believe it, J. T. said.

— Well I was born and bred on the place, Kate said, and I never heard of it.

— There was an article about it, J. T. said. In the thingummy transactions.

— Out-house really. Just a shelter for feeding-store cattle. That's all I remember it. And as a slaughter-house of course.

— That was centuries ago, J. T. said, raising his voice.

— All right, Kate said. We haven't all had as much education as you've had.

She turned her head to look at Gwyneth.

— Not everybody's interested in history, she said. We can't be forever living in the past.

19

WITH HIS TONGUE out, the small boy was drawing at the kitchen table. His straight hair hung down over his eyes and his left leg was bent underneath him. Jenny Leyshon also had her elbows on the table and as she stretched her neck like a teacher to see more closely what Vernon was doing, her bead necklace swung to and fro. A draught from the back door had started a black patch on the glowing mantle of the Aladdin lamp[87] and a tongue of yellow flame was edging through it, but Jenny was too intent on Vernon's pencil to notice. He was drawing a castle, the walls of which ran so close to the edges of his paper that the pencilled men who covered the battlements were very tiny, and the flags on top of the towers at each end were squashed squares with crossed lines on them. Across the bottom of the sheet arrows flew through the air in broken arches, and two lumps with four lines sticking out of the larger of them represented a dead horse.

There was also an oil-lamp on the wide mantelpiece above the fire-place and in an armchair Ronnie sat with a finger in his nose reading *The Boy's Magazine*. On the pink cover of the magazine there was a picture of British Tommies with fixed bayonets leaping down into a German trench. At the bottom of the page German soldiers in their sinister steel helmets cringed, and their shaded faces crumpled with abject fear.

At the other side of the fire-place Lydia sprawled in her chair, caught by sleep with one arm stretched towards the basket cradle in which her third child was sleeping; and with the other resting against the top of the high fire-guard. Her sleeves were rolled up as if she would wake up to find she had more work to do. From the oven there was a smell of a rice pudding baking.

Jenny looked over her shoulder and saw that Lydia was sleeping. She smiled compassionately and when Ronnie looked up from his comic, she put her finger to her lips and smiled. The boy looked down and continued reading without returning her smile. Jenny put her fist under her chin and smiled at Vernon who had begun to draw a large portcullis in the empty middle of the drawing. His pencil paused for a moment as he looked up and smiled and then continued to draw deep lines into the paper.

When the front door opened, the yellow flame spurted out of the mantle and Jenny put out her hand quickly to turn down the wick. J.T. was talking loudly and cheerfully to a companion, but Lydia slept on. Jenny went up to her and shook her by the shoulder. Lydia sat up quickly.

— It's your husband, Jenny said. He's got somebody with him. Lydia got up and felt along the mantelpiece for a comb.

— He's always doing this, she said.

She was frowning crossly.

— Is there anything I can do? Jenny said.

Lydia shook her head, looking down at Ronnie. She pointed at his comic with her comb.

— Put that out of sight, she said, or it will go on the fire like the last one.

Ronnie pushed the comic under the cushion of his chair.

— Have you finished your homework? Lydia said. He'll want to know, you know.

— I haven't got any tonight, Mam.

— Well find a good book then. Don't let's have any bother.

J.T. opened the door and ushered in a well-dressed youthful looking man with thinning hair. The visitor came through the door in two long steps and then stood to one side, modestly rubbing his hands together and smiling faintly. The flame of the table lamp was still lowered and in the shadows the visitor's light brown tweed glowed in cheerful contrast to J.T.'s sombre black rain-proof.

— Every time someone opens the front door that thing goes black, J.T. said.

He pointed at the table lamp. Vernon continued to be absorbed in his drawing, his head nearer than ever to the paper.

— They told us when we moved not to bother with gas. Electricity was due any day. It still hasn't arrived.

J.T. laughed cheerfully. He began to speak English.

— Now let me see, he said. This is our new doctor, Lydia. Doctor Cyril Brice. He doesn't speak Welsh, I'm afraid, but otherwise he's fully qualified. A native of Abergavenny.

The doctor moved nearer to Lydia to shake hands.

— And this is our great friend, Mrs Leyshon. I think . . .

— We've met, Jenny said.

She smiled and nodded approvingly until the doctor took her hand.

— This is Ronald, J.T. said. Our eldest. And this is Vernon, his brother.

J.T. put his hand on Vernon's shoulder as the doctor shook hands with Ronnie. Vernon went on drawing.

— Who's this down here?

The doctor squatted down on his haunches to take a close view of the sleeping baby. His knee touched the edge of the basket and the cradle tottered slightly on its mahogany rockers, but the baby did not wake up.

— Fine-looking baby, he said. Boy or girl?

— That is our Thea, J.T. said. Our little girl. Six months.

— Five, Lydia said.

— Is it really? J.T. said.

He sounded surprised, as if it were a baby in another family.

The doctor straightened himself and came over to the table to see what Vernon was doing. They watched in silence for a few moments. Jenny Leyshon joined them. She whispered to the doctor.

— He's our little dreamer.

Ronnie looked up sharply, trying to catch what she was saying.

— Interesting, is it not, what goes through a child's mind? J.T. said. All this hidden aggression. Where does it come from? These comics are full of it, of course.

The doctor nodded.

— How old is he?

He turned this time to Lydia. His questions sounded clinical. His manner was gentle and yet deeply serious. He rarely smiled.

— Six and a half, Lydia said.

— Doctor Brice is all for the clinic[88] J.T. said. He has a very good idea too. Since you are here, Mrs Leyshon. Both you ladies I mean . . .

His finger waved between Lydia and Jenny.

— Shall I tell them?

He grinned at the doctor. Ronnie moved so as to get a better view of the doctor's face. He seemed fascinated by the stillness of the doctor's mouth.

— He thinks you two ought to go down and give evidence at the County Council. The Memorial Hall is finished. What better use could it be put to, say, two or three mornings a week? A mother's clinic! I was telling Doctor Brice as we came along, his predecessor, old Doctor Parry, was a splendid man in many many ways, but he just pooh-poohed this clinic idea from the start. More of a country squire he was than a scientist, I would say. Always wore breeches and thick stockings and boots, seven days of the week. A keen churchman he was who never went to church. Never in a hurry.

— Well that's always a good thing.

The doctor spoke so quietly they all looked at his face as if to make certain he had spoken. His lips were still again.

— The study fire is very low, J.T. said to Lydia. Would you mind if we had a cup of tea in here?

— No, really.

This time Dr Brice spoke more loudly and lifted his hand to forestall any activity.

— I must get back. My sister is expecting me. This meeting lasted much longer than I expected.

— Have a cup in hand, Lydia said.

She had woken up fully now and she was smiling.

— Next time.

He turned back in the doorway and gave a smile which was the warmer because it was unexpected. J.T. followed and overtook him in the passage in order to get to the front door first. Lydia touched Jenny's shoulder and motioned her into the back kitchen so that they could speak without being overheard by the children.

— He's very nice, isn't he? Jenny said.

She peered closely into Lydia's face. The light from the small lamp on the nail above the sink was very dim.

— Jenny, Lydia said. Don't say anything in front of Joe about the money.

—You mustn't worry, Jenny said. Of course I won't.

— I'll give it you back next month. I just couldn't bear the boys not to have new boots. I just. . .

Jenny put her hand on Lydia's arm.

— Now listen, she said. We're friends, aren't we? So not another word about it.

WYNNE BANNISTER WALKED backwards down the stairs. His arms were raised and his hands were held apart the width of a coffin. At the corner he tapped the narrow end of the stair-treads with the toe-cap of his brown boot.

— They'll need to be very careful on this corner, Miss Jones, he said.

Kate frowned anxiously and bit her lip. She opened the stair-door wider, the fingers of her right hand clutching awkwardly at the door's edge.

— Oh dear, Kate said. I wouldn't want . . . it would be awful if. . .

—You mustn't worry, Mr Banister said.

He continued to move backwards carefully. A briar pipe that stuck out from the corner of his mouth wagged up and down as he spoke. He stood still and let his hands rest on his hips. The sleeve buttons of his jacket were undone so that his shirt-sleeves could be turned up. The backs of his hands were freckled like his narrow face. He passed a strong hand over his thinning ginger hair.

— I'll go over it very carefully with them, he said. No mistakes. No accidents. Everything taken care of.

He reached the bottom of the stairs and placed a fatherly hand on her shoulder.

—You've had a very trying time, I know, he said. I've seen a lot of sorrow, a lot of grief. In the war you know, my best friend was shot. Right beside me. I just couldn't believe it. I put my head over the parapet. I didn't care whether I'd get shot or not. I wanted to kill the man who killed my best friend. I was older than the others, you see. That's why they made me a sergeant. They offered me a commission, but I didn't want it.

— Would you like a cup of tea? Kate said.

— If it's no trouble, Mr Banister said.

In the kitchen he stood by the dresser while Kate made a pot of tea. He wore a brown suit and his arm was stretched out along the dresser in a self possessed but friendly attitude, so that his physical presence loomed large in the room.

— It's been a terrible shock for you, Mr Banister said. A terrible shock. And none of your brothers home any more. And your sister living in South Wales.

Kate pressed the kettle on to the coals of the fire, resting her forehead against the back of her hand which lay flat against the oak chimney beam below the high mantelshelf.

— The doctor said he had no pain, she said. I'm glad of that. He was afraid of pain.

— Everybody respected him, Mr Bannister said. Everybody. Lords and tramps. Liberal and Conservative. I know this doesn't sound right, but I'd like to tell you a funny story about him. Doesn't seem right though now, does it?

— I don't mind, Kate said.

He moved away respectfully as she approached the dresser to reach for cups and saucers.

— It's an old story of course, Mr Bannister said. I dare say you've heard it. About the watch and the threepenny bit?

— Oh yes . . . yes. I have heard it.

Kate smiled sadly. Mr Bannister watched her pouring the tea.

— I have a suggestion about the bearers, Miss Jones, he said. Your poor father was a justice of the peace for many years. Now I remember very well when I was a lad working in Ruthin I saw a funeral and all the bearers were policemen in their uniforms. It looked very fine, I thought. I don't know whether your brothers would approve but I think it would be . . .

— I think it's a very good idea, Kate said. I know I would like it.

But who would . . .

— You could leave all that to me, Miss Jones.

— Well I don't. . .

— It's most important for you not to worry.

Kate handed him his cup of tea and held the sugar bowl towards him. He took three teaspoonfuls of sugar. He seemed to read a degree of surprise on her face.

— I'm afraid I've got a sweet tooth, he said.

Kate lowered her eyelids and pressed her hands together, tightening her lips.

— You must take a cup too, he said.

— I couldn't, Kate said. I really couldn't.

— Well . . . he said sighing.

He smiled and put the cup of tea down on the kitchen table, opening his right hand with the palm outwards and the bowl of his pipe wedged between his fingers. His thin cheeks creased many times and his clean false teeth seemed to add to his charm.

— If you don't, he said, I won't.

Kate shook her head slowly.

— The trouble with you is you're too hard on yourself. Come on. Let me pour it.

He stretched out a hand towards the teapot on the table. Kate picked it up and poured herself a cup of tea. She added very little milk and no sugar.

— Do you mind if I sit down?

They sat at each end of the table; Mr Bannister on the settle, set at right angles between the window and the door that was three steps up; Kate in Pa's chair at the narrower end of the kitchen, nearest the fire.

— There's nothing like the sadness of a bereavement.

Mr Bannister spoke after a long silence when only the noise of the teaspoon stirring the teacup disturbed the afternoon silence of the house.

— Sometimes people think we're hard. Measuring and all that. They make jokes about it. I'm a builder first, as you know, and an undertaker second, but that is something I can never understand. It's the sadness . . . The long farewell . . . I'm not a very religious man as anybody can tell you. The war did something to me. But I'm a loyal churchman. I know your religion means a great deal to you, Miss Jones. My mother was a Methodist and she was a very pious woman.

But death is no joke, Miss Jones, it's one great . . .

He held the teacup in one hand and sketched a curving gesture with the other.

— . . . one great cloud of sorrow for those who are left behind. When I lost my dear wife, Miss Jones, you know I never thought I'd lift my head up again. We married so young you see. There I was with three young children on my hands. I never thought I'd survive. Not for one minute. And yet I made my mind up. I built a business. My father left me nothing you see. I built up a business from nothing. It's bigger than I can manage to tell you the truth. I shouldn't be sitting here now. I should be in Rhyl by rights, on the site. Men slack, you know, if they think you're not keeping an eye on them.

— It was very good of you to come, Mr Bannister, Kate said.

— Oh no, no, no. The least I could do for your father's memory. I told Birch down at the works, I said, 'I'll see to this one myself out of respect.'

— Is that Maldwyn Birch? Kate said.

—That's right. One of my foremen. Good lad. Do you know him? He's from here of course. This very village. They tell me his mother used to drink and still does on the quiet. But I've never held that against him. He's a good worker. Conscientious. Never late. And a real craftsman. Has a feeling for wood.

— He used to sing, Kate said, didn't he?

— I believe he's a precentor at the Wesleyan chapel at Llan.[89] A very good man.

Kate looked at her hand as it lay on the table, and nodded. Bannister was silent. He tapped his lower lip with the stem of his pipe and then lifted the cup of tea to his lips, his blue eyes taking a look around the room and then coming to rest on Kate's lowered head. It was so quiet they could hear the slow tick of the grand-father's clock in the hall, and outside in the back yard beneath the water cistern, the clucking murmur of a broody hen.

—You know what would give you a lot more light in this room, Miss Jones? A nice little window at the end there.

He pointed shrewdly with the stem of his pipe to the narrow wall beyond her head.

—You'd get the sun you see in the afternoon. And you could see everything that went on in the yard from where you're sitting.

Kate pressed her chin against her chest. It seemed several moments before he realized she was sobbing. He jumped to his feet, but she pushed her chair round so that her back was turned to him. She held one hand rigidly over her right eye while her other searched the two pockets of her dark skirt for a handkerchief.

— Miss Jones . . . he said.

— I'll be all right. Just leave me be.

—Yes, of course . . .

He touched her shoulder. She shook off his hand.

— Leave me be, she said. Leave me be.

—Yes, of course . . .

He stood still. He sighed deeply.

— I know what sorrow is, he said. I was left alone. Utterly alone. I've seen the depths, Miss Jones. But if you want me to leave, of course I'll go.

He paused. Kate did not look up.

— I'll just make one suggestion. For your benefit I think, or I wouldn't make it. I'll go outside. With your permission I'll walk to the rise above the orchard and I'll wait for you there. Then perhaps we could take a walk down to the old school. My mother went there, you know, long before you were born of course. She used to tell me they used to eat the water-cress that grew in the tiny stream at the bottom of Argoed Wood. Now we could go down together. Perhaps not as far. But in the open air we could talk, Miss Jones. You've got to talk at a time like this. Much better out of doors on a day like this, with death in the house.

He stopped abruptly. On the dresser in the hall he picked up his hat. The staircase door hung open. Tactfully he tiptoed back to close it. He looked into the kitchen. Kate still sat facing the narrow wall and she still held her hand pressed against her eye socket. On tiptoe again, he made for the front door, his brown boots squeaking, measuring silence. He opened the door quietly. A grasshopper leapt off the warm flagstone before the door and settled on the wall of the house. He stepped forward without closing the door and turned to look at the windows with the blinds pulled down. He broke off a piece of grey-green shrub, called 'old man's memory', that grew alongside the path and held the fine leaves to his nose to enjoy the smell.

AS IT MOVED off from the village square the broad-bottomed bus backfired so loudly that the children standing outside the General Stores all jumped and a terrier dog that had been sniffing the exhaust pipe scampered off down a side street, whimpering with fright. Inside the swaying vehicle the Reverend T. Machno Jones grabbed the luggage rack and smiled down at J.T., who sat next to the window. J.T. was wearing a grey hat and coat and clasping an umbrella between his knees.

— I'm not sure that I should sit next to you, he said.

T. Machno Jones was tall and thin. He was ten years older than J.T. and when he addressed him in the second person singular, he made it sound as if he were talking to an irresponsible young person. J.T, folded his arms and made more room on the hard seat.

— Doubts, J.T. said, are part and parcel of faith.

— Not everybody rushes into print with them, T. Machno Jones said. It's our business not to confuse our flocks, in my opinion.

He turned his head to look at J.T. and smile again. He hitched up his well-pressed trousers.

—You see I'm being perfectly frank with you.

J.T. had begun to blush. He breathed deeply and then grasped his ribs tightly with his outspread hands.

— The church isn't an ostrich, he said. The world is being pulled inside out. We can't close our eyes and say nothing is happening.

— The gospel is the gospel, T. Machno Jones said. The same yesterday today and forever. Saving men's souls. That's our task. I shall be speaking today, Miles. I'm glad we are making the journey down together. I want you to understand there is nothing personal in any attack I may feel compelled to make on your position. Everybody agrees that you are a good man and an excellent pastor. You are popular. Your people are with you and that is always a good thing. Some people suggest that you are dragging politics into the church . . . .

Protest burst out of J.T.'s lips.

— But I never, never . . .

— I know this is untrue. And I shall say so today. I shall say so.

— Bad housing is immoral, J.T. said. Making people starve is immoral. Near me there is a district of over two hundred houses, two families in most of them and more than sixty per cent of the men out of work. The average income is thirty shillings a week, the average family five and the average rent seven and sixpence. That's immoral.

— Quite so. Quite so.

— And it's our job to say so.

—Well it's not quite as simple as that, is it?

T. Machno Jones turned his head stiffly to look at J.T. and smile again. Their bodies bounced in their seats as the bus drove over pot-holes in the narrow road.

— You know, Miles, I may be called 'dry as dust' by people who should know better, but I do claim to have a clear mind. As I see it our denomination is threatened by two diseases. One is heresy. And the other is sentimentality. And of the two, I think the latter is the worse. Soft religion is bad religion, just as soft apples are bad apples. Look at this man Thomas. The most popular preacher we have today. And what are his sermons? Sentimental anecdotes from start to finish. I heard him last night at Forth. It was appalling. That story about not shooting any crows flying from Llantrisant. 'Don't shoot any living creature that comes from the direction of Llantrisant.' 'Why not, sir?' says the hired man. 'Because mother came from Llantrisant.' The people loved it of course. Absolutely loved it. Now I maintain stuff like that can silt up the river of faith faster than the time it takes to spread it abroad. There are eight deadly sins in Wales, Miles. Eight not seven. And the eighth is sentimental vulgarity.

J.T. frowned until his eyes were shut. He breathed deeply and shook his head.

— There's been so much poverty, he said, and so little education. I attach more and more importance to the Sunday School. Marxism is making tremendous headway among the young people who think. They talk all the time about the realities of power and the class war. We must bring them back into the church. In a few years' time, in two years' time, it will be too late.

— Sin demands the consequences of sin, T. Machno Jones said. I tell you how I see Marx. I'll tell you exactly. The voice of Beelzebub. You may smile. I am being quite serious. *Paradise Lost*. Book Two. It's all there. In the great council of the fallen angels, Beelzebub advocates an invasion of Earth . . . 'Possess all as our own, and drive, as we are driven, the puny habitants, or if not drive, seduce them to our party . . . to confound the race of Mankind in one root,' Miles, and 'Earth with Hell to mingle and involve, done all to spite the great Creator.' It's all there, Miles. 'Whom we shall send in search of this new world?'. . . I've got a very interesting sermon on the subject. It doesn't sink in of course. People are so ignorant.

— What do you mean by 'sin demands the consequences of sin'? J.T. said.

— 'A child who is left to have his own way, shall reduce his father and mother to shame and tears,' T. Machno Jones said. It's the same with the human race as a whole. The greatest sin of all is to usurp the authority that belongs to the Lord God alone. Disobedience. The consequence will be the most terrible consequences. War. Famine. Plague. Death.

J.T. began by nodding as he listened as if giving assent and ended by shaking his head in excited disagreement. When he spoke the words tumbled out faster than he could enunciate them.

— God is a God of Love, he said. The New Testament is a testament of Love. That is the constant recurring theme, isn't it? Love God. Love one another. Love your neighbour. Love your enemy. It's all there, Mr Jones. It's all there.

J.T. held out his hand triumphantly and sucked back the accumulation of saliva at the corner of his lips. His companion raised his eyebrows. Noisily the bus had halted to pick up a passenger. It stopped outside the middle of a long row of terraced houses. T. Machno Jones bent his head to look through the window.

— Look at that, he said.

A shop window had been painted green on the inside so that the stationary bus, trembling as its engine turned, was reflected in it. Above the window, instead of a trader's name, was painted 'TREDWR WORKINGMEN'S CLUB.' The premises were in darkness and the front door locked.

— Another one, he said. That's the enemy, Mr Miles. He pointed with a stiffened index finger.

— Drinking clubs spreading through the valleys like a skin disease. We are not active enough. Not vocal enough. We must stamp them out. There's the enemy for you. It's a straight fight, Mr Miles, but have we got the light of battle in our eyes?

— Well . . .

J.T. was thinking hard.

— It's a clear-cut issue. We must take a stand.

— Well . . . J.T. said again. This is my whole point really. It's as simple as this. We must make the chapel a place where people like going. On a week-night in the vestry make the place warm, bright and cheerful and let the women knit if they want to and the men smoke. That's why I have my club for young men in the store room behind the Cross Inn Stores. It isn't a secret society or anything like that. It's a meeting place for me to meet men who normally wouldn't come to chapel.

— A political cell it's called, T. Machno Jones said. Two miners' agents there. They say they're making use of you, Miles. You are the false front. The respectable veneer.

— That's untrue, J.T. said indignantly. It's my club. I started it. It was my idea.

— I'm only telling you what people say.

T. Machno Jones bowed his head. The bus driver was shouting loudly at a woman with a man's cloth cap on her head who stood with her bare arms folded, leaning against the doorpost of her terrace house. The words reached her above the noise of the engine. She suddenly became animated and waved her arms as if to order the bus away, half-smiling, half-angry. The driver leaned out for a parting shout, lifting his foot off the large clutch pedal. The bus bumped on its way.

NED LIFTED HIMSELF from the milking-stool by pressing his head against the cow's flank. One of the cats walked between the cow's rear legs, miaowing for milk. Lydia stood in the empty stall at the end of the shippon. Both doors were wide open and through the slatted windows the rays of the setting sun illuminated the hay dust on the cobbled floor. A cow stamped and rattled her chains as if something unfamiliar had disturbed her. At the other end, from squeezed cow teats, the drumming of milk on the bottom of an empty bucket ceased, and Glyn Brain pushed his head out to look down the row of eleven cows and see what was happening.

— It's the little girl, he said. He sounded cross.

— You'd better call her. Wouldn't be nice for a kick to spoil her beauty.

— Thea! Come here. Come to Mummy, *cariad!*

The little girl stood hesitating, her finger in her mouth. Ned bent to take her hand in his and steered her towards her mother. He straightened himself and said in English.

— Keep away from the cow's legs, my girl, whatever you do. Your cousin had a kick in his jaw when he was just the same age as you. He added in Welsh, looking at Lydia,

— Rowland's boy that was.

He bent down again to pour a drop of milk into the cat's tin and looked up at Lydia.

— I don't know why I should have to talk to her in English, he said.

— Oh she understands everything, Lydia said.

She caught Thea by the shoulder and pressed her against her leg.

— The Welsh down there is so different, she said.[90] I speak English with Mrs Leyshon the schoolmaster's wife.

— I should have thought she would have spoken Welsh with the minister's wife. If only as a mark of respect.

— Oh Ned, don't be so old-fashioned. It's not a bit like that down there.

— No respect?

Ned straightened himself and ran his hand around his crumpled waistcoat. He seemed to be composing a suitable comment.

— You're putting on a lot of weight, Ned, Lydia said quickly. She smiled.

— You're thin enough, anyway, Ned said. Thin as a tin whistle, that's what you are.

He looked down at the bucket of milk and then called out to his farm worker.

— I'll leave you to finish, Glyn, he said.

The cow Glyn was milking stamped her leg and Glyn shouted.

— Stand still, you black bitch!

— What's the matter? Ned said.

His tone of voice was strongly disapproving. He walked purposefully to where Glyn sat milking.

— Her teats. They're cracked, Glyn said.

He spoke as if it were just one among a thousand faults he could find with the herd and with the whole farm.

— I've told you, Ned said. You're a wet milker. You wet their teats to milk it easy and that makes the cracks worse. Be sure to put the salve on before you let them out. It's very important.

He held out his bucket to Glyn, who tipped in the small quantity of milk he had taken. He shifted his milking-stool and nudged the cow with his head and as Ned walked away from him he muttered to himself, In the yard as they avoided the cow muck that had still to be cleared, Ned said,

— You know who he is?

Lydia swung Thea from the ground and carried her across the yard in her arms.

— He sounds bad-tempered enough, anyway.

— I keep him for his father's sake, Ned said. He's Jac Brain's son.
Poor old Jac. Can't hear or see now you know. Pity to see him. He's
been the backbone of that little chapel up there for donkey's years.
He was a marvellous man with the horses. I remember when I first
took this place, the wagons used to stop outside the road gate to give
the horses a breather after pulling up the long hill . . .

— Come along, Ned, come along now!

Outside the kitchen Bessie his wife was mixing calf-meal with
water from the rusty pump. The squealing and groaning of the iron
handle had brought the four young calves bellowing to the nearest
gate. Lydia put Thea to stand on the stone wall so that she could see
the calves being fed. Ned took the buckets from his wife and added
a quantity of milk to each one, stirring them briskly with a length of
old brush handle. There were geese and turkeys in the paddock. The
geese waddled down from the top of the cinder-heap where they
had been foraging among the nettles. Further away, in the pigsties
beyond the line where Bessie hung out her washing, the hungry pigs
began to snort. Thea gripped her mother's shoulder. Her eyes were
bright with an excitement mixed with fear, but she stood firm on
the wall and shook her head when Lydia offered to take her in her
arms.

— Everything's hungry, she said to her mother.

Bessie looked up for a moment, smiling. The smallest calf nuzzled
into the bucket she held while she kept the others at bay with the
length of brush handle.

— What did she say?

— She said everything is hungry.

Lydia lifted her voice above the din; the rattle of buckets, the
lowing, the hissing and the grunting in the background. Ned was
getting hot and irritable as if the work was crowding in on him too
fast.

— Where's John Henry?

— He's taken Ronnie for a walk. They're gone up the mountain
to see the old mines. I told you.

— Well it's time he was back. He's twelve years old for goodness'
sake. When I was twelve I was doing a day's ploughing.

When the calves were fed they were driven off from the gate. They
jumped about in the paddock and settled down to sucking each

other's ears. Ned hurried off to attend to the pigs. Thea put out her arm to show she wanted to go with him. He paused to allow himself to smile a brief smile and advise his niece to stay with her mother, Lydia picked Thea up and followed her sister-in-law into the kitchen. The child seemed to consider putting up a struggle, until her attention was taken by the large black kettle hung from a thick chain over the open fire. It had begun to boil. With confident strength Bessie lifted it off the hook and set it on the hob.

— Sit down, my dear.

Bessie pushed Lydia towards the rocking-chair in the corner between the table and the fire.

— We'll have a bite to eat.

She looked down at Thea.

— Everybody's hungry, she said in English.

She laughed unsteadily in her throat. Bessie had a goitre and she wore a thin band of black velvet around her throat. Lydia sat down.

— I ought to be helping, she said.

— You are on your holidays, my girl, Bessie said. And not having enough to eat down in the South there. It must be a terrible place.

Thea stood balanced in the middle of the kitchen floor so that she could move her head to watch her aunt intently as she bustled about preparing a meal, talking in her warm and friendly tremolo as she hurried in and out of first the dairy and then the pantry.

— I do like this old house, Lydia said. It's a better house than Argoed, Bessie. I always thought so.

She lifted her voice and spoke more loudly. Bessie was in the echoing dairy, rinsing the buckets under the solitary cold-water tap.

— Well, Bessie said, once more in the kitchen. Well it's very laborious I know that much. Nothing but work from morning till night. No electric here.

She tugged at a table drawer, put in her hand and pulled out a fist full of knives and forks which she dropped on the table with a clatter that brought Thea trotting to the other end of the table to peep over the edge and see what was happening. She gazed fascinated at the speed at which her aunt's hands moved, and when she hurried out again into the whitewashed dairy Thea followed her. Bessie scooped out a hunk of butter from an earthen-ware pot, slapped it into an enamelled dish and pushed the pot back with her knee under a slate working surface. From another large pot covered with a flour sack she extracted a large homemade loaf which she tucked under her arm. Thea stood on tiptoe and saw that the pot was filled with big loaves. She looked up at her aunt.

— Can I carry one? she said.

Bessie laughed, opening her wide mouth. Her goitre seemed to roll about under the black velvet neck-band.

— Well carry this one then.

Thea grabbed the loaf eagerly, but it was so big it obscured her view as she tried to follow her aunt. She dropped the loaf and jumped back as it bounced on the clean dairy floor. Her aunt laughed again and snatched up the loaf.

— Is she getting in your way, Bess?

Lydia called from the rocking-chair in the kitchen.

— No, indeed.

Bessie held her hand on the latch of the dairy door while Thea ran out under her arm. She closed the door.

— She's a little pet, Bessie said. I wouldn't mind if you left her here all the year round. I always wanted a girl to tell you the truth.

— Come on now. Come on now!

Ned bustled in, his hands dripping wet after rinsing under the pump outside the door. He dried them vigorously on the roller-towel behind the door.

— Let's have tea, my love, before that Glyn Brain finishes. He likes to have the table to himself, then he can drink his tea out of his saucer.

— I'm in your chair, Ned, Lydia said.

She swung forward and stood on her feet. Ned nodded approvingly. The chair rocked backwards and forwards until he sat in it and bent forward to take off his leather leggings and boots. Thea stared at his legs as they came into view. They were very large and there was an expanse of white drawers between the tops of the woollen socks and the bottom of the voluminous breeches. Thea moved nearer to examine the inside of one of the leggings. She seemed fascinated by the furry texture of the interior and the metal clasps at the top and the bottom. Ned watched her for a moment.

— Try them on, he said. Thea looked at him, hesitating.

— Go on, Ned said.

He turned his chair to face the table.

— Come on, come on, come on, he said good-humouredly.

— Don't take any notice of him, Bess, Lydia said. It's what comes of being the eldest.

Ned suddenly looked serious. He lifted his hands to see if they were clean, smelled them discreetly and then lowered them with the tips of his fingers pressed together.

— I'm worried about Kate, he said.

Bessie had settled down to cutting bread and butter with great speed and skill.

— It's all Pa's fault, Lydia said. Dying without making a will.

— It's hard to understand. My father was such a responsible man. Ned sighed and shook his head.

— He just couldn't bear to write down something connected with his own death, Lydia said.

— Come, come, Ned said.

— Well he was an awful baby, Lydia said. And what provision is there for me? I signed that paper because you told me to, and Argoed is hers. She deserves it. She's the one who has stayed home and kept the home fires burning. All right. We all sign this paper and give up our rights. She's my only sister and I don't grudge it her. But what happens if she gets married?

— Is that likely? Bessie said.

She held her knife still for a moment while she said it, and then carried on cutting without waiting for an answer.

— Well, that's what's worrying me.

Ned shut his mouth firmly and bent his head, waiting for their undivided attention.

— I went to see old Mary Parry Price, down in the lower village, on my way up from the station. Poor old thing doesn't look half well. Her arms look awful. Like matchsticks. Pa was very fond of her, you know. After they turned to religion in '04, her and old John Parry Rice, Pa could forgive them anything.[91] Old Mary told me that Bannister has been in Argoed very often these last few weeks. Very often. Now she knows. She has a nephew who works at Plas-y-Bryn and he comes home around supper-time. He's seen that green car of Bannister's in the yard on several occasions.

— Do you mean Wynne Bannister? Lydia said. The undertaker? Ned nodded solemnly.

— Good gracious me, he's old enough to be her father, Lydia said.

— He's not as old as he looks, Ned said.

— He's married anyway. He's got children . . .

— His wife died, Ned said.

— Gracious!

Lydia exclaimed loudly and then looked down to see if Thea had heard. The little girl was absorbed in trying to put her uncle's leggings on, and in finding out how the inside clasps worked, at the top and the bottom.

— I've heard things about him, Lydia said in a very quiet voice. Mrs Bayliss at the office used to say things about him.

— Everything isn't as it should be there, that's certain, Ned said.

— Well good heavens, Lydia said. She's never said a word to me. When we were there last Sunday. Not a word. She just asked if Ronnie could stay on for another fortnight to keep her company. They get on very well, I know, but I miss him myself to tell you the truth.

All three looked at each other, so that their concern seemed to circle above the table in a way that kept them still and speechless for so long that Thea looked up. When she let it go, the stiff legging fell from her legs and rolled over on the floor.

— Everything is hungry, she said.

— Isn't she a clever one? Bessie said.

As she laughed, she folded a round of bread and butter and bent down to put it in Thea's mouth.

— Kate is so deep, Lydia said. It's since she lost her eye, I suppose. I think I'd better go up there tomorrow.

ON THE STEPS of the large chapel and in the forecourt and finally on the road itself men in black moved restlessly, forming themselves into many groups that sometimes tightened and cohered and sometimes fell apart. In the street there were six motor cars. A man with a heavy camera stood on the steps of the new war memorial trying to take a picture of the scene outside the chapel. The sky was blue, but few people seemed to notice what a fine day it was. The village school was closed for the holidays and there were many children about. At the moment they were quiet with curiosity, and their mothers watched them from the open doors of their terraced houses. J.T. stood with his back to the railings of the chapel forecourt, surrounded by a group of younger ministers. At his side stood James Foster Jones who was quivering with excitement. He kept repeating,

— I'm with you, J.T. I'm with you all the way. It's got to be revised and it must be revised and you were absolutely right to bring it up.

— I don't want to cause dissension.

J.T. was speaking to a tall man in a long overcoat who kept his hands deep in his pockets in spite of the fine weather. J.T. seemed anxious to break the intense gloom that had settled on the broad, pale face that was bent down towards him in an attitude of concentrated attention.

— I don't claim to be a theologian, J.T. said. All I know is that the idea of total corruption flowing with the seed from father to son is primitive and barbaric and it leads in the end to making us morally impotent and unable to respond to the full challenge of the New Testament that we are supposed to preach. That's all I'm saying.[92]

The tall man cleared his throat three times before speaking.

— Well that is quite a lot, isn't it? he said.

— Does it have to be part of our confession of faith? Something that actively impedes the work of the Kingdom? The whole document urgently needs revision, not only in the light of modern knowledge but in the light of the New Testament and modern Biblical scholarship.

The tall man pursed his lips and moved away, his head swaying slowly from one side to the other so that it was impossible to know whether he was shaking his head over what J.T. had been saying, or looking about to decide what other group had a fringe to which he could attach himself.

— You know what Machno Jones said to me?

James Foster Jones looked up at J.T., smiled and prepared to imitate Machno Jones's dry manner of speech. He lifted his voice so that the whole group could hear.

— He said, 'I know sin exists, Jones. If it exists, it must come from somewhere. That means it has origins. That means it is original sin.' But I said, 'In the light of present-day knowledge can you believe that Adam's seed is the original source, and natural generation the method of propagation?' 'Well,' he said, 'you could hardly think of a more efficient method, could you?' He's very dry of course, but he has got a sense of humour!

A young man with a pencil and a notebook halted the other side of the iron railings. He was bareheaded and he kept on pushing his lank hair out of his eyes. He poked J.T. in the shoulder with his pencil.

J.T. turned. The young man had a stammer.

— I'm from the *Western Mail,* he said. You are the Reverend J.T. Miles? Could I ask you some questions?

J, T. turned to face the reporter. The small group became a line of men behind the railings, all listening eagerly,

— I'm with you, Mr Miles, the reporter said. I'm . . . I'm . . . with you all the way. I think you know my brother, Esmond Prosser. I'm Rhys Prosser.

They shook hands warmly through the railings.

— You have been invited by the East Carmarthen Labour Party to become their parliamentary candidate. Are you going to accept, Mr Miles?

J.T. looked thoughtful. His companions watched his face impatiently.

— You'd better ask me something else, J.T. said at last. I still haven't had time to read the letter of invitation. It only reached me this morning.

— About your book *Honesty and Dogma,* the reporter said.

— It isn't a book at all, J.T. said. It's just an address really. It's an address I gave to a W. E. A. rally at Ammanford.[93]

— It's a pamphlet, James Foster Jones said. That's what it is. A pamphlet.

— It wasn't really a rally, J.T. said. It was a public meeting held in the evening after a one-day school on 'Church and State in the Modern World'.

— Haven't you read it? one of the ministers said.

He had a deep voice and the reporter looked alarmed.

— I haven't seen it, he said. I don't usually . . . not . . . use . . . use . . . al . . . y.

He stood in the grip of his stammer. The row of ministers watched him sympathetically.

— Take your time, son, one of them said, nodding solemnly.

— I'm new, the reporter gasped.

— Here you are.

The minister with a deep voice had taken a copy of the pamphlet out of his pocket. It had a pink paper cover which crumpled easily. He held the pamphlet out through the railings. The reporter took it eagerly, nodding his thanks,

— I don't know, J.T. said. I don't think I want it printed in a daily newspaper. I'm not sure it should ever have been printed in the first place. It's very hastily written. It's an answer really to a question put to me by one of my own church members. 'Do you have to believe in the Immaculate Conception in order to believe in the divinity of Christ?'

The young reporter stuttered.

— Do you ... do ... you?

— I don't think so, J.T. said. I really don't think so.

The reporter turned his back on the ministers. From the steps of the war memorial the photographer was waving and beckoning. The reporter put his head on one side, opened his mouth and listened to the voice in the distance. The photographer waved more impatiently. The reporter nodded hastily and turned to speak to the ministers.

— He wants you to come out and have your photographs taken in front of the chapel, he said. So ... so ... you don't look in a cage.

Two or three of the group began to laugh and make jokes. James Foster Jones began to nod and gesticulate.

— He's the leader, he said.

He pointed at J.T.

— That's the photograph you should take in my opinion, he said. Isn't that so?

He turned about to seek nods and demonstrations of agreement. Most of the ministers were in full agreement, but one of them said in a measured way.

— Well now, wait a minute. What are we committing ourselves to? Are we all agreed that there should be what you might call a formal left wing or modernist movement, whatever you like to call it ...

— The issue is clear, James Foster Jones said.

He lifted his closed hand, the ends of his fingers pressed in the palm.

— J.T. has spoken out, he said. He is our spokesman and he is our leader.

J.T. was shaking his head.

— I'm not eloquent enough, he said. It's one thing to want reform. It's another thing to bring it about. In any case I don't want to cause splits and dissension. Honestly.

He was facing the other ministers.

— If you'd just come around to this side of the railings, the reporter was saying. Inside there it will ... 1 ... 1 ... look funny. These bars are so high ...

J.T. shook his head and turned to look at the chapel.

— I want to think, J.T. said. I don't want my photograph taken.

IN THE BEST bedroom at Argoed, Kate lay in the double bed which had been her father's. She lay on her right side with her hand covering the empty socket of her right eye. There was a gold wedding-ring on the third finger. The night was so quiet an owl hooting as far away as the tall clump of trees in the field across the road that led to the village, sounded very close. The glass of the enlarged photograph of her mother that hung above the fire-place glimmered in the dark, and moonlight from the low window showed up the rug between the fire-place and the bed.

Downstairs someone was fumbling with the locks and bolts on the back door. Kate seemed to hold her breath to listen harder. She turned suddenly in bed and sat up to peer at the clock on the mantelpiece. She threw aside the bedclothes and stepped across to the fire-place, picked up the broad clock and carried it to the window in order to read its face in the moonlight. The time was twenty-five minutes to one.

She stood still by the window holding the clock against her hip so that her flannelette night-dress was hitched up and the moonlight shone on her leg. She took the clock back to the mantelpiece, replacing it quickly but carefully in its usual place. There was the noise of footsteps on the stairs. A man in his stockinged-feet, moving with care. Candlelight appeared in the crack under the door. Kate flew across the room to turn the key in the lock before he could open the door. She pressed her hand over the lock. The key was missing. The door could not be locked.

As he opened the door she pressed her body against it. He kept his knee forwatd to prevent the door closing. His narrow face was illuminated by the light of the candle he was holding. His thin red hair was ruffled and he was smiling in a very friendly manner. His pipe was in the corner of his mouth, but the bowl was upside down.

— Been shuting up the shop, he said.

His speech was very amiable, but slightly slurred.

— Where is the key of this door? Kate said.

— Pom-pom, pom-pom, he sang cheerfully. Never been twenty-one before . . .

— Where is it?

— 'In the lily-pond, I saw it fall'. . .

He continued to sing and then suddenly thrust his free hand through the gap to give Kate an unexpected tickle. She jumped back with a scream and the door swung open.

— There we are then, he said.

—You're not sleeping in this room, Kate said. Not in your condition. Not in this bed.

He walked forward and put down the candle on the wash-stand. He peered at the clean water in the ewer and stirred its surface with his finger.

— It's a beautiful night, Kate, he said. I came through the orchard. I stopped. Didn't breathe. I heard a ripe apple fall and land with a plop in the grass.

He took off his brown jacket and ran his thumbs up and down his braces.

— Did I ever show you my trick with a pack of cards. Dropping them, you know . . .

He held his hands on his behind to represent a tail.

— Make a noise like a cow, he said. You'll catch cold if you stand there in your nightie. Let them fall through your fingers. The cards, you see. Get into bed there's a good girl.

—You won't get round me, Kate said. I don't want you in this room.

Her voice was becoming shrill.

— Oh, Mrs B, make me some tea, he sang. 'Oh Mrs Bannister. Open up your canister.'

— I never knew what kind of a man you were, Kate said. You tricked me. You cheated me. We've been married four months and you've paid me exactly five pounds towards the housekeeping. Five pounds in four months.

— My dear girl!

For the first time he sounded serious.

— Five pounds in four months!

— Listen to me, will you! This isn't a joke, he said. I've explained the position. My business is a long-term business. The County Council owes me eight hundred pounds. Just think of it. Eight hundred pounds! I've waited. The question is . . .

He paused dramatically and pointed at Kate where she stood on the other side of the bed.

— Can you wait?

Kate said nothing. She climbed into bed and pulled the clothes up to her chin and her left hand continued to travel up until it covered her eye-socket, as if lying down made her more aware of her missing eye. Wynne Bannister let his trousers fall to the floor. He pointed at Kate again.

— It's a question of confidence, he said.

Kate made no answer. He put his striped pyjama jacket over his vest and buttoned it up to the neck. He snuffed the candle out with finger and thumb. The smell spread through the bedroom.

— I've been married before, he said, climbing into bed- You've got to be straight about these things. You've got to talk it out, thrash it out, man to man and face to face.

— You put bottles in Pa's cupboard. You threw those magazines on to the midden without even asking me.

— They were so old, Kate fach, Bannister said. Eighteen seventy-one and all that. The mice were nibbling at them.

— Bringing bottles into this house, Kate said. You told me you never drank.

— I told you I was church, Bannister said. Wasn't that enough? I'm not a Methodist, thank God.

— How can you say that in my father's old bedroom.

— For goodness' sake calm down. Calm down!

He put out a hand to take her arm and pull her down. She wrenched her arm free.

— Come on.

He was trying a coaxing note.

— Come on, my beauty. Come down to old Wynne and he'll give you something you like. Something very tasty.

— Don't talk to me like that. . .

— Come on, old beauty. It's nice and warm down here. Just the place for a bit of . . .

Kate swung herself out of the bed and stood on the rug, her arms tightly folded.

— I'll sleep in my old bed, she said.

— Oh come on . . .

— It's not aired, she said. I'll sleep between the blankets. She slammed the bedroom door behind her.

20

J.T.'S BOOTS SANK into the spongy heather as he climbed the last slope at the head of the valley. His companion, Bayley Lewis, had already reached the top. He was standing on a heap of stones, his hand on his hips. His mac hung over his arm and it blew about in the strong breeze. He was smiling. The fringe of silver hair around his bald head glistened in the sun. He waved cheerfully and J.T., lowering his head and quickening his pace, waved back. On the slope there were sheep that had recently been sheared. Immediately below was a derelict coal-mine. Further down, a street petered out on the hill-side and a snaky line of small terrace houses crept down into the hidden valley.

Bayley Lewis was making expansive gestures. He pointed north-wards and seen from J.T.'s view point he looked like a public monument on its plinth.

— I couldn't hear, J.T. said. He was out of breath.

— We mustn't take it all for granted, Bayley Lewis said.

His tenor voice was cultivated. It sounded sweet and patient. He always seemed to smile as he spoke.

They both looked northwards. A vast landscape stretched to hills a great distance away and above these the clouds were coiled thickly, and towards them across the open sky, broken cloud formations swept, pursued by the prevailing wind.

— Look how simply the problem is stated.

Bayley Lewis turned to address J.T., who balanced unsteadily on the small space that was available on the heap of stones. He held out the palm of his white hand.

— About the camps you mean, J.T. said. Camps for the unemployed?[94]

— About everything.

Lewis made a comprehensive gesture with both arms.

— They all want to be near a beach if possible, J.T. said.

He frowned and stretched his lips as he studied the great landscape, ready to pick out landmarks.

— The perspective is clear, Joseph, he said.

J.T. nodded, anxious to follow what was being said. No one else ever called him Joseph.

— The task is clear. We must get them out of there.

He stretched his arm downwards towards the valley.

— And put them out there. He waved his arm northwards.

— I know what you're thinking, Bayley Lewis said. Impossible. Impossible. Sit down on these stones, Joseph, and let me tell of an experience I had last winter.

They sat down side by side, looking northwards. As he listened, J.T. scratched at the bare patch of soil between his feet with a small stone.

— We were decorating the Community Hall, Bayley Lewis said. It was too wet on the Park on the Long Tip. Three colliers came rushing in. Two of them were men I knew well. The third was a communist. They had come straight off the shift. The one pit left working, you see. 'Y Foel'. It was threatened with closure. They wanted me to join a deputation to the owners. It so happened that I knew the chairman, Lord Dykes. We were at Balliol together. A hard, but just man. Off we went to London. He received us very courteously. Put all his cards on the table. His board was opposed to keeping the pit open. He pointed out that the miners took £200,000 a year in wages. Why should they lose it all in order to save an annual deficit of £20,000? He appealed to us for help to keep the pit open. He put it very simply. Even I understood it.

Bayley Lewis smiled to show how prepared he was to laugh at himself. J.T. scratched away at the soil.

— We worked out a scheme. Wages under two pounds to be left untouched. Over two pounds a week, a shilling in the pound to go into a central fund to guarantee the pit against future deficits. Then we had to go back to the men and persuade them to accept the plan. Well . . .

Bayley Lewis drew a very deep breath and lifted his eyebrows. They were black in striking contrast to his white hair and bright blue eyes. He took a glance at J.T. from the corner of his eye, but J.T. did not look up.

— Well it was an anxious meeting as you can imagine. Before the deputation left the little room behind the platform, Edward Williams suggested I should offer up a prayer. A fine old type, Edward Williams. From Meirionydd originally. Came down to work in the pits as a young boy. He had the task of putting the scheme to the men. He was wise and slow and he made a good impression, but there were men there ready to turn the whole affair into a political demonstration. Then old Edward asked me to give some of my own first-hand experiences of the terrible conditions of the depression in the Rhondda. There was a great deal of excited talk after this. But Edward kept the meeting under control. A vote was taken. And the scheme was accepted. I suggested the meeting should close with the singing of a hymn. Ever since then Joseph, the relations at 'Y Foel' between management and men have been the very best. Grace and goodwill won the day. More of this, I say, and the impossible becomes possible. More of this, I say, among all the affairs of men and a new world becomes a reality. This is the way of reconciliation.[95]

— The sacrifice was one-sided, J.T. said. It's always the poorest who have to pay. This is what I don't understand.

— The weak must show the way to the strong, Bayley Lewis said. He sounded triumphant.

— This is their strength, their very great strength. This is why I am a pacifist, Joseph. This is the New Way. This is the way that cannot be suppressed, either by the power of money or by the power of arms. We who have nothing except the spirit of Christ will do more for these men than any government, any parliament, any political party. You believe this in your heart, man, and that is why we are here together on this glorious afternoon. And why our desire to bring these people out of the dark valley into the fields of light will be fulfilled. By faith and by prayer. Shall we pray, Joseph?

Obediently J.T. went down on his knees on the patch of bare earth between the stones.

— O Lord God, give unto thy servants the infinite strength of love. Give unto us the faith no greater than a mustard seed, so that we may move mountains and lead thy people out of the valley of darkness into the world of light. Amen.

Together they knelt in silence. Invisible above their heads a curlew sent out its long call.

THE DOCTOR SAT on the edge of Thea's bed. Her bedroom was so small Lydia stood in the doorway. His thermometer case had a clip on it and he was replacing it in his waistcoat pocket. Thea lay very still, but her eyes followed everything the doctor did and she winced when he pressed the lock of his bag and it closed with a snap.

— Now then.

He stretched his arm across the bed so that he could talk straight down at Thea, his head poised above hers.

— You are a good girl, aren't you? Thea nodded nervously.

— You will stay in bed for two days. All right?

Thea nodded again.

— You'll be a good girl and keep still. And keep nice and warm. Mummy will bring you nice hot drinks and you will take your medicine like a very good child, without even pulling a face. All right.

— She got up to see, Doctor, yesterday evening, Lydia said. You couldn't blame her, really, there was so much coming and going with the annual preaching festival. You may as well have taken the front door off its hinges.

The doctor did not take his gaze away from Thea's face as her mother spoke. He stared at her with hypnotic intensity, and the little girl studied his forehead in detail as if she were counting the neatly brushed hairs of his thinning hairline and then moved her eyes to watch the corners of his steady mouth, waiting for them to move.

— She said she could hear the preacher, Lydia said. When we lived in the terrace we could always hear the singing of course. Perhaps she remembered that, although it's nearly two years since we lived there.

— What was the preacher saying, Thea?

The corners of his mouth were moving like dimples in his plump cheeks.

— Telling everybody to be good and not to tell lies, Thea said.

The doctor nodded seriously and got to his feet.

— He was a good preacher then, wasn't he? he said.

He picked up his bag and offered Thea his hand. She took it.

— Goodbye, he said. I'll be back to see you the day after tomorrow.

He stretched out his arm to motion Lydia from the doorway.

— We'll leave the door open, shall we? he said. And you can call if you want anything. But don't call unless you have to, will you? Or you'll tire your mother out, running up and down stairs.

Lydia put her hand on the banister to stop herself from running downstairs. The doctor seemed to make a point of always moving at an even pace.

— She'll be all right, he said.

They were standing in the small hallway.

— But what about you?

He looked intently at Lydia's face.

— You look anaemic. I'd better take a look at you, I think. Anyone in there?

He pointed to the study door; which was closed. Lydia shook her head.

— Joe is at the Settlement, she said. There's trouble with some of the men. Communists I suppose. They don't want to go on with this public gardens scheme. And they don't like Bayley Lewis. I must say for once I don't blame them. I don't like him either.

The doctor opened the study door. Outside, the sun was shining on the roofs of the houses across the street, but the front garden of the little manse was in the shade. J.T.'s desk in the bay window was covered with open books. His slippers were on the brown tiles of the hearth and the study smelt of stale tobacco.

— He comes in the house as if everyone here ought to dance attendance, Lydia said. Joe says he's a saint, but it gets on my nerves the way he smiles all the time. I'm awful, aren't I? I can't help it.

She stopped talking while the doctor took her by the arms and steered her around into the light from the window. He placed a forefinger on her high cheek-bone and drew down her lower eyelid to study the inside of the lid. Her skin twitched with the desire to blink and her eyeball rolled from one side to the other. The doctor removed his finger and stepped back.

— Stretch out your arms, will you? he said. Close your eyes.

Lydia closed her eyes and sighed.

— Spread your fingers, he said.

The sensitive skin of her well-shaped hands was covered with lines and fissures due to manual labour. The fingers trembled very slightly. He took one hand and bent it to examine her finger-nails. He placed his hands on either side of her head and lifted her hair to observe the lobes of her ears. He moved her head slightly from one side to the other. Her eyes were still closed. Tears bulged through her long eyelashes. When he saw them the doctor said:

—You'd better sit down.

Lydia obeyed. The castors slipped back as she sat heavily in J.T.'s mahogany desk chair, with her back to the window. She lowered her head.

— If you send Ronnie down to the dispensary about tea-time, he said, I'll make up a tonic for you. You've been overworking. Probably worrying too much, too. That doesn't do any good.

— I hate this place. I hate it.

The doctor pushed his hands into the deep pockets of his

mackintosh and smiled faintly.

— *Hiraeth*[96] for the north? he said.

— It's no joke trying to bring up three children in the middle of all this. I've spent nearly twelve years of my life in this awful place and I hate it more now than when I first came.

— Do you really mean that?

— Of course I do, or I wouldn't say it, would I?

Lydia tried to wipe the track of tears from both her cheeks.

— I'm sorry, she said. I didn't mean to be rude.

The doctor stood in the middle of the study floor and studied his patient with care.

— Have you talked about this with your husband?

— Him.

Lydia gripped the curved ends of the chair-arms.

— He's much too busy to talk to me. He's got all the miners to worry about. And Bayley Lewis. And the Settlement. And the chapel. And the state of the world. You don't think he's got time for his wife and children?

The doctor stood still and silent, visibly considering a problem he had not expected to encounter.

— You should talk to him, he said at last.

— Why should I? If only I had some money I'd take the children and leave him tomorrow.

The doctor had become pale.

— I suppose I shouldn't talk like this. In my own house. A minister's wife. A man whom everybody respects. A good man. Everybody calls him a good man. I want you to know.

Lydia looked up at the doctor's face.

— I live in this house. I make his meals. I clean his boots. I sleep in his bed. And most of the time I can't stand him. I can't stand him.

The doctor stood motionless. Lydia jumped to her feet as if she had suddenly acquired a new lease of energy.

— You'd better go, she said. People will be noticing how long you've been here.

— He's a very good man, Lydia, the doctor said.

— So everybody keeps on telling me, she said.

She opened the study door. Upstairs Thea was calling in a weak voice.

— Mam! Mam!

— Coming dear. Coming.

She turned back to speak to the doctor.

— You can let yourself out, can't you, Doctor Brice?

She ran up the stairs and called

— All right, darling. I'm coming.

KATE WAS MAKING pastry. By the friction of her finger-tips the lard and and the flour blended into each other inside the large mixing bowl. Flour covered her hands up to the wrists. She stirred the crumbling mixture with her finger. A cup of cold water stood alongside the bowl. A ginger kitten rubbed against her legs. She turned for a moment to glance at the fire, and she saw Tomi Moch through the new window at the narrow end of the kitchen. He was trotting up the outcrop of rock towards the archway. He stopped suddenly as if he were surprised to see the new window, and through it, in the warm kitchen, Kate standing at the bare table making pastry. As Kate picked up the cup of water, Tomi tapped the window-pane with the long nail of his index finger. It was a cold March day and a drop hung from the tip of his sharp nose. He appeared to be smiling, but since the benign expression on his face hardly ever varied it was always difficult to know what he was feeling. Kate leaned towards the window to study his small eyes. If the pupils could be seen trembling it was always a sign of emergency or alarm.

— Come inside! Kate said. He could not hear.

— Come in!

She shouted and beckoned. He stood back and pointed at his boots. They were dark with wet cow dung. She swung her arm to indicate he should pass under the archway. She wiped the loose crumbs of flour and pastry from her hands as she walked up the three steps to the churn room. Tomi had opened the back door. He leaned inside, clinging to the latch handle and the doorpost.

— What's the matter, Tomi? Kate said. What is it?

She always spoke to him now in a sharp, kindly tone, like a school-mistress addressing a backward pupil for whom she has finally developed a certain affection. Tomi lifted the thumb of the hand that held the latch and nodded behind him.

— It's them, he said. They're quarrelling. Like a couple of kids.

— Who? said Kate sharply.

— Mr Bannister and Mr Dan. Up by the old house. I was with

the pigs and I could hear them shouting. They were waving their arms about and their coats were open. You know what Dan's like with his temper up.

Tomi grinned with undue familiarity, but Kate was putting on her mac from behind the door and did not bother to rebuke him. With her foot she sent the kitten down the three steps and closed the kitchen door.

— I don't know what this other feller's like, Tomi said. You know him better than me.

— Come on, Kate said sternly, banging the door behind her and making for the orchard.

— This way's quicker, Tomi said.

He jerked his thumb over his shoulder towards the archway and main yard. Kate hesitated.

— Go through the threshing floor, see, Tomi said.

He waited for her to make up her mind, and when she moved back, waited for her to pass, before trotting behind her.

— He's a one for jokes, isn't he?

Tomi stood watching as Kate fumbled with the lower half of the heavy door that opened into the threshing floor.

—You can't always tell whether he's serious. I expect that's it. This morning he asked me if I had a vote. I didn't know whether he was serious, but I said since I was thirty I'd voted Liberal same as your father, and he said, 'How old are you now, Tomi? Eighty next birthday?' I just laughed you know. I wasn't going to tell him, was I?

The wind caught Kate's skirt as they crossed the rickyard and she forced it down impatiently with both her fists. Beyond the rickyard gate and into the lower paddock they could see the old house. It stood alone on the brow of the hill, windowless and doorless, but the roof still intact. Even from the distance the great corner-stones of the sturdy foundation could be seen standing out from the hill. There were no men in front of the house.

— Where are they? Kate's mouth hung open.

— Inside I expect, Tomi said.

Kate began to run up the hill and Tomi followed, his loose leggings knocking against each other. Three yearling calves that were grazing the young grass between them and the Old House also began running.

Inside the Old House, against a pile of hay that half hid the carvings on the wide chimney-piece carved in local stone, Dan Llew was punching Wynne Bannister, who had his arms raised to protect his head.

— Stand up and fight like a man, Dan Lleew was saying.

He was panting and breathless with his effort. His mac and his jacket lay on the floor that was inches deep in dung and hay. This was where the yearling stores had taken shelter all winter.

— He's still very strong, isn't he? Tomi said.

He pointed at the biceps of Dan Llew's pale arms. As if Tomi had told her what to do, Kate waded forward through the drying dung and took hold of Dan Llew's upper arm with her cold hands.

— He's gone mad, Wynne Bannister said.

He peered around the ground for his pipe.

— Won't do your blood-pressure any good, friend, he said. Not when you are nudging fifty.

Dan Llew worked his arm up and down, but Kate did not let go.

— I'll kill him, Dan Llew said.

He turned his angry face towards Kate's.

— You married him, Dan Llew said. You married him on the q.t. without telling anybody. Look what you've landed yourself with.

Wynne Bannister found his pipe. It had been trodden into the dung. He turned to the pile of hay and tugged out a handful to wipe the pipe. He held out the handful of hay towards Dan Llew.

— Now then, he said. Mind what you're saying. There are one or two facts about you, my friend, I've got under my hat. So mind what you're saying.

— Dan, Kate said. Dan, what's the matter?

— He asked me to clear my stores out of this field, Dan said. That's what's the matter. I pay you two hundred pounds a year rent for this farm, just for the use of it, my old home, just to help my sister, and he asks me to keep the animals out of this paddock. I've been waiting for this!

Dan Llew tightened his mouth and stepped back to address them both more publicly. Tomi stood in the doorway, watching everything with deep interest, moving his head about like a hungry bird so as not to miss any detail of behaviour. Wynne Bannister drew in his breath rapidly and pointed at Tomi.

— If you paid him a living wage for a start, he said.

— Just listen to this, Kate. Just listen. For you to understand what kind of a man you've married. He wanted this paddock clear to rebuild this place. Something for visitors, he said. A holiday house.

— It's a good idea, Bannister said. You agreed it was a good idea . . .

— He wanted to borrow the money from me, Dan Llew said. I said you pay our Kate the housekeeping money you owe her first, I said.

— How did he know anything about that?

Bannister walked heavily through the hay-covered dung towards Kate. When he stood in front of her, he asked her the question again. She turned and walked out of the building. Totni Moch almost fell as he moved out of her way. He put out his hand against the wall to steady himself. Bannister ran after Kate, who was walking with her head down towards the orchard above the house. He took her arm and made her stop.

— Listen. Listen, Kate, he said. You haven't heard my side. You listened to him. Why don't you listen to me?

Kate lifted her head. Her hands were deep in the pockets of her old mac.

— I've got the rest of my life to do that, haven't I? she said.

J.T. PUT DOWN his fountain-pen and rubbed his eyes. His slipper dropped off his left foot and lay on the fat Concordance that was open on the floor. The wind lashed the rain against the bay window of his study. He opened his eyes and across the street he saw a paper-boy hopping over puddles as he dashed from one door to another. His gaze returned to the sermon paper and the green notebooks scattered over his desk. On the paper he had written down the text, 'He telleth the number of the stars; he calleth them all by their names . . .' Psalm 147. The rest of the paper stretched blank from the tip of his finger to his shirtcuff. With his wrist balanced on the base of the pad he stroked the air with his fingers as if he were outlining concepts that he could not put into words. He straightened his back and shifted his buttocks on the polished seat of his oak desk chair. He leaned back, closed his eyes and exercised his neck. He stopped suddenly when he heard a knocking on the wall between the study and the kitchen. He kept still, listening intently. The knocking was repeated. He could hear it distinctly beyond the bookcase that stretched from floor to ceiling. His face looked puzzled. He pushed back his chair and made for the door. He stopped to look around for the slipper missing from his left foot. He hobbled through the cold room that was only used for enter-taining visitors. Through the open door and across a short passage he saw a fire burning cheerfully in the kitchen Triplex grate. There was a white cloth on the kitchen table and a place laid for one. He saw Mrs Jennie Leyshon kneeling before the oven to extract a covered plate. The smell of a hot dinner made his mouth water.

— Come along, Mr Miles, Mrs. Leyshon said.

Her voice seemed more modulated than ever. Often when she spoke Mrs Leyshon sounded as if she were reciting.

— The grass widowers of this world must be fed, just like anyone else, she said.

— Dear me, J.T. said,

He watched her remove the cover from the plate of meat, pota-toes, brussel sprouts and gravy.

— Now it won't be up to Mrs Miles's standards, Mrs Leyshon said, but it will feed the inner man. Do come and eat, Mr Miles.

Obediently J.T. sat down. Mrs. Leyshon opened a drawer in the dresser and extracted a napkin rolled in an amber ring that J.T. always used. He thanked her as he took it from her and spread the napkin over his knees.

— What about you, Mrs Leyshon?

J.T. waved a knife to show concern.

— I've already eaten, Mr Miles. I told Morris I wanted to bring a hot meal across to you and he went back to school early. He's got the end-of-term reports to do, so that will keep him busy.

— You are very kind, J.T. said.

— I can see how hungry you are, she said.

— I'm most grateful.

He nodded as he chewed.

— I hope the meat isn't too tough, she said. You know me. I always say what I think. I warned Lydia not to go and leave you alone.

She clapped her hands and laughed.

— I did you know. We are very frank with each other, Lydia and I.

Suddenly she became serious and sat down in a chair between the dresser and the fire. The food was very hot and J.T. pushed it about a great deal with his knife and fork. Mrs. Leyshon lifted her head and spoke.

— Tea, she said. That's what you need. I'll have a cup too. The kettle has boiled.

She put the kettle back on the fire. From the pantry across the short passage she brought a tea pot and a tea canister.

— This is a good deal better than the old house, isn't it? she said. I was absolutely determined the move should be made this year. In that other poky terrace place with a growing family. I told them there was absolutely no sense in it. Strange, isn't it, even in this day and age, men hate being told something by women. It was hard on Lydia. They could see that — with three children. But I told them it was hard on you too. To be a preacher and a leader, a man mustn't be worrying from morning till night about his wife overworking and about his children's health. Mr Miles is a wonderful man, I said, but you mustn't expect too much from him.

— Did you say all that?

J.T. stopped chewing.

— Yes I did. I shouldn't embarrass you by telling you, I know, but I couldn't help myself. I just wanted a bit of credit. That's all.

Mrs Leyshon bit her lip as she poured out the tea. J.T. watched her face. For a moment she lifted her head, so that her eyes, enlarged by the lens of her spectacles, gazed earnestly into his.

— From you I mean, J.T., she said.

J.T. began to blush. He had never heard her address him as J.T. before.

— I made it sound extreme and silly, but I was very discreet really. I would never cause you a moment's anxiety by behaving unwisely in public. I think too highly of our relationship for that.

J.T. swallowed and looked down at the cup of tea she pushed towards him.

— I always feel I can speak so freely with you, she said.

She sat down and stirred the sugar in her tea.

— I feel I share the same idealism, somehow. It's all so difficult to put into words. Last night in bed I found myself lying awake and thinking how much I would like to address you as 'ti' — in front of other people even — and how gladly I was prepared to give up such a simple pleasure for the sake of those we both love. I think that is something other people would never never understand, but I can tell you, because you understand.

Mrs Leyshon sighed and sipped her tea. J.T.'s teaspoon clanked nervously against the inside of his cup as he stirred his tea.

— You mustn't let me go on if I embarrass you, she said.

— Oh no, J.T. said. Not at all. Please go on.

— The relationship between men and women must change, she said. I have more in common with you than anybody else I know. But because I am not your wife I'm hardly ever permitted to speak to you freely. Men talk to each other endlessly, about politics and the world situation, but a man and a woman are only supposed to talk about one thing. Now that is barbaric. Don't you think so?

— Yes, J.T. said. Yes I do.

— There's nothing I wouldn't do for you or for Lydia or one of the children, because I love you all. I believe I love you all equally. But I could never say this outside. Anywhere. To anyone else. People already say I'm a crank because I won't eat meat. Goodness me. If they heard me now they'd rush me off to the police station. They would, you know. They really would.

She put down her teacup and rose to her feet.

— I'm upsetting you, she said. I know I am. On a Saturday too and you've still got your sermon to write. It's about the stars, isn't it? Morris is quite excited about it. He's got his charts all ready. It's a revolutionary Sunday School. Everybody over sixteen sitting there listening to a lecture followed by a sermon. Where else could it happen? Where else? Will Bayley Lewis be coming?

— He might, J.T. said.

He was frowning.

— Is there something worrying you?

— It's just that I'd like more time to prepare, J.T. said. There's so much I haven't read. I'm not really competent to deal with the subject . . .

— Just say what you feel yourself, Mrs Leyshon said.

— What does it matter what I feel? J.T. said. Who am I to . . .

Mrs Leyshon held out her hand. J.T. hesitated.

— Please take my hand, she said. Cautiously he took it.

— It does matter to us, Mrs Leyshon said. You are our minister. We know you are a good man.

She leaned forward and lifted his hand until it touched her cheek. Then she let it go.

— I'll leave you to get on with your work, she said.

THE NEGRO WAS wearing a purple uniform. Ronnie and John Henry stared at him with their mouths open. They gave the tiny red veins in his large eyeballs all their attention until he stretched out his hand again and they stared at his pink palm.

—You bin in, you pay, the negro said.

The word 'inspector' was embossed in gold braid above the peak of his cap. For the third time Wynne Bannister plunged his hands into his trouser pockets and rummaged about, leaning first on one side and then on the other.

— Funny, isn't it? he said. You can never find it when you want it.

He put down his head and looked at the negro over the top of his gentlemanly spectacles.

—What part of the States do you come from? he said.

— Alaska, the negro said.

He pushed his thick lips in and out.

—You goin' to pay? he said. I ain't got all night.

— Now then, Wynne Bannister said.

He made himself as tall as he could, but the negro still looked down at him.

— Haven't you got any money, Uncle?

Ronnie whispered anxiously and turned to see if his mother was coming. The great roundabout that swung around in the heart of the fairground seemed far away where the light of the lamps and the flares glistened on the wet ground. There were no shadows moving down the muddy path to the menagerie.

— Wasn't much better than a Cheap-pots Stall anyway, Wynne Bannister said.

He was looking in the same direction as Ronnie and he spoke in a low voice.

—Was you sayin' somethin'? the negro said.

— Ronnie! Ronnie!

Lydia's voice was calling out of the darkness.

— Here, Mam! Outside the menagerie.

She ran towards them out of the darkness. When she spoke she was out of breath.

— For heaven's sake. Where have you been? I thought I'd lost you for ever.

— Lydia, fach, Wynne Bannister said, we thought we would take a quick look at the lions. Didn't want to see anything else really, did we boys? It wasn't much but it seems we have to pay.

The negro rolled his bloodshot eyes. John Henry shuddered as if he felt the cold and Ronnie shut his eyes.

— Could you lend me a ten-bob note, Lydia, until we get back?

— How much is it? Lydia opened her handbag and lifted it close to her face. The electric light at the solitary turnstile that led into the row of cages was depressingly dim.

— Sixpence each, the negro said.

— Don't they get in for . . . they're both under fourteen, Wynne Bannister said.

— That's for trying to get in for nix.

The negro gave the rebuke with weight and dignity, and the boys shuffled guiltily behind their uncle.

— Thanks, Lydia.

She had given Bannister half a crown.

— Here we are then. No bones broken.

The negro shook the loose change in his trouser pocket without smiling. Lydia put her hands on the boys' shoulders and started to steer them back towards the centre of the fairground. Ronnie looked back to see what was happening to his uncle. Lydia pushed him on. Their feet crunched on the cinders that had been spread over the wettest patches. Wynne Bannister was laughing when he caught up with them.

— Where's the change? Lydia said.

— Told him to keep it.

He lifted his soft hat, looked inside and replaced it on the back of his head. His well-worn mac with the collar up blew behind him in the rising breeze as he searched his pockets for his pipe. The bottoms of his trousers were rolled up. He looked like a well-to-do farmer at a cattle mart. He put his hand on Ronnie's cap and pushed it forward.

— He's a good lad, Lydia, he said. Ronnie looked up and smiled at his uncle.

— You should have called the police, Lydia said.

Bannister found his pipe and stuck it quickly between his teeth.

— Good God, he said. I wish my brother Jack had been with us. Jack is a U.S. citizen. Now he wouldn't have dared open his mouth in front of Jack. I remember the year of the Wembley Exhibition. Jack was over. We went to see a big circus in Chester. By the racecourse. There were blacks there. There was one in charge of the queue where we were standing. People were fed up with waiting. And he got cheeky. Jack showed him his badge.

He stood still and turned out the lapel of his jacket. They were near a fruit stall and there was a smell of over-ripe oranges that made John Henry swallow and pull a face. The naphtha flare above the stall was blown about by a gush of wind and the shadows danced on Bannister's face. He took the pipe out of the corner of his mouth.

— I never saw a man change so quickly, he said. I thought he was going to drop on his knees and kiss Jack's feet. Without a word of a lie. Now that's the way to treat them.

They walked on through the fair. Bannister tried to urge Ronnie to stop and buy a water-squirter disguised as a rose. He mimed inviting someone to smell it and then getting a squirt of water in the eye. Lydia waved them on impatiently, and then lifted her foot to examine the state of her shoes. Bannister put his arm on Ronnie's shoulder. Ronnie straightened himself and glanced to his left to check if he were taller than his cousin, John Henry. Bannister became serious again.

— The white man must show himself master, he said. His teeth were clamped firmly on the stem of his pipe.

— The moment he forgets that he's done for . . .

— Where is your motor-car? Lydia said.

Ronnie looked up at his mother's face. She sounded cross.

— 'The night is young, and we are far from home . . .'

Bannister lifted his eyebrows and sang in a tuneful tenor.

— It's time these boys were in bed, Lydia said. It will be very late by the time we have taken John Henry back to Cefn.

— John Henry, John Hen-rey . . .

Ronnie began to laugh, but Lydia said,

— Oh come on for heaven's sake, where is it?

They passed through the centre of the fairground. The proprietor of the roundabout was making a last effort to stir up excitement. Music had begun to pour out from the steam organ. People talked more loudly and there was much gesticulating and signalling among the young men as if the time was coming for them to take over. Lydia kept her hand firmly on John Henry's shoulder. Ronnie was shepherded in a jolly way by his uncle, who tried to shuffle and sing whenever he could in time with the music. He had a brief conversation with a group of young men with flushed faces and he left them regretfully when Lydia came back to touch his arm. She made no attempt to speak, the noise was so great.

He had left his motor-car in the back yard of the 'White Goat', an old coaching inn on the outskirts of the village. They stumbled up a lane that led, Bannister said, direct from the fairground to the back of the pub. They hurried forward through the darkness, their arms held out in front of them to meet any unseen obstacles. Bannister advised them to keep close to the hedge, treading the grass verge, until he himself tripped over a large stone and landed laughing on his back in the hedge. When they got to the yard he stretched forward to grasp the big handle of the cover of the back seat and pulled it open with a gesture of triumph.

— Boys in the dickey seat! Up you get!

Ronnie and John Henry scrambled up into the back seat and covered their knees with the travelling rug.

— Snuggle down, boys! That's the style. I'll just pop in and say good-bye to Cecil the Goat.

He spoke to Lydia.

— Just thank him you know for letting me leave the old car in his back yard. Why don't you come in? Have a nip of port and lemon? I'd like to introduce my sister-in-law. I told you Cecil and I were in school together. Lydia opened the door of the car on the passenger side.

— Please hurry, she said. I'm getting worried about these boys. He nodded towards the car to reassure them and lifted his arm as if to direct them to wait in their seats until he got back. They heard him scraping his boots outside the back door of the pub.

— He'll be drunk, John Henry said, when he comes out.

Ronnie looked at his cousin's face.

— He's pretty safe I should think, Ronnie said.

— He's been in a ditch with it twice for me to know, John Henry said. I'll be grateful if I get home in one piece, I can tell you.

He sank further down under the rug.

Ronnie leaned forward to see what his mother was doing. He peered through the small rear window in the roof of the coupe. His mother was sitting bolt upright, her hands clasped together in her lap so tightly her knuckles shone in the dark.

IT WAS A FINE day and on two sides the canvas walls of the marquee had been rolled up, so that those who sat at the trestle-tables facing westwards could see, beyond the bell tents that were pitched neatly among the flowering gorse bushes, a margin of sand where the land dipped, and a curtain of open sea.

Bayley Lewis, together with the visiting M.P. and the arch-deacon, was moving between the tables, serving tea from large brown enamelled teapots. The porridge and syrup course was almost finished and the tin plates were being scraped noisily by the hungry men. J.T. sat between Bill Mabon, a silicotic miner from the Aman Valley, and Walter Silin, a lecturer in Welsh History at the University College of Cardiff. Bill Mabon was pointing his spoon in the direction of Bayley Lewis, who smiled as he poured out tea.

— He means well see, Bill said. But he doesn't really begin to know what it's all about.

With his spoon he tapped an empty 'Force' packet on the bare table in front of him. The young man sitting opposite him stopped stirring the remains of his porridge in the shallow bowl and tried to hear what Bill was saying.

— He's like him, Bill said.

He tapped the picture, on the packet, of a smiling gentleman leaping over a five-barred gate. Walter Silin lowered his copy of the *Manchester Guardian* and leaned forward to listen. Bill turned the packet around to show J.T. the figure more clearly. He was smiling as if he were already amused by what he was going to say. His thin face was glistening after his morning shave and there were still traces of soap on the lobes of his ears. He seemed susceptible to cold. He was the only man on the table wearing a jersey and long trousers. The others were dressed in shirts of all shapes, colours and sizes and football shorts.

— He is propelled by a degree of optimism, Bill said.

Then he paused for breath and smiled again, lifting the spoon so that no one should interrupt him.

— That would be dangerous if he had any more intelligence.

— You mean he has faith, J.T. said.

— Last night now, Bill said. Giving us a sermon on strikes. The goodwill approach. He just doesn't know what he's talking about.

J.T. was going to speak, but Bill turned and gripped his arm while he spoke.

— Listen, man, he said. I've seen soldiers with fixed bayonets charging down the workers. I've seen it with my own eyes, man, and I know men, railway men now — not miners — railwaymen with bayonet wounds in their buttocks. You can't kid me with all this goodwill stuff. The class war is a war, and don't you forget it.

Bill tapped his empty porridge plate with his spoon.

— I came here for a square meal and a bit of fresh air. I don't want you to think I'm here under false pretences.

J.T. pressed his lips together and nodded several times before he spoke.

— This is an experiment, he said. It's an experiment in living together. We don't know whether it will work, but we believe it would be wrong not to try.

— It's just scratching at the edges, Bill said. Scratching at the edges. There's a revolution needed. He lifted his arm in an abbreviated wave, and struggled for breath.

— What does all this mean in the context of 'The Coming Struggle for Power'? New bottles, Mr Miles, for new wine. Do I have to tell you?

J.T. began to laugh. Bill raised his spoon again.

— The fact that I'm smiling, boy, doesn't mean I'm not serious.

J.T. leaned back to allow Walter Silin to speak directly to Bill Mabon. Bill looked at him over his steel-rimmed glasses.

— Here he comes, he said. Our tame nationalist.

— I just want to ask you one question, Silin said.

— Get in a college, Bill said, and be safe outside the struggle. Cosy place a college . . .

— You're not going to make me lose my temper, Silin said.

A blush had begun to rise up his narrow face to the roots of his springy hair.

— Just answer me a simple question, he said.

— Go on then. I'll buy it.

Bill looked at the young man sitting opposite him and gave him a heavy wink.

— Are you a Welshman?

It appeared as if Silin were making a special effort to keep his head and tongue still after putting his simple question.

— Don't be bloody daft, man, Bill said.

He turned to J.T. and said,

— Sorry, Reverend. What do you think I am, an Eskimo?

— Are you?

— Of course I am. As good as you are any day.

— Has the Welsh nation got a right to exist?

— A nation is a collection of people, boy. All people have got a right to exist. I don't know why I argue with you really. You're so elementary.

The men who were listening laughed and Bill tugged contentedly at his leather belt, a humorous expression on his face.

—You don't believe that the Welsh people should be responsible for the life of the Welsh nation?

— Oh, Duw,[97] of course I do. And look what a mess they're making of it.

— In London.

— Aye in London. In London or Cwmscwt.[98] What's the difference.

—You don't admit any responsibility for the language and traditions and literature of your own country?

— I knew we'd get back to this, Bill said.

He smiled again, but this time Silin thumped the table with his small fist.

—Why don't you answer!

He spoke so loudly everyone looked in their direction. Bayley Lewis lifted a bare leg over a bench and holding the teapot in front of him came trotting down towards them. He wore a khaki shirt with its collar up and a pair of white rugger shorts. There were varicose veins on his legs and there were holes in his plimsolls that were still wet with the morning dew.

— It's your job, man, Bill was saying. You've got a vested interest there. Academics . . .

The young man opposite Bill held out his mug for tea. Bayley Lewis filled it carefully, his eyes lifting quickly from the mug across the table to the two men arguing. He looked down again to see how the mug was filling and looked up meaningfully at J.T. He smiled when he spoke and his tenor voice sounded loud and sweet. He bent forward and nodded towards Bill.

— I was just saying to the archdeacon before breakfast, Bill, You are the very man we need to lead the discussion group on 'The Future of Education'. As you know he'll be leaving us this afternoon and he agreed with me, you are the very man to take his place.

Bill shook his head. He appeared to be modest.

—We know you can do it. That's why we are asking you.

Bill closed one eye with the effort of thinking, and then nodded.

— On one condition.

Bayley Lewis raised his eyebrows and continued to smile.

— Completely free hand.

—Within the limits of practical democracy, Bill, a completely free hand.

They shook hands across the table. Bayley Lewis squeezed Bill's hand tightly and then let it go.

— I must be about my business, he said, or the tea will get cold.

Walter Silin stood up. He rolled the *Manchester Guardian* into a thin cylinder and used it to slap his palm. He was a short man who found it difficult to be still.

— Would you like a walk?

He tapped J.T. on the shoulder with the newspaper.

— Coming, Bill? J.T. said.

— Got to stick up the teams for the morning game, Bill said. Regular busy bee, me. Teacher's favourite.

Silin and J.T. stepped into the sunlight. J.T. blinked in the bright light and he would have tripped over the guy-rope had not Silin held his arm. They walked briskly towards the path that wound down between the cliffs to the sea. They passed the cook-house that was built of corrugated iron over a wooden frame. Washing up had begun, in the open air in a row of enamelled bowls on a tresde. The cook stood watching the fatigue party. He was waiting his chance to tease the more inept of the handful of undergraduates at the camp, where everyone from Bayley Lewis downwards took his full share of the chores. The cook's heavy moustache completely covered his mouth, but it was possible to tell from the lines about his narrowed eyes that he was smiling. He waved to J.T. and Silin as they passed, and J.T. waved back. Although he was so much taller than Silin, he had to walk briskly to keep up with the little lecturer, who kept on banging his naked calf with the rolled-up newspaper as he hurried along. They had reached the top of the path when he stopped suddenly and looked back at the camp.

— I can't stand him, Walter Silin said.

— Now wait a minute, J.T. said. Bill's a fine chap, really. And a good Welshman too. You know it.

— Not him.

Silin spoke impatiently.

— I meant Bayley Lewis. He's a poseur. Everything he does is for effect.

— How can you say that? J.T. said. What right have you to say it?

Silin threw up his thin arms and plunged down the sandy path. J.T. watched him as if the rapid increase of distance between them were a strange phenomenon he was observing for the first time. Silin ran on until he was a tiny figure standing in the middle of the empty sands. He turned back and waved. J.T. did not wave back. Silin lifted his roll of newspaper again and waved and called, until J.T. moved down the path. It was so steep and soft, J.T. broke into a run. His feet twinkled over the crumbling surface of the path as it flowed out broadly into the beach. He gathered so much momentum that he ran on past Walter Silin and did not stop until his feet were splashing in the ridges of wet sand left by the ebb tide.

Walter Silin trotted over the sands to join him.

— You keep pretty fit, he said. Clean living and high thinking!

They walked towards the edge of the sea. It was a long beach and the tide spilt itself slowly in shallow waves that seemed to flounce up to their feet.

— I want to know what you've got against Bayley, J.T. said.

He stared out across the sea. There was a small ship on the horizon.

— You've got to see people exactly as they are, Silin said. Take a close look at him.

— He lives for other people, J.T. said. He spreads goodwill. He has a mission for peace. He brings men together. Look what he did during the General Strike. And what he did for Ireland. He brought De Valera and Lloyd George together.[99]

— He has his uses, I've no doubt. He's a go-between dressed up as a saint.

— He is a saint!

J.T. sounded indignant, and his voice rang out as he turned to look sternly at his companion.

— He's also a snob, Walter Silin said. He wants everybody to know how friendly he is with Lord Harlech and Lord Salisbury. You can't talk to him for more than ten minutes before he mentions both of them. And a show-off. He's playing a part all the time. But the worst thing of all about him is the harm he does.

— What harm for goodness' sake? Everything he does is constructive. He is a practical Christian.

— He pours a syrup of muddy, wishful thinking all over Wales!

— Wishful thinking! J.T. said. What about your economics? Back to the middle ages, Welsh autarchy. Feed Wales on Welsh wheat.

— You don't see any nearer than your nose . . .

They were facing each other, both red-faced and unreasonable.

— I've seen a working man sitting up all night with a little coffin on his knees so that the rats don't get at the body of his dead child!

J.T.'s lower lip trembled with his efforts to control his excitement.

— And I know, he said.

He stabbed the air between them with a bony forefinger.

— I know that good hard wheat from Manitoba or the Black Earth region or anywhere would have kept that child alive.

— People like you are made use of, Silin said. Men of goodwill. That's what you think you are. Look what happened at the Disarmament Conference[100] . . .

— I'm not talking about that, J.T. said. I'm talking about the simple realities of everyday life. A family of six eating a saucepanful of pig potatoes poured in a heap on the table and the children eating with their hands![101]

— That's exactly what I'm trying to tell you, Silin said. Charity begins at home. God helps them who help themselves. Oh damn, we've reached the proverb stage. Any minute now you'll be talking about reconciliation and I've heard enough about that this week.

— There's no point in you and I talking, J.T. said. We've been over all this before.

He turned to look back at the cliffs. Men were running and shouting down the path. A rugby ball had been kicked high in the air and those who were already on the beach looked up in admiration as it hung in the air. J.T. began to move away from the sea as if he wanted to join the men in their game.

— You've got to make a choice!

Walter Silin raised his voice.

— One day whether you like it or not, Miles, You'll have to choose. People like you will find you can't have it all ways . . .

Someone had given the ball a strong kick. It had begun to move before the wind had carried the noise of the impact of the boot on the leather within their hearing. It flew out towards the shallow waves on their right. J.T. took his hands out of his pockets and ran as fast as he could to intercept the ball. When he caught it, he was so; out of breath he had to bend down and wait a full half-minute before he could gather enough strength to kick it back against the morning breeze.

21

KATE ROLLED UP her sleeve again and thrust her arm into the flue at the back of the new stove. Inside, she twisted her wrist around bringing down the soot that was beginning to harden already against the chimney wall. It tumbled with soft thuds into the space at the back of the ashbin.

Her husband lifted the latch of the kitchen door. He was unshaven and without a collar and tie. Under his arm he carried a faded travelling rug and in his hand he had a copy of the previous day's newspaper.

— Can I come in?

He was ill and thin, but he smiled and looked over the tops of his spectacles to create a jovial impression. Kate looked over her shoulder, her arm remaining in the chimney flue.

— You should have stayed in bed, Kate said, I was bringing you some beef tea.

— I got fed up in bed, he said. I'm like my father. 'In bed good as dead,' he used to say. Has the post been?

— Go back to bed. You can get up after dinner.

— He's been then? Any letters?

— Were you expecting any?

She withdrew her arm from the chimney and blew the soot particles that clung to the hairs of her forearm in the ashbin.

Wynne pulled a comic face.

— Not really. Just thought I might have won the Irish sweep.

He came into the kitchen and made for the steps leading up to the churn room.

— Don't open that door!

Kate spoke sharply.

— You're not fit to go out there. There's a draught like a knife from the dairy.

Wynne lifted his finger.

— Bathroom, he said. Bathroom, Mrs B.

— Oh, is that what you call it.

Kate sank on her knees and began to rake the soot and ashes forward with a blackened raker.

— It just looks like a hole in the wall to me, she said.

— I thought I'd have a look, he said. See what they're up to.

— They're up to nothing, are they, Kate said. And never will be until they're paid.

He clutched his rug and paper and came to the table, pulling out a chair.

— It'll add two or three hundred to the value of the house, Kate, he said. Now that grate was a success, wasn't it?

He pointed at the grate with the hand that held the newspaper.

—You've said so yourself.

— Well it's all paid for, anyway, she said. Don't sit yourself down there. Go back to bed. I've told you I'm bringing you beef tea.

— I'm an active man.

He slapped the paper on the table and opened it out.

— I don't like being ill and I don't like being in bed. There's nothing wrong with me really. If I could get rid of this stomach trouble I'd put my name down for a monkey gland!

He leaned over and stretched out an arm as if he wanted to tickle Kate as she bent forward to rake the back of the fire vigorously. The effort was too much and he leaned back in his chair and slapped his hand over the paper. He read for a few seconds and then he said,

—This chap Hitler's got some good ideas you know. Work camps for young men. The best of army life without the killing and the snags. Good idea that you know. Clean up the country in no time with a few ideas like that. Probably pinched the idea from Lloyd George. It's a quick way to conquer unemployment you see. That's the man we need, you know, if you ask me. Get Lloyd George back. If I had more spare time you know, Kate, I'd go in for politics. It's men like me the country needs you know, really. Experienced. Been in the trenches. Been in business. Knowing the practice and principles of several trades. Now they want men like me to put new zest into building. Bring new life into stagnant industry. Men like me.

— Be quiet a minute.

Kate held up her head, listening.

—What's the matter?

— There's someone knocking at the front door.

— The front door? This time of the morning?

— Listen.

He listened intently. They looked at each other. Kate rose to her feet and looked at her black hands. Her husband looked apprehensive.

— I can't very well go . . . like this, he said.

He moved his head uneasily and smoothed out the newspaper with the side of his hand. She lifted her soot-covered hands and seemed to study them briefly, lifting her sack apron between finger and thumb and letting it fall again. As if there were nothing else to be done she walked briskly out of the kitchen, down the dark passage. The old front door was ajar and she levered it open by raising her knee. Wynne Bannister had altered the portico. It was now enclosed, with a glass-panelled door on the left side. Through the glass panel Kate saw the back of the new minister. He wore a mac over his overcoat and there were bicycle clips on his trouser-legs. His hat was tilted back slightly and he appeared to be examining the branches of a sycamore tree that grew out of the hedgerow on the far side of the garden. He held his hands behind his back and twiddled his fingers. Kate grasped the knob of the new Yale lock firmly between her fingers. At the first sound of the door being opened, the minister swung round, his mouth already open to give a salutation, which was suspended as his eyes dwelt through the thick lenses of his spectacles on Kate's blackened hands and forearms. As Kate pulled the ill-fitting door open and said 'Good morning, Mr Owens' he stepped back and held out his arm stiffly.

— Mrs Bannister, bach, he said. I'll call again.

— Come in, Kate said.

She spoke calmly as if nothing could upset or excite her. She still inclined her head to one side when she spoke as she had done when she was a girl, but now it appeared an old habit that had ceased to be based on curiosity or wonder.

— If you'll wait in the parlour, Mr Owens, while I wash this stuff off my hands.

— Well really . . . Mr Owens said. I do apologize.

— Sit down, Kate said.

He sat down obediently in a chair near the window. He looked at the piano. There was a large hymn-book open on the music-rest, but the lid of the keyboard was closed.

— I won't ask you to take off your coat, Kate said. It's so chilly in here.

Mr Owens moved his hands in opposite directions, as if one said that the room was most comfortable and that he would have safely discarded both his coats, while the other still emphasized the fact that he had been perfectly willing not to come in and to call again another time. He smiled benignly and nodded as Kate left the room.

In the kitchen, still seated at the table, Wynne Bannister held up his head like a man with acute hearing picking up signals of sound in order to appraise a situation. His right arm still lay over a photograph of young Germans stripped to the waist, working in the sun.

— Owens, is it?

As he spoke he was nodding as if encouraging Kate to say yes. She moved briskly to the fire-place and lifted up a kettle full of hot water. She carried it in her left hand and reached up from the bottom step to open the churn-room door.

— You'd better get back to bed, she said. It will be very cold in here with this door open.

She filled the enamelled wash-bowl that stood in the churn-room sink and with a bar of rough soap and a scrubbing brush worked on her hands. Through the small window there was a side view of the rainwater cistern and the small yard outside and the archway that joined the corner of the house to the nearest out-buildings. Kate scrubbed hard, but the soot was deeply ingrained into the lines and the palms of her hands and under her finger-nails.

Wynne stood on the second step, holding the travelling rug over his shoulders with one hand and keeping the door sufficiently open with the other.

— It's about the new bedroom in the manse, he said. I didn't mention it, did I?

Kate stopped scrubbing.

— Lewis Davies the plasterer left one wall unfinished before he left me. I told the Trustees, you know, it was a patch-up not a proper job. The whole wall wants knocking down, but they weren't prepared to pay. Mean lot you know.

— Why didn't you get someone else?

— They're not so easy to come by. Good craftsmen, I mean, not unskilled labour. As you know I haven't been well.

Kate began drying her hands on a roller-towel that hung behind the back door.

— It's not finished then, she said. Like our new bathroom.

— I want you to see my side of it, Wynne said.

— You always do.

She took off her apron and hung it up on a nail in the back of the door.

— You're blaming me already.

He swayed on the step as he turned. She hurried forward and caught his arm.

— Bed's the best place . . .

She waited for him to pick up the newspaper and watched him climbing the stairs slowly. She felt her hair and hurried back to the parlour. The minister got to his feet as she came in.

— You'll have to excuse my appearance, Kate said.

She sat down in the chair on the other side of the window.

— I heard Mr Bannister wasn't at all well, the minister said. His round face showed deep concern.

— He isn't well, Kate said.

She sat erect and very still except for her hands. They lay in her lap and she was using a nail of one hand to remove soot from the nail of the index finger of the other.

— I hope it isn't serious.

Kate did not answer. They could hear faintly her husband shuffling about in the bedroom above them.

— It would be a great sorrow for the whole church if anything happened to anyone connected with the good family of Argoed.

He began to smile to indicate that he was about to turn to a more cheerful aspect of the same subject.

— How are they down South?

— They are fairly well, I think, Kate said. Thank you.

— Your brother-in-law was always very independent, you know. I remember my first term in college he was making a great stand for peace. I was a youngster of course, but I was very impressed. I don't remember your brother at all. I think he must have joined up by then. Strange, isn't it? Two friends. Two points of view. So firmly held. And yet they understood each other. There's a lesson there.

He paused as if for the first time trying to check the spate of speech that flowed on because Kate would not speak.

— I had hoped to see Mr Bannister, just for a moment, he said.

His face was growing red. His wide mouth opened in a smile which found no response.

— About the new bedroom in the manse? Kate said.

— My wife and I were hoping, the minister said, if he could manage it, to get it finished soon. My wife's father isn't too well and we'd like to have him with us for a few weeks . . .

— He's in bed, Kate said.

— Please don't disturb him about it now, the minister said. Kate stood up.

— I'll tell him about it, she said. I'll see it gets done, Mr Owens.

— Thank you very much.

The minister jumped to his feet. He was smiling again and seemed to be searching for an excuse to laugh. Then he became serious. As they stood in the portico he dropped his voice.

— Well now then, he said, what does the doctor say?

Kate hesitated before she answered. She tugged at the old front door, but held the door-knob with one hand so that it should not close, only help to muffle what she was saying. The brass doorknocker gleamed behind her head. The minister stood with one foot outside the open doorway and his body twisted towards Kate as he waited for her to speak.

— He's got cancer, Kate said.

The minister's face showed horror and astonishment. He shook his head in sorrow.

— Please keep it to yourself, Mr Owens, she said. I don't want him to know.

The minister put his finger to his lips and nodded.

HERBIE WATTS HAD one foot in the road and the other on the uneven pavement. Unlike most of the houses in the side street, the front door of the manse was closed. In front of two of the terraced houses across the street there were heaps of coal lying, waiting to be carried in. An old woman sat outside her open door, knitting in the sun. At the blind end of the street children were playing, jumping on and off a broken wall. Some of them stayed in the thistle-thick field trying to talk to the old horse. Herbie Watts moved his position with a little jump so that the foot that had been on the pavement was now in the dry gutter. He shook his head sadly. Listening, Ronnie also shook his head.

— I can't understand it, he said. History yes. But Chem no. I never thought I'd come down in Chem. Honestly. I got sixty-eight in the Christmas term. Why should I pip it?

— What will you do?

Herbie's hands hitched up his badly-fitting grey flannels. Ronnie frowned sympathetically.

— Go back, I hope. Do Welsh matric next January.'[102]

— You mustn't leave, Ronnie said. Where would we get a new hooker?

— Plenty waiting to get in the team.

Herbie muttered with determined gloom.

— Acka Davies says you're the best hooker the school's had since he's been there.

Herbie's face broke into a delighted smile.

— Honest? When did he say that then?

— When I bust my ankle. I was standing by him on the touch-line.

Ronnie stopped speaking. He was listening to a new sound coming from the house behind him. A door banged and from the open window of his parent's bedroom he could distinctly hear his mother's voice rising in anger. Ronnie suddenly began a spasm of noisy coughing, Herbie Watts stared at him wonderingly.

— What did he say then?

— I was standing next to him when he said it. I've got to go in now, Ronnie said.

He opened the iron gate as noisily as he could and shook it unnecessarily as he closed it. He even clattered the latch up and down until Herbie looked down to see what he was doing.

— Maisie Philips did very well, Herbie said. Did you hear what her marks were?

— No. No I didn't. This gate gets stiff.

Ronnie spoke loudly.

— Well, I'll see you down the Rec then, Herbie. Tonight. Okay?

— Okay then. Congrats again, Ronnie.

— Thanks.

The front door was locked for some reason. Ronnie waved to Herbie who had started to walk away.

— Looks as if I'll have to go around the back! Ronnie said.

He rushed around, although he could see that Herbie had stopped farther down the road with his hands in his pockets, waiting for him to repeat what he had said. In the back garden Thea was standing on the green bench under their solitary apple tree, playing some game by herself. The runner beans which were his father's chief crop were in red flower. The grass grew thickly around the old privy, and beyond the wooden fence a particularly well-cared-for section of the allotments was visible, with clear rows of broad beans, peas, beetroot, parsnips and onions. Ronnie hurried into the house and stood listening and holding his breath at the bottom of the stairs. Their voices had subsided. He paused for a moment, looking down at the worn stair-carpet. Then he put his hand against the wall and began to climb the stairs as quietly as he could. His mother's voice was urgent and full of reproach.

— I suppose you think you're perfect, she was saying. Absolutely perfect.

— Good heavens, no. Of course I don't.

— And everybody else has got to be perfect. Everybody to speak Welsh! Everybody pacifist! Everybody Welsh nationalist! Everybody teetotal!

— Lydia, this isn't what we are discussing.

— Oh isn't it?

Her voice was heavily sarcastic. There was an ominous silence. At the top of the stairs, Ronnie held his breath. Then J.T. spoke again, as wearily as a tired ploughman about to open yet another furrow across a long field.

— I merely asked you where this necklace came from.

— You went snooping around in my drawer . . .

— I did nothing of the sort. The drawer was open, So far on your own admission everything you have told me has been untrue. Now please, in a spirit of quiet and reason and understanding, just tell me where you got it.

There was no answer. Ronnie looked up at the ceiling above his head. There was a trap door leading to the roof and the heat of the afternoon seemed to be pressing down on him. He had begun to sweat.

— If you won't tell me, J.T. said, this thing will always be between us, poisoning our relationship. Like a lie in the soul . . .

The word 'lie' seemed to touch off a fresh burst of anger. Lydia raised her voice so loudly, Ronnie stretched out his hand as if to implore her to keep her voice down.

— I don't know what you're talking about! This is how you always are. Full of words and phrases as if they have mattered more than anything else. You aren't like a normal man at all. You live on words and phrases. That's all you care about. You don't care about me or about the children. We've got to stay down here on this coal tip, in poverty and meanness, all because of your words and phrases. You know how much I hate it. I hate South Wales. And you know the doctor has said it's bad for Thea's health. But you don't care. You don't take a job in the Extra Mural Department because it will look as if you're deserting the church in its hour of need. And I have to borrow money from a woman I can't stand in order to get new boots for my children. But you don't mind. You've got all your little words and all your little phrases intact so you don't mind. You can sit on your bottom in your own little study, making up new words and phrases and we can go on existing like beggars who have to say thank you to a lot of working-class people for every crust we eat.

— Lydia. Will you please listen . . .

— No. You listen to me. I'll tell you where it came from. Edgar Berry gave it to me. He gave it to me for my birthday last year. When I was staying with Kate. He took Thea and me to Shrewsbury Flower Show. I happened to mention it was my birthday, so he bought it. And I took it. I thought it might come in handy — something to sell for a new pair of shoes.

Lydia slopped. J.T. sounded utterly puzzled.

— But what was he doing in North Wales?

— I should think he had plenty of excuses. He's a rich man. Is there anything else you want to know?

Ronnie heard his father move. He stepped as fast and as quietly as he could into the back bedroom, which he shared with his brother Vernon. He picked up a thick book and stood at the window, so that it should appear he was reading if they saw him. Outside Thea was still playing under the apple tree. She had tied a small length of rope to a branch. She stood on the bench and then swung herself off and held on as long as she could before dropping into the long grass. In the allotments two old miners stood smoking. They flourished their pipes at each other's crops. Ronnie turned the book in his hands so that he could study an illustration: *Fig. 95.— Wheatlands of the world. Europe (except Russia) eats more wheat than she can grow.* On the opposite page there was *Fig. 94. A photograph of an enormous wheat-field in*

Alberta Canada. Note that it stretches as far as the eye can see. He closed the book and lifted his head. His father was talking. He threw the geography textbook on to his bed. He stood on the stairs as if he were uncertain whether or not to go on listening. He stretched out his arms so that his elbows pressed against each wall of the stairwell and when he lowered his head, he looked imprisoned.

He was in this attitude when someone lifted the knocker on the front door and rapped sharply on it. His knees sagged. He seemed about to collapse in a heap at the bottom of the stairs. Then he recovered. Upstairs the talking had stopped abrupdy. He heard his father open the bedroom door. He shifted himself to the doorway of the living-room and called upstairs as if he had just come through from the back.

— It's all right, Dad. I'll open it.

As the door opened Mr Emrys Leyshon stepped back and smiled, looking up at Ronnie. Behind Mr Leyshon stood a man in a clerical collar. He carried a black hat in one hand and his closely cropped hair was parted in the middle. Mr Leyshon lifted his arm cheerfully.

— Hello, Ronnie! The hero of the hour. Matriculated! Is your father at home?

Ronnie blushed. Both men were watching him closely. He became conscious of a visible pulse in the pit of his neck and he stroked the whole of his neck with his open hand.

— I've brought an old college friend along to see him.

Mr Leyshon stood aside so that Ronnie could have a clearer view of his companion who moved forwards, offering his hand.

— I'd better shake hands with him, hadn't I? Taller than his father I shouldn't wonder. Must keep on the right side of him.

Mr Leyshon laughed loudly. J.T. was coming down the stairs. He was buttoning up the waistcoat he wore underneath his alpaca jacket. He held his head to one side as he frowned as if to demonstrate that he was expecting nobody and was preparing himself for the shock of recognition. Ronnie tried to move out of the way. His father put a hand on his shoulder.

— Frank, J.T. said. Frank Morgan! Where did you spring from? Emrys, how are you?

He shook hands with them both without removing his left hand from Ronnie's shoulder.

— Well it was rather remarkable really.

Mr Leyshon waited for them to settle down and listen.

— There was an N.U.T. meeting in Cardiff and I had promised to take Walters, the National School, Pen-y-ffordd. Who should be staying with Walters but Mr Morgan here — his brother-in-law! Mrs Walters is Mr Morgan's sister.

J.T. thrust his head forward to show he was listening closely.

— I happened to mention our minister in the course of conversation and of course Mr Morgan pricked up his ears. To cut a long story short, I promised to bring him here to see you, this very day. I understand he is returning to Luton tomorrow . . .

Morgan nodded to confirm the statement.

— I didn't want to vanish without snatching the chance of seeing you, J.T.

Morgan touched at J.T.'s sleeve and plucked at it as if to make certain he was there.

— And now I see your son as well. And he's as tall as you. And better looking.

They were all smiling. Ronnie pressed the back of his head against the door-post. His father was making an effort to show as much interest and excitement as his unexpected visitor.

— Good gracious, come inside, come inside, J.T. said.

He led the way into the study. He moved some books from one of the chairs so that Emrys Leyshon could also sit down. Ronnie closed the front door and came to stand in the study doorway.

— Well, well, J.T. said.

He bent down to pick up one of his pipes from a yellow dish on the hearth tiles.

— It's only shag, I'm afraid.

He held out his tobacco pouch to Frank Morgan, who took it with a grateful nod, having held it first to Mr Leyshon, who waved his fingers, smiled roguishly and said that he did not smoke.

— You haven't changed a bit, J.T., Frank Morgan said.

They used the second person singular to each other and seemed to acquiesce very willingly in such an arrangement. It was proper that men who had been in college with each other should use the closer mode of address.

— I don't remember that mole on your cheek either . . .

— That's something that grows with the years. Like hair in your ears! Their laughter was noisy and explosive. Ronnie stared at his father as if he were seeing him as a completely new person.

— Where's Lydia?

Frank Morgan looked around him urgently. J.T. took his pipe out of his mouth. The tobacco clouds were already gathering in the tiny study.

— Go and see where your mother is, Ronnie, will you?

Ronnie nodded obediently, glancing quickly at Mr Leyshon and the other visitor.

— Tell her Mr Morgan is here. Frank Morgan who used to come to Argoed with Uncle Griff . . .

— But not as often as your father did!

There was a fresh outbreak of laughter. Ronnie closed the door. The laughter died down.

— Well tell me about yourself, J.T. said. Are you married for instance? I don't remember hearing any news of you for goodness knows how long. Talk about the days of long ago. Did you know Platt Rees was in Australia? I had a letter from him last Christmas. A big church in Melbourne. Married a rich widow . . .

Frank Morgan was nodding to show that he knew.

— Now I think that's something every minister should try and do. They all burst out laughing again. J.T. was flushed and excited and his eyes gleamed. He laughed until tears began to appear in the corners of his eyes.

— Well, well, he said. I don't suppose we laugh enough these days, do we?

Frank Morgan leaned over to touch Mr Leyshon's sleeves.

— Hang on . . . he said, speaking to Leyshon and keeping an eye on J.T.

— I don't really know yet, do I, that he's going to speak to me? Now listen, you old Methodist. Before we start. I'm a parson now. A parson in the Church of England.

J.T. sobered visibly, raised his eyebrows and began to nod with demonstrable tolerance.

— After the war, Frank Morgan said, I was chaplain in a camp in Yorkshire. I met my wife there. Now she was church you see. And to cut a long story short I've been in English parishes ever since. But I keep in touch, mind you. I always try to get to the Eisteddfod. And I get the magazines that interest me. It isn't the same of course. I'd like to come back. I saw the Bishop of Llandaff last week. It isn't easy you see at my age. And the wife. We've got two boys at Mill Hill. I couldn't go to any old parish.

J.T. sighed. Mr Leyshon looked at him anxiously.

— Do you still write verse?

J.T. spoke very gently.

—Very little. Very, very little. Mind you, there are lot of Welsh folk around Luton. There isn't a day passes I see someone . . . Most of them from down here of course. Hwntws. Young people mostly. Very go-ahead some of them. There are several societies. There's an Eisteddfod too.

He was frowning and his voice was harsher.

— That's exactly it, J.T. said. Wales is the last thing that counts.

— What do you mean?

Frank Morgan looked surprised. Mr Leyshon cleared his throat and looked uncomfortable.

— Over half a million men and women gone, J.T said. Driven out of their native country by unemployment. All the youngest and most active. The flower of the working class you could call it.

Morgan made a tutting noise.

—You're not one of those, he said. Not a Welsh nationalist?

— I'm with them all the way, J.T. said. I'm against that bombing school in Caernarvonshire[103] and I'm against the draining away of our young people to London and the Midlands and Luton too.[104] And I'm against a lot of other things too. And I'd like to do something about it. Before it's too late. I wouldn't want to go on living in the middle of a dying country.

— You haven't changed a bit, Frank Morgan said. As impractical as ever. I suppose you don't believe that England and Wales are the same country?

— Of course they're not, J.T. said. You know it as well as I do. You haven't changed either. You were always the one for the most comfortable armchair.

— I didn't come here to be insulted, Morgan said.

He was trying to smile, but already his cheeks had gone pale. Mr Leyshon coughed again and smiled uneasily.

— I'm sorry, J.T. said. I'm sorry. I've had a trying day. That's no excuse I know. This morning we . . . there are nearly a hundred small children in this valley alone suffering from rickets . . . well this morning we . . . the government refused a special grant to pay for converting a private house that had been given to the committee into a hospital and rehabilitation centre.

There was a knock on the study door. Ronnie opened it. When they looked at him he said,

— Mam is in bed. She isn't feeling very well.

Frank Morgan jumped to his feet. He looked flustered, anxious to remain amiable and yet still angry. Mr Leyshon also rose, frowning in sympathy with the news of Lydia being unwell.

— I think we'd better be on our way, Mr Morgan said.

—No! No!

J.T. spoke vehemently.

— Not without a cup of tea. And what's the hurry anyway. I can't let an old friend go without a cup of tea. Just a cup in hand. Sit down, sit down. Or would you rather go in the garden? Ronnie, put the kettle on, will you? As much of a garden as we've got. Where's Thea? Where's Vernon?

J.T. made his visitors sit down. Ronnie closed the door

— We've got three, J.T. said.

He stood above Frank Morgan's chair.

— Ronnie. And Vernon. A bit slow he is. Bit of a dreamer. And Thea. Living image of Lydia. You'll see her in a minute. How old are your boys?

— Francis is sixteen and Stephen is twelve.

— Time flies, J.T. said.

He sat down heavily in his chair.

— *'Who sees it, sees the wind.'*

Mr Leyshon looked at them both and they acknowledged his apt quotation. Mr Morgan adopted a poetic tone.

— *'As it was in the beginning so it must ever be;*
  Time never stays until he stops with me.'

— That's very good. Is it your own?

— Well . . .

Mr Morgan nodded grudgingly.

— In a way. I translated it really. Very freely.

Their conversation petered out. Once or twice Mr Leyshon sighed audibly. Mr Morgan crossed his legs and gripped the bowl of his pipe with both hands, puffing hard until his head was wreathed in smoke. In the distance there was the noise of children playing on the broken wall at the end of the street.

— That's it really, Mr Morgan said. You don't get it in England, but in Wales it's the note you always hear. Regret. Always regret. For a lost kingdom. A city under the sea. Arthur sleeping. Old friends. Old memories. It's always 'what was' not 'what's to come'. Even in this day and age. It's in all the poetry I read.

There was a light tap on the door.

— Come in, J.T. said.

Lydia opened the door. She looked fresh as if she had just washed and changed. J.T. had been smiling, but as he stared at the thin gold necklace she wore round her neck his smile faded. Lydia offered her hand to Frank Morgan and he leapt to his feet.

— Frank, she said. How wonderful to see you.

He held her hand and they smiled at each other.

— I'm sorry, I was lying on the bed when you called. I had the most terrible head. But it's much better now.

— You haven't changed, Frank Morgan said.

He turned to J.T.

— If I may be allowed to say so, more beautiful than ever.

Mr Leyshon stood up, waiting to be greeted.

— Good afternoon, Emrys. You haven't brought Jenny with you?

— I left her in Cardiff, Mr Leyshon said. She had some shopping to do and she wanted to go and see her sister who lives in Rhiwbina.

Lydia nodded understanding. As soon as Mr Leyshon had finished, Frank Morgan said eagerly.

— How's your sister? Do you remember her hat blowing off on the prom at Rhyl? And old Platt Rees and me, racing to be the first to pick it up. How is she?

Mr Morgan spoke impatiently as one who cannot wait for news.

— Well that's quite a long story, Lydia said.

Ronnie appeared in the passage behind his mother. His hands were plunged deep in his pockets and he looked worried.

— Look at him!

Frank Morgan pointed dramatically.

— Towering over his mother! 'Behold a giant am I!' Is he going to be a preacher, like his dad?

— Well . . .

Lydia smiled as the three men laughed and Ronnie smiled uneasily.

— Well, I think you can safely say that's one thing he won't be, thank God.

When the men stopped laughing, Lydia brought her hands together and said,

— Now you all sit down and chat about old times. Ronnie and I will have the tea ready in no time at all.

FROM THE TOP window of the Old House, Thea was waving at her mother and her aunt. Lydia lifted her arm to wave back and Kate went on talking. They were standing by the row of deserted pigsties that backed against the long shippon. It had been raining and they trod carefully in the young grass. The sun had driven its way through the high cloud and both lifted their hands from time to time to protect their hair from the gusty wind. Lydia's hair was hobbed and waved, but Kate still wore a bun.

— I can't think what possessed you, Kate said.

She put her hands on the pigsty door and waited for an answer.

— I haven't said a word to a soul, Lydia said. Not a soul.

— What about J.T.?

— He can say what he likes. After all I've got Thea with me. Gone home on a visit.

— What did you say to him?

— I said 'I'm going to see Kate and I'm taking Thea with me and you needn't expect me back.' Lydia looked at Kate as if she were hoping she would smile or show some sign of approval.

— What did he say?

— What do you expect?

She tried to sound angry and contemptuous.

— What did he say?

— Nothing. He went in the study and shut the door.

— Where are the boys?

— I told you. They were all at school. When they came home when I gave them their tea, I told them you'd sent for me and that I was taking Thea.

Lydia looked back at the Old House. Thea had disappeared inside.

— Do you think it's safe for her to play in there?

— Why didn't you say something at the funeral?

— Poor old Wynne.

Lydia shook her head sadly.

— He was a good sort.

Kate did not speak. She waited for an answer.

— I didn't want to worry you at a time like that. And Joe was there. It wasn't a time to speak. Joe was assisting at the service. There wasn't a chance really.

— I had to clear up the mess.

Kate muttered so quickly Lydia did not appear to hear. They walked on towards the gate that led into the stackyard. The farm was strangely quiet. Grass grew right up to the doors of a row of outhouses where calves used to be reared. Lydia stopped to look over the top of a double door. Young nettles were already growing at her feet. The interior was dark and silent. Kate had walked on. Lydia raised her voice.

— I can't think what Dan Llew is doing with this place. He's letting it run to rack and ruin as far as I can see. Honestly, Kate, you ought to speak to him. After all the place is yours. If I know him, all you're getting is a very low rent, I dare say. Just look at this stackyard. Pa would turn over in his grave if he saw it.

Kate turned to look at her sister who had been making gestures appropriate to a public speaker and then jerked her head towards the house.

— You'd better come in, she said.

— What about Thea?

— She'll be all right. You come in with me. I want to talk to you. Lydia walked behind Kate as they crossed the yard.

— I wish I could see it all as it used to be, she said. I never thought I'd miss it so much. Look at poor old Tomi.

Tomi Moch sat on a box in the empty cart-house, sharpening a scythe. When he saw Lydia wave, he wagged the piece of whet-stone in his hand and grinned and nodded.

— I suppose Dan isn't paying him a penny more now than he did ten years ago.

Kate walked under the archway without giving any reaction to Lydia's words. By the back door she pointed at the cake of mud on the heel of Lydia's left shoe.

— You'd better scrape that off, she said. No use carrying it into the house.

While Lydia was scraping her shoe clean, Kate paused to look through the door from the churn room to the dairy that Bannister had planned to convert into a bathroom. The hole in the outside wall had been filled and roughly plastered over. But there was no bath in the room and no water ran into the taps above the isolated wash-basin.

— The old fool!

Lydia heard her as she closed the back door.

— He wasn't such a bad old stick.

— Wasn't he?

Her smile faded as Kate glared at her.

— I'll tell you what he was like. He stole every penny I had. Every single blessed penny. I'm only living here now, my girl, because Dan Llew lets me.

Her face had flushed and her eyes had filled with angry tears.

— He told lies, Kate said. And he cheated. I wish he'd died before I ever set eyes on him. I never trusted him. Never. I should never have let him through that door. Never.

— But Kate. You married him . . .

— What else could I do? Nobody else cared about me. All the rest of you were busy with your own lives. I was left here alone. Expected to die an old maid, I suppose. Alone in this house. You all took it for granted that was what I wanted. I suppose I only married him to make the lot of you sit up.

— Oh Kate . . .

— I hated it, I can tell you. I couldn't bear him to touch me. The smell of him used to turn my stomach.

— Even in the beginning . . .?

— And his voice. I couldn't bear his voice. He couldn't open his mouth without starting to lie. I can tell you I used to dread it when he came down to breakfast. The moment when he would open his mouth.

— Oh Kate . . .

— Every penny I had he took from me. Every security. He even managed to mortgage this house. I didn't know half the things he'd been up to until he died. And that bank manager, Thomas. Helping him take everything I'd got.

— The fat one at the funeral? The one who was talking about his new house?

Kate was absorbed in her own anger.

— If only I could turn this place inside out and scrub away wherever he put his dirty fingers. Instead every time I go in or out I've got to look at that.

She pointed dramatically at the unfinished bathroom.

— That's his monument, Kate said.

Lydia began to smile.

— I'm not joking, Kate said.

— I had no idea things were so bad.

Kate walked down the steps into the kitchen. Lydia stood at the top of the steps as if the position would give her all of Kate's attention.

— Listen, Kate. Let's set up house together. Just as we used to.

We'll even take that blessed stair-carpet up on Mondays. Just for old times' sake. I mean it. Honestly I mean it. I can't go back to Joe. I'd rather bring the children up here. We'd have a marvellous life. I mean they're old enough to do a lot of work. And we could be together. There's nobody in the world I'd rather be with than you, Kate. Honestly.

— The way you talk.

— I'm serious, Kate. Why couldn't we run this farm, the two of us? Our own home. We worked here long enough for other people. You've given your life to this place and to other people. Well now, let's live for ourselves. Thea and Vernon with us, Kate, to keep us young. And Ronnie can come here for holidays from college. Live the way we like it. Do you I know what I mean?

— Don't talk soft, Kate said. And come down from there. You look as though you're preaching.

She moved from the dresser against which she had been leaning, to attend to the fire. She began to rake away at the dead cinders at the bottom of the grate.

— I'll put the kettle on, Kate said. And we'll have some tea.

— As far as I can see, Lydia said, in this world women are slaves. That's all they are. Just slaves.

Kate lifted the heavy kettle on to the fire.

— You don't say anything about what I'm suggesting. I'm serious you know. Deadly serious.

Kate sat down in the high-backed chair that used to be her father's. Lydia waited for her to speak.

— You can stay as long as you need to, Kate said at last.

Lydia's eyes grew big. Her cheeks began to redden.

— What d'you mean?

— Sooner or later you'll have to go back, she said.

Lydia began to raise her voice.

— Why should I? Just tell me, why should I?

— He's your husband, Kate said. You can't leave him. Whatever else he is, he's a good man.

They eyed each other across the kitchen table. Lydia clenched her fist like a woman who is wondering whether or not to say the most wounding thing, and the whole house seemed to listen to their breathing. Outside, faintly, they heard Thea calling for her mother.

—You don't want us.

—That's got nothing to do with it.

—You're afraid we'd be a burden.

— Think what you're doing, Kate said. You're leaving your husband. You want your children with you. What has he done wrong?

— I've told you. I can't stand it any more. I can't stand that place. I can't stand him.

— People won't take that as a reason.

Lydia exploded.

— People! she said. People!

— Don't raise your voice, Kate said. I'm trying to be reasonable, so don't make me lose my temper. It isn't just what people say, it's what your own family will say. Think for a minute, girl, before you say anything. Think. What would Dan Llew say if you settled down here and people began to ask why you didn't go back to your husband? Two of us here for the rest of our lives. What would Ned say? What would Rowland say?

— I don't care what they say, Lydia said. And you shouldn't care either.

— They'll say you were dragging the family name in the mud, Kate said. That's what they'll say.

— Let them say it. Let them say it. I don't care.

—Well I care!

Lydia nodded her head slowly, menacingly.

—Yes, she said. That's it, isn't it? That's it exactly.

—What do you mean?

—You know exactly what I mean.

Kate's temper flared out suddenly.

— No I don't. And in any case nobody asked you to marry him. Nothing else would do.

Thea clicked the latch of the back door with her finger and I scraped her shoes noisily on the iron bar outside the door.

— Mam!

As she spoke her eyes moved from her mother's face to her aunt's, as she fingered the detachable white collar on her blue serge dress.

— Get your coat on, Lydia said abruptly, when she skipped down the steps. Get your coat.

Thea looked at her, her mouth open and her eyes wide with surprise.

— We're not staying here.

— Lydia.

Kate spoke softly in Welsh.

— Don't make a scene. For her sake. It can make a terrible impression on children.

— I'm not making a scene.

She spoke to Thea.

— We'll get a bus from the cross-roads, she said. There's a bus at four o'clock. If you wouldn't mind, Kate, we could leave our cases here until we could give you a forwarding address.

She turned to Thea impatiently.

— Go and get your coat.

— I don't know where it is.

— Don't know. Don't know.

There was a trembling in Lydia's voice.

— It's with mine of course, where it should be.

She hurried through the dim passage to where the coats hung in the hall.

— Lyd. Don't be soft. You can't go.

Lydia forced the glass-panelled front door open. It was beginning to sag slightly on its hinge. She took Thea's hand and almost dragged her down the paved garden path. Kate overtook them near the mounting stone. From his box in the cart-house Tomi Moch leaned forward to watch them with frank curiosity. They took no notice of him. Kate stumbled on an outcrop of rock and gripped her sister's arm tightly.

— Look it's going to rain, Kate said. It's going to rain any minute.

— We'll be all right, Lydia said.

Thea looked at her mother's face anxiously, as if she were searching for some clue to her behaviour, and then she looked up at the clouds in the sky and back at the house. She seemed very reluctant to leave.

— Now come back. Come back, Lyd. I'm begging you. Can you

hear me. I'm begging you. Come back to the house and we'll talk it all over calmly.

Lydia stared at her sister.

— You've never forgiven me, have you? All this time and you've never forgiven me.

— Of course I have. You know very well I have. You're just making a fuss for nothing and you know it.

Lydia tried to free her arm but Kate held on. She seemed annoyed to find that Kate was stronger than she was. As she tried in vain to free her arm, she spoke with difficulty.

— All I can say is . . . she said.

— Don't say it. Whatever you do don't say it . . .

— Say it?

— Look, Lyd, I'd go to Dan on my bended knee and beg him to let you stay here with me, if I thought it would do any good. You know I would.

Lydia kept her arm still. At last Kate's urgency seemed to have impressed her.

— I'd sell the place if it would help. Keep a boarding-house. Anything. He'd like to have the house anyway. Annie Grace told me, he wished he had a bailiff living there.

— I never could stand that woman, Lydia said.

— Come inside, Lyd. We'll talk it over.

Lydia looked down at Thea and seemed to notice the anxious expression on her face.

— I've never let you down, have I? We'll talk it over. You can have the boys up here for the holidays. I'll come down there and stay with you. In any case he could take a call from a church nearer here. I'll talk to him too if you like. You'll see, we'll manage.

22

THE FISHERMEN SAT in the shade of the harbour wall. A woman carrying a large basket stopped to talk to them. Children played at the water's edge. The little harbour was crowded with fishing vessels. J.T. tipped his panama hat over his eyes and pulled out a watch which hung by a leather strap from the lapel buttonhole of his alpaca jacket.

Near him Walter Silin sat with his back to the harbour, reading *L'Action Française*[105] of the previous day, and also watching the dark doorway of the small hotel across the cobbled street.

— He's gone inside.

He murmured so quietly J.T. had to ask him to repeat what he was saying.

— The gendarme. He's gone inside.

The newspaper rustled in the still air as he turned it over.

— You watch. He'll be here in a minute.

J.T. slipped his watch back into his pocket. He looked worried.

— I think I ought to send Lydia a telegram, he said. This crisis. It looks more like war every day. We ought to go home.

— Home or abroad . . .

Silin turned over a page.

— Shouldn't think our being here will influence Mr Hitler, one way or the other.

— The issue is peace or war. I don't know how you can read that paper.

— What do you mean?

— Its so unreal. Day after day. Reports on the situation. Hitler sends a note to London. Musslini sends a note to Hitler. The Poles send a note to Paris. You say reading that is one of the pleasures of life, like wine or good food. It's a monstrous game. The way you rush out every morning to buy that paper and the way you study it. You are playing at it too.

— You're sorry you came?

— I'm not talking about that, Of course I'm not.

— What did I tell you? Here he comes.

Silin lifted his newspaper to study it more closely. The gendarme had emerged from the Hôtel des Voyageurs. He had paused under the awning as if to enjoy the shade a moment longer before crossing the cobbled road and walking briskly towards them where they stood in the hot sun.

— Good morning, gentlemen. Could you show me you passports, please?

He seemed to bow as he saluted. He was smiling and friendly. He waited patiently while J.T. took out the entire contents of his inside pocket. He examined their passports with care.

— You have friends in Brittany?

He did not look up as he spoke.

— Yes we have.

Silin answered. J.T. did not speak.

— Yesterday you visited the house of Monsieur Tedecq. Did you speak to him?

— I called to collect some books, Silin said. As you can see from my passport, I am a university lecturer. I take a great interest in Brittany, her literature, her language, her traditions.

— Monsieur Tedecq is an engineer, the gendarme said.

He turned the passports over in his hands. He no longer smiled.

— You know that he was released from prison three weeks ago? He was imprisoned for writing and distributing seditious pamphlets. You know this?

— I know it. But it is nothing to do with me. I visited him because he is an old friend.

— Did you speak to him, monsieur?

— I spoke to Madame Tedecq, Silin said. I told you I collected some Breton books I need for my studies.

— Can one see these books?

— They are in my room in the hotel. Shall I get them for you?

The gendarme considered for a moment. The passports were still in his hands.

— Do you have many friends involved in the Separatist movement?[106]

— Oh yes.

— And you, sir?

The gendarme looked at J.T., who had become red in the face.

— Not really. This is my first visit to Brittany.

— How long do you intend to stay?

— The news is bad, J.T. said. I think we will start for home as soon as possible.

The gendarme nodded gravely. He handed J.T. his passport. He spoke to Silin again.

— May I ask you one question monsieur. Do you favour the aims of the Separatist movement?

— To a certain extent. Yes I do.

The gendarme looked severe. He did not speak and yet he did not move away.

— Their aims I'm speaking about, Silin said. I say nothing about methods.

Abruptly the gendarme handed Silin his passport. He was about to speak when the shrill note of a siren pierced the stillness of the air. The startled fishermen scrambled to their feet and from the quiet houses people began to emerge to stand in the streets. Their gestures were visible but their voices were drowned by the long-drawn wail as it rose and fell above the roofs of the town. When at last it stopped there was a moment of leaden silence as if every heart in the place had stopped beating. Then the voices began again. Mothers rushed out to call in their children. There was a general movement towards the little public square in front of the church with its towering spire. A group of fishermen approached the gendarme. One of them, a man in his fifties, had pushed up the sleeves of his jersey to display an old wound that had disfigured his forearm. J.T. stared at the long scar.

— War, then? they said. Is it war?

The gendarme was shaking his head.

— Not yet. That was the order for general mobilization.

He made a face to suggest there was nothing to be done.

— It might still not happen.

— Hope, J.T. said.

— That's it, monsieur, Hope.

The fishermen listened closely to their words and then went off towards the square, arguing. The gendarme turned to address the two foreigners who were clutching their passports.

— There is a train for Paris at three o'clock. I would advise you both to catch it. It is possible that after that passenger services will be suspended.

— It's not war yet, Silin said.

The gendarme shrugged his shoulders.

— Not war, he said. There is still a little hope, for those who want to hope. The train is at three o'clock.

When the gendarme left them J.T. and Silin looked at each other without saying anything, both self-conscious, neither knowing what to do with his hands. Silin rolled his newspaper up tightly and smote it against the palm of his hand like the rod of a teacher chastising himself.

— The fools! The mad fools!

— Who?

J.T. was looking at his hands. He clasped them together.

—Tedecq, Lorien and the other. You heard me tell them they were wrong?

— It was all very unreal, J.T. said. I had a curious feeling there you know. In that cottage, when Madame Tedecq took out the bundle of *Breiz Atao*[107] and said she was going to bury them in the hen-run. A strange feeling of unreality. The house was real enough. And that heavy oak furniture. But the people were ghosts, talking about war in 1942 and the dismemberment of France as if it had already happened. It occurred to me, you know, this is one dilemma of our times. The way science makes it possible for unbalanced people to realize their fantasies. You know what I mean? The nonexistent wars and diplomacy that went on in those people's heads. The shifts in this or that . . . You know what I mean?

— You heard me tell them? Silin said. The Germans would use them and then shoot them. You heard me say that?

—We'd better go and pack, J.T. said. And then we'll send telegrams home.

Silin seemed reluctant to move from the harbour wall.

— You know what Tedecq said to me. 'The difference between you and me, Silin,' he said 'is simply this. I don't mind being shot.' He didn't mean to be insulting. He smiled when he said it. As if he were taking about the weather.

— I had the feeling, J.T. said, they were out of touch with reality. Maybe as a result of prison. Brooding over their wrongs. We'd better go and pack.

Two army officers emerged from the hotel and stood in the shade of the awning. They seemed aware of their uniforms and obliged by them to look both calm and knowing.

— Those were the two we saw at breakfast, J.T. said. They were very quiet, weren't they?

— All over Europe, Silin said, the police and the army are taking over. Uniforms! It's the end of an era, J.T.. The end of your bourgeois liberty!

— I remember August 1914. J.T. said. That was very sudden. An explosion. This has been creeping along like gas. For a long time. Would you rather we went to the Post Office first?

— Remember the chapel at Kermaria? The painting on the walls? This is it, J.T.. You can hear the orchestra tuning up. The Dance of Death is about to start.

— I'm worried about Ronnie, J.T. said. Vernon and Thea are alright. They are with Lydia. Staying with my sister-in-law at Argoed. But Ronnie's in Italy. With a friend from Queen's. A harum-scarum type, I'm afraid. Very Red of course. Been to Spain.[108]

Silin led the way across the road and J.T. followed him.

— There's nothing you can do about it, Silin said. Western man is moving to his doom like a sleep-walker, and there's nothing can stop it.

The army officers stepped aside politely, to allow them to pass through the door. In the dim hallway they saw that the office door was open.

— I'd better have a word with her, Silin said. Tell her we're going.

J.T. waited outside, leaning on the counter of the little reception desk. The hotel seemed entirely empty. He saw the backs of the two officers and beyond them a glimpse of the harbour and the open sea. Everywhere seemed warm and peaceful. He could hear the muffled voices of Silin and the proprietor of the hotel in the little room she called her office. When they emerged he turned round and saw that the little woman had been crying. There were tear stains on her round cheeks. She was shaking hands with Silin. J.T. offered her his hand.

As they climbed the stairs he murmured to Silin.

— What was the matter?

— Her son. Her only son. He's been called up.

They walked down the dark corridor to their rooms. Silin opened his door.

— Her brother was killed at Verdun.[109] And her husband was gassed. It's the same everywhere.

Silin went into his room. It was narrow, bare and very clean.

J.T. went to study the view from the window.

He saw the church and a corner of the town square.

— I heard them singing last night. From my bedroom window. Down in the café. A train-load of farm boys with their little black kit-bags. Drowning their sorrows and their home sickness. Singing Breton songs.

Silin had begun to pack his suitcase.

— What will be left of it all? he said. These little countries. In an age like this. How will they survive? How can they? These little countries.

Suddenly he sat down on his bed and held his head in his hands.

J.T. was still looking through the window.

— We ought to get back, he said. There's nothing we can do here.

Then he turned and saw Silin rubbing his face with his hands.

— I know it's unlikely, he said. But there's still a possibility. You can call it hope.

THE OLD TRACTOR made so much noise, there was no point in talking.[110] J.T. balanced his Gladstone bag on the seat which was wrapped in an old sack. The driver, a melancholy faced man, explained he could not sit down himself because he suffered from piles. His bent knees served as shock-absorbers against the violent vibrations of the machine. J.T. clutched his hat with the hand that also held the umbrella and nodded sympathetically. Where the hedges were trimmed down, J.T. cautiously lifted himself to peer into the fields on the left side of the road as if he expected to see someone he knew. It was a hot day and he held his face gladly to the slight breeze caused by the tractor's progress.

The narrow road took them to the gates of Plas Mawr; there was a glimpse of an unkept drive disappearing between the dark trees. The tractor driver pointed to a gate to the left of the white-washed lodge.

— Down there you go! That's the way to Allt Goch!

He shouted above the engine and J.T. showed his gratitude for the lift by nodding vigorously, tapping the man on his back, praising his Pembrokeshire Welsh, and getting himself and his belongings off the tractor as quickly as he could so as not to waste the man's time. For a moment the tractor driver looked at him suspiciously and then he smiled.

At the gate J.T. turned to wave. The driver waved back and steered his tractor through the gates, so that the noise of his engine was muffled abruptly by the trees. The track to Allt Goch appeared to pass through the gates of a series of fields, each gate to be opened and shut. J.T. closed the first gate and breathed deeply and listened to the warm sounds of the early afternoon. He touched the long foxgloves that grew out of the hedgerow, the ruts of the cart track were baked hard. Wearing his hat and dark mackintosh and carrying his bag and his umbrella he moved into the field in order to walk more comfortably. The field had been over grazed and it was covered with crusted cowpats and clumps of well-grown thistles.

He passed a muddy pond and an oak tree under which sheep were resting among their droppings on the cold earth. Then came a hay field that had been cut and carried. He put off his mackintosh and jacket and folded them to carry them over his arm. His face had already begun to glisten with sweat. In the next field he leaned against the hedgerow and seemed to consider taking a rest. He folded his arms and looked critically at the rows of swedes that stretched down the field. The leaves were perforated with the nibbles of insects and butterflies. As he walked on he looked down at his boots. By now they were covered with a film of dust. He changed his bag from one hand to the other as he walked. It was not large but there were books in it that made it heavy. Also the pockets of his mackintosh bulged with small parcels.

Alongside the next gate there was a tall stile. J.T. studied it carefully. He was able to clamber up without putting down any of his load. The summit of the stile was higher than the top of the gate and he balanced himself carefully on the narrow stone. The air was cooler and sweeter and there was a clearer view of the way ahead. After the width of two fields the land fell away and there was just a glimpse of the slate roofs of the farm among the trees. Beyond that, the woods on the opposite side of the valley merged in a blue haze. The view was so pleasing it made him smile.

He was also able to see over the wild hazel hedge on his left. A square five acre field had been closed off with a mixed crop of oats and barley. The crop was maturing too early because of the dry weather. It was when he turned back to look at the way he had come, that he noticed two human figures lying in the corner of the five acre cornfield. They lay in the long grass of the headland that had not been ploughed. A soldier and a woman, totally unaware that he was looking at them. The soldier's tunic was a pillow under the woman's head. The woman was naked from the waist down and the soldier's sunburnt arm stretched carelessly across her white thighs as if he were asleep. J.T. looked back at the rood tops of the farm. He peered up at the sky where an invisible skylark was singing. He looked again at the couple in the corner of the field. He was close enough to see that although the soldier was asleep with his face in the grass, the woman's eyes were open. Her white belly and her black pubic hair that were meant to be hidden, had become the centre of the whole landscape. She had not seen him. Instinctively he bent his head as if he himself had urgent need to hide. The soldier was stirring and might at any moment sit up and see him. At the foot of the stile his mac fell to the ground and he dragged it along for some yards before stopping to pick it up.

Trees became more frequent as he came nearer the farm and kept it entirely in the shade, with a cool rustle of air in the leaves. For the last three hundred yards they grew on either side of the stony lane. His foot dislodged a stone and it tumbled forward down the lane that now sloped more steeply and J.T. had to bend his knees to keep his balance. A dog barked and he could hear it pulling at its chain. The back door of the farm house was in sight. The approach now was roughly paved with flag stones.

The back door was open. Still grasping his case, with his jacket, mackintosh and umbrella over his other arm, J.T. called out in a cheerful voice. It was quite clear the house was empty and yet every door and window was open. He walked through to the front door and saw the excited sheepdog that rattled its tether in a corner of the yard sheltered from the sun. A layer of flaked dung covered the sloping yard and the doors of all of the outhouses were open. It was a prosperous farm that had been allowed to decay. At the side of the house there was a neglected orchard. The branches of the apple trees were covered in moss and lichen. Beyond the orchard there was a stony field that appeared to be over-grown with sorrel. In a corner of the orchard that had been cleared a pet lamb was grazing. Outside the barn there was a load of corrugated zinc sheeting and seasoned timber. A restoration seemed in hand.

J.T. put down his coats and his case on the low wall that protected the narrow garden at the front of the house. He looked back as if considering whether or not to go inside the house again. He seemed deeply interested in everything he saw. He moved out into the middle of the yard. The dog stopped barking and watched him anxiously. He was drawn to a gate at the bottom of the yard. There was a view of the long narrow valley immediately beneath the farm. He leaned on the gate and saw the way in which the woodland on either bank, of the little river was gaining ground on the neglected water meadows. The hedges between the meadows were overgrown and the irregular fringe of the woods could be seen spreading into the fields, a darker green, except where the breeze caught the light leaves of the sapling alders. In the furthest distance it was possible to see four

or five men working, clearing the shrub and the woodland, and opening drains and ditches. Sometimes the sunlight seemed to flash on
the blades of their mattocks. He shaded his eyes with his hands,
steadying his elbows on the top bar of the gate.

— Can I help you?

A woman's voice called. He turned and saw her standing in the
open doorway of the farmhouse. He walked back to the house with
apologetic haste. The woman wore a skirt and blouse of the same
silky material. It was the woman he had seen in the field. She ran her
hands which were red from the housework through her hair, which
had been dyed jet black. Her face was older than her body. It was not
a young girl he had seen in the field. On the bridge of her nose there
was a weal which showed that she usually wore spectacles. The pupils
of her eyes were so distended they made her blue eyes appear black
and added to the air of anxiety that underlay her cultivated manner.
She was an Englishwoman in her middle thirties.

—You must forgive me.

She offered her hand tentatively.

— I've lost my spectacles. I just can't find them anywhere. It's such
a nuisance.

— I'm Vernon's father, J.T. said.

— Of course you are. You look just like him. Or vice-versa I should
say. My name is Dorothy Colinson. We haven't met, but I think you
may have met my husband . . .

Her polite smile faded slowly. For a while he had been staring at
her, speechless, and now as he turned his eyes away, he was blushing.

— It's very pleasant here, he said.

He pointed at the pet lamb in the orchard as a piece of evidence
in support of his statement.

— Oh but the mess is terrible. Usually I have help but for the last
three weeks I've had to manage by myself. Of course these days one
mustn't grumble. Anyway, listen to me talking about myself. You must
come in. We've got a big surprise for you. Someone you know very
well.

J.T. followed Mrs Colinson into the house. It took a few seconds
for his eyes to accustom themselves to the gloom. In the kitchen, in
a low armchair near the open hearth that stretched across the furthest
corner of the room, he saw his eldest son, Ronnie.

He was smoking and as he got up he exhaled the smoke from his cigarette, moving his head sideways to avoid bumping against the low beam. He pushed down a box of matches in the pocket of his battle dress tunic. He seemed self-possessed and at the same time his politeness was awkward.

— What are you doing here?

— I'm on leave, Ronnie said. They're carrying on the war without me for thirty-six hours.

— I'll leave you two together and get on with my work, Mrs Colinson said. You'll have a lot to say to each other.

Across the passage she began to move pots and pans in the dairy as if to demonstrate that she wasn't listening.

— By the time I arrived it would be time to start back, Ronnie said.

— You ought to write oftener. Your mother gets worried.

— I'm sorry, Ronnie said. I'm a rotten correspondent, There's always more I don't want to say than what I want to say.

— What do you mean?

— It was a joke.

— A joke?

Ronnie shrugged his shoulders and spread out his hands. J.T. moved his head to study the gesture closely as if it would give some clue to his son's character. They stared at each other.

— I think you're losing weight, Ronnie said. How are things in the chapel. Any more resignations?

— Your mother isn't at all well.

— She never is, is she?

— What do you mean?

Ronnie threw his cigarette away and stretched himself lazily.

— Nothing would do except a nice little middle-class church, in a nice little North Wales watering-place.

— I don't like to hear you talk like that about your mother.

— I lost my rugby and she gained her rheumatism. Or whatever it is she's got.

— She isn't at all well, J.T. said again.

He sat down suddenly. Mrs Colinson was marching in and out of the dairy. Buckets clanked noisily as she set them up on the wall beneath the trees. She hurried about like someone making up for lost time. There were hens in fold-units in the field beyond the trees. She hurried over the low stile to feed them. J.T. could see her through the small kitchen window.

— Who is she?

He spoke so quietly Ronnie could barely hear him.

— Dolly? Dolly Colinson. You met her husband in Eights Week.[111] Don't you remember?

— Where is he now?

— God knows. Ronnie said. They've separated. As you can see she's a woman full of ideas. I think he's in Intelligence, She's down here looking after a bunch of back-to-the land conchies.[112] Including our Vernon of course. I must say he thrives on it. Have you seen him?

— How could I?

— Brown as a berry and as strong as an ox. Doesn't smoke. Doesn't drink. Takes after you.

J.T. turned his head as he heard Mrs Colinson climb over the stile. The stone paving between the wall and the house was dappled with the trembling shadows of the leafy trees. On the window shelf there was an old wireless set and a carbide lamp. Ronnie leaned across the table to switch the wireless on. There was nothing to be heard except oscillations and crackling. He switched off again.

— The news is terrible, J.T. said.

— Best news possible, Ronnie said. He had to break out to the East. If they can hold on for the next few months, the Russians will crush him.

— I'm thinking of the men, women and children who will be slaughtered, J.T. said. That's what I'm thinking about. The cities in ruins. The countryside destroyed.

— From now on, we've got a real chance of winning. Best news for years.

— Nobody wins a war, J.T. said. Nobody.

He spoke vehemently.

— Don't let's start, Ronnie said. Not now.

— I can't stop bearing witness to what I believe is right because it isn't fashionable any more.

— Not now, Dad. Please.

— I've seen war, my boy. I know what war is. This time it will be so much worse. Wales won't survive this war you know. What are you smiling at? I'd rather not live in a world where Welsh wasn't spoken. What are you smiling at?

— You are so muddled . . .

— Wales doesn't matter of course.

— What's Welsh got to do with it? What's Welsh got to do with war?

— That's all it means to you?

— We are dealing with a war. And if it comes to that, what's pacifism got to do with Nationalism, for God's sake?[113]

— Everything, J.T. said. Everything.

— This is how you've always been, Dad. Logic can't get anywhere near you. If it had you would have been a socialist M.P. With you it's all emotion and exhortation. Don't you know the Age of Exhortation is over? It's the time to do things now. Look. You always talk about power as if it were something dirty. It's an instrument. Something to be used. I can remember saying all this to you when you stopped me going to Spain. It's still just as true. It isn't that I'm any cleverer than you or anything like that. There are certain facts you refuse to see because you wish they didn't exist. Anyway now is the time to fight. There is nothing else we can do. The issue is so simple. On any level. It's him or us. And he is evil. You admit that he's evil?

— No man is entirely evil, J.T. said.

— And worse than that, he's probably mad.

— It's ordinary Germans you'll be killing, not him.

— If he's mad and they all follow him, they're all tinged with madness. If they came here, people like you would be the first to be strung up. Luckily for you they'll never get here. Because people like me are going to stop them. And while we're on the subject I'll tell you something else. When it's all over, I'm not coming back. I don't want to live in an open-air museum. I want to go where ideas are made and where the future is shaped. Wales suffocates me.

— Then what are you doing here?

The question burst out so unexpectedly. J.T. poked the table angrily with his stiffened index finger. They heard Mrs Colinson taking her feet out of her clogs at the back door. They listened to her running through the passage and up the stairs in her bare feet.

— I suppose you expect me to believe you've come to see Vernon?

— Don't let's quarrel, Dad. Please.

You won't see the wickedness of war, J.T. said. The wickedness and the horror.

— I'm not afraid of dying. That's all. Not like poor old Vernon.

— He's no more afraid than you are, J.T. said.

—There you are you see. You can't see anything right in front of your nose. He's scared stiff. That's what all the talk boils down to.

— You're talking about you own brother.

— I know I am. I think the world of him and as far as I'm concerned he can go on talking about the holy soil of Wales as long as he likes. All I'm trying to point out to you is there is no more defenceless creature in the world than a chapel-bred Welsh poet. He has two skins less than anybody else.

— All you do, J.T. said, is to harden you heart to the suffering of others. That's all you do. Your own mother is ill and you won't come home to see her.

—There you are! Always the same! I can do nothing right. Not a thing. I am totally corrupt.

— Oxford, J.T. said.

—Yes, thank God. You weren't all that keen on my going there. Mam's bit of middle-class snobbery was a big help there.

J.T. had no answer.

— You know, Dad, I don't think you've ever really forgiven me since I said Bayley Lewis was a homosexual. Something a boy of sixteen shouldn't think, let alone say. Certain things should never be talked about.

Ronnie's mood changed suddenly. He laughed and slapped his father's shoulder.

— Oh dear, oh dear. We've had some rows in our time, haven't we? What's the news from the chapel front? How's that little squirt Dr Emrys?

J.T. jumped up from his chair. He opened his mouth and then closed it. He turned on his heel to leave the kitchen. The passage was darker than it had been earlier because Mrs Colinson had shut he front door. He groped his way forward. When his eyes got used to the gloom, he saw that she had also hung his dark mackintosh and jacket on the row of hooks on the passage wall. His Gladstone was on the stone floor immediately beneath them. J.T. reached his jacket and put it on. As he did so he saw the inside of the front parlour. The door and the window were wide open but even on this summer day, the room smelt damp. There was a table in the centre of the room and on the floor stacks of books waiting to be put in the empty bookshelves on either side of the fireplace.

J.T. set his Gladstone bag on the table and opened it. He pulled out a bundle of new Welsh books. There was also a piece of home-made slab-cake in a tin and a new shirt. In the passage he held up his mackintosh as he tried to pull out the packages that were wedged tightly into the pockets. Mrs Colinson appeared on the stairs. She s wearing a shirt now and a pair of breeches.

— Let me help you, she said.

— I've brought something for Vernon, J.T. said. Can I leave them on the table in there?

— Yes of course, Mrs Colinson said.

Ronnie appeared in the passage. He put his hand on the banisters.

— A cup of tea would be nice, he said.

— Um.

Mrs Colinson nodded girlishly and smiled. She pushed her fingers through her hair as if she were acutely aware of her appearance.

— I wish I knew where my specs were, she said. I can't get used to being without them.

She bent down and peered at Ronnie with exaggerated short sight.

— Where are you? she said.

— Oh Grandma, what big eyes you've got!

Kindly never refer to a lady's age, Mrs Colinson said. I'm nobody's grandmother, thank you.

They were ignoring J.T. He took down his umbrella from the hook, picked up his bag and put his coat over his arm. Ronnie looked at him and grinned. He spoke to his father playfully in Welsh.

— You look as if you're off to a preaching engagement, he said.

J.T. did not smile. He spoke in English.

— I'd better be going.

— Going?

— Would you tell Vernon his mother isn't too well.

He spoke to Mrs Colinson and she nodded. She tried to steal a glance at Ronnie but J.T. was looking at her intently so that she was obliged to pay him her full attention.

— If he could ask for some leave, he said. I'd like him to come up and see her.

— Look, Dad. This is downright stupid. You can't leave without seeing him!

— He knows where we live.

Ronnie slapped his hand against the banister and raised his voice.

— I'm stationed less than fifty miles from this place, he said. I told you. It would take me all my leave just to get home and get back.

— I'm not blaming you. You're old enough to . . .

— Blame! What's it got to do with blame? Everything's a moral issue with you. It's nothing to do with right and wrong.

— We would like to see you both whenever you can manage to get home, J.T. said.

— Don't start making a noise as if you were forgiving me. I've done nothing wrong and I don't want to be forgiven thank you very much. If you want to go off in a huff, you go off in a huff.

Ronnie stepped aside and made a gesture of showing that the way was clear for J.T. to go.

— A cup of tea, Mrs Colinson said.

She was confused.

— There is so much to do in this place . . . I've taken on too much really . . .

— Good afternoon, J.T. said.

— Mr Miles . . .

Ronnie held her by her arm.

— Let him go, he said.

J.T. halted in the back doorway. Ronnie walked towards him. J.T. swallowed and closed his eyes tightly for the fraction of a second. He appeared to want to speak again. He turned to look at Ronnie. The longer they waited the more difficult it became for either to say anything. At last J.T. turned and walked briskly towards the leafy lane.

THROUGH THE PANEL of frosted glass Thea saw there was someone at the front door of the manse. She tightened the cord on her gymslip, glanced at the ink on her fingers and examined her fingernails. She stepped back into her father's study, picked up a fountain-pen and then went to open the door. The little man turned to smile and speak. His faded coat was open and he carried a small case.

— Good morning, he said. Here I am at last.

Thea stared at his pallid cheek. He had a ginger moustache, but his brushed back hair was white. He was asthmatic.

— I'm the piano tuner.

He still smiled, but the smile showed signs of fading.

— Oh.

Thea sounded completely taken by surprise. She began to smile and then bit her lip. Dimples appeared in her cheeks. She moved the hair from her eyes with the back of her hands.

— I've come to tune the piano.

He sounded prepared to extend his patience. She looked at his brown shoes. The uppers were well polished but covered with small cracks. The soles were thick. They were practical shoes. Heavy, for long walking. She took a quick glance down the street. The small market town seemed very quiet. Down by the crossroads two women with shopping baskets were waiting for a bus.

— There's nobody ar home except me.

She spoke as if she expected the piano tuner to say he would call again. He did not move. His neck straightened. She could hear his asthmatic breathing.

— If I could just get at it . . .

He sounded cross. Hastily she opened the door wider.

— I know where it is, you know.

He sounded more cheerful once he was inside.

— It's a beautiful day, isn't it? 'No sooner does April blossom, than May overwhelms the world.' It's my favourite month.

He took off his coat and threw it over a chair. He paused for a moment to stare at a large landscape that Lydia had hung on the wall to the left of the piano to hide a patch of damp. Then he opened the piano briskly and began to remove the front panel.

— That's an oil.

He nodded towards the picture as he put the panel down. He spoke quickly as if to give himself more time to breathe.

— Could be valuable, he said. Could be worth money.

— Oh I don't think so, Thea said. My mother bought it in a sale-room in Caernarvon.

— Well there you are, he said. That's how it happens.

He removed the lid of the keyboard and paused again to study the picture.

— I don't know where it is do you? Nowhere around here, or I'd know it. Could be Bala Lake, and that mountain behind. I don't think it is though. Could be South Wales of course. You coming from there.

— Would you like a cup of tea?

Thea stood in the doorway that led to the kitchen, with her hands and her heels together like a girl giving a recitation. The piano tuner lifted his hands as if he were about to conduct an invisible choir.

— A nice cup of tea, he said. That's one thing I never refuse.

He opened his little case and took out a tuning-key. He shut it quickly and Thea shifted her gaze before he looked at her. He held the tuner like a meat-hook and looked at it with a smile.

— There's my tool for what it's worth, he said. Wouldn't be much use without it.

— I'll put the kettle on, Thea said.

She closed the door of the parlour. While she was filling the kettle she heard the first chords being hammered at. As she tilted the cowl of the oil stove to light the circular wick, she pulled a face. She took out an oval tray with a wicker rim. She smelt her hands. The piano tuner had begun to play a noisy chromatic ragtime of his own. The noise obviously displeased her. She opened the parlour door. He looked up from his stretched fingers and smiled as if she had come back to admire his playing. His foot was planted down firmly on the sustaining pedal.

— Do you take sugar and milk?

He nodded cheerfully. Then he stopped playing.

— Who plays?

The noise he had made seemed to have given him pleasure. He spread his hand over his thighs and breathed with difficulty as if he had just run a race.

— I play, Thea said. And my brother plays. It's an awful piano.

— Awful?

— The keys, Thea said. You have to hit them so hard.

— It's the type you see. You get a lot of these round here. Made for hard wearing. Did you hear the bombs last night?

He began tuning again, tapping one note over and over again as he made adjustments with his tuning instrument that seemed to use up all the strength in his right arm.

— Liverpool again. Second night running.

Thea stood still and listening.

— I thought to myself coming this morning on the bus, you know. Such a lovely day. You know when I got out at the crossroads and the bus had gone, I could hear I don't know how many different birds singing. And I thought to myself on a day like this. After a night like that. My wife and I sat up in bed listening. And I mean Liverpool must be sixty miles away as the crow flies. It made the doors of our house rattle. Did you hear it?

Thea shook her head slowly.

— Did you hear them going over? Must have been hundreds of them. Did you hear them?

Thea bit her lip and shook her head.

The piano tuner was staring at her so intently she began to blush.

— We could hear the baby next door crying. Woke him up all right. Kettle's boiling, my dear.

Thea rushed out to make the tea. As she poured the hot water into the teapot there was a knock at the back door. Thea looked around quickly for the lid of the teapot. When she had found it, she hurried to open the door.

— Oh hello!

— Hello.

The round-faced girl who stood outside had tight curls at the back of her head.

— Come for a ride on the bikes?

She looked slyly over her shoulder and revealed a packet of cigarettes in the pocket of her summer frock.

— I thought we could go down to the beach. Take sandwiches if you like. Thea made a face to show that she was sorry but she couldn't go.

— School tomorrow, the girl said. Awful, isn't it? How's your mother then?

— We haven't heard. They tried to phone last night. They couldn't get through.

— Wes William's father was in Liverpool yesterday. Terrible, he said. He couldn't get through. They turned him back at the Mersey tunnel. The police. Is your father in?

— He's gone to Liverpool. With my uncle from Rhyl. They're going to move her in an ambulance.

Once more the girl looked secretive.

— What's the matter with her, Thea? Is it something to do with the womb?

— I don't know. Look, I've got to go,

— I had a walk with Wes last night. He's hot stuff. He said he'd take me for a ride in his father's van. Last time, he said. He's being called up next week. Do you want to come?

— I don't expect they'd let me, Thea said. I've got to go, Louie.

Suddenly Louie took Thea's hand and began tickling her palm.

Thea looked puzzled. Louie giggled and let her hand go.

— Bet you don't know what that means.

In the house the piano tuner had begun working fortissimo.

— Who's that? Louie said.

— The piano tuner.

— The little one? Little moustache and a bad chest?

Thea nodded.

— I must go, she said.

— You want to watch out for him, Louie said.

She began to giggle again.

— He's got wandering hands. Be all over you before you can say doh. Ta'ra then. I'll call again after tea, all right? That is if Wes doesn't fetch me, I don't expect he will though. All right then?

Thea closed the door. She took the tray into the piano tuner. She stood holding the tray and looking at him intently. When he turned his head he was surprised to see her.

— Oh there you are, he said.

— Would you like some tea? Thea said.

— Never say no to a nice cup of tea.

He rubbed his hands together while she poured the tea.

— Pity your Dad's not home. I always have a chat with him about religion. He's a very easy man to talk to. We talk about the war, you know, and about religion. He's got a mind of his own, hasn't he? Modern, that's what he is.

He nodded gratefully as he spoke and dipped his spoon in the sugar.

— Shan't take much, he said. Rations are rations. If I'd finished the job I'd ask you to give me a tune. How old are you, love?

— Fourteen, Thea said.

— Is that all? I wouldn't be surprised if you told me you were as tall as your mother . . .

Thea ran to the window. She had heard a car drawing up outside, in the road, beyond the garden railings.

— It's my uncle, she said excitedly. I must go and open the door.

The piano tuner took a hasty sip of tea. Thea left the front door open and ran down the short path to open the gate. She saw her uncle get out of the driving seat. He was wearing a crumpled mac and his face was unusually pale. On the other side she saw her aunt. She was wearing a dark hat and her face was also pale. It was obvious she had been crying for a long time. She was making impatient gestures at the back seat of the car.

— Bring my bag out, Dan, she said.

— Just a minute . . .

They sounded impatient with each other.

— Hello, Aunty.

Kate kissed her briefly.

— Hello, Uncle.

Inside the back of the car Dan Llew lifted his hand in greeting.

— Did you see Dad? Thea said. He said he'd call on his way. Did you see him?

Kate nodded and her mouth began to twitch with the effort of not crying.

— Did they stay then? I thought Mam was going to stay with you at Argoed to convalesce.

— Go inside, my dear.

— Aunty . . . What's the matter.

— Go inside, there's a good girl. We can't talk like this in the middle of the road.

Dan Llew brought Kate's suitcase. He lifted an arm to shepherd them both through the gate.

— Are you coming to stay then?

— Shut the door, there's a good girl. Shut the door.

Kate walked into the parlour. She was preparing to speak, but when she saw the piano tuner she said nothing.

— Good morning, the piano tuner said.

He smiled and nodded, still holding his cup of tea.

— She makes a first-class up of tea, he said.

— Would you like a cup, Aunty? Would you like one, Uncle?

Dan Llew and Kate were looking at each other.

— What's the matter?

Thea's voice became strained with anxiety.

— In the kitchen, Kate said. Let's go in the kitchen.

— Why don't you tell me what's the matter?

— Hurry up through, there's a good girl.

Dan Llew put his hand on her shoulder and gave her a gentle push. The piano tuner swallowed his tea hastily as if to demonstrate that he wished to get back to his work without wasting time. When Dan Llew closed the kitchen door carefully, he began again tapping insistently on a high note.

— Are you coming to stay?

Thea spoke pleasantly. Kate stared at her and as if overcome by the innocent pleasure on the young girl's face she collapsed into a chair by the table and let her head sink into her outspread arms. The brim of her hat, pressed down by the weight of her forehead levered the crown of her hat away from her uncombed hair.

— What's the matter?

— It's your mother, Dan Llew said.

His voice was trembling and out of control.

— It's your dear mother, Thea fach. She's . . . she's dead. She's been killed, my dear. In the hospital. In the raid.

— A bomb . . .

Thea uttered the word as if she had used it for the first time and was still unfamiliar with the sound.

— But I thought Dad had gone there to move her? He went there yesterday . . .

— He was too late, Dan Llew said. It had already happened.

His voice was under control, but he spoke unwillingly, impatient of conversation.

— Where's Dad?

— You could see it, Dan Llew said. From the orchard. You could see it all. Night after night.

— Where's Dad?

— He's stayed in Liverpool. It's the shock. I don't think he's realized it properly yet. He said he wanted to stay to help.

The piano tuner had begun to thump out chords again. He seemed to want to demonstrate how much power was left in the old piano. Kate took off her hat and felt her hair with her hand. Her mouth was slack and her face blotched with weeping. Thea turned away suddenly. She lowered her head and rushed past her uncle. When the door opened they saw the piano tuner sitting side-saddle on the piano stool. He turned to look at Thea. She closed the door and hid him from view once more. They listened intently as they heard Thea running upstairs.

— You'd better tell him to go, Dan, Kate said.

— Vernon will have to come home, Dan said. I'll send him a telegram.

Kate was wiping her eyes,

— I can't believe it, she said. I just can't believe it. We were so close. Just the two of us. Two girls.

— I could see it all you know. From the orchard. The fires and the searchlights. I told you, didn't I? That first night. We'll have to move Lydia, I said. Do you remember? The first night. We should have gone there straight away. She should never have been sent there anyway.

— The operation . . .

The piano tuner started work again.

— Send him away.

Dan Llew began to smile.

— Old Lyd . . . She'd be the first to see the funny side.

— Send him away.

Kate spoke so sharply he hurried to the parlour door.

— Dan!

She gestured to him with the hand that held her wet handkerchief. He raised his head to hear what she had to say. She looked at him as if she were seeing his characteristic attitude of impatience freshly through someone else's eyes.

— You'd better draw the blinds.

23

BECAUSE THE SOIL was sandy and the trees and flowering shrubs had not long been planted, the bungalow was still not hidden by its surrounding garden. Its name was fixed on the road-gates, printed on a steel plate on raised chrome letters: ARGOED.

When he saw it, J.T. muttered the name twice.

— *Argoed . . . Argoed. Y mannau dirgel.*

— What's that, Uncle?

Gwyneth leaned backwards. The engine of the car was ticking over and it made her head shake slightly. J.T. repeated the line again and shook his head meaningfully.

— I'll get out and open the gates.

Kate jerked herself out of the low seat. As she strode forward, the movements of her head showed which way she was looking with her single eye.

— She's wonderful, isn't she Uncle? Gwyneth said. Like a two-year-old.

— She does too much, J.T. said. Puts too much strain on herself. The doctor has warned her. I keep at her as much as I dare . . . but of course I'm the one that causes her all the trouble.

Kate returned to her seat in the car and slammed the door so hard that Dan Llew woke up. He had been asleep in the back seat with his head lolling back and his mouth open.

— She's in the window.

Kate muttered as if she were sharing a secret with the driver, Gwyneth forced the gear lever into its gate and the car edged forward through the gateway. The tyres crunched over the thickness of the gravel. Having moved forward, they saw a dark blue Mercedes parked on the drive where it began to curve towards the further gateway.

—Whose is the posh car, Uncle?

— Car, car. What car?

Dan Llew pulled himself up and peered beyond the back of Gwyneth's head as if it were an irritating obstruction.

— Oh that. That's Norman's. All the stock in the window.

He seemed very alert after his sleep.

— That's Norman opening the front door. Been on his holidays. I suppose I shall have to hear all about it. Come on, come on.

— I'm waiting for the car to stop, J.T. said.

He had his hand on the door lever.

— Here we are then.

Kate wound down her door window and Norman looked in.

He resembled his mother, Annie Grace. A narrow face and the tip of his nose always a little red, as though it was permanently exposed to cold weather. His eyes moved restlessly and his precise lips were stretched in a worried smile.

— I was up in Rhyd-y-gwaith, he said. There's been some trouble on the site there. Terrible weather this for poor old builders. I got here as soon as I could.

Dan Llew had opened the door on his side. J.T. got out more slowly.

— You know your cousin Gwyneth, don't you? Kate said. The Aunty Addy side of the family.

Norman bent down lower to put his arm in the car and shake hands with Gwyneth.

— We meet in funerals usually, don't we? he said.

Gwyneth chuckled and nodded.

— I'm awfully grateful to you, Norman said. He's a bit of a trial sometimes, isn't he Aunty?

— She's in the front door. Don't turn round.

Kate was whispering, moving her lips as little as possible,

— My goodness she was upset, Norman said.

He raised his eyebrows and turned down the corners of his mouth like a sad-faced clown. Gwyneth raised her hand in a half-hearted signal to the woman standing in the open doorway of the bungalow, She was Mrs Wilson, Dan Llew's housekeeper. She clutched a silk scarf around her neck and she lifted her other hand to show it contained a handkerchief. Her stance suggested that she preferred to endure being talked about than venture out on the drive and go through the process of encountering Gwyneth through the medium of Kate. The soles of her felt slippers could have been screwed to the parquet floor of the hall. Her hand suddenly became animated. With one foot outside the door she signalled vigorously in the direction of the way the car had driven in. Dan Llew was walking away briskly. J.T. was bending down to smell some flowers on the edge of the lawn.

— Well would you believe it, Norman said. He's off again.

Simultaneously Gwyneth and Kate tried to swivel their necks to see behind them. Norman shouted.

— Hey, Dad! Where do you think you're off to?

Dan Llew stopped. Even at a distance it was possible to see he was frowning.

— To close the gate, he said. Where do you think? I can't bear gates being left open. You can drive in and out of my place. I've seen to that.

He pointed to the further gateway. Norman waved a signal of approval and relief. J.T. straightened and said,

— I'll do it.

Dan Llew made a gesture of impatience and tramped off at speed to close the gate.

— Well, Norman said. If it makes him happy. Aren't you two coming in? I tell you what. I'll show you my colour transparencies. I was going to show them to Dad anyway. He loves looking at them.

— Where did you go?

— All over the place really. A sort of alpine tour. In and out of

Germany, Austria, Switzerland and Italy. I had to take the boys some-where. To take their minds off things.

Norman looked intently at Gwyneth, who blushed as if she had been caught in some embarrassing position.

— I suppose you've heard. Gwyneth nodded sympathetically.

— I did hear something, she said. I was very sorry.

Norman looked at his aunt. Kate was staring straight in front of her, not prepared to advance comment or opinion. Dan Llew was walking back across the front lawn. He was examining its surface carefully. He stopped and J.T. went to see what he was looking at. His brother-in-law had begun to rub the sole of his boot against the surface of the lawn.

— Ants, Dan Llew said. Ants. They're everywhere. When the human race stops working, these little buggers will take over.

J.T. laughed. Dan Llew looked annoyed. He kept rubbing the ant-sifted soil with his foot.

— I'm not joking, he said.

In the doorway of the bungalow, Mrs Wilson had begun to smile and was making gestures of invitation with her plump and flexible forearm.

— Are you coming in? Norman said. I can't promise a feast. You know what she's like. But I dare say coffee could be forthcoming.

He smiled his sad smile. J.T. was advancing towards the bonnet of the car, one hand on his hip and the other smoothing down his white hair. He looked as if he might pat the car's bonnet as though it were a pony's head.

— He could stay, Kate said, looking at J.T. We could call for him on our way home, couldn't we Gwyneth?

— What ever you say, Aunty, Gwyneth said. I'm at your service. This is your day out.

— If we could go back so that I could cut old Hobley's hair, Kate said. We could be off then and call here this afternoon after tea on our way back. How would that be, Norman?

Norman nodded slowly as if the plan had been unfolded a little suddenly, but presented on the whole an agreeable prospect.

— It's a pity you can't stay, he said.

— They'll be company for each other, Kate said.

J.T. had placed his hand on the bonnet of the car. He was smiling benignly at them.

— Did you hear that, Uncle? Would you like to see my film show?

J.T. moved to stand near Norman. He bent his knees to talk to Kate.

— What about lunch? he said.

— We can have a bite here, Norman said.

He leaned forward to whisper.

— Mrs W. can open an extra tin.

Gwyneth laughed but J.T. still looked a little puzzled.

— Do you think we ought to leave the house?

He spoke to Kate.

— If you're going out, I mean.

— It won't run away, will it? Kate said.

— I've got some letters to write. Thea will want an answer, you see. And there's this business in Llangefni. Ifan Cole's timepiece. I'd rather like to go there.

He looked pointedly at Gwyneth.

— Well it's not exactly urgent, is it? Kate said. The man's dead and buried.

J.T. sighed and shook his head.

— Poor old Ifan, he said.

Norman made a comic face.

— It looks as if I'll have to start paying people to come and see my picture show, he said. Oberammergau, Uncle. Does that appeal to you?

— Oberammergau.

J.T. fastened on to the word.

— I nearly went there in 1926, you know. With poor old Bayley Lewis. They were holding a Peace Conference there.[114] I was chosen for the Welsh delegation. I would have gone but for the General Strike. I couldn't leave my people at a time like that.

— Well there you are then, Kate said. We'll be back soon after tea.

Mrs Wilson had lifted her handkerchief to her mouth and placed her other hand on the doorpost. She moved aside as Dan Llew walked past her into the house. Kate was watching him as she spoke to J.T. and Norman.

— Did you see that? she said. Did you?

— What?

J.T. turned to look at the bungalow. Mrs Wilson had gone inside.

— He didn't recognize her, she said. Not from Adam. Walked straight past her.

She seemed pleased.

— It's just as well you're staying with him if you ask me.

— I can run Uncle home, Aunty, Norman said. There's no need for you to come out of your way.

— Well there we are then. Very kind of you, Norman. We'd better be on our way.

Kate had begun to wind up the window even before the car had moved off.

NORMAN WAS HAVING difficulty in closing the new curtains that reached from near the ceiling to the parquet floor. His fingers pulled first at one cord and then the other. Outside there was a terrace and in the middle of the back lawn there was a circular rose garden, with a bird-bath in the centre. Behind Norman, J.T. and Dan Llew sat where he had told them to sit, side by side on the heavy settee which had been moved to face the screen Norman had set up at the other end of the room. Behind the screen the curtain had already been drawn across the small window that looked out on the front garden. Norman frowned up at the curtain rails. He was shorter than his father and his shoulders seemed frail inside his dark jacket as he brought them together.

— I'm sure this hasn't been put up properly, Norman said.

Dan Llew jerked back his head as if he'd been tapped on the shoulder.

— You're the builder. You should know.

— No. I mean this new curtain fitting.

— The sun's coming out, Dan Llew said. I knew it would. Couldn't we see them in the garden?

— These curtains, Norman said. I'm sure there's something wrong with them.

— Mrs Wilson!

Dan Llew shouted loudly. There was the sound of a lavatory being flushed. Across the hall a door opened and Mrs Wilson appeared, looking alarmed and brushing down her dress of floral chiffon with the back of her hand.

— Norman can't work the curtains, Dan Llew said. He always had more fingers than thumbs.

— I'll close them then, shall I?

Mrs Wilson's voice was soft and held back, as if she always wanted it to sound soothing and comfortable.

— Just a minute.

Dan Llew stood up and reached over to the television set, which stood beyond the end of the settee where J.T. was sitting. It had a twenty-one-inch screen. He bent down and switched it on.

— Dad, what *are* you doing?

— There's Welsh on this now, Dan Llew said. I like the Welsh.

— Surely there isn't, Norman said. I'm sure there isn't. Sit down. I'm just going to show you my pictures. Switch it off, Dad. There isn't any Welsh now.

Norman leaned over and switched off the set himself. As he did so, he whispered in J.T.'s ear.

— He's got no idea about time.

—Who?

Dan Llew spoke sharply. His face looked angry and suspicious.

— Sit down, Dad. I want you to see my colour pictures.

—Well don't talk about me as if I wasn't here.

Dan Llew sat down heavily on the settee.

— It's no joke growing old, he said.

— I'm closing the curtains now, Mrs Wilson said.

The room grew dark. No one spoke. Dan Llew lifted his head apprehensively.

—You know I don't like the dark, he said.

— Not to worry, Norman said. Can you switch the light on a moment, Mrs Wilson? I want to see what I'm doing.

— Certainly, Mrs Wilson said.

She stumbled over an occasional table before getting to the switch. When the light went on she fingered her hair and her dress, although no one was looking at her.

— It's nice to have pictures in your own home, she said.

— People sitting in the dark. It's daft. I never liked the pictures. Never saw anything in them.

— Now where are we . . . ?

Norman was studying the boxes that contained his slides. He switched the projector on and off.

—You'll like some of these, Uncle. I'm afraid I haven't really had time to set them in order. I'll do my best to explain as I go along.

A great rectangle of blurred colour appeared and jumped about on the screen. Greens and blues flashed and flicked.

—What's that? Dan Llew said.

— Wrong picture. Start again. It's out of focus. This machine is second hand I may add. Lights out, Mrs Wilson.

J.T. laughed obligingly.

— Brings these things along so that he doesn't have to bother to talk to me, Dan Llew said.

— I'll ignore that one, Norman said.

His disembodied voice came out of the darkness of the room.

— Where are you for goodness' sake, Dan Llew said. Let's get it over.

There was a sudden lurid picture of the garden of a hotel, garish with red flowers.

— This is the hotel we stayed in on Lake Garda. That little figure in the top left-hand corner is me. Gareth took this one so I'll blame him . . . Here are the two boys together.

They had their arms over each others shoulders and they grinned at the camera in front of an azalea bush.

— This is Innsbruck I think . . . This is an Alpine shepherd's hut. Look at all the flowers . . . This is Gareth and Geraint again . . . This is Romeo and Juliet's house in Verona. Gosh I have got them mixed up, haven't?

— It's very interesting, J.T. said.

— This is . . . it must be the Brenner Pass. I think it is anyway. Not very good. The light was bad.

A picture of a blonde woman playing with a large dog on a lawn appeared. The camera had caught them both with their mouths open and their teeth bared.

— It's that bitch Marjorie, Dan Llew said.

— They're all mixed up.

Norman switched the light on. He looked pale and unhappy. Mrs Wilson patted Dan Llew on the shoulders as if to calm him down.

— The boys look very well, J.T. said.

— It's Gareth I'm worried about. He doesn't say much, but I know he's missing his mother. After all it's only natural. He's only ten you see.

— Bitch, Dan Llew said.

Norman looked at his father sadly, then he picked up another box of colour slides.

— I bought these in Oberammergau, Norman said. I thought you might like to see them.

— Oh yes, J.T. said. I would indeed. Very much. Norman smiled at him sadly.

— Nice of you to be so patient, Uncle, he said.

— As I was saying, I nearly went there in 1926. A long time ago. Dan Llew looked at J.T. as if he were seeing him in a new light. Mrs. Wilson's hands were still on his shoulder.

— Do you think we could give this man a bite of dinner, Mrs W?

— It's a light lunch today, Mrs Wilson said.

— You know I'll say this for my father, Dan Llew said, he was very tight with money but he always gave the minister real hospitality. Best bedroom and a good table. I like respect for the cloth.

He poked J.T. in the arm.

— Can't think why you don't wear a proper collar.

— Hold tight, Norman said. I'm putting the light out again. Now these are properly organized. I thought myself the place was over-commercialized. There wasn't anything on there, but we were shown round. We saw all the robes. Hundreds of them.

— Who is it? Dan Llew said.

— That's Mary the mother of Jesus, Mrs. Wilson said.

— I'll say this for Mrs W., Dan Llew said. She can't cook but she knows her Bible. In English of course.

— Oh Mr Jones, Mrs Wilson said.

She slapped Dan Llew playfully on the shoulder.

— That's our Lord carrying the Cross, Mrs Wilson said. That's the Last Supper. Oh that's beautiful. Isn't it beautiful, Mr Jones? Look at the expression on his face ...

— We saw him, Norman said. He's got a shop in the village. They all do very well out of it you know.

— Oh look at that ... oh just look ...

Mrs Wilson's head was lowered so that she was speaking softly near Dan Llew's ear.

— Our Lord carrying the Cross. Look at his eyes turned up to Heaven. Look at the Crown of Thorns.

Dan Llew lifted his head slowly to pat Mrs Wilson's hand on his shoulder.

— Have you got a hanky?

Mrs Wilson extracted a hanky from the sleeve of her chiffon dress. She placed it under Dan Llew's nose. He snatched it from her and it dropped in his lap.

— Look, she said. The Crucifixion. Our Lord crucified between two thieves.

— Put the light on, Dan Llew said.

He was groping between his legs for the handkerchief.

—Not big enough to wipe a gnat's nose, women's hankies. Put he light on, Norman. It's a soft thing to have your curtains drawn in he middle of the afternoon. Open the curtains, Mrs W. There's the sun outside.

— Wait a bit, Dad. There are more pictures.

— Open, Dan Llew said.

Mrs Wilson turned around and drew back the curtains, settling them in their folds with pride and care. The sunlight made Dan Llew screw up his eyes. He blew his nose on Mrs Wilson's handkerchief.

— 'Behold the Man who was crucified by the Jews.'

He put his hand on J.T.'s arm as if he were sharing a confidence with him.

— 'Crucified by the Jews.'

Dan Llew shook his head sadly.

— Not at all, J.T. said. His voice was brisk and didactic,

— He was crucified by the Romans. By the temporal power, He was crucified by the full power of the state; by the law, by the army, by the police. And it was the Church that handed him over. The Jews represent the Church. People like you and I.

— Like me?

Dan Llew stubbed a finger into his own chest.

— I'm a bad man,

— I didn't say that.

— No, but that's what you meant. Trying to talk clever to show me I'm as bad as the worst. That's how you've always been you know. All along. Everybody else is bad and wrong and you're always right.

J.T. shook his head.

— I'm just as worthless as you are, he said. And as weak. It's precisely because we are weak and worthless that we have any value. That is the true measure of our value.

Dan Llew looked up at Mrs Wilson.

— What's he talking about? he said.

— Really, Mr Miles, Mrs Wilson said. That's the last thing anyone would say about Mr Jones, He's not weak and he's certainly not worthless. He still has business interests in both towns. And he has a family that loves him.

— Which is more than you've got, Dan Llew said.

He turned his head to glare at J.T.

— You've always looked down on me because I don't read books all day. He never liked me you know.

He turned to look up at Mrs Wilson's face and when she saw he was looking at her she pouted in a way that made her fat face look strangely girlish.

— It's a mystery, J.T. said. And yet it must be simple enough for simple people to understand.

He put out his hand in Dan Llew's direction and began to tick off points.

— You accept that we are all sinners?

— I've lived a good, straight hard life and I've worked hard and I deserve a rest.

— Of course you do, Mr Wilson said.

— It's an old-fashioned term today, but it has its usefulness. We all feel the need for salvation. It's part of the way we breathe . . .

— 'To save an old rebel like me . . .'[115]

Dan Llew began to sing in a trembling tenor. J.T. nodded eagerly and interrupted him before he finished.

— That's it exactly, J.T. said.

— I know all about that!

Dan Llew slapped his knee with his hand.

— I was brought up on it.

— But not to see that the gospel is wide enough and deep enough to provide mankind with a new way of living. A society that gives and not a society that takes. A society that creates, not a society that destroys. . .

— He's off again, Dan Llew said.

He lifted an arm to draw Norman's attention.

— Out comes the old soap-box. Always the same,

— Why don't you listen? J.T. sounded angry.

— How can you expect to learn if you never listen?

Dan Llew pushed away Mrs Wilson's restraining hand and struggled to his feet.

— Learn! Learn from you!

He swayed on his feet and his brown boots creaked.

— Mr Jones, Mrs Wilson said. Now don't upset yourself.

— He's got three children and they hardly ever come to see him from one year's end to the other.

— Now steady on, Dad, Norman said.

— If that doesn't show what they think of him. I'm a plain speaker you know. Always was. I can say what I think and I don't have to jump up in a pulpit to do it.

— I had a letter from Thea this very morning, J.T. said.

He lay back in his corner of the settee and looked at Norman.

— Wants your aunt and I to go and spend the winter in Italy.

— That's very nice, Uncle. Are you going?

— Your aunt isn't very keen.

— Of course she isn't, Dan Llew said. She's got more sense. I'll tell you one thing, Miles, and I say it to your face. The worst thing that ever happened to my poor sister was the day she married you, and if the truth were known the poor thing lived to regret it.

J.T. seemed to consider what he should do or say, and then he tried to rise with speed, but the settee was so soft and low he only got up on the third attempt.

— He doesn't belong to our family. As far as I know he never had a family. He's a nobody from nowhere.

— Are you all right, Uncle?

— It's a bit hot in here. The curtains kept the air out. I'll be off I think, Norman.

— I'll take you in the car, Norman said.

— I can catch the bus . . .

— I wouldn't dream of it, Uncle.

— You never met her, did you?

Dan Llew had turned to Mrs Wilson and had placed his hand on her shoulder as if he were pushing her away from him to be able to see her better.

— You never met my little sister.

Mrs Wilson took his arm and he allowed her to guide him to the corner of the settee where J.T. had been sitting. His voice was beginning to break with emotion.

— She was . . . she was a lovely girl. Full of humour you know. Always laughing.

In the hall Norman turned around to see what J.T. was staring at. Dan Llew's foot was lying in Mrs Wilson's lap as she unlaced his brown boots. The boot fell on the carpet with a thud. Mrs

Wilson peeled off Dan Llew's sock and his white foot lay in her hand.

24

IN THE MORNING service there were fifteen people in the congregation. They were scattered far apart in the pews. The gallery which projected from all four walls was empty, apart from the elderly precentor and the lady organist, who sat facing each other, with arms folded, heads inclined downwards towards the preacher, who sometimes glanced upwards from the pulpit, at each in turn, during his sermon as if to remind them that they were both still part of the service.

J.T. sat with his son Vernon, who kept yawning and blinking, as if he had difficulty in keeping himself awake. Vernon's white shirt was crumpled as if it had not been ironed, and the dark blue suit he was wearing fitted him badly. His dark hair fell down over his forehead. On the yellow wall above the end of their pew there was a marble tablet giving the names of the nine members of the church who had been killed in the 1914-18 war. The verse carved underneath said: 'But ye shall die like men, and fall like one of the princes. . ,'

The preacher's voice was high-pitched and husky. He was a tall man burnt thin with a zeal which expressed itself in a physical restlessness and an uncurbed eloquence. When J.T. broke out into an Amen of unqualified approval, he surged forward on a rising tide of argument, as though the chapel contained a congregation of many hundreds instead of fifteen scattered among the empty pews. As the sunlight poured in through the stained glass, he hardly paused to clear his throat.

— The Christian church has failed and is failing because it has never realized the magnitude of its task. I would say it lost the initiative in Europe even before the communist manifesto was published. It has failed because it has never dared to put its own doctrines to the test. What if the love of power was really confronted with an organized power of love?

J.T. made a noise of approval. Vernon's head jerked. He opened his eyes wide and stole a glance at his father. Vernon had large eyes and the kind of looks that did not suffer from his sleeping in his clothes and hardly brushing his hair.

— And what other power would someone like to tell me will bring peace and order and understanding to replace war, and bloodshed and famine and fear? Perhaps you will tell me to try the reasoning powers of men of goodwill. Try the power of reason!

His husky voice was drowned by the siren. It was fixed to the clock tower of the town hall, in the main street. The chapel seemed too small to contain the expanding noise. The sparse congregation exchanged troubled glances. The preacher's words were completely drowned. Impatiently he took off his glasses and began to polish them. Vernon showed signs of being thoroughly woken up. He looked at his wrist-watch, cleared his throat, and then gazed innocently at the preacher who by now was blowing his nose. At last the ear-splitting wail began to die away. The preacher was anxious to continue.

— Reason creates weapons of ever-increasing power, he said. But how much does it do to control them? The love of power demands unconditional surrender from the enemy. Does the voice of Reason dare to make itself heard and demand a negotiated armistice? Reason can always find good reasons for continuing to do what is evil. I say as a Christian we have in this world only one unconditional surrender to make and that is to the power of love as expressed once and for all time in the uniqueness of Christ. This is our message. . .

The menace of an engine in the sky had already taken the attention of the congregation. As the clatter and splatter came nearer, they raised their eyes to the curved ceiling where the plaster mouldings had been painted yellow and blue. There was no way of telling from the sound the exact course the flying bomb was taking. In the gallery the precentor and the organist looked at each other, nodded, got up from their seats and tiptoed quietly towards the stairways that led down into the body of the chapel.

— I must be simple, the preacher said. It isn't just something for intellectuals only — or for priests and ministers only. Or for God-fearing mothers only. This is a universal message, for every man, woman and child in this world. And that includes Hitler and Goebbels as well as Winston Churchill and the Archbishop of Canterbury. As an English poet has put it 'We must love one another or die'.[116]

The engine in the sky was still spluttering loudly. An elderly woman in black grasped the back of the pew in front of her and began to lower her bulk sideways to the floorboards.

— My friends, the first step is repentance! The whole world will have to kneel . . .

The engine had cut out. The world seemed to hang on a thread of silence. The preacher kept his mouth open. There was a sudden scuffle as most of the congregation took to the floor. The preacher remained standing. J.T. closed his eyes and held his breath. He toppled sideways as Vernon tugged his arm.

The explosion when it came was violent. The floor shook and there came the crash of shattered glass. When J.T. lifted his head, the chapel was hidden in a cloud of grey dust. There were pieces of moulding from the ceiling along the seat of the pew. Dark figures were beginning to pick themselves up. Anxious voices were speaking in whispers because they were still in chapel. J.T. peered in the direction of the pulpit.

—What about Pierce? he said. Is he all right?

He pushed Vernon in front of him down the aisle. The chapel, which was Congregrationalist, had no special seating for the deacons.[117] Mr Mathews, the senior deacon, was groping about under the pulpit. He was grasping his chest and coughing. Vernon took him by the shoulders and led him towards the back of the chapel where someone had opened the doors. J.T. stepped on the lowest stair leading to the pulpit. The fallen plaster crunched under his feet.

— Pierce, he said, Are you all right?

Pierce was sitting on the floor, holding his forehead in his hands.

— Can't see much.

He too had begun to whisper. It was as if he wanted to demonstrate he was no longer exercising the function of preaching.

—There isn't much point in carrying on with the service, is there?

J.T. was helping him to his feet.

— Do you think we might sing a closing hymn?

J.T. shook his head. The dust was subsiding. A woman sat in a pew by herself, dusting her new hat. Quietly she was crying. The elderly woman in black was pulling herself up to her feet. She waved at a friend at the other side of the chapel, who waved back. At the back, near the open doors a young man in khaki and a sidesman were pointing and grinning at each other. A stout man crawled out of his pew into the aisle, picked himself up shaking himself like a dog and marched out.

— It's shock, J.T. said. Nothing but shock.

He was helping Pierce down the pulpit stairs. The stout man reappeared suddenly in the doorway of the chapel. He smiled apologetically.

— Just for you to know, he said. There's another one coming.

J.T. and Mr Pierce stood blinking in the chapel doorway. The Chelsea street was bathed in the calm Sunday morning sunlight. Mr Mathews was sitting on the steps and Vernon was kneeling beside him. Across the road a man in a torn dressing-gown was standing in the doorway of his house, a cigarette hanging from his lips. He was looking at the sky and he held a bottle of milk in his hand.

— Is he all right?

J.T. spoke to Vernon, who nodded and pointed to a great column of black smoke that hung in the air above the tall houses across the main road. Pierce was looking in the opposite direction. From the south of the river a dagger-shaped machine with a tail of flame had appeared.

— An angel of death, Pierce said.

J.T. nodded and stepped down into the street to get a better view of the course the flying bomb was taking. The congregation clustered on the chapel steps as if they had been disturbed in the middle of having a photograph taken, and standing in the roadway with his legs apart, J.T. might have been the photographer. He had an arm up to show he was listening to the engine of the bomb, which was veering westwards. He was waiting for the moment when the engine would cut out. Down the main road, three red double-decker buses jerked along, one after the other. The bomb pursued its course until its engine could no longer be heard. J.T. looked puzzled. Vernon seemed satisfied that Mr Mathews was all right. He came into the road to speak to his father.

— I'm going over to see what I can do, he said. I'll just get my bike up from the basement.

The congregation lingered on the steps, uncertain what to do. The stout man suddenly shook hands with everyone near him. He laughed as he spoke, lifting his thumb over his shoulder.

— Got to go see if my dairy is still there, he said.

Mr Mathews had got to his feet. He brushed the seat of his trousers automatically. He seemed unaware of the dirt on his jacket and face.

— Your hat and so on are in the vestry, Mr Pierce, he said.

Vernon held his bike above his head as he climbed the steps from the basement.

— Hey!

The young soldier tapped Vernon on the shoulder.

— Give us a lift on your cross-bar.

Mr Pierce's eyes were gleaming and he spoke excitedly in his husky voice.

— Well, where is it?

— Never go anywhere without this.

Vernon patted the saddle of his bike. Mr Pierce looked at it critically.

— Vernon is with the Friends, Pierce, J.T. said. Due to be sent abroad. Wish I could go with him.

— There's work to be done now, Pierce said. What about it, boys?

Mr Pierce led the way. Before Vernon could stop him he rushed across the main road and was almost run over by an ambulance. From the chapel steps, J.T. could see the three of them arguing about the quickest route to the bombed building. Mr Mathews touched his arm.

— Terrible mess inside, Mr Miles, he said. And if it wasn't difficult enough to keep the cause alive in days like these. Do you know, in some ways it's worse than the Blitz. I may be wrong of course. My nerves may have something to do with it.

— I think I'll follow them, J.T. said. There must be something we can do.

— Mr Pierce has left his hat and coat in the vestry, Mr Mathews said.

— I'll tell him.

J.T. limped as he ran, and turned at the corner of the street to wave back as if to reassure his friends there everything would be all right.

The side street in which he found himself was narrow and the buildings on the east side kept out the sun. There were few people about and they seemed to be going about their normal business, already oblivious that a flying bomb had fallen in the vicinity. He slowed down and seemed to be wondering whether he had taken the wrong turning. At the end of the street he was still undecided which way to turn. He looked up in search of the traces of black smoke. He sniffed. The acrid smell of the explosion still hung in the air. He seemed to take his bearings by sniffing, and he moved forward into more shadowed side streets that were obviously strange to him. At the end of the street he saw two N.F.S.[118] men clamping a hose to a fire hydrant. He ran forward, but they took no notice of him. The area of damage was still invisible. And then suddenly through a gap between buildings he caught a glimpse of a smoking hole in a large block of flats, and on the lawn in front it looked as if a garden fete had suddenly been thrown into confusion. A fire engine had reversed fiercely into a flower bed and the hose was still being unwound across the grass. From where he saw it the whole scene seemed abnormally quiet.

He wandered nearer, with an arm half raised in front of him as if he were preparing to go forward and touch the disorder. He stood staring at the flames from a gas main that flared up in the smoke. A special constable took him by the arm and led him away.

— You don't want to get too near, mate. You don't want to get clobbered with falling masonry.

— It's bad.

J.T. was very pale.

— You look as if you could do with a cuppa char.

J.T. had turned to follow the progress of an elderly woman in a summer dress. Her forearms had been slit open by blast. She was being led across the lawn by a fireman and she kept looking at her arms and then shaking her head in quiet wonder. They passed a row of bodies that lay still on the lawn. Blankets covered six bodies that had already been recovered.

— They're working very hard, J.T. said. Very hard.

— What number was your flat?

— Amazing the goodness in human nature, J.T. said.

J.T.'s eyes were filling with tears.

— You got somebody in there, mate?

— I was in chapel, J.T. said. Over there. Somewhere over there, when it fell.

The constable pointed along a path that led away from the smouldering building.

— Down there, he said. Ground floor of the next block. People from the Rest Centre. They'll give you something useful to do.

— I'm glad it's not a hospital, J.T. said. You know for a moment I thought it was a hospital.

— Keep away from the wall, there's a good chap. Breathe on it, see, and you'll have it down and you'll be one more to collect. Now, as I say, you go down to the Rest Centre people and they'll give you a job to do.

J.T. nodded obediently and hurried down the path. The french windows of the first flat had been swept away in a heap and in the opening a man in uniform with a Red Cross band on his arm was standing behind the table. He had black bushy hair and a complexion of crushed strawberry. He seemed to be enjoying issuing staccato instructions. He gave J.T. a keen stare and then sent him down the corridor to a flat which had been thrown open as a temporary shelter for people suffering from shock. In the kitchen of this flat tea was being brewed on a large scale by women in dark uniforms. J.T. was handed two mugs of steaming tea. He looked around the living-room for someone who was not already nursing a mug. In a corner he found a frail woman with a fine face and large eyes, nursing a blue Persian cat. She lay on the floor, partly hidden by a standard lamp with a massive shade, and a blanket was spread over her legs. Her eyes were following everything that went on with lively interest.

— It's so absurd, she said to J.T. when he kneeled down to offer her a mug of tea. They just won't function. There's nothing wrong with them except that they won't function.

She tapped a leg with a free hand and laughed at herself.

— Oh dear, oh dear. I am in a mess.

— Would you like some tea? J.T. said.

She examined the mug critically.

— Pity you haven't a saucer. Bit hot for the cat.

— You, J.T. said. You drink some yourself. She sipped it carefully and pulled a face.

— Awful stuff. You're Welsh, aren't you?

— Yes. How could you tell?

This seemed to amuse her very much. She laughed so much, J.T. was compelled to smile as well. The muscles in her thin neck were stretched to their utmost and her mouth which was wide and full trembled. She was physically old, but very youthful in manner and spirit.

— Rest assured in this wicked world no one will ever suspect you of being anything else.

J.T. was looking at her suspiciously.

— Don't be alarmed, she said. I meant it as a compliment. It's very romantic really.

— You've lost your home?

— I'd been with my Clio here to pick up the Sunday papers. Silly of me at my age. But there you are. I'm incurably curious. Always want to know what's going on. I was just getting into the lift actually.

— And your home's gone.

— I suppose it has. I was too dazed to look. I never liked the place anyway. There's an awful restlessness about old age, you know. All sorts of things I still want to do. Don't I, Clio?

She lifted the cat to her face and pressed her cheek against its fur.

— What do you do?

— I'm a minister, J.T. said.

— What sort?

— Welsh Calvinistic Methodist.

— That's a new one on me.

She smiled as if to take any offence out of the remark.

— Welsh Presbyterian. I'm up here to see my son.

— Ah.

She made signs of comprehensive understanding.

— Is there anything I can do?

— Not really. I'm rather glad it's happened from my own point of I view. That sounds a horrible thing to say. But I feel like one of the lightly wounded. Relieved, you know. A little less responsible for all the misery in the world.

— Could I get in touch with your family?

— Not very easily. My husband is dead. He died before the war. At first I thought I'd die of loneliness. We had no children and we were very attached to each other.

J.T. tilted his head to listen sympathetically.

— We used to write detective stories together. Martha Tree. Did you ever read any?

— No. I'm afraid not.

— I'm rather glad he never lived to see this war. We had a private joke about human nature. He used to believe people were essentially good and I believed the opposite. Very effective for our detective stuff. Anyway, here I am. High and dry. Pretty useless, but still awfully interested in things. Now what about you? Tell me about yourself. Are you married? Of course you are.

J.T. bent his head.

— My wife is dead. She was killed in the big raids in Liverpool. She was in hospital there at the time.

He struggled to keep his voice steady. The frail woman continued to study him with interest.

— Have you got children?

— Three.

J.T. swallowed and lifted his head.

— A girl in school. I have a boy here. Helping with the rescue work. And my eldest son is in Italy. With the Eighth Army.

She nodded approvingly.

— You have a lot to live for, she said.

— Oh yes. Oh yes.

J.T. nodded wisely. His accent and his manner seemed to intrigue her. She stared at him with continued interest, as if he belonged to a species she had not come into close contact with before. Her smile was daring and playful.

— You know you make me want to say things to shock you, she said, and I don't even know your name.

J.T. opened his mouth, but she shook her head.

— I don't want to know either, she said. And you shan't know mine. Do you still miss her? Every day? Her physical presence?

— I haven't got over it, J.T. said. I don't think I ever will.

— You understood each other?

— Oh yes.

— You must forgive my asking. It helps. To compare. I know I'm less than half the person I was. When I look at my ration card, I don't honestly believe there's enough of me left to deserve having one.

She had begun laughing again. J.T. looked at her.

— My wife was very fond of joking, he said.

— I'm going to give you some advice. I know you've got three grown-up children, but you look awfully young to me.

She lifted a thin finger.

— Don't pass by a chance of getting married again.

J.T. rose to his feet. He was shaking his head as one who had given an idea the most impartial consideration before rejecting it.

— Don't tell me, she said. You have missions and messages. I know your sort. At least the English variety. Now just look at her. She's been hanging about the whole time I've been lying here.

A tiny old woman was shambling about in the corridor, carrying an ancient shopping bag on her arm. Her dress was torn and her stockings were falling down.

— Lives in the Council Buildings. About as useless as I am. She's always wandering around.

—What's her name? J.T. asked.

— No idea. Never wanted to know to tell you the truth. But I think something ought to be done about it. I don't expect she ever eats properly. These doodle bugs are very upsetting for old people.

J.T. followed the little old lady down the corridor. He tapped her gently on the shoulder. She turned to peer up at him short-sightedly. At close quarters she had an oddly masculine face with wisps of white hair on her chin. And her mouth was set in a suspicious grin.

—Yes? What is it you want?

Het voice was sharp and full of authority.

—Would you like to lie down? I could bring you a cup of tea.

— No I would not. Who are you anyway?

— I'm a minister. Would you . . . for your shopping?

J.T. put his hand in his pocket. She shook her head. She frowned angrily and then she lowered her chin as if struck by a deep thought.

—What day is it?

— Sunday. Shall I get you a cup of tea?

—What happens to people when they die?

She looked at him from the corner of her eye.

—Well, J.T. said. Well. . .

—You don't look to me as though you know.

— St Paul says that there are . . .

The old lady waved a hand impatiently.

— Listen. Listen. There are more coming.

Once more he heard the splutter of a flying bomb approaching.

— Reprisals.

She looked at J.T.'s face.

— I know about politics. My brother James was in the Government. Listen.

They both listened together.

—They'll go on slicing people out until there's nobody left. That's politics. My brother James always said politics was based on fear. You brutalize. That's the word he used to use. And out of that grows order. This is my seven-hundredth-and-eighty-third raid. Do you know how I keep count? I have my own system . . .

The spluttering engine was noisy overhead. It distracted her. She pulled a worried face.

— Don't like these. Don't like them at all.

She pressed herself against the wall and clasped her hands together in what could have been taken to be an attitude of prayer.

— Keep away from the glass! I shan't be able to help you.

— I think it's passing over.

— My mother was afraid of going to Hell. My brother James said it was nothing to worry about. Nor the Day of Judgement. What is your opinion?

— The engine has stopped.

J.T. spoke very quietly, but she heard him. Her clasped hands began to tremble. When the explosion came, it was some distance away. Her face lit up with a radiant smile.

— Well there we are, she said.

With her weight against the wall, she slid down to the floor and opened her shopping-bag to make a slow examination of the meagre contents.

25

THE SURFACE OF the drive to the hall of residence was covered with frozen snow, and down the centre the sliding students had polished out a river of ice that flowed through the main gateway and turned sharply left to join the main road. To avoid the ice, J.T. walked close to the shrubbery and each time his elbow touched an evergreen there was a shower of powdered snow. The end of his nose poked out redly above the grey muffler he wore around his neck and his hat was pulled so far down, his ears stuck out inside the upturned collar of his overcoat. His progress was made more difficult by the shape of the parcel he was carrying. Brown paper concealed a biscuit tin and it was clear that he felt compelled to hold the tin upright.

The wide steps which led to the front door had been carefully swept. When he had rung the bell, he stamped his feet on the red tiles. A short maid in an overall opened the door.

— I want to speak to Miss Miles, he said. The maid seemed uncertain what to do.

— I'm her father.

After the silence of the frozen garden, the interior was warm and filled with the noise of young women and from the kitchens there came the unappetizing smell of boiled cabbage. The maid ran up the oak staircase. She was wearing rubber-soled shoes that thudded heavily on the uncarpeted oak treads. Half-way up there was a huge pre-Raphaelite picture of a draped female figure leaning against a garden urn.

Carefully J.T. put the biscuit tin down on the table which stood in the centre of the hall. He bent down to look at the open ledger in which the women students put down their names for late passes, together with their reason for wanting to be late. He looked at the episcopal bench against the panelled wall as if he were considering sitting on it. Girls who came hurrying down the wide staircase gave him curious looks. He took off his grey woollen gloves and blew on his cold fingers.

— Tada!

Thea's voice was full of wonder and surprise. He turned and saw her standing on the stairs, with one leg already stretched forward for the final run down the last flight. She was wearing a black polo-necked jersey, an old grey skirt, thick black stockings and worn slippers. Her hair was cut short, curled and seemed a lighter colour than it used to be. Without make-up her face was anaemic. There was a pimple on her chin that she had been squeezing. He stared at her intently as if he were seeing her for the first time. She put her arms around his neck and pulled his head down so that she could kiss him warmly on the cheek more than once.

— You're the last person in the world . . . when she came in and said 'Your father is here,' just like that, you could have knocked me down with a feather . . . What's that?

— Some eggs. And two pots of marmalade. Mrs Willie Lloyd packed them for me.

— I can just see her. How is she?

— 'Remember me to her, remember me to her.'

J.T. was making a weak effort to imitate Mrs Willie Lloyd's effusive manner, but Thea laughed so loudly the sound echoed through the bare hall and she clapped her hand over her mouth.

— I can't take you up to my room. You're a man. If there's a fire in the drawing-room it will be full of chattering girls. Have you got enough money to pay for our lunch? Beans on toast. Anything. I know this isn't exactly the season, but you can get ice-cream now in the café lounge of the Plaza. And it's warm there too . . .

Even as she spoke, Thea hurried down the corridor and opened one of the doors that led to a long drawing-room. She peeped in, closed the door hurriedly and came back to her father with her nose wrinkled up with distaste.

— Like a hen house. Let's go out, shall we? I'll be as quick is I can. Are you sure you've got enough money?

J.T. began to put his hands in his trouser pockets. Thea tapped the end of his nose with her finger, picked up the biscuit tin and hurried upstairs. He continued to examine the contents of all his pockets with care, until he seemed satisfied that all was as it should be. He sat down on the bench and folded his arms. His chin sank down into his muffler and he appeared to be deep in thought. A tall girl with a narrow self-absorbed walk and restless eyes that seemed to want to take account of everything around her hurried past and then stopped, and approached him at a much slower pace.

— Excuse me.

J.T. looked up, startled.

— You must be Mr J.T. Miles. I heard you at the Llandudno Conference last August. Forgive me for saying so, but I thought it was an inspiring address. Does Thea know you are here? No, please don't get up. I just thought I would go and get her if she didn't already know. My name is Valmai Stevens. I've got no right to introduce myself really, except that I'm one of Thea's friends.

They shook hands.

— Do sit down, Mr Miles. If you like I'll keep you company until Thea comes down. She's awfully popular. I admire her really. It's wonderful to have such a mind of your own and still be popular. Are you writing anything now, Mr Miles? I thought *Jesus Today* was a wonderful little book.

— That's very kind. Fancy you having read a pamphlet like that.

— Don't I look serious enough?

— Forgive me. Of course you do. I always imagine only old ministers read things like that.

— I saw it in Thea's room one day. I asked if I could borrow it.

— Did you really? J.T. shook his head and smiled.

— Did you really?

— Are you coming to see Thea playing Viola?[119] I think she'll be marvellous. Everybody says she's the best actress this place has ever produced. A lot of the girls are jealous of her. She does tend to say just

379

exactly what she thinks. She isn't conventional, is she? I hope to goodness this weather improves or people just won't be able to get here.
It's awfully bad luck on the Labour Government this weather, isn't
it?[120] Not that I'm Labour of course, but I think one can quite see...

— Tada!

Thea was wearing a fur hat. J.T. stared at it as if he were wondering where it came from. Valmai Stevens bent a knee to make herself
shorter and looked avidly from father to daughter.

— I say, Thea! What a marvellous hat! I've just been awfully bold
and introduced myself to your father. You're both so alike somehow.
I don't know what it is. But I mustn't keep you.

She offered J.T. her hand.

— Goodbye, Mr Miles. It's been wonderful meeting you.

Thea's face was hastily made up. Her lips smudged with lipstick.
When she pulled a face it was ruefully comic distaste that she showed.
Outside on the steps she gripped her father's arm firmly.

— Why don't you like her?

— She's what I would call an Exo Lesb.

— What's that?

She looked up at his puzzled face.

— You don't know much, do you, Joe Miles? After all these years.
Come on. I'm hanging on to you, mind. Don't let me go.

The warmth of her breath issued in clouds from her mouth on
the cold air.

— My leg aches in this weather, J.T. said.

A car churned past on the main road, the chains on the wheels
slapping the packed snow.

— I've been wondering why you've come today of all days. Have
you got a meeting or something?

— I had a letter from Ken, Thea. Yesterday.

Thea stood still. She closed her mouth tightly.

— That one!

— He's a very nice boy, Thea. Quiet and hard working.

— That's what he's like with you. All pious and chapel and 'Cym-
raeg am Byth'.[121] Just because he's learnt Welsh you want to give him
a halo.

— He said you'd written to the Director of the Repertory Company in Wor ...

— What if I had! I've never made a secret of it. I always said I was going to act. I only came here to please you. I told you in September, Tada, I wasn't going to do Honours. A pass degree is good enough for me.

— Ken said you'd told him you were going at the end of the month.

Thea shook with laughter as she held on to her father's arm. Her head when she looked up at him was wreathed in the traces of her breath.

— He's such a creep, she said. I can't think what I ever saw in him. Since he's been elected Secretary of S.R.C.[122] he pads about with files under his arm like a Minister of State.

—You're not going then?

J.T. sounded deeply relieved.

— He was getting on my nerves so much. 'You get a good degree, Thea,' he said, 'and we can get married next summer. We'll go to Ceylon for our honeymoon.' 'Ceylon?' I said. 'Why Ceylon?' 'That's where the World Conference of Students is next year.' Can you imagine it?

As they laughed together, they stepped carefully among the heaps of frozen snow on the pavement.

— I wouldn't marry him if he was the last man on earth, honestly.

Thea hugged her father's arm.

— It's a pity I can't marry you. You're my pin-up boy. I'd keep house for you and you could write sermons about the sins of Wales. Pity the law's against it. Silly old world, isn't it? What's the matter?

J.T. was looking solemn.

—There was one matter I wanted to discuss with you.

— If it's getting married again, I won't hear of it. I'll write to Ronnie and say you're threatening to bring disgrace on the family.

— I'm serious now.

The hill going down to the centre of the town was steep and slippery. J.T. steadied himself with one gloved hand against the garden wall that surrounded the old part of the hospital and Thea let go of his arm to jump on and off the mounds of frozen snow.

— I've been invited to take up the pastorates of Engedi and Nant-y-Wrach.

—Where on earth are they?

— Not very far from Argoed. They're very small churches, but I don't mind that. In Engedi there are some men who work in the ironworks and in the new plastics factory on the coast, but Nant-y-Wrach of course is entirely rural.

— Whose idea was this?

— Mine of course.

Thea stood on a mound of snow and pointed at her father accusingly.

— Are you sure?

— It's a sort of semi-retirement. I'll be sixty in less than three years. My children have all left home.

— You sound as if you're giving in. I don't like it.

— A biggish church is an awful responsibility for a man without a wife. . .

— Do you want me to come and be your deputy?

— I'm serious, Thea.

— So am I.

He looked at her and shook his head sadly.

— You're not cut out for it. Any more than your mother was. You're very like her, you know.

— The thing is, I take it, you'll be able to live at Argoed. And Aunty Katie will be able to keep house for you.

— They have offered me a car, J.T. said. I don't know whether I'll be able to learn to drive it.

— It sounds like a retreat to me.

— No indeed it isn't. It will give me more free time to read and think and write. It's a desperate sort of crisis everything I believe in is faced with: Christianity, Wales, the Christian way of life. I want to think about it more deeply. And I want to write about it.

Thea jumped down from the mound and took her father's arm.

— Come on, she said. This cold is making me hungry.

J.T. moved forward carefully, still pursuing his train of thought.

— After all, Argoed would be somewhere splendid for you all to come to. On your holidays and things like that. A sort of centre for the family. Vernon and Dorothy are going there for Easter. Ronnie and Sheila were there last summer.

— And Aunty Kate will be there all the time to keep an eye on you.

— What do you mean?

— There won't be any stray widows floating up from South Wales with pots of lemon cheese and pullovers knitted with their own fair hands. . . So long as you know what you're doing, Tada.

— I've given it careful thought, J.T. said.

Thea pushed her head down and turned towards him so that he could see her looking over a pair of imaginary spectacles.

— Permission granted, she said.

KATE BENT DOWN low to lift the rear wheels of the maroon pram up the concrete steps. She had passed her wrist through the loop of string around the brown-paper parcel she was carrying in order to free both hands to grasp the back axle of the pram. The parcel scraped along the grimy floor.

— No, Aunty, please don't.

— I'm used to manual labour!

Kate's English sounded gruff, but she was smiling to show Vernon's wife how glad she was to help.

— It would be easier if you didn't. It's a knack.

Kate stepped back and Dorothy began to pull the pram up the stairs, first one wheel and then the other.

— I used to leave it down in the corridor. But that woman's cats went nesting in it. And worse. Ghastly pong.

Kate held her head to one side as if she were hard of hearing.

— Smell.

— Oh, I see. Why don't you use the lift?

— Can't get it in. The pram's too long. Or the lift's too small.

— It's hard work for you . . .

— Never mind. He'll soon be big enough for a push-chair.

The passenger in the pram hung his head over the side and a chain of dribble suspended from his open mouth as he stared at the jerky revolutions of the pram's wheels. The uncarpeted stairs ascended around the lift shaft. Vernon's wife was pregnant with her second child. She was a big cheerful-looking girl with short fair hair and a freckled face. She used no make-up and the blue of her maternity coat drew attention to the blue of her eyes.

— Let me pull it then, Dorothy, Kate said.

She had paused for breath at the top of the first flight of stairs. Kate's voice reverberated in the stair-well. Dorothy smiled briefly and shook her head. She made for the short flight that led to the first floor. Her mouth was set determinedly as she made the effort. She wore no stockings and in spite of her pregnancy her legs were shapely and powerful and seemed to gleam with life and vigour on the gloomy stairs.

On the first floor Dorothy used her head to indicate the closed door of a flat with No.7 on it. Kate stared at the door and then opened her mouth as if she were about to ask questions. Dorothy frowned and Kate looked at the door again, shaking her head, an expression of fascinated horror on her face. Down on the ground floor someone was shutting the noisy gates of the lift.

— Just to think. . . in this place . . .

Kate's voice boomed out and Dorothy hurriedly put a finger to her lips. They watched the lift ascend to an upper floor. They caught a glimpse of a pallid-faced young man biting his nails. He looked at Dorothy as if she were about to ask who he was. Dorothy grinned at Kate and pulled up the pram more energetically so that the baby rolled from side to side in his straps. The movement made him gurgle and laugh and his mother began to speak to him in baby talk.

— Is he laughing? Kate said. I don't see him.

Dorothy nodded as she continued to communicate with her son by pulling faces and making noises. Kate turned to look down the stairs. She could still see the closed door of flat No. 7. It seemed to fascinate her.

— I can't get it out of my mind.

— What?

— The bloodstained carpet.

— Well. . .

Dorothy hesitated, clearly wanting to speak and yet uncertain what exactly to say.

— I didn't like the look of that one going up in the lift either. He looked a criminal if ever I saw one.

Dorothy looked too serious to notice the smile Kate was preparing to make. She lifted her newly-cut latch key and paused before pushing it home into the lock.

She put her ear against the door.

— There's someone with him, she said. One of his prisoners, I suppose. Really, he never stops. He knows you're coming perfectly well.

— He's just like his father. Kate sounded tolerant.

— Listen, Aunty.

Dorothy held the pram steady with one hand and bent to put her head as close as she could to Kate's. Kate frowned as she tried to follow Dorothy's hurried whisperings.

— He's got no qualifications, Aunty. None at all. He'll be twenty-eight next birthday and by then we'll have two children not one. What kind of a future will they have? He's just taken out quite a heavy insurance — it's the least he could do of course — and we'll have an awful time making both ends meet. And it isn't as though he hasn't got the ability. If you could talk to him, Aunty and make him see sense.

— Don't talk so fast, Kate said. It's difficult for me to follow.

Dorothy's hand that held the pram tightened until her knuckles showed white.

— I'm sorry to pour all our troubles over your head before you've got through the front door . . .

— I don't mind that, Kate said. If you'd just talk a little more slowly. Remember English is my second language.

Kate was studying Dorothy's face and Dorothy smiled.

— It's not that I'm out of sympathy with his work, she said. It's just that the time has come to think of the children and to think of the future. This man Shelley wants him to go to the Middle East and organize rehabilitation centres for refugees and he wants to go, Aunty. I've got to tell you about it, because he thinks it's wonderful and he just thinks I'm lacking in a sense of adventure, but I tell him it will only last two or three years and then where is he at the age of thirty-one? With no qualifications and no money. He was talking about medicine until this came along. Well, who can start medicine at thirty-one and then go on to specialize in child psychology? I'm awfully worried, Aunty. I just can't sleep, worrying about it. Did Ronnie say anything?

— He wants to see him, Kate said.

Dorothy scrutinized Kate's face anxiously.

— Well there you are, you see. He won't listen to Ronnie. It's horrid really.

— What?

— The way they are with each other. Suspicious. Finding fault all the time.

Dorothy's face was flushed.

— It's no way for brothers to behave. I can't think really why father doesn't see it. After all he's supposed to understand people. He writes books about peace and all that, doesn't he? I can't read them of course.

— I don't think he realizes. . .

— That's just it! He lives in a sort of cocoon. Anything unpleasant or disturbing and it's got to be kept from him.

— No use him worrying about something he can't do anything about.

— That's just it. He should be able to. And they do their best to keep it from him. I've seen them with my own eyes. In front of him, they act as if they're the best of friends. It's almost ridiculous. I'll never understand it. Is it something to do with being Welsh or something?

— It could be.

Kate looked stern. Dorothy turned her attention to getting the new key to turn in the lock.

— What a place to live, she said. Everybody in the block had to change the locks on the front doors at a week's notice.

She steered the pram carefully into the flat. Because of her size, her movements in the confined space seemed rough and noisy. In the kitchen she banged cupboard doors to, filled the kettle and slammed it on the gas cooker, while Kate made the pram swing on its springs with her finger.

— You'd think he'd at least have put the kettle on, Dorothy said. Still I've made the tea really. I hope you like banana sandwiches, Aunty. I do. And my inevitable flap-jacks. It's the syrup I get with my sugar ration.

Kate nodded towards the parcel she had put on the chair against the wall.

— I've bought two shirts for Vernon.

Dorothy made a noise of pleasure. She was pulling at the straps which kept the baby safe in his pram and she turned her head for a moment to look at the parcel. As she did so she pinched the baby's arm with a strap and he began to cry.

— Oh blast! Now look what I've done. My little sugar.

She picked the baby up and clutched him tightly to her breast. His bare feet kicked against her swollen belly. When she had finished rubbing, sucking and kissing his chubby arm she lowered him down so that his feet explored the linoleum of the kitchen floor. He stamped the soles of his feet so energetically that his mother laughed. With both hands clutching her skirt he looked up for her approval. She smiled down on him dotingly until she heard Vernon's loud yet gentle voice in the corridor, reassuring the last mumbled doubts from the Irish discharged prisoner he was seeing out.

— Don't worry, Rosco, and give me a ring between eleven and half-past tomorrow morning and tell me how it goes. Okay? Right! Cheerio!

Vernon banged the door and called out cheerfully,

— Is my Aunty Katie there?

— Don't make so much noise, Dorothy said. This little boy's trembling all over.

Vernon kissed his aunt. She lifted the lock of black hair out of his eyes. Dorothy held her cheek out for him to kiss and then he picked up Martin and turned to look at Kate and say,

— What do you think of this one?

— I want to change him, Dorothy said. He's sopping.

She snatched a nappy from the fire-guard that she kept around the Ideal boiler for airing purposes and put it against her cheek.

— You might have put the kettle on, she said.

— Sorry, Vernon said. How's the old prophet in Israel?

Vernon spoke to his aunt in Welsh. Dorothy had a safety-pin in her mouth and she was frowning as she took the baby out of Vernon's arms.

— This is an awful place to live, Kate said.

— It's better than most, Vernon said. Can't complain really.

— A murder downstairs. And prostitutes upstairs. Dorothy's been telling me about it.

Dorothy took the pin out of her mouth and said.

— Are you talking about Father?

Vernon laughed loudly.

— Not yet, but we soon will be.

— I was telling him this was no place to bring up children, Kate said.

— He's too young to notice yet, Vernon said. He can't tell margarine from butter.

— I'm serious, Kate said. You ought to think of your father too.

— He'd love it, Vernon said. I remember during the war I used to notice how different he was when he was up here. More positive somehow. And more cheerful. He didn't have that look on his face. You know. I've-got-the-sins-of-Wales-on-my-back sort of look.

— He'll have to retire one day, Kate said. What could be nicer for him than having you all near him?

— What would I do there, for goodness' sake?

— And you could bring the children up Welsh-speaking.

Vernon lifted his finger playfully.

— My goodness. You've got it all worked out. You two have been talking.

— Indeed we haven't.

Dorothy handed the baby to Kate so that she could make tea. The cloud of steam shot up from the teapot. Her actions like her gestures were all brisk and large.

— It's the sight of this place, Kate said. Especially compared to Ronnie's.

— We can't all be dons, Vernon said, and we can't all marry rich widows.

— I'm serious, Kate said. Look at the chance in life Sheila's children will be getting. Both of them. And what chance will Martin have in a district like this? Shall I start giving him his feed, Dorothy? Do you think he'll take it from me? I'm not an expert of course.

She settled the boy comfortably in her lap and dragged the heavy feeding plate, which was decorated with gambolling rabbits, within her reach. She began to mix the food with a spoon.

— If you wanted, she said, you could quite easily live in Argoed for a few years. You could study in Liverpool or Bangor. There's enough room there . . .

— Oh Aunty . . . That would be wonderful!

Dorothy was beaming with pleasure. Kate appeared to be absorbed in her task of mixing the baby food to the right consistency, putting the correct quantity on the end of the spoon and lifting it temptingly to the baby's mouth. Vernon was shaking his head gratefully.

— It is a great offer, Aunty.

— I haven't said a word to your father. I only got the idea this minute. But it's my house, not his, isn't it?

Kate looked up smiling, pleased with her joke.

— At least it's partly mine. Dan Llew keeps on offering to buy me out. It's that John Arnold you know. I never liked him. He drives up in the yard in those cars of his as if he were the Lord of Creation, just because he's making a bit of money. His brother Norman is a much nicer boy.

— I've been invited to take up a job in the Middle East, Vernon said. I'm rather keen on it to tell you the truth.

— Well I'm not!

Dorothy shouted so sharply the baby stopped chewing and looked up from the loaded spoon, its mouth full and open. Kate unloaded the spoon into the feeding dish and used it to glean the lumps of mixture that hung about Martin's mouth with delicate care. In the silence it was possible to hear the noise of children being chased down the stairs by an angry woman and the noise of the lift doors opening and shutting on the floor above.

— How are our rich relations?

Vernon tried to sound amiable. Kate pointed at the brown-paper parcel on the kitchen chair.

— I've brought you two new shirts, she said. I pinched some of your father's clothing coupons.

— Can I open it?

Vernon had picked up the parcel eagerly. He seemed pleased to have thought of something to do. He pulled hastily at the string and the paper.

— I got them in a shop in Regent Street, Kate said. Sheila helped me choose them. Wouldn't dare go wandering around London by myself.

— Shirts by Nessus, Vernon said.

— Is that a make?

Kate looked at him innocently.

— He's trying to be clever, Dorothy said. It's always the same when he wants to avoid talking about something.

— She's not exactly fond of me, is she?

— What makes you think that? Kate said.

— Her first husband was killed in action. She's not really sure that I'm entitled to be still alive. For all I know she may well be right. I'm not blaming her.

— That's just a convenient form of self-pity. You just want to avoid the whole problem as usual.

— Do you think I wouldn't enjoy it? Explore my Welshness. Find the answers to life's mysteries hidden under the hills?[123]

— It's no joke, Vernon.

— I'm not joking. I'm talking about myself for once. This isn't self-pity either. There's a part of me that longs to go back. Ronnie's the same you know. We've both got the Arthur complex.

— What on earth are you talking about?

— Maybe it's too big a challenge. There's too much lost and too much to put right. It needs more guts than anything I can think of.

— More than looking after a wife and family properly?

— Can I take a sandwich?

Vernon pushed a banana sandwich in his mouth.

— Aunty has made a wonderful offer.

Vernon nodded, his mouth full.

— Are you going to take it?

— Well . . .

— Are you? Are you?

— I'm not a big enough type to go back. I'm not equipped to . . .

— I'm not talking about anything, Vernon, except us. I'm sorry, Aunty, to shout in front of you, but this has got to come to a head. You've got to say, Vernon, here and now that we're going back. And you're going to qualify.

— This isn't very nice, Vernon said. I haven't seen Aunty Kate for goodness knows how long . . .

— I've explained everything to Aunty. She understands.

— I've promised.

— You had no right to promise without consulting me!

— Please, Kate said. Don't quarrel. You'll frighten the baby.

— I can't stand it.

There were tears of anger in Dorothy's eyes.

— Listen . . .

— No. I won't listen. I'm sorry, Aunty. You talk to him. I'm going out. You talk to him, please.

She left the room so quickly that Kate and Vernon did not look at each other until the front door banged and the baby started crying.

SHEILA'S HOLIDAY TAN was exposed by the backless dress she was wearing, but the evening was cool and she seemed to be trembling slightly as she stood at the foot of the staircase with the eager young lady from the newspaper, who managed to hold a notebook and pencil as well as a cigarette and glass of white wine, and to dangle her patent leather handbag on her wrist.

— You could say it was the only double staircase in Croftwood, Sheila said.

As she laughed she turned the corners of her mouth down to show that she attached no importance to what she was saying. She seemed to have trained herself to calmness, as the hairdresser had imposed elegance and order on her tough springy hair. When Ronnie came up to her and put a hand on her bare shoulder she inclined her head to listen to him without turning round. His voice was quiet but urgent. His back was turned on the young woman reporter and his dark protruding eyes seemed to be keeping track of the man and woman from the caterers who were putting the last touches to the buffet meal in the long dining-room. He could see them through the half-opened door.

— It's our au-pair girl, Sheila said to the newspaper reporter. She should be helping with the wine and she's nowhere to be seen. Would you excuse me? Do make yourself at home. There are some nice pictures upstairs if you want to see them. Just go wherever you like.

— If I could have a list of the guests...

— It's in your study, isn't it, darling?

— Yes. I was going to wait a little longer and cross off the names of the people who haven't turned up ...

Ronnie gave the reporter all his attention and a charming smile that seemed to suggest he was apologizing for not having taken proper notice of her before.

— Don't tell me you've got more parties to attend this evening?

— No. This is the only one.

The girl suddenly became much livelier.

— Well there we are. Please stay as long as you like. Would you like me to introduce you to the Vice-Chancellor?

The guests were congregated chiefly in the drawing-room and the conservatory that was next to it. Ronnie held the girl reporter by the elbow and stretched himself to peer over their heads.

— He doesn't appear to be here. I can see his wife. But you want to avoid her. She's a bit of a bore.

The reporter giggled, and Ronnie gave her another understanding smile. She seemed to enjoy the protective manner he had adopted towards her.

— You weren't ever a student of mine, were you?

— I'm afraid I never went to college.

— How wise of you. Now let's have a look in here.

Ronnie opened the study door. They saw the Vice-Chancellor talking to Ronnie's father, who sat in a leather chair in a corner of the room, nursing a glass of lemon juice.

The Vice-Chancellor was a large man who was economical with his movements. When he smiled he looked downwards so that his amusement seemed secret. His buttocks weighed against the edge of Ronnie's desk.

— Sorry to interrupt, Ronnie said.

— Well it's your study of course, the Vice-Chancellor said. I've been having the most interesting discussion with your father.

— I think, with a little effort, I could just guess what it was about.

Ronnie's manner was extremely agreeable. The Vice-Chancellor shook gently with contained amusement.

— This is Miss . . . oh dear . . .

Ronnie looked at the girl at his side who smiled at him forgivingly.

— Lucy Jaynes, she said. You're not supposed to know.

— Miss Jaynes from the *Post*. . .

— From the *Mail,* the girl said.

— Well . . . I'm doing this very badly. She very much wanted to meet the Vice-Chancellor.

— Talk to him, the Vice-Chancellor said, pointing at Ronnie. He's going to be our first Professor of Sociology and Industrial relations. There's a bit of news for you.

— Headlines!

Ronnie lifted the glass he was carrying. The Vice-Chancellor seemed very taken with his charm of manner. J.T. looked quietly pleased.

— This is an extremely talented family, the Vice-Chancellor said. And since I'm almost half-Welsh myself I'm going to bask in reflected glory. Your father was just telling me, Miles, about your sister's tour with the Old Vic.[124]

— Do you mean you were not talking about the state of the Welsh nation?

Ronnie spoke with humorous exaggeration. The girl reporter was gazing at him with excited admiration. He shifted about slightly on the soles of his feet as if he were casting about for a chance to sparkle. J.T. lifted his hand wearily.

— Let's not talk about that, he said.

— This is terrible, Ronnie said. My father doesn't want to talk about Wales. What is the world coming to?

— Have you seen his new book, Miss Jaynes? The Vice-Chancellor pointed at Ronnie.

— *Mobility and Social Structure*. A very important little book.

The girl scribbled the title in her notebook. The Vice-Chancellor clasped his hands together in his lap. The fingers as they intertwined were large and white against the dark blue cloth.

— Now if you dipped into that, he said, you might find a headline or two.

— There you are, Miss Jaynes! We academics are all the same. We toil away in obscurity, secretly pining for notoriety. You must do your best for us.

— It's about change, your book, is it?

Miss Jaynes had stopped smiling. Her pencil was poised as she looked at Ronnie.

— Yes. I suppose it is.

He gave her a quick nod of approval.

— I was just thinking . . .

Miss Jaynes turned to address J.T., who was sipping his lemon juice.

— . . . You belong to a generation that has seen fantastic changes, Mr Miles.

Her Midlands accent lent a seriousness and an intensity to what she was saying. Ronnie extracted a small packet of cigarettes from his trouser pocket and as he lit a cigarette turned to study the girl, as if what she had just said had revealed a totally new aspect of her personality. As he exhaled smoke he regarded his father, who was nodding wisely. He lifted a hand and rattled the box of matches in his direction.

— You'll have to do better than that, he said. Here's a unique opportunity to make a statement to the English press on the Welsh way of life. Isn't that so, Miss . . .?

— Jaynes.

He gazed at her intently as if he were regretting having let her escape from his spell.

— All change passes me by, J.T. said. I've reached the age when I can't really adapt any more.

— Well now that's absolute nonsense.

Ronnie modulated his voice to reduce the harshness in the words.

— Your brain is as good as ever and physically I suspect you are fitter than I am.

J.T. did not speak. The girl's questions and his thoughtful silence seemed to be driving out the gaiety that had been in the room.

— It's just that you insist on living in Wales. This is the basic error. We want him to live here.

J.T. made no response. Ronnie gave his attention to the Vice-Chancellor.

— Do you know I once thought of doing a study of the Welshman in England? As soon as he gets away from the Welsh condition he becomes a different animal. I recall when I was making a mobility survey in the Coventry area, all the foremen seemed to be Welshmen. Outside Wales, you have a positive individualist, a leader, a man with all his abilities liberated, a pleasure to watch; a Bevan,[125] a Lloyd George. Inside Wales a guilt-ridden negative man with no initiative, weighed to the ground by a sense of cosmic doom, bent under a load of dead-wood tradition.

— Dead wood!

J.T. sat up erect in his chair.

— This is it, you see. This is it!

He looked up at the Vice-Chancellor as if Ronnie had just proved a point he had been making earlier.

— Wales is the last place that counts and the last thing that counts.

Ronnie spread out the fingers of the hand that held his cigarette.

— Emotional overtones at once. It's always the same. A conditioned reflex.

— Of course it is. And there is a very good reason. Old Ambrose used to say that nationality was a question of loyalty.[126]

— Who was that?

The Vice-Chancellor sounded alert. He looked with great interest from the son to the father.

— William Ambrose.

J.T. shook his head sadly.

— First-class writer. He's been dead ten years, and it still hasn't occurred to anybody to prepare a decent, critical biography.

— Well don't look at me as if it were my fault, Ronnie said. I don't even know who he was.

— There you are! That's exactly it.

J.T. seemed suddenly energetic.

— How can there be any faith or meaning or purpose without loyalty? This is the basic question.

— And what does loyalty mean?

Again Ronnie held out the open hand that held his cigarette. It was a characteristic gesture.

— To become a spiritual Red Indian living in a language reservation? An air-conditioned wigwam? There was once a tribe of gentle nonconformists who played happily in their native hills, safe in the custody of a great empire, emasculated by their sentimental religion.

He smiled and glanced at the girl who was scribbling in shorthand.

— I say, he said. You're not taking this down, are you?

— The treason of the intellectual, J.T. said, is to have no loyalties at all.

— Now wait a minute. Wait a minute. Would you agree that any idea of a nation or indeed any ideal — let's make it as broad as we can — must bear some relation to reality? Reality being defined as 'things as they are', or 'that which is the case'?

J.T. lowered his head to consider Ronnie's statement.

— Let me give an example. English or Welsh, what difference does it really make, in reality? We eat the same food, we wear the same clothes. We travel in the same motor-cars. We pay the same taxes. We read the same newspapers . . .

— Ah!

J.T. put up a finger.

— Language? Ronnie said. It boils down to that? Now you've read the *Manchester Guardian* every day of your life since I can remember. I suppose you would prefer a daily edition printed in Welsh?

— Yes I would.

— Can you see it happening?

— I don't see why not, if the demand . . .

— That's the crucial word. Demand. That's exactly when the big let-down comes. The Welsh people don't want it. . .

— This is hypothetical, J.T. said. And in any case a substantial minority, which includes me, does.

— They don't want a language that is dying, or any of the fantasies that go with it. This is the reality.

— Dad.

Christopher, Ronnie's stepson, tapped him on the shoulder to attract his attention. The girl reporter turned to study the new arrival, but Ronnie continued to concentrate on his train of thought.

— It is, in fact, a world of fantasy related to something that might have existed before 1914. It's living in the past on a large scale. A stubborn refusal to grow up, so that whole lives are spent in a sort of Welsh dream. I agree the language is the real issue, because this is the symbol. This is the letter that kills and keeps out the spirit that gives life. It lies on a new generation like a corrosive dust that stops them breathing and gives them no chance at all of making something new.

He paused triumphantly for breath.

— I don't know why . . . J.T. said slowly, why my own son . . .

— Dad.

Christopher shook his father's shoulder urgently.

— Mum wants you in the kitchen. It's the police. They've arrested Bodil.

— Arrested? What on earth for?

Ronnie was forced to speak loudly to maintain an appearance of balance and control.

— It's our au-pair girl. She's got herself arrested. She's terribly nice, but she really is monumentally stupid. You must excuse me.

Chris followed close on Ronnie's heels. He was fair-haired and his fresh cheeks had uneven patches which showed where colonies of pimples had recently receded. His sister Helen was hanging anxiously out of the kitchen doorway, waiting for some sign from her brother so as to know whether to laugh or be very serious. She jumped out of the way so that her step-father and brother could march in without decreasing their speed.

— SHALL I GO up and have a chat with him?

Christopher sounded so responsible that Ronnie tapped him warmly on the shoulder. They were both standing at the foot of the double staircase. The party had reached the point where it was running itself. Warmed by the wine, in every room leading off the hall people were talking and laughing. Those who were still hungry lingered in the dining-room and idly picked up tit-bits from the table as they continued to listen attentively to their companions.

— He was a remarkable man, Ronnie said. When I was your age I used to think what a marvellous leader he would have made.

— *Taidi*

— I used to go through agonies watching him preach at street corners . . .

— Did he do that?

Christopher looked up the stairs and shook his head with unconcealed wonder.

— It must have cost him something. A shy man really. And not really eloquent. Just sincere. Are you sure he heard her?

— Mummy's got such a penetrating voice. If I heard her, he must have.

— Wasn't he talking to anybody?

— No. I was keeping an eye on him like you told me to. I was all set to go and chat him up, but he looked so content I didn't want to disturb him. He must have heard.

— Urn.

Ronnie looked worried.

— Well . . . here goes.

He took the stairs in wide strides and hurried along the corridor with his head down, until he came to the room which was occupied by J.T. He tapped on the door, opened it quickly and found J.T. on his knees alongside the bed. He was packing books away at the bottom of a large suitcase. The volume in his hand was called *The Fourth Gospel*.

— What are you doing?

— Packing books, J.T. said.

— I can see that. What for?

— I'm a bit worried about your aunt. She isn't very well. She doesn't like being left alone in that old house. I was going to tell you only you were so busy. I'd better be off home tomorrow.

— But you said you'd stay until the end of the month. This room is yours. To come to whenever you like.

— That's very nice of you, J.T. said.

— Who am I going to argue with if you're not here?

Ronnie stood in the room where his father could see him smiling, but J.T. looked at the torn dust-jacket of the book in his hand. From his trouser-pocket Ronnie extracted a packet of cigarettes. As he lit one, he said,

— Have you taken the huff?

J.T. looked up.

— Good heavens, no.

—You don't want me to treat you with exaggerated respect, do you? If we can't say just what we think . . . Our opinions are bound to differ . . .

— Of course they are. Of course.

—Well, what is the matter?

J.T. was still on his knees in front of the open case.

— You are, in effect, packing your bags. Now I am entitled to know just exactly why.

— I'm getting old, I suppose, J.T. said. Don't worry about it.

— But I am worrying. Is it anything I have said or done? Or anything Sheila or the children have said or done?

J.T. got to his feet. His knees were stiff.

— Sheila thinks I'm going to be a bit of a problem as I grow older. With all my Welsh nonsense.

— She didn't mean . . .

— She always says what she means. She's always been able to afford to. Ronnie shook the cigarette between his fingers.

—We are all problems as we grow older. It's true. It's not tactful, but it's true.

— Of course it is. Of course.

—You keep on saying 'Of course'. You think she's a hard, materially-minded woman, determined to push me on . . .

— She wasn't very nice to your Aunty Kate.

— I explained that to you fully at the time. It was a misunderstanding. In any case, it's ancient history.

— Even if she didn't like her, it wasn't polite to expect her to eat in the kitchen . . .

— Sheila just thought she would have been bored with the people we had in. And Aunty is very narrow about alcohol anyway. We've been over all this before. The fact is, you think it's wrong to have any money and it's wrong to spend it. You set impossible standards. You make impossible demands and then you condemn all of us outright because we don't fulfil them.

— I don't condemn anybody.

—You do. Your whole attitude is one of condemnation. I mean, when I opened that door and saw you kneeling on the floor . . .

— I was packing my books.

—You wonder what I am. You can't understand this and you can't understand that and all the time this was at the root of everything.

When I was a child I could never reach the standards you set. I could never win your approbation. That's why I am what I am. A man like you should never have children. I mean, look at Vernon.

—Vernon is doing wonderful work, J.T. said. You should be proud of him.

— Oh I am. I am. And you should know why he's doing it.

— There are always motives we don't know about ourselves.

— There certainly are.

— I wonder why you and your wife . . .

— Don't call her 'your wife' for God's sake. Her name is Sheila and I've been married to her for twelve years.

—Why you both encouraged Dorothy to leave him?

— Good gracious me.

Ronnie roamed about the bedroom with a cigarette stump between his fingers, looking for an ashtray. When he found one on the dressing-table, it contained his father's collar-studs and spare cuff-links. He tipped them out and stubbed the cigarette-end which was burning his finger.

— I don't understand your attitude to your own brother . . .

— Oh but you do. From an early age I was insanely jealous. That's why I was a soldier and he was a pacifist. That's why I had to stand up and get shot at and that's why he's got to go on toiling in foreign fields. In your view it's an interesting variation on Cain and Abel.

J.T. sat on the edge of his bed.

With his hands in his pockets Ronnie walked across the room and gazed down into the open case on the floor. He was smiling.

— Now you see how childish I can still be. There just are these terrible immaturities lurking about in all of us. You mustn't take any notice of Sheila. She's an honest old thing and kind hearted too, but like most of her kind lacking in imagination. We've got too much. They've got too little.

J.T.'s shoulder seemed to sink when Ronnie touched it.

— She thinks the world of you really. She wants you to retire and come and live with us. Aunty Kate could go and keep house for Uncle Dan Llew. It would be an ideal arrangement. You'd be your own master here. There's the life of the university. The library. You always wanted to be a scholar anyway.

J.T. shook his head.

—You sound just like your mother sometimes.

— How?

— Persuasive. J.T. smiled.

—You don't think it's true?

— It doesn't matter. It's time I got back to the Reservation! When I'm there I know more or less where I stand. That's my reality. Not this.

J.T. waved his hand around the room and the gesture seemed to wipe out the expensive wall-paper, the curtains, the new furniture, the fitted carpet, the pictures on the walls.

— There you are!

Ronnie's indignation made the blood come to his face. He rubbed the back of his head.

—You're at it again.

—What?

— Condemning. Everything we do and everything we are. Really it's intolerable. Perpetual judgment.

J.T. put his hands on his knees and lifted his head to look at Ronnie.

— I wasn't judging you, he said. It's as much as I can do to look out for myself.

He smiled to show Ronnie that he was joking.

— It isn't easy to be always defending . . . One can never do enough.

— There you are.

Ronnie's face brightened.

—You've put your finger right on it. Welsh this, chapel that, every minute . . .

J.T. waved him to silence.

— It's very nice here. I've enjoyed myself very much. I like meeting your friends. I like Christopher and Helen. But in the end, this isn't where I belong.

— MIND THE STEPS, Kate said. They're very slippy. It would have been better if you'd have brought it through the front really.

—You know, Aunty, I could never get used to using the front door at Argoed. I used to love coming through the churn room when I was a kid. Especially if you were cooking.

— No point in cooking unless there are mouths to feed.

— I never get used to that window either.

John Henry nodded towards the narrow window that had been

put in by Wynne Bannister.

— Didn't my grandfather always have books there? In a kind of recess?

— How is my brother Ned? Kate said.

John Henry, Ned's son, set the tape-recorder down carefully on the kitchen table. His upper lip was covered by a closely clipped moustache and he wore rimless spectacles. His hair, which was thin, was carefully parted, brushed and oiled.

— Not at all bad, Aunty, thank you. He has to take it easy of course. I couldn't bring him today, and this thing!

He slapped the tape-recorder with the palm of his hand and laughed.

— He's a handful you know. I caught him the other day sneaking out with a sickle. Hey, I said, where do you think you're off to? Goodness me, he was cross when I stopped him. But it's his heart, you see, Aunty. He gets on well with Gwenda, you know. That's a great help. He's still mad with me for putting caravans in the bottom meadow. The fact is he doesn't really believe I work at all. The other day he went into my new place down by the Beach, J.H. Jones Electrical Equipment, and you know what he said?

Kate shook her head.

— 'To think a son of mine has started keeping a toy shop'

John Henry laughed, and Kate smiled.

— How's Uncle J.T.?

— He's not at all well. He's been doing too much. Far too much. He took four young lads and they started painting the vestry. He was trying to teach the deacons a lesson, but he won't admit it. He was determined to show them. Those boys were too young to be any good and you know he's got no control over young people. It was too much for him. The smell of the paint really finished him. The doctor says he's not to get up this week. And there it is. Goodbye to my holiday.

— Well, well.

John Henry sat down. He looked as if his plans had been upset.

— I saw John Arnold yesterday. He didn't say anything.

— I'm not surprised. Did he say anything about seeing me?

— No, not a word.

John Henry looked up at his aunt expectantly. She appeared to be about to make a revelation.

— I'm not surprised. That fine gentleman is trying to smoke me out.

Because of Kate's tone of voice John Henry seemed obliged to show an expression of exaggerated horror.

— He wants the house, Kate said. He had the nerve to come here and make me an offer. 'I want to buy you out, Aunty,' he said. 'Do you?' I said. 'And what does your father say to that?' 'He says he'd be willing if you were willing.' 'Does he indeed,' I said. 'Well I'm glad to hear it. Well you can tell my brother Dan, my home isn't for sale.' 'There's going to be a new housing estate in the Cross-Roads field,' he said. 'We've sold the land.' 'We,' I said. 'Who's we?' 'My father and I,' he said.

— Gosh, John Henry said. He didn't say a word to me.

— He's like his father, Kate said. Only worse. He worships nothing but money. Never goes near chapel. And I dare say it will be his brother Norman who will build the houses.

— Norman's a good sort, John Henry said. I like Norman.

— It's always business with them.

— Norman's very sensitive.

— I can see it all. This house is in the way. I haven't said anything to J.T. It would upset him too much in his present condition.

— Do you think I'd better not see him?

Kate looked thoughtful.

— With this thing? What do you want it for?

— I thought you both could record a message. For Uncle Hugh and my cousin Sally. In North Dakota. I had the idea you know. Something to keep the old family together. I think my grandfather was a bit narrow really. Just because Uncle Hugh married a Catholic . . .

— He had his principles.

— Well. . .

— Well what?

— I'm sure you're right. But it doesn't seem the same to us today Anyway, it all turned out for the best, I suppose. Sally's a lovely girl. Do you know Herman her husband gives her a hundred pounds a week! I couldn't get over it you know when she told me.

— Money isn't everything, Kate said.

— Yes but he's only a truck driver really, who's gone into livestock transport. Very nice, but no education at all. It amazes me.

Kate switched on the electric kettle.

— I'll make tea, she said. I'll just take J.T. a glass of hot black currant juice. It does him good I think.

— I'll come again next week, Aunty. So long as I send the reel off in time for Christmas. They think a lot about the old home you know. Especially Uncle Hugh. He doesn't say much, but you can tell what he's thinking.

— It seems a pity after you brought the thing, Kate said.

— I'll tell you what. I'll leave it here if it isn't in the way and then I'll pop up next week one evening. Would that be all right, Aunty?

HE LAY ON his side in the single bed as still as an alabaster effigy on a tomb. The creases in the pillow running towards the hollow made by his head were almost stylized in their stillness. Only his eyes moved as he watched John Henry trying to straighten a twisted strand of tape. His gaze lifted from the effort of the big hands to the sunburnt face which wore the almost pained expression of a man struggling with a delicate and unfamiliar apparatus. John Henry's dress, like his moustache, glasses and hair style, seemed designed to give an urban effect; but his skin remained robust, weathered, out of doors and his hands powerful as any agricultural instrument.

— Fiddling things, John Henry said.

He smiled briefly at J.T.'s still figure.

— I've always been interested, mind. In mechanical things you know. Even as a lad. Could never get my father to see it. He thought because I couldn't do French and Latin like Ronnie I was no good. If only there'd been a Tech somewhere near. Not that my father would have let me go. I always tell him as far as he's concerned the Industrial Revolution hasn't taken place. He believes in sweat for sweat's sake.

He spoke as if he were repeating things he had said many times because they were worth repeating and as much part of the flavour of living as the quaintness of his father's character.

— You have to agree to disagree, don't you, if you want to live together under the same roof. Mind you it isn't always easy. He gets on very well with Gwenda you know. That's a great help.

— I knew her father. Very good family in chapel.

J.T. whispered throatily.

— She's patient you know, Uncle. Much more patient than I am. It isn't always easy you know. Living under the same roof. My father was always a man who liked his own way. He was very quiet about it, mind you, but he was always the boss. He still misses my mother you know. She's been dead six years now, but he hasn't got over it. I don't suppose . . .

At this point, he noticed the tears welling up in J.T.'s eyes. The flow of his reflections petered out. He held up the reel of tape.

— Make an unusual Christmas present I thought. They're mad on this sort of thing out there. That's where I got the idea to tell you the truth. It's a wonderful country, Uncle. It is really.

— You mustn't take too much notice of me.

J.T. spoke without moving his head. The tears were rolling slowly down his cheeks. Sooner or later they would drop on the white pillow and create round patches of wetness.

— There's nothing wrong with me really, only I get these depressions. It's much better now than it was. It's like a cloud descending, a heavy cloud. And it wraps itself around me. And I can't move. It began about three weeks ago. And it got heavier and heavier . . .

John Henry nodded frequently.

— I'll put this on then, he said. Then you can record a message into the little speaker.

The tape-recorder was on a chair alongside the bed.

— It's a German machine, John Henry said. Can't beat the Jerries at this kind of thing, can you?

— I thought at first it was my heart, J.T. said. But it isn't physical at all you see. It's the mind really. It's not giving way or anything like that; but it's these terrible depressions . . . I had something very similar a few years ago. When the Americans melted an island with a bomb and it disappeared under the sea.[127]

John Henry frowned as if it were an event of which he had no recollection.

— I didn't mention it to your aunt or anybody. I was on the square in Caernarvon waiting for a bus to Waunfawr. I was checking my watch by the Post Office clock and this little man from the chemist shop ran up to me and said, 'Mr Miles, have you heard about Bayley Lewis, he's hanged himself!'.[128] I don't think I said anything. I got on the bus. It wasn't very full. It wasn't a long journey. But when we got there I couldn't straighten my legs. The conductor came up to me and told me I was crying.

John Henry began to test the machine. He held the portable microphone in front of his mouth and said,

— Testing, testing, testing. One, two, three, four, five, five, four, three, two, one —

He began to press switches so that the reel spun backwards and forwards. His cheeks bulged with a satisfied smile when he heard a sound that resembled his own voice being reproduced faintly through the small speaker.

— I'm like a kid with this thing, I'm afraid, Uncle. A new toy. Ever heard your own voice, Uncle?

J.T. shook his head with the minimum of disturbance to its position on the pillow.

— Bit of a shock you know. The first time. I never thought my voice was so metallic, you know. I told Gwenda you know. 'It sounds like a corn-crake in a corned beef tin,' I said. You'll have to sit up for this, Uncle. Sit up and speak up.

— Who are you sending it to? J.T. said.

— My cousin Sally. My cousin Sally in North Dakota. I had a wonderful welcome there, Uncle. They arranged everything for me. Absolutely everything. Uncle Hugh was so glad to see me. It isn't true though that the farm is called Argoed. It's not a farm anyway, the way we understand the word. It's a ranch. Fourteen hundred acres. A cattle ranch. The address is just, Hugh Jones, Little Brunswick, North Dakota. Little Brunswick's the sort of town with a drug-store and all that. Mostly of German extraction around there. Clean, hard-working. Uncle Hugh's the only Jones. But it isn't called Argoed. People just say the Jones place. I was struck by one thing uncle. I'd never seen Uncle Hugh you know, to remember. He looks very like a thinner version of my father. But I was struck by one thing. He hadn't a good word to say for my grandfather. All that trouble because he married a Catholic. And Aunty Joyce is the nicest little woman you could ever want to meet. But it was Sally the daughter I got on with best and her husband Herman. Wonderful the way we got on. On the same wave-length you know, Uncle. We spoke the same language. Now then, what about sitting up?

J.T. moved slowly and stiffly. He dug his elbows into the mattress and lifted with all his might as if the bed clothes were made of lead.

— Can I give you a hand?

He shook his head and drew himself up into a sitting position. When the upper part of his body was erect, it began to sink slowly forward like a clasp-knife shutting itself, and he had to fasten his hands over his knees to prevent this happening. He seemed to hold his head up with difficulty.

— I told Sally her cousin Ronnie was a professor and her cousin Thea was quite a well-known actress. Pity they're not here really. I was thinking of sending Ronnie the tape for him to add something. Do you think he would? I'm telling you I'm doing what I can to keep the old Argoed breed together.

— I'm much better than I was, J.T. said. Three weeks ago I wouldn't have been able to sit up like this. I think you know in a way it's been a crisis of faith with me.

John Henry looked at his uncle anxiously. He held the small microphone in his hand and seemed to be wondering how best to capture his uncle's speech under such difficult conditions.

— Shall I sit on the edge of the bed, Uncle? Then I'll hold the microphone and you can speak into it freely. It isn't as though you're unaccustomed to public speaking, is it?

— I was telling the doctor I had an overwhelming sense of failure. I was telling him that wholesale slaughter and misery is to be stopped before it happens, not afterwards. That's why the followers of Christ must be sacrificed, must sacrifice themselves. Because the whole future of mankind rests on love as the ground of our being.

As he looked at John Henry, J.T. made an effort to smile.

— I'll tell you something they would like, Uncle, say something in Welsh. She won't understand, but Sally's very proud of being Welsh you know. Lovely girl, Uncle. She really is. I was telling Aunty Kate downstairs that she's the image of Aunty Lydia. Same laugh exactly.

J.T. stared at the little microphone intently as if he were preparing himself to welcome a new member in church. His features began to form themselves into another smile.

— Hang on a minute, Uncle.

John Henry stretched out towards the machine on the chair.

— I'll just switch it on. As soon as I've switched on you can start speaking.

J.T. turned his head with difficulty to watch John Henry's hand press the key-switch on the machine. He saw the tape spool begin to revolve. John Henry nodded in encouragement and moved the microphone as J.T. moved his head. J.T. cleared his throat carefully and frowned as if he were composing something to say. John Henry looked anxiously at the tape being paid out from one spool to the

other. When he spoke, J.T. sounded strangely old and unlike himself.
John Henry moved the microphone nearer to his mouth.

— This is your Uncle Joseph speaking . . .

J.T. cleared his throat and began again.

— This is your Uncle Joseph speaking. It is strange to think that
my words will be reaching you across the wide ocean by means . . .
by means . . . by these means. I don't know you and you don't know
me. But I am very happy to send you a message because we are closely
related. We are bound into the same family by the bonds of love. You
know I am a preacher so you will not blame me for preaching. After
all, this is a message and any message I send you should be worth
having . . . Just as the distance between us is annihilated by this device
and I am speaking now in your hearing, so it is with the means of
salvation that quicken our lives with purpose and meaning . . .

J.T. was overcome by emotion. His mouth opened and shut as he
wept, and the microphone was recording nothing but the faint sob
in his heavy breath. John Henry slid off the side of the bed and
switched off the machine. J.T. nodded as he stared at the spools which
were now still.

— If I have a short rest, he said, I shall be able to continue.

— I don't want to put a strain on you, Uncle, when you're not
well. . .

— No indeed. It helps me. It really helps me.

— If I were you, Uncle, I'd lie back and rest. There's nothing like
sleep, is there? I don't know where I'd be without my solid eight
hours. The business would have gone to pot long ago.

— I'm getting better, J.T. said. Three weeks ago I wouldn't have
been able to do it at all.

— You can rest, John Henry said. I'll get Aunty Kate to say something and then we'll do the rest when you're feeling stronger.

— No. Just wait a minute. I'd like to finish that message.

26

KATE HAD HER HANDS CLASPED TOGETHER ON THE
TABLE. Through the spokes of the old spinning-wheel in the
window, there was a view of the public convenience at the entrance
to the car park.

— It's nice, isn't it, Aunty?

All the tables were taken. Three ladies in tweed skirts and pink twin-sets were sewing. A notice planted in a small tub said 'Morning Coffee'. Gwyneth was pointing at a large copper kettle on a stone shelf which had been built where the old fire-place had been filled in.

— They make their own cakes.

Gwyneth looked with admiration at the plate of cakes set in the centre of the round table.

— Mustn't be long, Kate said.

— Well here's the coffee anyway.

Two shallow cups of white coffee were set in front of them. Gwyneth exchanged gestures of recognition and a few words with the lady who served. As Gwyneth spoke the lady put her palms against each other, smiled and swivelled on the ball of her foot, like a games mistress with a large class of small children, studying the state of other tables.

— I know how busy you are, Gwyneth said.

As she moved away Gwyneth leaned towards Kate to pass on quick whispered information.

— That's Marian. She shares the place with Dolly and Margaret. It's off the beaten track a bit but near the car park, as you can see. Dolly's husband's a doctor. It's quite an adventure for them really. I remember them choosing the name.

Kate sipped her coffee carefully. It was hot. She put down her cup.

— I like rhe big blue cups, don't you? Gwyneth said.

— They're a bit heavy, Kate said.

Gwyneth picked up the plate of cakes and held it nearer Kate.

— I don't think so, Kate said. They look very nice. But I had a nasty turn first thing this morning. Nausea.

— Oh that's horrid. I get bilious attacks you know.

— To tell you the truth, Kate said, I thought I was dying.

— Aunty!

Gwyneth sounded a little alarmed, but Kate smiled as if she were preparing to tell a joke.

—We all want to go on living when it comes to the push. You know what I was thinking? What a silly place to die, sitting on the doormat. I was telling myself I didn't want to miss the trip in Gwyneth's car over the Denbigh moors.

Kate's shoulders shook and then she turned her head furtively to see if her amusement had been observed.

— Does Uncle know?

— Oh for goodness' sake . . . Let sleeping dogs lie!

Gwynefh frowned. Her gaze was drawn slowly to the cakes.

— Do you think there's time? Just one of those lemon cheese things. I know I shouldn't. It's home-made.

She picked the cake up gently. It was delicately made and liable to break at the touch.

— Poor old Uncle. He looked so innocent somehow. Going into Uncle Dan's. I've often wondered, Aunty. He's such a nice man. I've often wondered why he never married again.

Kate was holding the coffee cup with both hands. She stared sternly into the coffee.

— He thought the world of my sister. He's always been true to her memory.

Gwyneth cut up her cake into small pieces, which she transferred one by one to her mouth with finger and thumb. She did not take her gaze away from Kate's face, so that her mouth opened as soon as her hand began to lift the piece of cake.

— I heard my mother say once a widow from South Wales came up after him . . .

— Mrs Leyshon?

Gwyneth had begun to smile and sink her chin between her shoulders, but Kate looked grim.

— That was Vernon's fault, she said. He was on leave and he went to see her.

Gwyneth made a round 'O' of surprise with her mouth while her fingers assembled together the crumbs on her plate.

— He knew very well I'd send her packing. She came with some people in a car. When everything was still rationed after the war. Came for sympathy because her husband had died. Awfully bold she was. She came in the kitchen when I was making tea and asked if she could stay the night. These people were going to visit relatives in Anglesey. Well, I said, I'll arrange somewhere for you in the village but you can't stay here. I hadn't much patience with her. Fancied herself with opinions. On everything you could think of. From God to fighting.

— Where is Vernon these days, Aunty?

Gwyneth asked the question very quietly, as if Kate could either answer it or ignore it as she wished.

— She always used to spoil him when he was a child. Did a lot of harm I think. Made so much difference between them. I don't think Ronnie's ever got over it.

— When was Ronnie over last?

— They haven't been this summer. His wife has bought a cottage on some Scottish island.

— Nice to be well off, Gwyneth said.

— They haven't got all that much, Kate said. They've written to Thea and asked to borrow her place. The boy has cost them a lot you know. If you've finished, Gwyneth, I think we ought to go.

NORMAN HAD PARKED his Mercedes on the quiet stretch of road between the hospital and the sand-dunes. J.T. sat listening to everything he had to say, with his head lowered and tilted sympathetically. Norman's hands were clutching the steering-wheel. A party of children suddenly appeared on the ridge of the highest dune. Norman's eyes were following their manoeuvres as he spoke.

— I trusted him, you see, Uncle. That's what gets me. He was my best friend after all. Marjorie used to say she couldn't bear him and I used to stick up for him. And there they were in the back of this car. I thought I'd never get over it. I don't think I have, to tell you the truth. It's the boys I'm worried about. I took Gareth to the psychiatrist in London. I mean he's only ten, Uncle, and it's affected him very badly. He tells lies all the time and he wets the bed at least once a week. For his sake I should take her back. But how could I see her sitting in this car when I know they used to use it together? I could sell it of course. Won't get all that much for it second-hand. But Phil won't move you see. He says it would damage his business. And I'm not boasting, Uncle, but his business would have been nowhere but for me!

Norman struck the steering-wheel with the palm of his hand. He stared intently at J.T. as if he wanted to see his own expression of horror mirrored in J.T.'s face.

— There they are, both of them together, in the next street! It's the most terrible mess, Uncle, and I can't stop talking to myself about it from morning till night. My business is suffering too. One minute I want to divorce her and the next minute I want her back. But if she comes back he'll have to move. I've made that a condition. But he won't move. He says it will harm his business. And so it goes on. Some days I think it'll drive me mad. Sometimes I think if it wasn't for the boys I'd commit suicide and get it over with. What shall I do, Uncle? What shall I do?

J.T. lifted his hands and spread them out in front of him. There were tears in his eyes.

— Behold the lamb of God, he said, which taketh away the sin of the world!

— What does that mean, Uncle?

— You know I used to wonder why mothers taught their children such a difficult verse. But they were so right. In their simple faith they were so right. It's one of the keys to the Christian faith, Norman.

He ticked off items on his fingers.

— The innocence. The sacrament. The messenger. The sacrifice. The link between the eternal and the temporal. It's all in that little verse. The whole wonder of living.

— I'm afraid I don't understand, Uncle.

— How it reaches you?

J.T.'s voice was full of excitement.

— Just as it reaches me. A condition of living. You can trace it from the infinite to the finite. From the vastness of time and space down to your own little problem which seems to you at this moment to be vaster than time or space. Do you follow?

Norman's fingers were caressing the curve of the steering-wheel. He nodded doubtfully.

— There's a story in the Old Testament, J.T. said. A wonderful story. I used to take it as my text very often when I was in South Wales. The story of Hosea and Gomer. She was unfaithful you see. She went off with other men. But Hosea forgave her. Just as God forgave Israel.[129]

— I don't know why she did it. I honestly don't.

Norman had tried so hard to follow what J.T. was saying, it seemed as though his concentration was dispersing and he couldn't listen any more.

— I may have neglected her. The business took all my time. My father and my brother were being difficult and I wanted to prove I could make a success of it on my own. I don't know what my deepest motives might have been. We never do, do we? Anyway I worked like a fool day and night. Building is a very chancy affair. Depends on the weather. Depends on the unions. Anyway I suppose I did neglect her. Not materially. She had the money. She had this car. I had to go to London once a week. Away from home. Every Tuesday. I had to spend the night in London. Every Tuesday she spent the night with Phil. For two and a half years. And she kept on telling me she couldn't bear him. I used to have to make up to her to get her to let him come for a meal. And all the time it was going on. If I live to be a thousand I'll never understand women.

— We are always called upon to make a sacrifice, J.T. said. It might be quite small. Our pride perhaps. Now what is pride?

— Uncle . . . What can I do?

— There is only one thing we can do. In this case you must 'love' her.

— You know, Uncle, I think she only married me because she thought I'd have money. My mother didn't like her, you know. They never got on. She couldn't bear the idea that Marjorie was just a hair-dresser. My mother was a bit of a snob really. And there was the Welsh of course. Marjorie wasn't Welsh. She had that against her. What do you think I should do, Uncle?

— I've told you.

— I know what you mean, Uncle, and I'm grateful. But it isn't so simple as all that. I think sometimes it would be better if I made a fresh start. A clean break. Get away from here. Take the boys with me. I've thought of going to Australia. Making a fresh start. What do you think?

J.T. did not speak. He shook his head as if he could not find the words that Norman wanted to hear.

— I'll be quite frank with you, Uncle, Norman said. Religion doesn't mean very much to me. It's a language I don't understand any more, to be quite honest — if I ever understood it. The way my father talks for example. It's all quite meaningless to me.

— You can't understand this existence without reference to an-other existence. This world and another world. Because we have imagination we can see things both as they are and as they should be — two worlds. Now . . .

— You know what I believe, Uncle, quite frankly? When we're dead we're dead. And that's the end of it.

— There are mysteries, J.T. said.

— I don't want to sound rude or anything like that, but I wonder sometimes how chaps like yourself — clever men, idealists, could keep at it, year in, year out.

The corner of Norman's mouth was raised in a tentative smile, which gave way to a look of anxiety when he saw that J.T. was opening the door of the car.

— Where are you going? I'm taking you home.

J.T.'s leg stretched out so that his foot could touch the pavement.

— I'll enjoy the walk, J.T. said. I've got all day.

— Have I said something?

J.T. shook his head.

— I'd like to move freely among the people. The common people. Talk to them as I used to.

— I was being frank with you, Norman said. On equal terms.

— Norman.

— Yes, Uncle.

J.T. seemed to be thinking hard.

— Think about other things and other people. You are the only one who can control what's going on inside your head. And try to be humble.

— Good heavens.

Norman smiled.

— I should have thought I was too humble.

— Religion or no religion, J.T. said. It's the only way.

He slammed the car door harder than was necessary and waved Norman on.

KATE STOOD IN the narrow passage of Miss Pickering's house between the coat-stand and a photographic view of the Sychnant Pass in an oak frame. Miss Pickering, clutching at the ends of her grey cardigan, was making an effort to remain calm but her chin kept dipping into her neck. She stood in front of the closed parlour door as if it were her intention to prevent Kate entering.

— He can still have a haircut, Kate said.

Miss Pickering's chin plunged into her neck and her pale face was suffused with irregular blushing.

— I don't think he should be moved yet. The doctor was quite positive about that.

The parlour door opened. Miss Pickering stepped aside. Mrs Hobley had taken off her hat and her grey hair was in disorder. She lifted a plump hand at Kate in greeting, and then put her finger to her lips while she closed the door.

— I can't think where he got it from, she said, looking at Miss Pickering. I asked him now. I said, 'John where did you get it?' He said,
'What?' And I said, 'That plastic bag?' And he said, 'It was in my pocket.
'What made you put it over your head?' I said. He laughed and said he
had no idea. We only left him alone for a minute. Miss Pickering took
me upstairs to show me the Jacobean fire-screen in her bedroom.

— Well if I'd have known . . .

Miss Pickering looked worried by guilt.

— 'He's very quiet,' I said to Miss Pickering. I'll just pop down
and see what he's up to.' And there he was with his head in the plastic
bag. He was smiling and his eyes were closed. I was only just in time.

Mrs Hobley moved closer to Kate.

— What am I to think? Was he just playing? Or what. . .

She stared at Kate, waiting for an answer.

— You can never tell what they're up to, Kate said. A trim might
make him feel better.

— I really don't think he should be moved, Miss Pickering said.

— I could bring my machine here. He always says he likes the feel
of the cold metal on his neck. You've heard him say that.

Kate looked at Mrs Hobley who turned to look appealingly at
Miss Pickering.

— You can put newspaper on the floor, Kate said. I'll clear it up
afterwards.

— Oh I don't mind about that, Miss Pickering said.

Mrs Hobley smiled at her, gratefully bobbing her head. She opened
the door to peep inside and see if her husband was all right. Kate
pushed the door open wider. He sat upright in the armchair, his thin
arms resting regally on the arms of the chair. He was already smiling
and he lifted a hand in greeting. He cleared his throat and sang in a
shaky tenor a line of a well-known hymn.

— 'To be alive is yet to wonder . . .'

Then his shoulders shook as he appeared to laugh at himself.

— Would you like a trim?

Kate spoke loudly. Mr Hobley was rather deaf.

— Nothing could be finer. Me first, the hedge next.

— He laughed again and this time Kate smiled.

— Well stay there, she said, and don't move till I get back.

— Where's the padre?

— He'll be back. I'll send him along to see you.

THE SAND AT the bottom of the wide ramp leading down from the promenade still bore the imprint of many feet from the influx of the previous day. A cloud had passed in front of the sun and the numbers of people on the beach seemed somehow less. There were children playing with the donkeys which were tethered near the breakwater. The donkey-man himself was deep in conversation with the white coated attendant of the palatial public convenience on the promenade. The weighing machine between them seemed to be listening to what they were saying. The attendant saw the children trying to mount the donkeys. He pointed. The donkey man began to shout and wave his arms. He felt his fly buttons and began to run. J.T., who had been paddling in the shallow water, stopped to watch the bow-legged donkey man chase the children away. His feet were still bare and he carried his boots with his socks rolled inside, in his right hand. He settled himself on the inclined base of the sea wall to brush the sand from his feet and put on his boots. As he pulled a handkerchief to and fro between his toes a small child carrying an empty beer bottle stood in front of him to study what he was doing. J.T. smiled at the child and said 'hello', but the child seemed more intent on the movements of his hands than anything he said or even the expression on his face. J.T. pushed a hand deep into a gray sock and flexed his fingers inside so that it looked like the struggles of a man tied in a sack. The child's chubby hand grasped the neck of the beer bottle tightly and nothing J.T. said could make him speak or smile or break the frown of concentration on his face.

— What's your name?

The child's lips were open but he would not speak.

— Where's your mummy?

The child watched J.T.'s fingers lacing his boots and he even leaned closer when the long lace squeaked as J.T. pulled it briskly through an eyehole. He wore a blue trouser that was buttoned to a white jacket of the same material. As he leaned forward he seemed to keep his balance with the prehensile grip of his bare toes.

— Well now, my little chap, J.T. said. I've got to say goodbye now. I've got to go. 'All away across the sea, To the fair isle of Anglesey'.

He bent his knees so that his face could be on the same level as the little child's, whose mouth had closed and begun to sag.

— Where's your mummy then?

J.T. placed his hands around the little boy's elbows as if he were about to lift him up and comfort him. The boy farted noisily and a dark yellowish patch began to spread over the seat of his trousers. J.T. continued to balance his forearms on his bent thighs, but his open hands stretched out emptily. He watched powerless as the child's face crumpled and his throat slowly assembled the strength to cry.

— There you are then!

A woman wearing a silk headscarf to conceal the coloured rollers in her hair leaned over the low wall above them where people could sit and look at the sea.

— Is he yours?

J.T. looked up and shaded his eyes with his hand.

— Just you wait till I get my hands on you!

The child howled. J.T. straightened up and the woman hurried along to the gap where the concrete ramp led down to the sands. The heels of her loose shoes clacked against the concrete as she ran down the ramp. One shoe came off in the sand and she continued to speak as she bent to pick it up. She waved the shoe threateningly.

— I was upstairs making the visitor's beds and the little bugger crossed the road. Doing it all the time. The minute my back is turned. If he were bigger I'd use this on him. Now my lad, where'd you get this from?

She snatched the beer bottle from his hand and threw it into the sand. Even as he cried, the little boy turned to see where the bottle had fallen.

— In the bin, I dare say. That's where you got it, wasn't it? She took his arm and shook it.

— Ooh, I'd like to . . .

— Don't hit him, J.T. said. I know you're upset but don't hit him. The woman looked up at J.T.

— What were you doing with him anyway?

— He came to watch me putting my boots on.

J.T.'s smile seemed to add to her anger. She shook the child with both hands. J.T. bent over to touch her shoulder.

— Don't, he said. You'll only be sorry. I remember once I was very angry with my daughter . . .

— You mind your own bloody business, the woman said. And I'll mind mine.

She had a wide determined mouth and the look of an experienced scold.

— The impressions that are made on them when they're small,
J.T. said. You know these impressions are huge and they last for life.
— Look, she said. If you go on, I'll call the police and I'll file a
complaint. So you watch what you're saying.
She pointed a rigid index finger.
— You bad behavin' boy, she said. Look at the mess you're in
stinkin' and smellin'.

GWYNETH WAS SITTING in a deckchair under the pear tree in
Miss Pickering's back garden. Her eyes were closed and she held her
face towards the warmth of the sun. Kate appeared in the back door.
She held her hair-clippers in her right hand and lifted them so that
she could blow away the white hair clippings from the back of Mr
Hobley's neck. Her eye caught the movements of a cat in the long
grass at the bottom of the garden.
— What's she got?
She spoke sharply. Gwyneth opened her eyes.
— What's the matter, Aunty?
— Listen to those birds twittering. Something's disturbed them.
— Sparrows?
— Listen to that one.
A small bird hovered twittering above the uncut hedge. Other
birds, unseen, joined in an agitated tribal chorus of distress. Gwyneth
got up from her deck-chair.
— What's the matter with them?
The cat swung out of the long grass, a dead bird hanging limp
from its mouth. It rushed down the side of the garden as Kate shouted
and waved her hair-clipper.
— It's that next-door cat, Kate said. As if I didn't give it enough
to eat. Killing for the sake of killing.
— Listen to that bird, Gwyneth said. It's doing everything except
talk, poor thing.
The flutter of wings and the tuneless agony of the bird's twitter-
ings seemed to fill the small garden.
— I've nearly finished, Kate said. D'you think we could have an
early lunch and then start out? I've just remembered I've got an egg
custard in the oven.
— Just as you like, Aunty. Is Mr Hobley better now?
Kate touched her niece's arm so that she should come closer.

— He's done it before you know. I didn't want to say anything in front of Miss Pickering. She's such a fusser. I don't know what gets hold of him. He can't be tired of life. You can see for yourself. He's always smiling.

— BUTTERMILK AT ONE penny a gallon!

The first few players had been allowed on the bowling green, which was protected from the wind and from the noise of traffic by a high beech hedge. J.T. belched quietly and put his hand over his stomach. Mr Bowen, who sat next to him, kept his eye on the woods as they rolled majestically down the green towards them, and continued to reminisce quietly as if he had heard nothing.

— Sheep's head, spinal cord, liver, lights and heart for eightpence. People had plenty to eat, you see. In a way it was the golden age.

There was a contented smile on Mr Bowen's face. The sun had come out and his bald head shone as if it had been polished. Geraniums in the ornamental borders also caught the sun.

— It's the need in man that is the measure of his worth, J.T. said. Just as the beauty of the world reflects the intensity of God's love for his creation.

Mr Bowen nodded wisely. His short arms were folded on his chest and they rose and fell as he breathed.

— We had very little freedom, of course. Never allowed to go for a walk after chapel. Not even on an August evening. But that was the custom. You've heard about the old college? The building is up for sale. Sad, isn't it?

J.T. belched again, more loudly this time and shook his head.

— Who's your doctor?

Mr Bowen leaned his plump body nearer to J.T.

— It's nothing, J.T. said. It's just getting near lunch-time that's all.

— I can't put my foot past the front door until twelve forty-five, Mr Bowen said. My daughter-in-law is mad about cleaning. Turns the place inside out every morning. Who's your doctor, did you say?

— Doctor Armstrong.

Mr Bowen made a noise of approval.

— Very friendly man. Very intelligent. He put a very interesting question to me the other day when he was examining me. I was lying there on the couch and he asked me had it ever occurred to me that there might be a hostile civilization on Mars.

A black ball clicked its way among the stationary spheres around the jack, changing the pattern of the game, as they both watched intently. Three small boys jumping and shouting burst into the quiet precinct.

— Boys!

Mr Bowen spoke so sharply he arrested their flight. They looked up with awe at the elevated bench on which the two elderly men were sitting.

— Off!

Mr Bowen spoke with the effortless authority of the retired schoolmaster. They scampered away.

— The imagination of children, J.T. said. As they play they become immortal gods immune from harm. Goodness knows what they thought this place was as they dashed in here.

— There must be order, Mr Bowen said.

A wood struck the jack gently and by a series of smooth clicks the positions were changed. Mr Bowen raised his arms to clap and the last bowler waved his mat contentedly as he waddled in his bowling shoes with his companion across the green to contemplate the result.

— I was thinking of going to Anglesey, J.T. said. A very dear old friend, old Ifan Cole, has left me his watch.

— There and back the same day? Mr Bowen sounded sceptical.

— Outside the Yellow Rose Garage there was a map of Anglesey. They were advertising a mystery tour. Leaving at one thirty, back at eight. Seventeen and six. Very reasonable. I've got the fare.

Mr Bowen looked disapproving.

— These things should be arranged, I think. A few day's notice.

— Gentlemen!

A young man with a white pigeon on his arm and a camera case swinging from his neck was offering to photograph them. He put the view-finder to his eye and lowered it again.

— This tame dove will perch on your arm or on your head, which ever you like and make a lovely photographic record of your holiday.

He smiled in the most friendly way and stretched himself on tiptoes to see over the hedge, whether on the promenade there were more potential customers approaching.

— Very cheap. Six shillings for a pair and reduced prices for half a dozen prints. Special opportunity. What about it, gents. On your head or on your arm?

— Not on my head, Mr Bowen said.

He passed his hand over his bald patch and shook gently with amusement.

— Just try it, the young man said. See how nice he looks on your arm.

Mr Bowen shook his head. The young man stopped smiling. He began to plead.

— One more before lunch, he said. Come on. Be a sport. Sun's come out. Bound to be a good picture. Business isn't good this morning. Just fill in this card and we'll send it to your home address.

He leaned forward to offer J.T. a card. J.T. stretched out a hand to take it and the pigeon flew across to land on his arm. J.T. looked at it with interest.

— Is this a pigeon or a dove descending? he said.

The young man frowned as if J.T. had spoken in a foreign language.

— Come on, gents, he said. Only a few shillings.

J.T. shook his head and extended his arm on which the white pigeon fluttered, unsteady on its perch.

— Take it back, he said. We don't want a picture, thank you all the same.

— We're not important enough, Mr Bowen said.

Once again he shook as he chuckled.

As the pigeon hopped back on the young man's arm he swore at it under his breath and walked on. Then he saw four youths wearing Mexican hats and waving lemonade bottles at each other, and he called out to them urgently. They were passing the bowling green on the further side, pretending to be drunk, but they stopped when he called to see what he wanted. As he ran around, a solemn bowler brought himself upright without discharging the wood balanced in the palm of his hand. Two of the youths began to push each other in some form of mock fight. The smaller ran around the perimeter of the green and began to shout as if he hoped the other would give chase. As he ran in front of them Mr Bowen leaned forward and ordered him to behave. The youth turned to look at the retired schoolmaster. Without stopping he put out his tongue and made a rude noise.

— Order! Mr Bowen said.

The youth dropped his hat. He paused to pick it up and put it back on his head. The photographer had captured the interest of the others. They called to the small youth to join them. Delighted by the notice they were giving him, he jumped on the green. Instantly, there was an angry howl from the four bowlers. For a moment he stood still and defiant. But when the four men began to advance on him flatfootedly, he tapped the wood nearest to him with his pointed toe-cap and ran away shouting. His friends pursued him and the photographer went, calling after them, trying to persuade them to stand still.

— There's the age for you, Mr Miles. If they had half the chance they'd rob us of the air we breathe. They've ruined the game.

Mr Bowen's eyes were enlarged with anger and his breath came in excited gasps.

— My eldest boy, he's an inspector of police in Manchester. You wouldn't believe the things that happen.

— I know, J.T. said. We must try not to be afraid.

— But for law and order, I can tell you, this country would be worse than the Congo.

— Fear is a bad thing, J.T. said. It holds us down like a force of gravity. If we could conquer it, and keep our imagination as sensitive as a child's, I think we could walk on water.

— There is no substitute for a strong police force, Mr Bowen said. That's what the world needs today. Right plus might, Mr Miles.

On the green after animated discussion, the players had resumed their game, absorbed in the rotations of the biased woods.

— To be completely without fear, J.T. said, would be to arrive at a mystical state. There comes a point where the spirit would have to leave the body behind. Now there is one of the creative functions of death. To put an end to what otherwise would be endless.

Mr Bowen took out his watch from his waistcoat pocket and consulted the time.

— It really is a disgrace. At this time of the year there should be men on duty . . . I mustn't be late for lunch.

— I was wondering, J.T. said. You wouldn't care to come to Anglesey for a trip? A mystery trip. Not as far away as Mars of course.

J.T. laughed in a friendly way. They stepped down from the concrete platform where the bench stood.

— I must consider my daughter-in-law, Mr Bowen said. She's very good to me. I wouldn't want to upset her.

He pointed eastwards.

— It's a very convenient place to live.

They raised their right arms in tokens of farewell. Having taken a few steps, Mr Bowen turned stiffly to watch J.T. marching alone to the garage that advertised mystery tours of North Wales.

AT THE TOP of the stairs, Gwyneth paused to look at Ma's photograph. Behind her, from the bathroom, there was a crescendo of rushing water as the lavatory cistern filled up. Gwyneth put her thumbs inside the belt of her dress and pulled in her stomach.

— My grandmother had one of these, Aunty. It was touched up with colour. I wonder where it is now?

— Everything looks different in the daylight, Kate said.

She had changed her hat and coat and her face was covered with a light coat of fresh powder. She closed the door of her bedroom. In a coat pocket she found a pair of thin white gloves.

— They were very fond of each other. Sisters can be you know. I always used to look forward to seeing Aunty Addy. That's your grandmother. Aunty Addy Denbigh we always called her.

— It's funny, isn't it? Gwyneth said. I love talking about the old times. It's no wonder I'm an old maid.

She laughed heartily. Her eyes closed and she showed her splendid teeth. Kate opened the door of J.T.'s bedroom and looked inside. She seemed satisfied with what she saw and closed the door again.

— I had such a funny dream last night, she said. If it was a dream.

She put a hand on the banisters and frowned with the effort of remembering.

— I'm always dreaming, Aunty, Gwyneth said. The daftest things really. No rhyme or reason. I dreamt last night I was in a submarine. That's the last place I'd ever want to go. Why should I dream of such a thing like that?

— It was my right arm, Kate said. 'My right arm O Jerusalem. . .'[130]

She smiled and lifted her arm and held it up so that Gwyneth could look at it.

— I was sitting up in bed and my arm had come off. I knew it was mine because of the mole.

Kate pulled back her sleeve to show Gwyneth the mole.

— It was hanging in the air in front of me. I wanted it back. I knew J.T. was sleeping in the next room. I only had to knock the wall. And then I can remember distinctly I said aloud. 'What am I doing in the same house as him?'

Kate was smiling so Gwyneth smiled too.

— At least I thought I said it aloud. I listened but nobody had woken up. The whole avenue was asleep. I wanted to get my watch and see what the time was. But I hadn't got my arm so I couldn't pick it up, could I? Then I got really frightened. I thought I was dying and I hadn't got a hand for anybody to hold. I was living in a watertight compartment and if I shouted nobody could hear me. Especially this one.

She pointed at J.T.'s bedroom door with her thumb.

— You know it's a funny thing to say, but if I really was dying, I wouldn't dream of waking him up. Life's a funny thing, isn't it?

Kate motioned her niece to start walking down the stairs.

Gwyneth stepped carefully down.

— I don't know what it's all about I'm sure.

Gwyneth paused on the stairs and looked up at Kate.

— Don't you believe in God, Aunty?

— I suppose I have to don't I? The world's in enough of a mess as it is. Nobody seems to want to die when it comes to the push. I don't know what it's all about I'm sure.

Downstairs before she opened the front door, Kate closed all the doors leading off the small hall.

— I don't know what it is. I don't like doors being left open. Even in a matchbox like this. Pa I suppose. Drummed the habit into me. He was never afraid of repeating himself.

— It's all very spick and span, Gwyneth said.

— I'm getting on, so it's just as well the world is shrinking.

Kate slammed the front door and then shook it by the brass doorknob to make sure it was locked.

— I've been thinking, Gwyneth fach, we can't leave J.T. with Dan Llew for the rest of the day. They're bound to fall out. I wouldn't be at ease. Do you think we could go and collect him?

— It's your day out, Aunty. I'll do whatever you say.

Kate squeezed Gwyneth's wrist gratefully.

— If you wouldn't mind it, we could just as easily go to Anglesey instead of the Moors. It's not all that warm is it? And he'd enjoy it so much. That's one thing he could always do. Enjoy himself.

Before they got in the car, Kate opened her handbag shook it and held it close to her face to inspect the contents. Inside it she turned a hand mirror to glance at her eye. She snapped the clasp and then from her coat pocket she took the letters that had come by the morning post. She whispered confidentially to Gwyneth over the top of the car.

— Letter from Thea. Tell you all about it.

Then in her normal voice she said,

— Got to have the address or we won't know where to go.

Note on the Text

I am indebted to my friend Professor M. Wynn Thomas for providing these notes to this edition of the novel. They illuminate both the text and the historical context from which it emerged.

E.H.

1.   'A present of some sort for my mother.'

2.   The name of the farm is also the title of a well-known poem (1926) by T. Gwynn Jones (1871-1949) concerning a tribe in a remote part of Gaul that lives a pacific pastoral life in tune with its ancient traditions. Unknown to the tribe, Rome has already conquered the greater part of Gaul, destroying its language, its customs and its cities. The tribesmen of Argoed discover this only when one of its poets is met with ridicule and incomprehension when he tries to sing his traditional songs in another pan of Gaul. When the Romans eventually attempt to tax the people of Argoed, the tribe sets fire to the forest rather than submit to foreign rule.

3.   Tomi Pigs.

4.   It is the practice in rural Wales to identify people with reference to the farms their families occupy. Sometimes the name of the farm may completely supplant the name of the individual — as happens on occasions later in this novel.

5.   Professor Henry Jones (1852-1922) was apprenticed as a boy to his shoemaker father, but went on to a very distinguished academic career. He was also a prominent Liberal and involved in educational reforms that included the Intermediate Education Act of 1889 and the establishment of the University of Wales.

6.   This legend of the 'cantref', drowned by the rising waters of Cardigan Bay — a story which recurs in Emyr Humphreys's fiction — dates in its earliest written form from the thirteenth century, but was recounted in the nineteenth century in several popular songs and poems.

7.   In July, 1879, British troops, led by Lord Chelmsford, defeated the Zulus at Ulundi, six months after 97 men of the 24th Foot (later the South Wales Borderers) had narrowly beaten off 4,000 Zulu warriors at Rourke's Drift.

8.   After 1870 a state system of non-denominational elementary schools was established, but until then Nonconformist Wales

had had to tolerate the Church of England's widespread control of education. The gradual integration of Church Schools into the state system, after the Balfour Act of 1902, was at first fiercely resented and systematically opposed by Welsh Nonconformity. Emyr Humphreys was himself educated in the Church School at Newmarket (Trelawnyd), Flintshire, where his father was headmaster.

9. North Wales Welsh for 'grandmother'.

10. For the education struggle see note 8 above. Welsh Nonconformist resentment at having to pay towards the upkeep of the Anglican church came to a head in the Tithe Wars of the 1880s, when tenant farmers refused to pay tithes. Disturbances followed, particularly in Denbighshire, and the young Lloyd George became a prominent figure in the anti-tithe campaigns in Caernarfonshire. The problem was largely solved by the Tithe Act of 1891, which incorporated the tithes into the rent, thus making them payable not by the occupier but by the owner of the land — which in Wales usually meant wealthy English or anglophile landowners.

11. Young Lochinvar is a dashing young hero whose story is told in the long poem *Marmion* (1808) by Sir Walter Scott. Both the poem and the story were popular during the Victorian period.

12. Only after the First World War did central government, through several stages of legislative action, slowly begin to assume responsibility for providing benefits for the sick, the needy and the unemployed. Until then such provision was the responsibility of local authorities that operated a centuries-old system of parish relief, coordinated, under the terms of the 1871 Act, by a Local Government Board. A Royal Commission, established in 1905, paved the way for the post-War reform of the system.

13. A capacious leather bag, much favoured by ministers from the end of the last century onwards. It was named after the great Liberal Prime Minister W.E. Gladstone (1809-1898), who was one of the great heroes of Liberal Wales.

14. Cattle shed.

15. Proverbs 26.14.

16. During the high Victorian period it was customary to place an empty chair in the centre of a family photograph, to signify the recent decease of a loved one.

17. My girl.

18. The reference is to Wordsworth's poem 'We are seven'.

19. Gracious, no.

20. The names of farms. See note 4 above.

21. Splendid (literally 'blessed').

22. The reference is to Wesleyan Methodism. Although this was the primary form of Methodism in England, established by the brothers Charles and John Wesley in the eighteenth century, it was always secondary in Wales to the largely 'native' Calvinistic Methodism (see below) which had been begun even earlier by evangelical reformers such as Howel Harris and Daniel Rowlands, whose work was reinforced from England by John Whitfield.

23. William Williams, Pantycelyn (1717-1791), was one of the leaders of the eighteenth century Methodist movement that transformed Wales, and a prolific writer of hymns some of which are now regarded as being among the greatest poems ever written in Welsh.

24. From its origins in the eighteenth century as an evangelical movement to reform the Church of England (see note 22), Calvinistic Methodism grew into an independent denomination that became the most powerful and influential of the Nonconformist sects of nineteenth century Wales. Its strength was most evident in the northern part of the country, but such was its hold nationwide that it became affectionately known as 'Yr Hen Gorff' ('The Old Institution'). During the course of the century the social and political outlook of the denomination changed profoundly from a Quietist conservatism to a campaigning Liberalism. Over the last two centuries many of the leading writers of Wales have been associated with this denomination, which is nowadays known as the Presbyterian Church of Wales,

25. *Luke* 16.25: The story of the rich man Dives and the poor beggar Lazarus concludes with Dives, now suffering in hell, amazed to see Lazarus resting in heaven, cradled in Abraham's bosom. Dives pleads that Lazarus be allowed to dip one finger in water to relieve his dreadful thirst. "But Abraham said, Son, remember that thou in thy lifetime receivedst the good things, and likewise Lazarus evil things; but now he is comforted and thou art tormented."

26. Habbakuk 2.1: "I will stand upon my watch, and set me upon the tower, and will look forth to see what he will speak with me, and what I shall answer concerning my complaint." The whole chapter is, in fact, relevant to the novel, for the prophet is told by God to inscribe his vision on tablets where all may see. The following verses seem particularly significant to the

disappearance of Argoed: "Woe to him that getteth an evil gain for his house, that he may set his nest on high, that he may be delivered from the hand of evil! Thou hast consulted shame to thy house, by cutting off many peoples, and hast sinned against thy soul. For the stone shall cry out of the wall, and the beam out of the timber shall answer it."

27. A church assembly, composed of ministers and elders, having jurisdiction over an area including several congregations.

28. Throughout the second half of the nineteenth-century, Welsh Nonconformists (who then outnumbered Welsh Anglicans by three to one) staged a determined campaign to abolish the privileged status of the Church of England in Wales as the official state church. Welsh Disestablishment finally took effect in 1920.

29. The teasing reference is to John Calvin (1509-1564), the great religious reformer who was one of the founding fathers of Protestantism, and upon whose central Pauline doctrines of grace and predestination Calvinistic Methodism was founded.

30. Henry Rees (1798-1863) was the most famous Calvinistic Methodist Minister of his time, the leading figure in his denomination and a notable preacher.

31. Almost from the outset, one of the hallmarks of Methodism, as the name suggests, was the elaborate system of internal organisation it established. Each church ran its own affairs, but above it in the hierarchy of government was the Monthly Meeting of the County, and above that was the Quarterly Association ('Session') of the province. South Wales and North Wales held separate Association meetings, but the supreme body was the all-Wales General Assembly.

32. These are theological controversies and social causes to which nineteenth century Nonconformists devoted a great deal of time and energy. In the context of this novel, the strength of the Temperance Movement in Wales is particularly worth noting. Its campaigns prepared the way for the Sunday Closing Act of 1881, which made the whole of Wales 'dry' on Sunday for almost eighty years. This situation was changed only by the Licensing Act which was passed in 1960, just three years before this novel was written — hence, perhaps, J.T.'s particular abhorrence of the 'House of Baal', the garish new local pub.

33. One of the favourite competition pieces in nineteenth-century eisteddfodau and singing festivals.

34. Known by the name of the village in Anglesey where he was a minister with the Calvinistic Methodists throughout the years of his fame, John Williams (1854-1921) was one of the greatest

figures in the Nonconformist pantheon at the beginning of this century. During the First World War he used his towering reputation and his charismatic power as a preacher to persuade Welsh youngsters to enlist in their thousands.

35.   Psalm 120: "I will lift up mine eyes unto the hills from whence cometh my help."

36.   Two more 'war-horses' beloved by nineteenth-century vocalists.

37.   In Nonconformist chapels the deacons sit on a single large bench at the front, directly under the pulpit, and turn to face the congregation during the hymn singing.

38.   *Acts* 4.12.

39.   Evan Philips (1829-1912), prominent Calvinistic Methodist minister from Newcastle Emlyn, who was one of the great preachers of his day.

40.   'And they came to Jerusalem; and Jesus went into the temple, and began to cast out them that sold and bought in the temple, and overthrew the tables of the moneychangers, and the seats of them that sold doves.'

41.   A wooden appliance, with two arms, and legs, used to stir clothes in a wash-tub.

42.   A backroom. Flintshire dialect from English *brew-house*.

43.   In Welsh the name for the Point of Ayr colliery, on the North East coast, is 'Y Parlwr Du' ('The Black Parlour').

44.   Roman Catholics.

45.   In the National Eisteddfod of Wales, held every August, a crown is awarded as a prize for the best poem written in any form other than the traditional strict meters *(cynghanedd)*.

46.   Denomination: i.e. Calvinistic Methodists.

47.   The allusion is to Jacob, who had to work for Labon for a total of fourteen years before he won Labon's daughter, Rachel, for wife *(Genesis* 29: 1-25).

48.   Strictly speaking the 'Awdl' (roughly 'Ode') competition in the National Eisteddfod is for poetry in the strict meters *(cynghanedd)* and the prize is a chair, not a crown (see note 45 above).

49.   Dog Latin for 'the poet's done a bunk'.

50.   Good God.

51.   O.M. Edwards (1858-1920) was the author/editor of several immensely popular periodicals and books that helped form a national consciousness in Wales by popularising Welsh history and literature. Following a period as tutor in History and Fellow of Lincoln College, Oxford, he was appointed Chief Inspector of Schools in Wales in 1907 and became a renowned educationalist. He is also remembered for his efforts to secure a

modest place for Welsh and the study of Welsh history in the thoroughly anglocentric education system of his day.

52. Raised in humble circumstances in Cricieth, Lloyd George (1863-1945), a lifelong Baptist, first became the darling of Nonconformist Wales by championing Radical causes like land reform. His popularity increased when, in his capacity as Chancellor of the Exchequer, he introduced the 'People's Budget' in 1909, and then went on to become the 'man who won the (First World] War'. During his period as Prime Minister (1916-1922) he consolidated his reputation as one of the greatest world statesmen of his era.

53. Pentir is here the name of a farm.

54. The fertile lowland region, west of Cardiff, and south of the industrial valleys, known as 'the Vale of Glamorgan'.

55. A miners' leader and founder of the Independent Labour Party, the Scot Keir Hardie (1856-1915) made history when, by winning the Merthyr Tydfil seat in 1900, he became the first Socialist M.P. to be returned for Wales. In retrospect, his victory can be seen as a turning point in modern Welsh politics, signalling the decline of the Liberal-Nonconformist alliance and heralding the conversion of the increasingly cosmopolitan workforce of south Wales to socialism.

56. The college at Cardiff was opened in 1883 and became part of the new federal University of Wales when that was formed in 1893.

57. Jesus from the North.

58. Throughout the war, elements in the unions and the socialist movement struggled, largely in vain, to counter jingoism by an appeal to the solidarity of the international working class.

59. Although the strong Welsh pacifist tradition, ingrained dislike of English militarism and admiration for German culture, predisposed Nonconformist leaders to oppose the war, most were caught up in the general war-fever, persuaded to participate in a religious crusade, or swayed by a sympathy for another small nation, Belgium. Only a rare character, like Thomas Rees, Principal of the Independents' Theological College at Bangor, continued to insist that "every war was contrary to the spirit of Christ". Still, the pacifist tradition remained sufficiently strong for Wales to supply approximately 1,000 of the 16,500 in Britain who registered as conscientious objectors.

60. Abraham obeyed God's command to offer his only son, Isaac, as a human sacrifice, but at the last moment God instructed that a ram be substituted for the boy *(Genesis* 22). Jeptha was the

leader of Gilead, who vowed, in exchange for success in battle, that he would sacrifice "whatever" came first from his house to meet him, on his return from war. He was met by his only child, a daughter, and after allowing her two months in which to mourn, he arranged for her execution. *(Judges* 11: 12-31).

61.   Calvinistic Methodist.

62.   Camel Lairds, Birkenhead, was a great shipbuilding and engineering company and the mecca of young North Walians in search of a good apprenticeship.

63.   My dear boy

64.   A keen attender of the eisteddfod, the annual, peripatetic festival of Welsh-language culture.

65.   Royal Army Service Corps.

66.   Benjamin Disraeli, 1st Earl of Beaconsfield (1804-81), was a Conservative Prime Minister and novelist. The son of an antiquarian and a man of letters, he was educated entirely at home.

67.   Baal is the name repeatedly given in the Old Testament to the false, cruel god of tha pagans who is the adversary of the true God of Israel, Jahweh. The worship of Baal is particularly condemned by the prophets Hosea, Zephaniah and Jeremiah, who deplore those who "commit fornication" after him. Particularly worth noting is the contest between the lone prophet Elijah and the 450 prophets of Baal, which begins with Elijah's challenge to his people: "How long halt ye between two opinions? If the Lord be God, follow him: but if Baal, then follow him". (1 *Kings* 18: 21)

68.   Lloyd George, who became Prime Minister in 1916, deliberately appealed to his fellow countrymen's patriotic sentiments. Propaganda was issued praising the warrior spirit of the Welsh, which was traced back to medieval heroes such as Owain Glyndŵr. And in order to encourage recruitment, a special 38th (Welsh) Division of the British army was formed and supplied with Nonconformist chaplains.

69.   The sixteen chapters of this epistle contain the very heart of Paul's message of salvation through the living Christ.

70.   These are two landmarks from the Dardanelles campaign (see below). The description of the lake is based on a paragraph in Tom Nefyn Williams, *Yr Ymchwil* (Gwasg Gee, 1949, 30), an important sourcebook for material in this novel (see notes below).

71.   See *Yr Ymchwil,* 31.

72.   The Dardanelles campaign, which included the Gallipoli landings, began in the spring of 1915. By mid-May the invading

force of 70,000 had suffered 20,000 casualties.

73. Royal Army Medical Corps.

74. Roath Park is in Cardiff.

75. This is closely modelled on a real-life incident reported in Tom Nefyn Williams, *Yr Ymchwil,* 39.

76. Kate dear.

77. Literally 'speckled bread'. A kind of fruit loaf.

78. A brand of cheap, strong cigarettes, particularly popular with working people.

79. In *Yr Ymchwil* Tom Nefyn describes the 'Gethsemane experience' that came to him as he lay wounded in no-man's land during the Gaza campaign in the First World War (41). In spite of the allusion to *Mark,* the quotation is presumably from *Matthew* xi.28: "Come unto me, all ye that labour and are heavy laden, and I will give you rest. Take my yoke upon you, and learn of me . . ."

80. Arnold's poem (1853) nostalgically narrates the seventeenth century story of an Oxford scholar "Who, tired of knocking at preferment's door,/ One summer morn forsook/ His friends, and went to learn the gipsy lore,/ And roamed the world with that wild brotherhood". Arnold views the scholar gipsy as the antithesis in spirit of the Philistine commercialism of his own time, and uses him to rail against "this strange disease of modern life,/ With its sick hurry, its divided aims,/ Its heads o'ertaxed, its palsied hearts".

81. Sir Ellis Jones Ellis-Griffiths (1860-1926), M.P.. A champion of Welsh Nonconformity. Also a Liberal Imperialist. Although they were in the same Party, Ellis-Griffiths never 'got on' with Lloyd George. His politics would be more to Pa's taste than the latter's.

82. Pentecostalism is a form of Christianity centering on the emotional, the nonrational, the mystical and the supernatural. It places emphasis on miracles, signs, wonders and 'the gifts of the Holy Spirit', including 'speaking in tongues', faith healing and 'casting out demons'. It derives its name from the account of the Feast of Pentecost (Acts 1 & 2).

83. The long term effects of the October, 1929 Wall Street Crash were felt in rural Wales, as throughout the western world.

84. From the haunting opening of the poem by T. Gwynn Jones (see footnote 2 above): "Argoed, Argoed of the secret places . . . / Your hills, your sunken glades, where were they,/ Your winding glooms and quiet towns?/ Ah, quiet then, till doom was dealt you, / But after it, nothing save a black desert/ Of ashes was seen of wide-wooded Argoed" (Tony Conran, ft, *Welsh Verse,*

Bridgend: Poetry Wales Press, 1986, 260).

85.   The Tudor holders of the English throne from 1485–1603 were descended from an aristocratic family from Gwynedd (north-west Wales). The founder of the English dynasty was Henry Tudor, who was crowned Henry VII after his victory over Richard III at Bosworth Field (1485). With his accession to the throne the Welsh supposed that the prophecies of the bards, that the 'Crown of Britain' would be restored to Wales, had been fulfilled. Emyr Humphreys has argued that this marked the beginning of the disastrous process of the assimilation of Wales to England, a process which has continued down to the present century, and which is exemplified in this novel by the careers of Ronnie, Thea and others. (See Emyr Humphreys, *The Taliesm Tradition,* Bridgend: Seren Books, 1989.) Elis Gruffudd (1500–1558?) was born in Gronant Uchaf, Gwespyr, Llanasa, Flintshire, not far from Emyr Humphreys's childhood home. A professional soldier (who was not knighted), he went to Calais as the servant of Sir Robert Wingfield and was present at the meeting, in 1521, between Francis I and Henry VIII on the 'Field of the Cloth of Gold'. He became a permanent member of the garrison at Calais in 1529 and lived there for the rest of his days. As well as being the author of a lengthy *Chronicle* of the history of the world (completed in 1552), he was a noteworthy copyist and translator.

86.   In January, 1558 the French laid siege to Calais and in eight days had expelled the English.

87.   An oil lamp.

88.   Women, burdened with the responsibility of raising families, were even harder hit than men by the conditions in the industrial valleys. As early as 1928 it was noted that "mothers of young children suffer to an extraordinary degree from general weakness and anemia".

89.   The precentor leads the congregational singing in Nonconformist chapels.

90.   The difference between North Wales and South Wales Welsh is not as great as Lydia makes out. This is a familiar excuse for turning to English.

91.   The religious revival of 1904–1905, led by Evan Roberts, was the last, and one of the greatest, to have been experienced by Wales. A remarkable phenomenon, still alive in popular memory, it began in south-west Wales but spread throughout the country, and even affected parts of England.

92.   The account in this section of the conflict between the right and left wings of the Calvinistic Methodist church conforms

in very broad outline to the account given in Tom Nefyn, *Yr Ymchwil,* of the Treherbert 'Sasiwn' in 1928 when he was officially condemned for his liberal, heterodox views (132-133).

93. The Workers' Educational Association, an organisation dedicated then as now to providing educational opportunities (mostly through evening classes) for the working population. In 1938 a total of 8,000 classes were held under its auspices throughout South Wales.

94. Ministers of religion (such as Alban Davies) played a prominent part in the efforts to alleviate hardship in the industrial valleys during the thirties depression. In camps, such as the one run by the Quakers, the unemployed were taught new skills.

95. This story seems to be based on "the reconciliaton and compact [during the strike of 1926] between Lord Buckland [colliery owner] and Noah Ablett, atheist and syndicalist, and author of *The Miners Next Step,* which had led the miners into uncompromising war against the owners". The part played by the minister John Morgan Jones in this remarkable episode is recalled in George M.Ll. Davies, *Pilgrimage of Peace* (London: Fellowship of Reconciliation, 1750), 62-63.

96. Longing.

97. O God

98. An apocryphal place-name, used in Welsh to denote the back of beyond.

99. George M.Ll.Davies performed a similar service in real life, after both he and Lloyd George had attended a meeting of the Methodist 'Sasiwn', in Porthmadog (1921). See *Pererindod Heddwch* (Dinbych: Gwasg Gee, 1945), 68-70.

100. The World Disarmament Conference opened on February 2 1932 and soon ran into difficulties. It was adjourned in December without any agreement being reached, and before it was reconvened in January 1933, Hitler had become Chancellor of Germany. The conference came to an end in utter failure in May 1934.

101. Official statistics show that in 1935, 14.6% of the children of the Rhondda were undernourished.

102. For those who failed to pass the Central Welsh Board exams in all the subjects required for proceeding to 'Higher' (sixth form work), the 'Welsh Matric.' exam represented a second chance.

103. The burning at Penyberth was one of the most significant events in the history of the modern Welsh nationalist movement, and it had a great effect on artists and intellectuals (including the young Emyr Humphreys). In spite of practically

unanimous Welsh opposition, the government had insisted on demolishing an old farmhouse in Llyn (Caernarfonshire), whose history dated back to medieval times. In its place they proposed to put an aerial-bombing range. Three leading members of Plaid Cvmru set fire to the building site on September 9, 1936 and immediately reported their action to the police. When they were tried in Caernarfon, the jury could not agree on a verdict. In order to secure a conviction, the unusual step was taken of transferring the case to England. At the Old Bailey each of the three (two of whom were among the finest Welsh writers of their generation) was sentenced to nine months imprisonment. About 12,000 people assembled in Caernarfon to welcome them after their release from prison.

104.   There was a mass exodus from the depressed south Wales valleys during the thirties — 50,000 left the Rhondda, and 27,000 left Merthyr. By 1951 there were 679,275 Welsh-born people living in England.

105.   During the thirties, the Action Française movement, primarily associated with Maurras, conducted a campaign against the French government and advanced a political programme in which strong, authoritatarian and anti-democratic central leadership would reinstate traditional social values and thereby restore France's greatness both at home and abroad. In the early thirties some Breton separatists were briefly attracted to the movement both by its authoritarian ideology and by its promise of federalism.

106.   Throughout the thirties, the Breton separatist movement, primarily associated with the Parti Autonomiste Breton (P.A.B.) and the Parti National Breton (P.N.B.) had been kept under close surveillance by the Francophone authorities and had periodically been suspected of involvement in terrorist attacks and with proto-fascist extremism. During the build-up to the Second World War, the anti-French and pro-German line taken by *Breiz Atao* (see below), accompanied by the violent activities of the armed Breton para-military force called the Kadervenn, provoked retaliatory measures by the French government. *Breiz Atao* was closed down in August, 1939 and the P.N.B. was effectively outlawed.

107.   Originally founded in 1919, the periodical *Breiz Atao* (Brittany for ever) had, by the late thirties, become synonymous with Breton separatism. It was by then the official organ of the P.N.B. (see above) and between 1937 and its suppression in 1939 its editorial policy was anti-French and pro-German.

108.   Artists and intellectuals, as well as miners and other members of the working-class, were among the 2,000 from Britain who fought in the International Brigade for the Republicans against the Fascists under Franco, during the Spanish Civil War (1936-1939).

109.   The defence of Verdun, which lasted throughout 1916, was a traumatic experience for the French. It involved about half a million losses on the French side alone.

110.   This section was not included in the original printed text of *Outside the House of Baal* (1965), although it does appear in the manuscript version of the novel. It was published separately, as a short story, in the periodical *Mabon* 1.1 (1969), 30-40, and collected in Emyr Humphreys' *Miscellany Two* (Bridgend: Poetry Wales Press, 1981), before being incorporated into the Everyman paperback edition of the novel (1988). The author cannot now recall why the section was omitted from the original edition.

111.   The week of competition between Oxford college crews.

112.   During the Second World War, conscientious objectors in Wales who refused to serve in the Armed Forces were required to appear before one of two special Tribunals, one being for the South and the other for the North, with a third acting as an Appeal Tribunal. The verdicts in these cases ranged from unconditional exemption to compulsory service (with prison as the penalty for those who refused to comply with the directive). Mostly, however, the men were either assigned to Fire Watch duties or sent to work on the land. Emyr Humphreys, having refused on both pacifist and nationalist grounds to serve in the army, himself spent four years — two in Pembrokeshire and two in Caernarfonshire — as an agricultural worker.

113.   After the burning of the bombing school at Penyberth in 1936 many pacifists, particularly of Nonconformist background, were attracted to Plaid Cymru (the Welsh Nationalist Party). The party's resolute opposition to rearmament projects in Wales was very much in line at that time with the policy of the Peace Pledge Union. Many members of Plaid Cymru (including Emyr Humphreys) remained committed pacifists throughout the Second World War, although strictly speaking the party's official policy was one of neutrality.

114.   George M.Ll.Davies describes the proceedings at the Oberammergau conference, held in the summer of 1926, in *Pilgrimage of Peace)* Ch.V.

115.   This Welsh hymn was a particular favourite during the revival of 1904-05 (see Note 91 above).

116.   A line from W.H. Auden's celebrated poem, 'September 1, 1939' — the day when German troops invaded Poland and World War II began.

117.   The Congregationahsts (or Independents) are one of the oldest of Nonconformist sects, dating back to the English Civil War. Unlike the Methodists, the denomination has no central organisation, each chapel being independent and democratically self-governing. Emyr Humphreys is himself a Welsh Congregationalist (Annibynnwr).

118.   National Fire Service.

119.   The leading female character in Shakespeare's comedy, *Twelfth Night*.

120.   A Labour government, under Attlee, was returned in the General Election of July 1, 1945.

121.   'Welsh (i.e. the Welsh language) for ever.'

122.   Student Representative Council.

123.   The reference is to the legend of king Arthur, who is said to be sleeping under a hill, awaiting the call to return and save Wales in her hour of crisis.

124.   The name of a famous repertory company, both in London and in Bristol.

125.   Aneurin (Nye) Bevan (1897-1960) has been decribed as "the most dazzling exponent of democratic Socialism ever produced in Wales". Labour MP for Ebbw Vale, he was instrumental in creating the National Health Service, during his period as Minister of Health in the post-war Labour government.

126.   Emyr Humphreys may have had W. Ambrose Bebb (1894-1954) partly in mind. A prominent nationalist and passionate Europhile, Bebb was a prolific author both of books on Welsh history and of books of travel, particularly in France and Brittany. The influence of the latter can probably be seen in the earlier section of this novel which deals with Brittany refugees in postwar Europe, and the spread of Stalinism — were more than his spirit could bear.

127.   On March 1, 1954, the U.S. tested a super nuclear weapon, the power of which was equivalent to 15 million tons of TNT Nuclear debris rained down on a Japanese fishing vessel 100 miles away, and a wave of panic swept through Japan when news spread that fish caught had been affected by radiation.

128.   On December 16, 1949, George M.Ll. Davies was found hanged in a ward of the hospital where he was undergoing treatment for clinical depression. His biographer believes that recent world events — including Hiroshima and Nagasaki, the

twelve million refugees in post-war Europe, and the spread of Stalinism — were more than his spirit could bear.

129. The prophet Hosea's wife, Gomer, was unfaithful to him. He divorced her, but found that his love for her was still strong. Realising that the love of Jahwah for Israel was similar to his love for Gomer, Hosea forgave her infidelity, and together they began life anew in the desert (*Hosea 2: 1-23*)

130. From Psalm 137. The whole passage is relevant: "By the waters of Babylon, we sat down and wept: when we remembered thee, O Seion. As for our harps, we hanged them up: upon the trees that are therein. For they that led us away captive required of us then a song, and melody, in our heaviness: Sing us one of the songs Seion. How shall we sing the Lord's songs in a strange land? If I forget thee, O Jerusalem: let my right hand forget her cunning. If I do not remember thee, let my tongue cleave to the roof of my mouth."

M.W.T.

A Note on the Text and Further Reading

The novel was first published in London by Eyre and Spottiswoode in 1965 and reprinted by Dent as an Everyman paperback in 1988, with the addition of a section, omitted from the original edition (see note 110 of the present text), which had been published separately in *Mabon* 1 (1969), 30-40 and then reprinted in Emyr Humphreys, *Miscellany Two* (Bridgend: Poetry Wales Press, 1981), 21-33. The present text is a corrected version of the augmented novel, except for one major emendation: section two ("The first time she ever heard his voice ...") and section three ("In the chapel house ...") of Chapter 8 as previously published are here transposed, in order to preserve the chronological time sequence of the narrative. This alteration is made with the full approval of the author.

There are two useful general introductions to Emyr Humphreys' work as a novelist: Ioan Williams, *Emyr Humphreys* in the Writers of Wales Series (Cardiff: University of Wales Press, 1980) and (in Welsh) M. Wynn Thomas, *Emyr Humphreys,* Llen y Llenor series (Caernarfon: Gwasg Pantycelyn, 1989). A brief summary of the novelist's life and work can be found both in Glyn Jones and John Rowlands, *Profiles* (Llandysul: Gomer Press, 1980, 313-319) and in Meic Stephens, ed., *The Oxford Companion to the Literature of Wales* (Oxford: Oxford University Press, 1986). For a detailed study of the present novel see Jeremy Hooker, 'A Seeing Belief: a study of Emyr Humphreys' *Outside the House of Baal', Planet* 39 (1977), 35-43, reprinted in Hooker, *The Poetry of Place* (Manchester: Carcanet Press, 1982), 93-105. There is also an interesting section on the novel in Roland Mathias, 'Channels of Grace: a view of the earlier novels of Emyr Humphreys', *Anglo-Welsh Review* 70 (1982), 64-88, reprinted in Mathias *A Ride Through The Wood* (Bridgend: Poetry Wales Press, 1985), 207-233. Reviews of the novel include *The Anglo-Welsh Review* (1966), 142-145; and the *Times Literary Supplement,* 27 May, 1965, 409.